PENGUIN TWENTIETH-CENTURY CLASSICS

RED STRANGERS

Elspeth Huxley was born in 1907 and spent most of her childhood in Kenya. She was partially educated at the European school in Nairobi, and then at Reading University, where she took a diploma in agriculture, and at Cornell University, USA. In 1929 she joined the Empire Marketing Board as a press officer. She married Gervas Huxley in 1931 and travelled widely with him in America, Africa and elsewhere. She was on the BBC General Advisory Council from 1952 to 1959, when she joined the Monckton Advisory Commission on Central Africa. Among her diverse writings are novels, detective stories, biographies, volumes of autobiography and travel books. Her publications include *The Flame Trees of Thika* (1959), *The Mottled Lizard* (1962), *Out in the Midday Sun* (1985), an anthology entitled *Nine Faces of Kenya* (1990) and *Peter Scott: Painter and Naturalist* (1993).

She died in January 1997. In its obituary, *The Times* wrote that 'She was not only a talented writer but an outstanding personality.'

Richard Dawkins was born in Nairobi in 1941. Educated at Oxford University, he was formerly an Assistant Professor of Zoology at the University of California at Berkeley, a Lecturer in Zoology at Oxford University and a Fellow of New College. In 1995 he became the first Charles Simonyi Professor of the Public Understanding of Science at Oxford University. Among his bestselling books are *The Selfish Gene*, *The Extended Phenotype*, *The Blind Watchmaker*, *River Out of Eden*, *Climbing Mount Improbable* and *Unweaving the Rainbow*. Many of his books are published in Penguin.

He has received many prizes and honours, and is a Fellow of the Royal Society of Literature.

ELSPETH HUXLEY

Red Strangers

With an Introduction by
Richard Dawkins

PENGUIN BOOKS

PENGUIN BOOKS

Published by the Penguin Group
Penguin Books Ltd, 27 Wrights Lane, London w8 5tz, England
Penguin Putnam Inc., 375 Hudson Street, New York, New York 10014, USA
Penguin Books Australia Ltd, Ringwood, Victoria, Australia
Penguin Books Canada Ltd, 10 Alcorn Avenue, Toronto, Ontario, Canada m4v 3b2
Penguin Books (NZ) Ltd, Private Bag 102902, NSMC, Auckland, New Zealand

Penguin Books Ltd, Registered Offices: Harmondsworth, Middlesex, England

First published by Chatto 1939
Published in Penguin Books 1999
3 5 7 9 10 8 6 4 2

Printed in England by Clays Ltd, St Ives plc

Contents

vi
CONTENTS
BOOK III: KARANJA

Introduction by Richard Dawkins

Elspeth Huxley died last year at the age of ninety. Best known for her vivid African memoirs, she was also a considerable novelist who, in *Red Strangers*, achieved a scale that could fairly be called epic. It is the saga of a Kikuyu family spanning four generations, beginning before the coming to Kenya of the British ('red' strangers because sunburned), and ending with the birth of a new baby girl, christened Aeroplane by her father ('His wife, he thought, would never be able to pronounce such a difficult word; but educated people would know, and understand'). Its 400 pages are gripping, moving, historically and anthropologically illuminating, humanistically mind-opening ... and, lamentably, out of print. I had an unrealized youthful ambition to write a science fiction novel. It would follow an expedition to say, Mars, but seen through the eyes (or whatever passed for eyes) of the native inhabitants. I wanted to manoeuvre my readers into an acceptance of Martian ways so comprehensive that they would see the invading humans as strange and foreign aliens.

It is Elspeth Huxley's extraordinary achievement in the first half of *Red Strangers* to immerse her readers so thoroughly in Kikuyu ways and thought that, when the British finally appear on the scene, everything about them seems to us alien, occasionally downright ridiculous, though usually to be viewed with indulgent tolerance. It is the same indulgent amusement, indeed, as I remember we bestowed upon Africans during my own colonial childhood. Huxley, in effect, skilfully transforms her readers into Kikuyu, opening our eyes to see Europeans, and their customs, as we have never seen them before. We become used to an economy pegged to the goat standard, so when coins (first rupees and then shillings) are introduced, we marvel at the absurdity of a currency that does not automatically accrue with each breeding season. We come to accept a world in which every event has a supernatural magical interpretation, and feel personally swindled when the statement, 'The rupees that I pay you can later be changed into goats', turns out to be literally untrue.

When Kichui (all white men are referred to by their Kikuyu nick-names) gives orders that his fields should be manured, we realize that he is mad. Why else would a man try to lay a curse upon his own cattle? 'Matu could not believe his ears. To bury the dung of a cow was to bring death upon it, just as death, or at any rate severe sickness, would come to a man whose excreta were covered with earth ... He refused emphatically to obey the order.' And, such is Huxley's skill that even I, despising as I do the fashionable nostrums of 'cultural relativism', find myself endorsing Matu's good sense.

We are led to marvel at the absurdity of European justice, which seems to care which of two brothers committed a murder: '... what does it matter? Are not Muthengi and I brothers? Whichever it was that held the sword, our father Waseru and other members of our clan must still pay the blood-price.' Unaccountably there is no blood-price, and Matu, having cheerfully confessed to Muthengi's crime, goes to prison, where he leads 'a strange, comfortless life whose purpose he could not divine'. Eventually he is released. He has served his time but, since he didn't realize he was doing time, the event is of no significance. On returning to his own village, far from being disgraced, he has gained prestige from his sojourn with the mysterious strangers, who obviously regard him highly enough to invite him to live in their own place.

The novel takes us through episodes that we recognize as if from a great distance; through the First World War and the ravages of the subsequent Spanish 'flu, through smallpox epidemics and worldwide economic recession; and we never once are told in European terms that this is what is going on. We see all through Kikuyu eyes. The Germans are just another white tribe, and when the war ends we find ourselves wondering where are the plundered cattle that the victors ought to be driving home. What else, after all, is warfare for?

Ever since borrowing *Red Strangers* from the library, I have been on a ceaseless quest to acquire a copy of my own. It has been my routine first question on every visit to Hay-on-Wye. Finally, I tracked down two old American copies simultaneously on the Internet. After so many years of restless searching, I could not resist buying both. So now, if any reputable publisher sincerely wants to look at *Red Strangers* with a view to bringing out a new edition. I will gladly make available one of my hard-won copies.* Nothing will part me from the other one.

*First published in the *Financial Times* in 1998. I am extremely happy that Penguin Books have risen to the challenge issued here.

Red Strangers

TO MY MOTHER

Who first suggested this book,
and helped to bring it into being.

Foreword

ALTHOUGH this is a novel, most of the incidents related are true. Part I has as its background the local history of a small area of East Africa, a section of what is now the South Nyeri district of the Kikuyu reserve, located on the southern slopes of Mt. Kenya at an elevation of about 7,500 ft. All the characters, without exception, are imaginary, but many of their adventures occurred to real people who related them to me ; and such events as smallpox outbreaks, famine and so on, are matters of historical record. The ceremonies and customs described are based in some cases on observation and in some on accounts given by elders, supplemented by such written sources as "*With A Prehistoric People*" by Routledge, and notes kindly lent by Dr. L. S. B. Leakey, whose authoritative work on the Kikuyu tribe is shortly to appear.

This book makes no claim whatever to scientific exactitude. I am not an anthropologist and have not been able to adopt the methods of long study and thorough checking and rechecking essential to that social science. The picture of tribal life is very far from being complete, and in a few cases I have erred intentionally for the sake of clarity. (For example, the eldest son is always named after his grandfather, and it would obviously muddle the reader if two characters were called by the same name. A son is in certain ways a sort of reincarnation of his grandfather, and for this reason is sometimes addressed as "father" by his own father—a habit very confusing to non-Africans. I have also applied the word "clan" to the extended family, where its correct use is to denote what I have called the "tribal group.")

The story of the coming of the white man is related as it was told to me by a number of people who were grown-up at the time. The first European they can remember who came into this particular district was John Boyes ("Kianjahé") ; the date of his visit was 1898. The submission of the elders to an agent of the British Government took place at Nyeri (then known as Tetu) on December 21st, 1902. While these landmarks are genuine, other events believed by the characters in this book to be equally historical are not necessarily true. For instance, by tradition the tribe originated in their present area, but in fact students believe that they reached it from elsewhere only within the last 150 years.

Finally, to forestall a possible, although absurd, misconception, I should like to disclaim any intention of speaking for the Kikuyu people or of putting forward their point of view. I have tried to describe the coming of the European to a part of Africa previously untouched by white influence as it appeared to one family of one tribe living in one small district in one part of Africa. But I am well aware that no person of one race and culture can truly interpret events from the angle of individuals belonging to a totally different race and culture. The old Kikuyu men, that rapidly dwindling number who remember life as it was lived before British rule, cannot present their point of view to us because they cannot express it in terms which we can understand. The young educated man—educated in our purely literary sense of the word—uses the thought-tracks of the European ; he is scarcely more able than his European teacher to interpret the feelings and outlook of the generation to whom the processes of European thought were always alien. It was the consideration that within a few years none will survive of those who remember the way of life that existed before the white man came, that led me to make the experiment of this book.

BOOK I: MUTHENGI
1890–1902

CHAPTER I

The Visit

I

MUTHENGI was fourteen years old when he first saw a column of shining-skinned young Kikuyu warriors swinging along the forest's edge towards the plains, like a ripple of wind across a field of ripening grain, on the way to war. Afterwards he could not remember the names of the warriors, nor the boasting words they had shouted to his father as they loped past, nor even the designs painted boldly in black and red on their long shields; but from that moment he became a warrior; his spirit marched with theirs, and dreams of battle filled his waking mind. While others of his age were preoccupied with their skill in games, with the herding of goats, or with bird-scaring among the millet, he would practise hurling sticks against the trunk of a banana tree; and in his imagination bronze-limbed Masai warriors surged in full retreat over the millet-fields, and captured Masai cattle flowed in a brown flood over the pastures of his clan.

Even his father caught a little of the excitement at the time. The family, all five of them—the two parents, Muthengi and his young brother Matu, and a baby sister slung in a goatskin on the mother's back—had just emerged from the cool shade of the forest to the edge of a sloping pasture that gleamed like a parrot's wing in the bright sunlight. They paused a moment to accustom their eyes to the white morning glare, after the soft forest shadows; and suddenly, away to the left, the blade of a spear stabbed the air with a shaft of deflected sunlight.

Waseru, the father, turned his head, and then Muthengi saw them, the warriors: lithe as the leopard, swift as the reedbuck, tireless as the elephant, moving in a silent column within the

3

shadow of the forest's edge. Their glossy black ostrich-feather head-dresses nodded and swayed with each long easy stride, and naked spear-points twinkled from the shadows as if the stars had been plucked from heaven to hang in the boughs of trees. The iron rattles, shaped like cowrie shells, that each man wore strapped below the right knee were stuffed with leaves to kill the sound.

This was no game, no warriors' display; it was a raid, the warriors' business. The lust for cattle and for glory was in every man's heart.

The movement of their feet disturbed Waseru's blood. He, too, belonged to the class of warriors on whose strength the safety of his people rested. A Kikuyu proverb came into his mind as his eyes followed them: "a young man is a piece of God."

They came on swiftly, and Waseru stepped back among the trees to let them pass. They seemed taller than men, in their nodding head-dresses. Each carried a spear in his right hand, and a long buffalo-hide shield hung from his left arm. A sword in a vermilion scabbard was strapped to his side, and a smooth-headed wooden club tucked into his belt. The right side of each warrior was newly greased with fat and brick-red ochre, and the left side, free from paint, shone like a dark polished chestnut. Many of them recognised Waseru, and raised their spears and greeted him by name as they passed.

"Is all well?" he called to one, a cousin, who saluted him. "Do you go to raid cattle on the plains?"

"Wa-Masai have captured Kikuyu cattle by the salt-lick and driven them across the river," the warrior shouted. "We go to get them back."

"Tonight we sleep by the salt-licks at Iruri," another added. The column did not pause. "On the second day we fall upon the manyattas * on the plain."

A third man completed the tale as the column moved on. "We shall bring back our cattle, for our spies have told us that

* Masai villages.

Masai warriors have gone across the plain to raid the Purko."

Waseru raised his own spear in a final salute. "Go," he called after the retreating column, "and tread upon termites!"

2

MUTHENGI'S body was rigid as a tree. Wide-eyed, he watched the warriors as if they had been a procession of spirits. His father's shout broke the spell. He darted out of the little group and ran after the young men, tripping over tree-roots and brandishing a stick, a wild rushing torrent of excitement at his throat. He hopped after the tail of the column like an ostrich chicken, every sense submerged in a tide of conviction that he was one with the young warriors, marching towards the plains for loot and glory. Then a hand gripped his shoulder, and pride and exaltation vanished like a dream at dawn.

"Come back, you senseless partridge!" his father exclaimed angrily. Then, remembering that no man must abuse his son, he dropped his hand, and continued in a calmer voice: "Do you know no better than to speak thus to the warriors—you, an un-circumcised boy!—and to run behind those who set out on a journey? Must you disgrace your parents before the young men?"

Muthengi made no reply. He followed his father back to the path, his head held low. Shame was in his heart, but the rhythm of strong swinging bodies pounded behind his eyes. "One day," he vowed, "I will be the greatest warrior of them all."

Dappled sunlight spotted his mother's brown goatskin cloak as though it had been a leopard's back. Matu, his young brother, stood by her side, silent and afraid.

"Ee, father, warriors will throw spears at you, thinking you are a dikdik, if you run after them!" Wanjeri told her son. Her voice was high and shrill. The shaved shiny head of the baby on her back bobbed up and down as she laughed.

"Soon he will be speaking of circumcision," Waseru remarked

to his wife. He adjusted the round ball of black ostrich feathers which capped the tip of his spear, to show that he travelled in peace, and hitched his short cloak of dressed goatskin more securely on his right shoulder. Iron bangles on his forearm caught flecks of sunlight from the shadows, and fine iron chains hanging from the lobes of his ears jingled as he moved. Small goat-horns containing magic hung by more chains from his neck.

"Circumcision!" his wife exclaimed. "And where will you find the fat he-goat to present to the elders, and the ox to slaughter for your son's circumcision feast? Are ownerless goats wandering like birds here in the forest, and oxen sleeping in the trees that you burn down?"

"Silence, wife!" Waseru said. He struck the butt of his spear on the ground and strode into the sunlight, following a path across the rich green pasture towards a cluster of golden-roofed huts that clung to the hillside like ticks on the flank of a cow. Muthengi's bare feet padded along the hard red path behind his bent-backed mother, but his spirit was with the smooth-limbed warriors gliding down to the beckoning, treacherous Laikipia plain.

The path leading to the homestead of Waseru's father wound along a steep green ridge that lay between two small rivers. A thick mat of short-cropped grass and clover clothed the crest of the ridge, and patches of bush and forest hid the full curves of the shoulders. The bush was thick and full of flowering shrubs. The glowing yellow of Cassia, pure as the note of a bell, mingled with the delicate mauve of muthakwa; down by the rivers the flame-coloured petals of a balsam seemed to reflect the brilliant wings of birds that came to sip the clear, quick-flowing water. Goats swarmed over the uncultivated land, sleek and shiny-skinned, nibbling at the aromatic leaves and juicy bark of young bushes. The tinkle of their iron bells was carried from hillside to hillside by a breeze that lightly stirred the bright-leaved banana-trees growing in the valleys. Millet, sprouting among the stumps of old forest trees, was knee high. The millet rains had fallen generously, the earth was moist and fertile, and the crop good. The air was light and clean in the nostrils, and the home of many birds. Waseru felt pleasure in his veins as he walked, for the sun was warm and satisfying after the cold shade of the forest where his new home lay.

The morning shadows were still long over the grass when Waseru and his family reached his father's homestead. A fence of closely-woven sticks surrounded a group of huts, and inside the grass was worn down to expose bare sunbaked earth. Although it was early the old man, Mahenia, had left already for a beer-drink; but his two wives had not yet gone out to their day's work in the shamba.* The younger of the two was kneeling before a large flat stone and grinding millet for the evening meal. Ornaments of twisted and polished iron hanging from her distended earlobes jiggled like a gazelle's scut as her body swayed rhythmically to and fro, and her silky skin, well greased with castor oil, shone like a polished gourd in the sunlight. She greeted Waseru and his family with welcoming shouts and laughter.

"Ee, you come from afar," she remarked to Wanjeri. "Men must find you irresistible, that your husband takes you where there is none but spirits to lie with you."

Wanjeri's rather sulky face creased into a grin. She threw back her head and laughed until her ornaments jangled.

"Are not spirits old men, too old for intercourse?" she retorted. "I tell you, it is lonely there. No strangers pass our gateway, and if the fire in my hut goes out, from whom can I take new fire?"

Mahenia's senior wife removed a screen of interlacing sticks from the door of her granary, a round hut made of sticks and perched on the top of four poles so that it resembled a beehive on stilts, and extracted from it a calabash of heavy green dough. The children stared at it silently, their eyes round as moons and black as buffaloes, with all the intensity of hunger in their gaze.

The wife broke off handfuls of dough and gave food to each in turn, beginning with Waseru, and ending with the youngest

* Cultivated land.

child. Waseru spat the first mouthful, the spirit's portion, to the ground, and ate the rest of his share standing a little apart; for it was not right to eat with women, even though a handful of dough hardly counted as a meal. The children gobbled greedily, licking the last traces off their fingers. It was a good rich paste of mashed bananas mixed with ground sorghum and two kinds of bean, and flavoured with leaves of the nettle nyani; and it was the most solid food the family had eaten for a month. Up in their forest home the granary was empty of everything save a small sack of millet, three bunches of bananas, and a few yams.

3

WHEN Waseru had eaten he strode with lighter feet along the narrow path, his short goatskin cloak and his sword in its red scabbard swinging as he walked. He was tall and shapely, his limbs smooth and long. His hairless skin was lighter than the average for his tribe, his cheekbones higher, and his nose less flat. A Masai grandmother, sold to a Kikuyu for two sacks of millet in the last great cattle plague, had left her stamp on his features. His hair was done in Masai style. It was divided into tufts, each one plaited with twine, thickly smeared with a mixture of sheep's fat and red ochre, and tied at the end farthest from the head. The front tufts dangled over the forehead; the back ones were gathered into a queue and hung down to cover the nape of the neck.

The hut of Irumu the mundu-mugu * lay beyond a banana plantation on the fertile slopes of the next ridge. Brilliant green fronds hung like the languid arms of dancers over the path, and in the shamba the tough tendrils of yam vines twisted themselves around low mukongogo trees. Irumu was at home, sunning himself outside his hut on a low three-legged wooden stool, and meditatively plucking a few stray hairs from his chin with a pair of tweezers.

* A magical practitioner.

His repute as a mundu-mugu stood high. Not only could he divine the cause of a thahu * and remove it with such strict observance of ritual that there was no danger of its persistence, but he could foretell the fortunes of warriors who contemplated a raid, he could make medicine to bring success in war or love, and he could remove curses—all, that is, save the deadly curses laid by smiths, which only a smith could abrogate. He was a man of great influence. When the council of warriors decided to make war, it was always Irumu to whom they sent to read the portents; and if he forecast success, they had no fears of failure.

Irumu was an elder of the ruling generation Maina and president of the senior council of elders, upon which only those with circumcised children might sit; but he still looked vigorous and full of nervous energy. He had a thin narrow face and a slightly hooked nose, and his eyes were several shades lighter than the usual sloe-black of his fellows. At times they could look as yellow as those of a leopard. His close-cropped woolly hair was dusted with white. He had long, flexible fingers and agile toes. He did not look like a Kikuyu at all; indeed, there were strange legends as to his origin. As a young man his father had migrated towards the east, to the country of the Ndia, and lived there for many years in order to escape from Masai raids. He had returned as an old man, with circumcised sons. Irumu had already become a mundu-mugu, versed in none knew what mysteries, for it was well known that Ndia was a land of magic; strange and dreadful practices of witchcraft and sorcery were prevalent in that savage country.

Waseru thrust the haft of his spear into the ground outside Irumu's homestead and entered, shouting as he did so that he came in peace. He greeted the mundu-mugu with great respect and sat down beside him, squatting on his heels. For half-an-hour they chatted leisurely of trivialities—news of wedding feasts, lawsuits, goat transactions, crops. Only then did Waseru broach the subject of his visit.

* Ceremonial uncleanliness, generally resulting from the breach of some prohibition, or of contact with some unclean person or thing.

He had come, he said, to ask professional advice. After harvest he was going to build a hut on his new land, and he wanted to know where to place it in order that his wife might be fertile and his crops abundant. And, more urgently, his second son Matu had fallen sick. The boy was growing thinner than a twig, and his stomach rejected food. Some malignant influence was at work. No doubt he would die, unless the cause could be revealed and the evil driven out.

4

IRUMU listened in silence, staring into the ground at his feet, his mobile lips curved in a half-smile. Even after the story was told he did not speak, but sat for so long without moving that Waseru thought he must have gone to sleep. Heat reflected from the red beaten floor of the compound pressed into their faces like a burning hand. Irumu liked to sit under the sky and feel the sunlight soaking through his skin and filling his veins with blood, as it fills the hard fruit of the tree with soft ripe juices.

Finally he stirred, unstoppered a small bottle of polished black wood that dangled from his neck on the end of a fine chain, and took a deep pinch of snuff. He rose without a word and, bending double to get through the door, vanished into the darkness of his hut. When he reappeared he carried a long, polished gourd, neatly stoppered with a baby gourd that fitted into the neck upside down. He squatted on his stool, arranged his heavy oxhide cloak around him, and spread a goatskin on the ground. Then he opened his gourd and sought the answers to Waseru's questions in the magic beans.

He tipped a random number of shiny black beans, fruits of the mubagé bush, into his palm, and counted them on to the goatskin in piles of five. Then he pushed the groups of five together into heaps of twenty, counted the number of beans left over, and poured them all back into the gourd. He shook the gourd slowly back and forth, tipped out another handful of beans and repeated the process. This he did several times. On each occasion he counted carefully the odd number of beans left over when the piles of twenty were made, for in their numbers lay—for those who could read the signs—the secrets of Waseru's future. At last Irumu spoke. He chanted in a low sing-song voice, striking the palm of one hand with the forefinger of the other to emphasize his points.

"The rains of the beans will be sufficient, and the millet rains after them," he said, "and your crops will be good. You will build a new house, but see to it that the door does not look towards the sunset; and if the gate of the compound faces running water your daughters will be barren. See that you bless the hut with beer, and do not cut the poles while the moon is dead."

"All that I shall do," Waseru agreed. "And now tell me why my son refuses food and grows weak as a stem of millet when the ground is hard as rock from lack of rain."

Irumu's chant went on, his long flexible fingers marking each point against a light brown palm. His amber-tinted eyes directed quick glances at Waseru's face, and then back again to the beans that glistened on the goatskin.

"Your son Muthengi will grow to be a great warrior," he said. "When he is circumcised he will go with the young men to raid cattle, and he will win great renown. One day he will kill a Masai warrior who has a spear with a notch in the haft, and he will bring back the spear for the council of warriors to see. That shall be known as a sign, and Muthengi shall become a great leader in war."

Waseru became excited over this, and exclaimed that his father had once been a great warrior who had captured many cattle and become rich. Muthengi, his son, would also capture cattle, and have many wives, and so the clan would grow in wealth and power. Then he remembered about Matu's sickness, and asked whether the boy would recover.

Irumu took another deep pinch of snuff, returned the beans to the gourd, and counted them, again, on to the goatskin at his feet. As he did so he addressed them softly, asking the cause of Matu's sickness. Two old men, passing Irumu's compound on the way to a beer-drink, came in and squatted on their heels to watch. Irumu paid them no attention. At last he spoke solemnly, repeating each sentence in slightly different words to emphasize its gravity.

"The fat that your son eats is turned into husks in his body," he said. "It cannot nourish him, and his limbs waste. He is sick because there is a thahu in his body. If it is not cast out, he will surely die."

Waseru's face remained impassive and he asked:

"What is the cause of this thahu, then?"

Irumu gathered up the beans, shook them, and set them out again in piles of five and then of twenty.

"The child has an evil thahu," he said. "The reason is here, but it is not yet clearly shown. It is a thahu that comes from a woman. Perhaps it came because milk from the breasts of a woman who is not his mother fell upon the child, and brought sickness into him."

"I do not know anything of this," Waseru answered, "but it may be so."

"The thahu comes from the child's mother," Irumu repeated. "Perhaps because her head was shaved after her child was born by a woman who had been suckled by a child not her own. Or perhaps because she was feeding sweet potato tops to a he-goat, and the he-goat licked her garments, and she did not go to a mundu-mugu to be purified from the thahu of the goat."

"She did not tell me of these things," Waseru said, "but they may indeed have been so."

Irumu gathered up the beans afresh, and asked again for the cause of the thahu to be revealed. "Perhaps the thahu comes to the child's mother from her parents," he went on. "Perhaps the woman's father is not satisfied with the bride-price and there was a quarrel between you and him. If the woman's father publicly cursed you because of this, a thahu would fall upon her child."

"It is true that the woman's father, Ndolia, claims more goats from me because his daughter has given birth to three children," Waseru remarked. "But before I left my father's house to cultivate new land in the forest, a he-goat was killed and the quarrel was thrown away in its entrails, and there is no bad feeling between us any longer."

Irumu's restless eyes flickered backwards and forwards from Waseru's face to the beans. "Now I will tell you which of these causes has brought the thahu to your child," he said. Again he gathered up the beans and shook them, and again he spread them out in black shining piles. He studied them for a long time before he spoke.

"The reason for the thahu is here," he said at last. "The woman's father is not satisfied with the number of the goats and the gourds of beer you gave him for his daughter. He claims more goats because she has borne you three children, and he has cursed you publicly because you have not paid your debt. The quarrel between you did not finish when the he-goat was slain, and it has brought thahu to your child. You must make peace with Ndolia, and pay him goats for the removal of the curse. And a goat must be slain for the purification of the child, or your son's body will wither like a plant whose roots are devoured by moles."

Waseru's face remained impassive, but dismay gripped his throat and stomach. This was the diagnosis that his heart had dreaded. Ndolia was a rich man and he, Waseru, poor. He knew that Ndolia despised him as a worthless son-in-law, and, worst of all, as one who neglected his duty towards his wife's father; yet he did not know how he could get goats to satisfy Ndolia's greed. Unless he could do so, the child would surely die.

"Truly, there is wisdom," he remarked bitterly, "in the saying : ' The rich man who eats with a stick does not know that the poor man who eats with his fingers is burnt '."

5

SHADOWS from the tall, slender-trunked trees that stood in clumps among the scattered shambas lay in long black bars across the green of grass and bush and millet when Mahenia's two wives returned to the homestead. The senior wife was bent almost double beneath a heavy load of sweet potato tops, strapped to her back with leather thongs. She was bringing them from the shamba to feed to a he-goat that was fattening in the darkness of a narrow pen inside her hut. A recently circumcised daughter plodded behind with a load of firewood on her back.

Wanjiku, the younger wife, arrived a little later. She carried two big gourds, golden in the slanting sunlight, on her back. Inside them water rolled a little from side to side as she moved with bent knees, in a sort of shuffle. Behind trotted a small daughter, four or five years old, naked except for a triangular piece of dressed goatskin hanging down in front. A few days before she had cried because she had nothing to carry, while a girl but little older than herself had been given a calabash of water by her mother. So Wanjiku had laughed, and handed the smallest gourd that she could find to her daughter. Now the little girl jogged happily up the hill steep from the river, the water in the half-filled vessel gurgling like a hungry stomach on her back.

The hut of Mahenia's senior wife was immediately opposite the entrance. To the left stood Wanjiku's hut, and on the right was a thingira * where men sat to feed and gossip, and where circumcised boys slept. All the huts were built of solid posts cut from the forest, joined with mud and thatched with pale dried grass. The domes of their circular roofs were slightly blackened, and blue wood-smoke drifted gently up through the thatch like a mist rising from a swamp at sunrise. The eaves hung lower than a man's shoulder and all who entered had to bend double to pass through the low narrow door. Surrounding the front of the hut, under the eaves, was a narrow veranda where the gourds were stored. Opposite the door of each wife's hut stood a round granary filled with the harvests of her shamba.

The air was full of the soft bleating of goats. They were nozzling eagerly at lumps of salt-impregnated earth kept in a

* Hut for men only.

trough made from the hollow trunk of a tree. The boys divided the goats into two lots and drove each contingent into the hut to which it belonged. Shuffling and jostling, the goats took their accustomed places in a warm, smoky pen screened off by hurdles of woven sticks. A fire burned in the centre of each hut, and around it were spaced four stout poles supporting the roof. They were encrusted with a thick layer of solidified smoke, and shone richly in the firelight like the black depths of a wise man's eyes. Beds of boards and sticks, raised on poles off the hard-beaten earth floor and covered with skins, flanked the sides of the huts. The air was densely charged with many smells: from the close-packed goats and their urine, strong and sharp; from the essential oils of wood, clean and bitter; from the red ochre and fat smeared on shining human limbs, sweet and rancid. A subtle compound arose also from porridge steaming in the big cooking-pot, and from bananas roasting slowly in the ashes.

The senior wife carried a smouldering log to the thingira and lit a fire. Waseru squatted over the flames on a low stool and waited for his father, talking meanwhile with his young half-brother Ngarariga, a newly circumcised youth now in the warrior class. Ngarariga was angry because he had been forbidden by the council of warriors to take part in the raid. He had been ordered to stay behind to guard the herds; and now, if any loot were taken, he would get no share.

As Ngarariga and Waseru speculated on the outcome of the raid, the thought of wealth and cattle filled their minds entirely, as hot beer fills the belly at festivals. The leaping fire was warm and caressing on their eyelids. In his interest Waseru forgot his own poverty and the loneliness that sometimes assailed him in his forest hut, separated from his own kin. Now he felt as a raindrop that has reached the river might feel when it merged itself in the great body of the stream; or as a bird that finds its way back to the forest after it has been lost for many days among the shadeless mountains.

6

MAHENIA, Waseru's father, was small and brittle. His face was networked with wrinkles as if a horde of ants had been scurrying over his skin, each one leaving a little furrow in its track. He had shrewd black eyes that darted swift glances about him like a forest rat. He was known as a quick-witted man who drove hard bargains in goats, and if luck had been with him he might have become rich. Fortune had been his match, but not his master. He was by no means a rich man, but he was comfortably placed and well respected in the council of elders. He himself, however, complained frequently of the misfortunes that had befallen his cattle, and of his worthless son's insatiate demands for the loan of goats. The lobes of his ears were distended with wooden cylinders, set with beads, as broad across as a man's palm. Small chain ornaments dangled from the upper cartilage of his ears, and necklaces of beads, shells and leather hung from his neck. He wore a cloak of chestnut goatskin, and his hair, as befitted an elder's, was closely cropped.

He greeted Waseru in a high, uneven voice and sat down by the fire on the three-legged stool, its wood darkened by long use, that hung over his shoulder on a fine iron chain. He grunted and belched with comfort as he sat, and rubbed his eyes and temples. The beer had been good and warm and liberally poured.

"Waseru," he said, "is all well with you? Have the millet-rains come plentifully to the new land that you have cleared, and does your wife cultivate with proper industry?"

Waseru replied that the rains had come and that the millet had sprouted knee-high among the stumps of felled trees. But there were many pigs in the forest, he added, and they came at night to eat the young stalks. And the cold was so bitter that it entered into the marrow of his bones; sometimes his limbs became as stiff as branches.

They talked intermittently by the fireside, pausing a long time between sentences as each theme was touched upon, weighed, and turned over slowly in the mind, as a full-bellied dog will prod a morsel of food with his nose before deciding whether or not to eat it.   They talked of many things, but Waseru did not mention the illness of his son, nor his consultation with the mundu-mugu; nor did Mahenia ask the reason for his visit.

Wanjeri, meanwhile, sat in her mother-in-law's hut, gossiping and helping to stir the big black pot.   How pleasant it was, she thought, to be again among the goats in the warm thick atmosphere of which she seemed herself to be a part; how pleasant to sense the familiar tang of goat sharp in her nostrils, to hear their scuffles and soft stampings in the darkness.   Eyes gleamed in the firelight on all sides, as if God had poured a little of the night into a calabash and let it stand with a circlet of stars floating around the rim.   In the forest there were no goats because Waseru was poor.   The hut was cold and empty, and the night outside full of spirits, angered and hungry for fat.

When food was ready Mahenia's senior wife carried steaming porridge in calabashes to the men.   They ate in silence, savouring the rich flavour of the heavy paste.   Wanjiku brought her husband a thin gruel made from ground millet left for a day to sour in a long gourd, and a platter of hot yams.   There were also large bananas, roasted in the warm ashes until they were hard and grey.   It was a good meal, the best that Waseru had tasted since he had left his father's compound.   He ate slowly, trying to conceal his hunger, but Mahenia was not deceived. The old man watched him covertly with darting eyes set deep in a cunning, leathery face.   Now he had no need to ask the reason for the visit of his son.

CHAPTER II

The Debt

I

WASERU left his father's homestead while the white strands of cobweb hanging on the bush were beaded with dew and early morning sunlight lay gently over new-washed grass.

From the green pastures below the forest's border he could see the majestic peak of Kerinyagga, that was hidden from his own dwelling by regiments of trees. The sun came up over the eastern shoulder and brushed its white tooth clean of darkness, while its immense shadow still lay like deep water over the roofs of huts and the grey cultivation below. The mountain of the ostrich, it was sometimes called, because the pure whiteness of its crown and the stark blackness of the rocks below gave it the appearance of a cock-bird's plumage. High and remote, the peak floated in the clean air above them, guarded from the impudent feet of men by many spirits. The Athi, those hunters who ate the flesh of game, had sometimes seen them, and reported them as small in stature, no higher than a man's waist. At night they would sit on cold black rocks and wail into the mists, malignant and lonely.

Above, on the far white crest where no man could venture, was the seat of God. There he dwelt, sending rain or withholding it according to his pleasure, blessing sometimes with abundance, showing his anger sometimes in pestilence or drought. He sent his messengers in the bodies of animals to accept sacrifices that old men left for him beneath sacred fig-trees, those trees whose roots grew down from heaven instead of up from earth as was the case with all other trees. Sometimes, when he prepared to go on a journey, men could hear him cracking his joints with a noise of thunder; at such times they would not dare to look up into the sky, lest they should glimpse his majesty and perish.

Waseru's father-in-law lived a full half-day's journey distant. At first the path followed the course of a twisting stream, through shambas carpeted with the dark, heart-shaped leaves of sweet potatoes and green with the stiff stems of millet and sorghum. Birds twittered and flapped everywhere in the warm, sweet-smelling bush. The three insistent notes of the bird called 'thrower-of-firewood' fell like raindrops out of the branches in a descending cadence: "Gai-ky-ngu; gai-ky-ngu; gai-ky-ngu."

As the sun climbed up the sky, heavy full-bellied clouds in changing shades of white and grey and violet rose from behind the earth and hung above the horizon like fantastic fruits, swollen with ripeness, suspended from the formless tree of heaven. Later in the day they would move slowly along the horizon with the dignity and sureness of old men proceeding at their leisure to a beer-feast. Waseru had heard it said that they were God's white oxen being driven by his wives over the deep pastures of the sky, but he himself felt doubtful whether oxen could be so transfigured.

As Waseru walked he reflected deeply on his troubles. Fortune seemed to have deserted him completely, he thought. Things had been good with him at first, after his circumcision. He had taken his place among the warriors, he had won renown at the dances, girls had looked on him with favour. When, after nine seasons, the time came for him to marry, his father had paid the bride-price without demur, even though the girl's father, Ndolia, belonged to a clan which was often feared because there were said to be many poisoners among its members. But his father had paid goats, his mother had brewed beer, the senior elder of his clan had allotted him good land, and he had built himself a hut. Soon afterwards his wife had borne him a son, Muthengi, and then, after the first had been weaned, a second son, Matu. He had owned a small herd of goats which was gradually increasing, so that the purchase of a second wife was not beyond his dreams.

2

THEN the first disaster had occurred. The land that Waseru had been given to cultivate on his marriage had been partially covered with forest. When weeds had begun to creep over his wife's millet field, and harvests no longer filled her granary to the roof, he had decided to plant his next crops on fresh soil. So he had declared war on the trees. The smaller ones he had felled with an axe, the larger ones with fire. He had hollowed out a place near the foot of each tree and started inside it a blaze of banana leaves. A stain of black had spread gradually over the white flesh of the tree; each stately giant had tottered like a drunken elder, and crashed to the ground with a mighty roar that had shaken the very foundations of the earth. The trees had smouldered slowly into ashes, and the sun had streamed down into the uncovered earth to warm it for seed.

Everyone had known, up and down the ridge, that Waseru was felling trees near the forest's border; and the boys had been told that goats must not be herded there. But one day a he-goat from across the river had strayed, and a boy had followed it into the forest's fringe where Waseru had been at work among the trees. The causes of the disaster that had followed were not yet fully understood. It was clear, of course, that some enemy of the boy's parents, or of his clan perhaps, must have laid upon him a powerful spell to guide his feet to the path of the falling tree. The last supports of the big makarimbui had cracked with a noise like bamboo poles bursting in a fire, and the trunk had smashed down on to the skull of the bewitched young goatherd. There Waseru had found him, later in the day. He had fetched his father, and they had stared fearfully at two black branches bearing no leaves that protruded from the foliage— two spindly, lifeless legs.

In the lawsuit that followed the victim's father had accused an enemy of killing his son by sorcery. The council of elders had sat in judgment for a long time. Waseru, as a party to the litigation, had found himself obliged to pay no less than three fat rams to the elders in court fees. And the payment of blood-money, forty goats, had stripped him of the last of his flock, forcing him to borrow from his father. At a single stroke he had been deprived of wealth that had taken eight seasons to amass.

His troubles, even then, had not been over. A third child had been born, and Ndolia had demanded payment of the balance of the bride-price. Waseru had hoped to borrow from his father, but the Masai had carried out a daring raid about that time, and Mahenia had lost all his cattle. The old man, distressed and angered by the heavy loss, had refused to help any further, and accused his son of idleness and sloth. Waseru had been deeply wounded by his father's attitude. When the millet crop had failed, and wild pigs had eaten his sweet potatoes, and on top of everything Ndolia had cursed him publicly as a worthless son-in-law unmindful of his duty, he had realised that the land he was cultivating and the huts in which he lived were charged with a very evil magic; and he had decided to move.

Waseru's clan had the right to hunt game and to gather honey in all that part of the forest lying between the two streams that bounded their land. Where cultivation lay the strip was narrow, perhaps six times as far as a man could throw a spear; but higher up the rivers spread out like the spokes of a fan, and the clan's territory stretched into the heart of the forest farther than man had ever penetrated.

Once, long ago, a race of wandering dwarfs who lived on the flesh of game had hunted there. They had slept in holes in the ground, like moles, and had worn long beards; their name, Agumba, meant "the people of the children's eyes." Some of their women had married into Kikuyu clans; but the men had retreated before Kikuyu axe and fire which had destroyed their shelter. The last of them, it was said, had changed into crimson-feathered plantain-eaters which could even now, on occasion, be heard talking the Agumba language in the dead of night. So the little hunters had vanished, and only elephants and deer, birds and monkeys, pigs and leopards, remained to stir the forest's silence with their restless motion.

The forest was the enemy of the Kikuyu; it was cold and dark, and barred rich land to the women's hoe. Only by labour and toil could trees be destroyed. Even then the forest lay in wait like an ambush of warriors, ready to surge forward if women were idle at their weeding. It was an enemy, but its only weapon was the slow persistence of growth, and that could not serve against the swift axe, the creeping fire, and the biting hoe. Steadily and inexorably the Kikuyu people were beating it back, foot by foot, and claiming the deep soil, rich with juices of vegetable decay, as their own. Although it was hard work to clear the forest the rewards were big; crops were heavy, and often there would be a surplus for exchange. And new land, Waseru reckoned, could scarcely be bewitched. So, fortified by a charm to protect the crops and a blessing from the senior elder of his clan, he had moved with his family from his father's homestead to the forest, to start a new shamba of his own.

3

THE sun, filling the sky with an exuberance that drowned its own body, was high overhead when Waseru reached Ndolia's homestead. The old man himself did not appear until the evening. Unlike most of his people he was fat and heavy, and his face wore a sulky, shifty look. He carried a staff of black polished mungirima wood and a fan of large leaves, badges of his rank as a member of the senior elders' council. He wore ear ornaments of flat metal spirals and a thick cloak of monkey skin. He was a rich man, with five wives living and two dead; and as an outward sign of his importance he displayed a long metal concave ring on the middle finger of his pudgy right hand.

His was a big compound, containing ten or twelve round huts. It was one of a group of eight which together formed a village enclosed in a high prickly fence and surrounded by a belt of forest. When shadows softened with the sloping of the sun it became a centre of great activity. Flocks of goats converged upon it out of the bush from all sides, like grey guinea-fowl hurrying to their roosting-places, and the air was filled with a gay noise of tinkling bells. Women and young girls padded homebound along the paths, bent low under burdens of sweet potato tops or green bananas, often with babies tucked into leather slings on their backs. A knot of slim young men, their hair plaited with twine and feathers and thickened by a paste of ochre and fat, arrived at dusk from the cattle boma. They carried long gourds that had been rinsed with cows' urine in order to thicken the new milk quickly into curds.

It was a warm night, and Waseru fed with Ndolia and several of his sons and nephews outside the thingira, under the stars. His father-in-law greeted him coldly, and spoke to him hardly at all. After the meal Ndolia, refreshed by frequent dips into his snuff-horn, listened to reports from his circumcised sons as to the disposition and health of the cattle. Waseru sat in silence, waiting for Ndolia's signal; but none came. He went to bed in the thingira on a skin-covered bed reserved for guests. Late at night a noisy group of young men came in from a dance, cracking a few last jokes about their amorous experiences. Then silence spread over the village and the tumbled land of ridges, and Waseru slept.

He waited two days, sitting silently on his stool in the sun or going with the young men who herded cattle, before Ndolia was ready to speak. All this time he looked respectfully at his feet when his father-in-law passed him, and turned his face away when one of Ndolia's wives approached. He was unhappy and apprehensive, for he felt dislike and contempt coming out of the minds of Ndolia's sons and nephews like the stench from a rotting corpse. And he was afraid, for sometimes it seemed that he did indeed detect an evil smell in the village, such a smell as could only arise where sorcery was practised.

4

ON the third morning he was summoned to an interview under a big, thick-foliaged fig-tree whose wide branches shaded the gateway of the homestead. Ndolia was seated on his low stool. Around him squatted a little circle of men of his generation, the ruling generation of the land. Waseru recognised them all as Ndolia's kinsfolk—his brothers, the sons of his father's brothers, and other more distant members of his clan.

Ndolia reviewed at length the history of the dispute. He recited the bride-price that Mahenia had originally paid, describing in detail the markings of each goat he had received, and recalling each brew of beer that Mahenia's wives had made. He held in his hand a bundle of short sticks and threw one to the ground to represent each goat, and then, in a separate pile, each brew of beer. He spoke then with great fluency of the many goats that were owing, of the progeny that these goats would have added to his flocks had they been promptly paid; of broken promises, of the disgrace of poverty, and of the undutiful behaviour of sons-in-law. It was a long recital, punctuated by a chorus of approval from those of his kinsmen who remained awake, and by the snores of those who had fallen asleep. When at last it ended Ndolia claimed seventeen goats, two fat rams, and ten brews of beer.

Waseru could hardly resist crying out in protest at this. The claim was far beyond his capacity to pay, and it was rankly unjust. He kept his temper, however, cleared his throat, spat, and started in a low tone to state his defence. He, too, reviewed the history of the case, pausing now and then to emphasise a point by hurling a stick to the ground as if he were projecting the argument into the skulls of his audience. He admitted a debt of two fat rams and four goats, but denied all obligations to produce more beer. He offered, however, to pay one fat ram immediately for a feast at which the quarrel should be thrown away, to provide one brew of beer, and to pay four goats and one more ram after the millet harvest was in. His offer was indignantly rejected. The argument grew heated, voices were raised, and the air was electric with hostility. Not until the sun was sinking through a red pool of cloud beyond the Masai plains did the discussion end.

Waseru was worsted, and he knew it. His child was ill; if the quarrel was not settled and the thahu exorcised, sickness would creep from the boy's stomach into the tips of his fingers and toes, as the parasitic fig entwines itself around the trunk and branches of the forest tree and stifles it to death. Ndolia's voice was unctuous, his face complacent. In his mind sleek, shiny-coated goats roamed to and fro, plucking insistently at the leaves of shrubs with their mobile leathery lips, crowding docilely into his huts at night—new goats, goats that would be his, goats that would bring more wealth and honour to his homestead.

A little before sunset Waseru threw down the stick representing the second fat ram with a gesture of mingled acquiescence and despair. He rose to his feet, rubbing the palm of his hand wearily over his face.

"I will bring the goats," he said. His voice was low and he did not look towards Ndolia. "But the curse laid publicly upon me and upon my children must be publicly revoked."

Ndolia could hardly resist a chuckle.

"Where the goats are, ill-feeling is not," he replied. "I have no quarrel with a son-in-law who pays his just debts."

He rose from his stool and walked majestically towards his huts, a knot of kinsmen following respectfully at his heels. A delicious smell of cooking beans and roasting sweet potatoes came out to greet them on the evening breeze. A group of young men stood by the gateway with gourds of milk in their hands.

"Come, brothers," Ndolia said, "there is food awaiting you, and for the son of Mahenia there is meat boiling in the pot, and good, juicy sheep's stomach."

There was a roar of laughter at this sally, for boiled meat and sheep's stomach were eaten only by women—never by men. Ndolia led the way through the fence's narrow opening in high humour. It had been a profitable day.

But Waseru could not bring himself to stay another night in the hostile homestead. He was sick at heart, his eyes were sunken into his head with chagrin and despair. He did not know how

C

he could get the goats. His father's small flock would disappear like water in a cracked calabash if this cruel demand were met. And where else could goats be borrowed? His was a small clan, and a poor one. His father's only living brother had run away, long ago, into the forest, and become a hunter of game. Even the muramati, the senior member of the clan, was not rich.

Well, let the boy die, Waseru thought; and a moment later felt ashamed at such an evil thought. Besides, the question was not only one of Matu's survival. Ndolia belonged to a strong clan, and his curse was potent; if the payment was refused, who could tell what magic would not be invoked? Waseru would be seized with sickness, his wife would become barren, his offspring would wither like the plucked tendrils of shrubs. No, somehow the goats must be obtained, and Ndolia's wrath appeased. Somehow a way would be found; for does not the young of the snake, he asked himself, bring itself up in a tree?

5

A MARKET was held at Karatina every other day. It was centred about a giant fig-tree whose foliage was black as iron and thick as beeswax. Usually it overflowed from the pool of shade on to the flat, sunflooded grassland that surrounded the tree. To the north, in the early mornings, the jagged white teeth of Kerinyagga bit into the soft blue of the sky. Later in the day they were buried in fat clouds of mother-of-pearl, and only the massive shoulders of the mountain, wearing rain-forest like a cloak of fur, could be seen above the foothills. The great mountain reared itself so lightly, so unexpectedly, from the clouds that it might have sprung out of the earth but a moment ago; and it stood there with such resolute majesty that it might have existed since before the world was made. God looked down from his bed of changing clouds directly on to Karatina, and none doubted that he saw much of interest there; for, like all old and wise men, he found in the driving of a shrewd bargain a zest which no other spectacle could afford.

Early in the morning streams of women, their backs bent under heavy burdens of millet and plantains, sweet potatoes and yams, pots and lumps of iron, converged on Karatina from all sides. Before the sun was overhead the market ground was black with bargainers, and the air full of shrill clatter. The women sat in groups on the ground, their wares spread out beside them, while elders leant upon their staffs in the shade gossiping of lawsuits and live-stock. Warriors did not waste much time with markets, which were affairs of peace; but one or two young men from the council of warriors patrolled the ground, clubs in hand (spears were not allowed), fully prepared to seize a thief or check a quarrel.

Wanjeri went to Karatina in a bad humour, for her needs were many and her means small. She had no goatskins, pots or grain to offer, nor could her husband bring sheep's fat or ochre. All she had was a honey-barrel that Waseru had made, as much firewood as she could carry, and some articles which she knew could be sold only by a trick : five skins of wild animals. The hair had been carefully scraped off with sharp-edged stones and the skin softened by rubbing with dung; the trick was to pass them off as goatskins. She had little hope that she would be able so to deceive any true Kikuyu, but there were always people from Ndia at the market, and people from Ndia were notoriously as slow in trade as they were crafty in magic.

6

SHE disposed of her honey-barrel early for a lump of red ochre and a sack of beans, and sold her firewood for a calabash of salt made from the ash of papyrus stalks. No one looked twice at her skins, but she did not worry; when the sun had passed its zenith and people began to leave the market, women whose produce was still unsold would think with weariness of the long walk home. Then was the time to drive a hard bargain. So she sat quietly, legs outstretched, in the fig-tree's shade. Near her people were offering newly burnt pots, fat and round and pink as the palm of a baby's hand; they were doing a brisk business with the women of Ndia. Farther off were the smiths, attracting the biggest crowds of all. They had a wide choice of goods to display: short, keen knives with wooden handles; tweezers for plucking hairs from the body; branding irons for burning clan-marks on cattle; rattles for warriors' ankles; bells for goats and cows; and a great variety of chains, ear-rings, bangles for arms and ankles, and coils of finely-drawn wire so much desired by women.

The market was beginning to empty before two Ndia men paused to feel Wanjeri's skins. She praised her wares, saying that she had worked for many days to make them soft and fine. One of the Ndia men, seeing the dikdik skins, asked if there had been an epidemic among her husband's goats, since several kids had died. The men were well-greased with fat and red ochre so that their limbs glistened in the sun, but they had harsh, coarse accents and uncertain, awkward ways.

"My husband is very rich," Wanjeri said carelessly. "He has many goats. I have sold the skins of the other kids that died."

"The skins are too thin," one of the men remarked.

"Thin! They should indeed be thin," Wanjeri answered, "for I have worked for many days to attain the thinness so much desired in our country. Do you not know that it is the fashion to wear cloaks that are light and soft? These skins are of just the right weight to make aprons to hang from a virgin's belt."

"Then they would find favour with the young men, for they would be as easy to tear as that which they cover," one of the Ndia remarked.

Both men laughed, and Wanjeri snatched away the skins in anger. These Ndia have no manners, she thought; whenever they speak it is an insult.

In the end they bought the skins, however, and called over a woman who paid for them with a woven sack of millet. The two bushbuck skins she sold to an Ndia woman for a large sack of sorghum and another of beans, with a small calabash of millet thrown in for good measure.

Here was their food until the moon had grown to fullness and dwindled again, she thought as she surveyed her purchases. If Waseru had been a good husband he would have given her a shamba near to his father's that would have filled her granary each season; then there would have been no need to cheat Ndia oafs with the unclean pelts of wild beasts. It was now four seasons since he had provided goatskins for a new dress. Hers was old and ragged, and no longer soft. Everyone could see that she was the wife of a poor man, and in the market-place she was ashamed of her husband's poverty.

The market dissolved slowly into divergent streams of women flowing from Karatina up the valleys towards the forest, and down the ridges towards the Sagana river. Those who had brought tobacco returned with firewood; the bearers of millet carried back pig-iron and yams suspended from their foreheads. Wanjeri plodded in silence along the red path that wound up the Ragati valley, sweating gently in the afternoon sun, her stiff cloak flapping against her bent and sturdy knees. She saw neither the ragged leaves of the bananas, nor the round-eyed children herding goats, nor the nests of weaver-birds hanging in the reeds by the river. In her mind's eye glittered only the smooth coils of drawn-wire ear-rings and the round, rare, and entrancing blue beads that had tempted her so greatly in the market, but in vain.

The Purification

I

THE company of other boys was more sweet to Muthengi than the curdled milk which was the food of men, and which he was sometimes allowed to taste. Because he was sturdy and strong, boys of his own age seldom dared to challenge him; and many of those who were older were circumcised, and herded goats no longer. So Muthengi, without close rivalry, became a leader. It was he who planned raids on the boys of neighbouring clans and divided the small force into fighting units like a warriors' band. Each member carried a spear and a club, both of wood and roughly fashioned, and a painted shield of bark.

Such games held little interest for the younger brother Matu. He was small and timid, with a belly as swollen as the bellows of a forge and limbs as spindly as the legs of a crane. His tongue was as sluggish as Muthengi's was quick. He was too young, or too feeble, to herd goats; all day during his father's absence he went with his mother to her cousin's shamba, where the women worked. There he would wander listlessly under the shade of the banana trees, or sit by himself under the tall survivors of the forest that stood in lonely clumps among the bush and millet, and listen to the soft monotonous fluting of the gai-ky-ngu. Sometimes he would take a small knife and squat beside his mother, helping her to dig out weeds. They grew in such profusion that it seemed as if the earth was a gigantic honeycomb, in which the soft fine soil was honey and the tough weed-roots were the comb. When he grew tired and listless Wanjeri would straighten her back and take him down to the sugar-cane plantation by the water, and there cut him a long stick, as thick as his arm, to chew. The juice, sweeter than honey and colder than a mountain stream, trickled deliciously down his small throat, and its strength flowed into his feet and fingers.

2

THE women weeded, for the most part, in silence. Farther down the hillside one of Mahenia's nephews was clearing a patch of bush, breaking the root-bound sod with a heavy digging-stick of fire-hardened wood. He had called a number of his nearby kinsmen to help. They came in the dress always worn for cultivation: a belt made from a single banana-frond, with other fronds crossed over each shoulder and a small leaf wrapped around the head.

Often, as they worked, they broke into song. One man, the leader, raised his voice out of the silence in a high strong chant. Before the last phrase was finished the others opened their throats to echo his theme in a resounding chorus. As they sang together, their red shining arms lifted the sticks and stabbed the earth and turned the sod, their glistening shoulders rolled to the rhythm, their throats vibrated like a singing bird's. The smooth rippling movements of their limbs, the vigorous chant, the rise and fall of the digging-sticks merged into a living unity; the song was as much a part of the breaking of the sod as the sharp bite of the stick, or the muscles that moved beneath the skin of the men's shoulders like fish swimming under water.

SONG OF THE CULTIVATORS

You who woke up early at dawn, who woke you?
When we woke we found that the grass was growing.
Mother, you are short as a knife-haft, yet you
    Cook for the workers.

You girls, you who weed in the garden, weed a
While, then turn your eyes to the sky—what hide you?

What lies hidden, what do you look for, oh you
    Girls who are weeding?

Men who dig beyond the swift river, we will
Shoot our arrows over the water, for your
Knives make sounds like knives of the women; you are
    Weaker than women.

Men who dwell across the broad valley, once you
Sold a sheep whose penis was like a man's, and
So we hurl these pebbles against you, now we
    Stone you with pebbles.

When you meet a man with a sore leg, bring him;
I will follow him by the flies that cluster
On the sores that cover him, find him when he
    Loses the pathway.

When you meet a girl who has sore eyes, bring her;
She was told no man would desire her sore-eyed,
None will lie with maidens with sore eyes, she will
    Stay with me always.

Oh you girl who walks on the path, stand silent—
Let me greet you, lest you be greeted by the
Lazy man who eats of the herb that lazy
    Mothers will pluck him.

Man who wanders far from the gardens, tell me,
We were friends, oh wanderer, why then did you
Break our friendship?   Can you remember now my
    Name, the hard worker?

I have taken life, but you must not ask me
Who is dead; the thing that I killed lies here, my
Knife has slain it, here in the shamba; now my
    Mother will praise me.

Behind the diggers followed the women, breaking heavy
clods with clubs, and pounding the soil into a coarse tilth.
As the day grew hotter the rhythm slackened.   When the sun
was overhead the song ceased and the diggers, moist with sweat,
worked slowly and with frequent rests.   Before the shadows
had grown to the length of a man they ceased work altogether
and lounged until nightfall under the trees, smacking their lips
over soured millet gruel and curdled milk, and talking of the
prodigious amount of work they had performed.

3

AFTER nightfall Matu clung always to his mother, and stayed with her in the women's huts. He was frightened of the strange dim shapes that lay over the grass in the night-time, of the hoot of the owl, of the spirits that came out of the ground, and of the distant voices of young men raised in laughter and song. While his father was away he was frightened, too, of the company of men in the thingira, of their wisdom and deep laughter, and of the shame that would fall on him if he offended these grave, all-powerful persons who governed the country and owned its wealth : the very rulers of the earth itself, and all that it supported.

But the soft talk of the women often bored him; and after the meal, hot and savoury from the cooking-pot, he would sometimes ask his mother to tell a story. Then, if she was in a good humour, she would recount some fable that she remembered from her own childhood. Matu would listen enthralled, especially if it concerned a very cunning squirrel, of whose adventures he never tired. In his career this squirrel experienced many setbacks, but never one to which his wit and ingenuity were unequal.

One day the squirrel stole a small he-goat and concealed it in a granary. But the store was full of good food and the goat ate until it became so fat that it could not possibly get out of the door. The squirrel, in great distress, went to seek advice from his friends. His first appeal was to the hyena.

"I should be delighted to come to your assistance," the hyena said.

"Thank you," the squirrel replied, "but before you help me, tell me what you will say to the he-goat when you are getting it out of the granary."

"I will say 'ow-u-ow,' " the hyena answered, and he howled loudly.

"No, that's no good at all," the squirrel said. "My goat would only be very frightened."

He ran off to the forest to find the bushbuck, to whom he told the story.

"Certainly," the bushbuck said politely. "I will help with pleasure."

"Before you do so," the squirrel asked, "tell me what you will say to my goat when you are setting him free."

"I shall say 'kya, kya, kya,'" the bushbuck answered, and barked sharply.

"That will not do at all," the squirrel said; and he ran off to find the porcupine. But the porcupine proposed to rattle his quills and stamp; and the Colobus monkey could only cry like a baby; and the elephant made a terrifying noise with his trunk; and the reedbuck whistled harshly like a boy; and the wild pig merely snorted.

But at last the squirrel met the leopard, a very cunning animal, who had a far more intelligent suggestion.

"I will say to the goat . . ." the leopard began; and then he whistled blandly and clucked his tongue.

The squirrel was delighted, and took the leopard to the granary to free the goat. But the leopard went inside and killed the goat by breaking its neck.

"Oh, what have you done? You have killed my beautiful fat he-goat!" the squirrel cried in bitter distress.

"Indeed my sorrow is great," the leopard said. "I killed it by mistake, because my claws are so big and sharp. Do not grieve, however, we will roast the goat and eat it."

So the leopard asked the squirrel to find a fire and bring back a burning log. The squirrel, however, was suspicious, and in a short while he returned to say that he could not find a fire. The leopard volunteered to look, and when he had gone the squirrel quickly cut up the meat and hid it in a tree. When the leopard returned and asked for a share of the meat, the squirrel refused; and so the leopard had to go away hungry, and very angry.

On reaching his home he said to his cubs: "Go to the pool

in the river that the squirrel visits every day to drink and hide in the bushes; and when the squirrel comes, kill him."

But the squirrel was very cunning. Whenever he went to drink he disguised himself as a bundle of leaves and the cubs did not recognise him.

"The squirrel is not there," they told their father, "but every day a bundle of leaves comes down to drink."

"That *is* the squirrel," the leopard said. "Next time the leaves come you are to capture them and bring them to me."

So the squirrel was captured and brought to the leopard, who said: "You cheated me over the meat, and now I am going to eat you."

"Very well," the squirrel answered.

The leopard took the bundle of leaves containing the squirrel to his mother and said: "Here is food, you must cook it for me; but you must not look at what is inside. You must put it straight into the pot."

"Very well," his mother answered.

When the leopard had gone away, his mother, who was full of curiosity, disobeyed her son and untied the leaves to see what was inside. The squirrel jumped out. She was so taken aback with astonishment that the squirrel was able to throw her into the big pot on the fire. Then he stirred the pot until she was thoroughly boiled.

When the leopard returned he called through the door of the hut:

"Well, is my food ready?"

The squirrel imitated the voice of the leopard's mother, and called: "Yes, my son, it is ready; come and eat."

The leopard entered, took the meat from the pot, and ate it.

"This meat is very bitter," he said. "There is something the matter with it."

"It is the meat that you gave me," the squirrel replied, still imitating the old leopardess' voice, "and you must eat it all up."

So the leopard did so. As soon as he had finished, the squirrel threw off his disguise, ran through the open door, and escaped. After that the leopard was an object of ridicule to everyone because he had eaten his mother. Wherever he went people pointed him out, and said: "Look at the leopard; he is the one that ate his mother." Then they would laugh till their sides shook, and the leopard was filled with shame.

4

MUTHENGI scorned women's huts and women's stories. At night he would sit in the thingira, hidden among deep shadows thrown by the red glowing fire. There, with thick warm smoke in his lungs and a heavy sense of masculinity wrapping him round like a blanket, he would listen to the talk of his elders: talk of goats and bride-payments, bargains and quarrels, lawsuits and charms and magic, and sometimes of war. Thus he learnt the ways of the world and its people, until sleep crept into his mouth like a caterpillar and thickened his tongue, and he crawled on to a pile of skins at the side of the hut to slumber.

Muthengi was a great favourite of his grandfather's. The old man talked to him often in the evenings, for he did not want his grandson to grow into an uncouth lad, ignorant of custom and tradition. He took delight in teaching Muthengi the names of all his goats, and soon found that he had a quick and willing pupil.

"When I am a man I shall have more goats than there are names for goats," Muthengi said. "I shall have ten he-goats called Kimaira and ten called Gicugu, and very many female goats of red, and white, and grey; some with spots on the head, or white stripes round the body, and others the colour of a guinea-fowl."

"The sound of the mortar travels far over the ridges," the old man said in rebuke, "but the mortar stays always in the village. Remember that boasting is the speech of fools." Muthengi was silent, abashed, but he could see from his grandfather's wrinkled face that the words were not spoken in anger. Later, Mahenia called him out of the shadows to squat at his feet, helped himself to snuff from a black wooden bottle that hung around his neck, and said :

"When the time is come you will be circumcised and become a warrior, and go with other warriors of your age-grade to fight men from Kutu's or from Kaheri's ridges; and yours will be the task of guarding the wealth of our clan from the Masai of the plains. The Masai are more terrible than lions, and when war-clubs are hurled against their shields the noise is louder than the noise of thunder. If you are to win renown in war your heart must be fearless, you must be stronger than the victorious buffalo that has trampled upon his rival."

Muthengi listened entranced, his eyes shining and wide, but he said nothing.

"When you are circumcised," his grandfather continued, "you must be full of wisdom as well as strength, for fools become poor men for whom none has respect—not even God; and men of other clans hurl insults at them across the river.

"There are many kinds of knowledge of which you must learn. There is knowledge of crops and of seasons; of the planting of millet at one season and beans at another; of the scaring of wild pigs and the trapping of porcupines. There is knowledge of the smoking of beehives so that the bees swarm in your barrels; and of cattle so that cows grow fat with calf; and of goats, that they may increase; and of trade, that you may exercise greater cunning than your neighbour. There is knowledge of magic, and of war; of love, and of good manners, so that you shall not pick quarrels with your kinsmen, nor disgrace your clan. There is evil knowledge of sorcery and witchcraft, from which you must learn to protect yourself; for the world is full of evil, and the ignorant man who lacks protection is like a lost kid who strays outside the goats' enclosure in a land that is infested with hungry hyenas. There are so many kinds of knowledge that I could not tell you the whole of it, even if I would; and all this you must learn.

" But now I shall tell you of one kind of knowledge which you must know before you are circumcised and become a man; and this is the knowledge of our people, the Kikuyu, and of how God created our people and the whole world; for even the Masai were created by God."

Mahenia helped himself again to the black powder from his bottle, and sniffed deeply. Points of reflected light jumped like dancing fireflies about the chains that dangled from his neck, the ear ornaments that hung below his shoulders and the bangles on his arms. His crinkled face looked wise and kindly in the firelight. Muthengi squatted by his knees, all sleep forgotten, his eyes wondering and rapt.

"In the beginning God made the world," Mahenia said. "First he mixed the land and the water, as women mix clay for a pot, and he made Kerinyagga, and moulded the world around it. And then God made the first man, whose name was Gikuyu, and sent him to dwell upon the earth at a place beside the Chania river. But the rainbow which then lived on the land, and was something like a snake, came and fought Gikuyu; so God gave him a wife, whose name was Mumbi, the creator, from whom all the people of our race are sprung. In time Mumbi bore nine daughters, and from the wombs of these nine daughters came the ancestors of the nine groups of our tribe. To-day the descendants of these nine daughters fill the world, and the men of each group are as brothers, for they come from the womb of one mother.

"When you are circumcised and go upon long journeys you will meet men of your own group, which is called Agachiku, and they will give you food and shelter and make you welcome. And you may not take a girl from your own group for a wife, because your ancestors and hers were the same; nor must you marry a girl from your mother's group, for her ancestors and the ancestors of your mother were the same.

"Now Gikuyu had a son Njiri, and told him divide the waters from the land. This Njiri did. He dug many channels, and the water flowed into them, and they became rivers. Then God imprisoned the rainbow in the waterfalls, where it lives to this day. Sometimes you may see it there, bound to a rock under the spray. At night it comes out of the water in search of goats or cattle to eat, and it climbs among the trees, but its tail must always remain in the water.

"At the beginning of the world the Kikuyu did not dwell on this side of the mountain; they lived on the side nearest the sunrise, where the Wakamba, who were then of the same tribe as the Kikuyu, now dwell. A long time ago an old man and his wife started on a journey across Kerinyagga. On the way they grew very hungry, and were about to die from lack of food. So the old man climbed up the mountain to see God and ask for food. God was sorry for him and gave him sheep and goats; and from these animals all the sheep and goats of the Kikuyu are descended.

"God gave him all the land on this side of the mountain, which was then forest, to cultivate; and he gave the plains below to the Masai for their cattle. Today the Masai drink from the rivers that flow from the hill they call Sattima, and the Kikuyu drink from the rivers that flow from Kerinyagga; but neither may drink from the rivers which belong to the other.

"God also created a race of hunters, the Agumba, who lived in the forest in holes in the ground, and fed upon honey and the flesh of wild animals. But the Kikuyu must never eat the meat of wild beasts, whether they are bushbuck or elephants, pigs or rats. Those who do so will become unclean, and fall sick, and die.

"And remember well that, because you are born into the Agachiku group, you must not work in iron as a smith, nor use the knife of the circumcisor; for if you do these things a deadly curse will fall upon you. Men of the group Mwesaga, also, may not work in iron; the eyes of the men of that group can see the rain before it comes from behind the mountain; they have a charm to stop rain. And you must beware if men of the group Eithaga should ever praise you, or your goats, or your crops; for they know the secret of a very powerful curse which they can use to bring sickness upon you, or your goats, or your crops.

"Now the generation which followed that of Njiri the son of Mumbi was called Mandoti; and the generation that came from the eastern side of the mountain was called Mathathi. After the Mathathi the rule of the country passed to the Chiera, and then to the Ndemi; during this age many trees were felled. Then came the generation Iregi, the revolters, when tall warriors came with spears from the north. My father belonged to this generation. When he grew old, he and the men who were circumcised with him relinquished the rule of the country to the generation Maina, which is my generation, and which still governs the land. One day the next generation, Mwangi, will take our places; and after that the generation Muirungu will follow. And the oldest men of the ruling generation, whose wives are past the age of child-bearing, are charged with the conduct of sacrifices to God, if he should be angry and hold back rain; for it is only the elders of the people, those who have finished with governing the country, who can speak with God and prepare sacrifices under the sacred fig-trees to please him. For God is very old; and yet he grows no older, and he lives alone."

"If God is so powerful that he can command the rain," Muthengi said, "he must have many cattle—more than he can count."

"God has no cattle," the old man answered. "He does not need them, for he has no wives nor sons. The Kikuyu are his cattle; and when they show increase he is pleased. Children are the wealth of the Kikuyu because they enrich their father's clan; therefore a barren woman is like a barren cow: she adds nothing to the wealth of her husband's clan. It is only through the evil magic of enemies that women and cows become barren.

"When you become a man you must walk in peace among your neighbours, show respect for elders at all times, and give no offence to strangers, lest they curse you. You must show courtesy to old women and step from the path so that they may pass; for old women beyond the age of child-bearing know a powerful curse to bring barrenness upon wives and cattle, and even upon goats. And you must respect the property of all men and women; for the child who steals food from his step-mother's granary will steal the goats of his neighbour when he becomes a man, and for this he will have to pay heavy fines. If he offends often, he will perhaps be slain by his kinsmen as the louse is slain between the fingers; or perhaps by a spirit that lives in the fire of every hut, whose eye is red and never closes. This spirit will rise up when a thief enters a hut, and suffocate him, and the owner will find the thief's dead body on the floor when he returns. Remember this, that the thief brings shame upon his clan; and remember too the saying : another person's ornaments tire the neck. Now you must sleep, for you are a child; but if you behave as I have told you, and obey your father's commands, when you are circumcised you will become a great warrior, and capture many cattle, and bring wealth and honour to your clan."

By this time Muthengi's eyes were heavy, and sleep was mixing with the wonder in his mind as rain mixes with earth.

"There is so much to learn," he said; "a man must have great wisdom to know everything."

The old man chuckled, and sucked up a deep pinch of snuff.

"When you are a warrior and your blood is hot, you will know everything," he said. "When you become one of the ruling generation you will know much, but less than before; and when you are old you will know little, save that growth follows rain, that the tree destroyed by fire cannot put forth new roots, that seed will ripen again into seed in its own time, and that no man can foretell the whims of God. Now sleep, for the moon is high and you are young."

5

WASERU returned to his father's homestead at noon, but the old man was at a beer-drink, and it was after nightfall before he appeared. He greeted his two sons cordially and sat down by the fire in the thingira to tell them all the gossip he had heard.

A man just returned from a visit to a kinsman, two days' journey down the rivers, had brought news of a disastrous Masai raid on the district called Wyaki's, after the leader of warriors in that region. He had observed, too, that many people were growing a crop, new to him, called maize. Seed had been brought during the rule of the last generation by tall, red-skinned men with hairy faces who came sometimes from a long way off to exchange elephant tusks for beads, wire and bangles, and for a kind of cloth that was stronger than bark. Because the big ears were wrapped in a thin green cloak, birds could not get at them, so the crop was an easier one to cultivate than millet. Waseru listened to this talk with great attention, for birds abounded in the forest. He had eaten maize and found it good. When he could get some seed, he decided, he would tell his wife to plant it.

At last, after the meal, Waseru's turn came. In a low tone he spoke of his journey to Ndolia's village. He talked of the state of the crops, the health of the cattle, the peace of the country; of Ndolia's wealth, and of the number of his wives. He spread his talk like a cloak to shroud the hard core of his tale. Little by little he drew it aside until his father could see the ugly shape beneath, the cruel outline of fact. It would have been difficult to say at what point the old man knew that Ndolia demanded seventeen goats, two fat rams, and ten gourds of beer; but before Waseru's soft voice had finished its tale, he knew the truth.

He sat for some time without speech, gazing at the fire. Then he said:

"The clan of Ndolia is rich and strong and owns many cattle and goats. Therefore Ndolia demands much from my father's clan, which is not strong, and has few cattle. It was ever thus; it is always the poor man's goat that is taken by the leopard. I do not think that the council of elders would grant these exorbitant demands."

"That may be so," Waseru agreed, "but Matu, my son, has a thahu. How can he be purified unless Ndolia's curse is lifted?

And how shall this be done unless Ndolia's demands are met?"

"Matu will grow into a man and add strength to our clan," Mahenia said. "It is not yet time for him to die. Goats shall be found to pay Ndolia, but not all at once. I shall pay him eight goats before witnesses, together with a fat ram and three full gourds of beer; then he will remove the curse and Matu can be purified. Then I shall dispute the remainder of his claim before the elders' council. It is enough. Tomorrow I shall visit the muramati. He shall witness the payment, so that there shall be no dispute."

Next day Mahenia selected the goats with great care. They must not be obvious weaklings, nor diseased, nor over-thin; but neither must they be taken from the fat and sturdy of the flock. They must be the poorest that Ndolia would be likely to accept, and their choice needed deep thought and nice judgment. The muramati of the clan had given his approval to Mahenia's plan and sent his son—a quiet, hard-working man of middle age called Gacheche—to witness the payment.

The women, meanwhile, set to work to make beer. Early in the morning Waseru and his brother Ngarariga brought armfuls of sugar-canes and laid them outside the compound, beside the big pounding-log. They stripped off the skin, cut up the white sticks, and threw them into round basins hollowed out of the prostrate log. Three or four women from nearby homesteads came to help Mahenia's wives. When all was ready the women ranged themselves along the log and began to pound the cane into pulp with club-ended wooden mortars, singing as they did so a high-pitched rhythmic song. Girls carried the pulped cane on big woven platters to a group of men seated a little way off, with open calabashes beside them. Each man took a handful of the pulp, tied it to a short stick with a length of twine, and squeezed the spindle-shaped bundle between his hands. Thick juice ran out into the calabashes in a cloudy stream. Thence it was poured into fat-bellied, thin-necked gourds into which dried alofa pods had already been thrown to start fermentation. The full gourds were taken to Mahenia's thingira and ranged around the fire, like rotund dwarfs immobile at a council meeting, to allow the beer to bubble and ferment until next morning.

A procession set out early for Ndolia's homestead. Waseru led the way, driving before him the eight selected goats and a fat ram. Gacheche followed, and then the three women—Waseru's wife and his two stepmothers—doubled under the heavy gourds. At Ndolia's they found a group of elders squatting in a circle in the shaded compound, waiting like vultures around a sick zebra for the arrival of the beer. When it appeared there was a stir among them as if a stone had been hurled among the vultures. The old men gazed with faded eager eyes at the gourds, their mouths watering in anticipation.

Ndolia was angry when he saw eight goats instead of seventeen, and even angrier when their blemishes were revealed to his experienced eye. A scrawnier, uglier lot of animals had never been seen, he exclaimed; they were forest rats rather than goats. Waseru defended them with passion, reciting the virtues of each one; and though Ndolia would have wished to reject them, or at least to argue all day, his kinsmen grew so impatient to broach the beer that he had to give way. He poured the beer into drinking-horns, spilt a little on the ground for his ancestors' spirits, and handed the horns to his eldest son to be passed around the circle. His cunning face was impassive, but satisfaction gleamed in his avaricious eyes. Eight more goats—not such bad ones, although he would certainly never admit it—and a fat ram; nine more goats and another ram to come; good beer; and victory over a poor unhonoured clan. No doubt about it, God was good.

Next morning he and a group of men of his own clan and generation gathered in a circle under the tall fig-tree outside the compound. Ndolia lifted his arms towards Kerinyagga and solemnly retracted the curse that he had laid upon Waseru's clan, crops and offspring. Then the fat ram was slain, and roasted, and a feast held to mark the end of the dispute.

6

THE purification of Matu took place outside Irumu's homestead, on an open piece of pasture shaded by a clump of trees. Waseru drove a goat before him, an old and skinny animal that was likely to die before long in any case; its skin would be the mundu-mugu's fee. Wanjeri followed with the baby on her back and Matu, spindle-legged and silent, trotted along behind.

Irumu scooped a shallow cup-shaped hole in the red earth with the point of his sword and in it laid two large banana leaves so as to make a basin. Waseru filled it with water from a gourd. Then he handed Irumu a small calabash of millet, the token payment without which no mundu-mugu could use his powers. Irumu sprinkled over the water a little powder which he tipped from three gourds, stoppered with cows' tails, that he took from his magic bag.

"You thahu, go away, grow thin and disappear," he chanted, "as this powder which I scatter on the water grows thin, spreads out, disappears. Now you must scatter away, you thahu, and grow thin, and dissolve like the clouds over Kerinyagga in the late afternoon." He added from a smaller gourd a few drops of a thick liquid said to contain the fat of a lion, of a leopard and of an ostrich, mixed with castor oil and the ground-up roots of a shrub. Matu, solemn and scared, was led up to the basin and told to squat on his heels opposite Irumu. His scanty cloak loosely covered his small thin buttocks, and flapped about his projecting ribs. His bones looked as fragile as the legs of a bird.

The goat was brought. Irumu took up a knife, split its nose, and rubbed powdered lime into the incision with the palm of his hand. He seized the goat by the shoulders and walked it on its hindlegs around the basin, once in each direction, so that it dripped blood in a circle as it went. All the time he chanted loudly that the thahu was to leave the child, never to return. Then he squatted down, dipped the goat's right forefoot in the water, and held it to Matu's mouth. The boy sucked off the liquid and spat it out to his left; then sucked at the left hoof, and spat to his right. All the time Irumu chanted in a high thin voice : "Vomit out, vomit out; let the thahu be vomited out."

The goat was taken behind Matu's back and its bleeding nose thrust in turn under each armpit. He licked the nose and spat out the blood and medicine to left and right. "If the thahu comes from under the left arm, if it comes from under the right arm, let it be vomited out," Irumu chanted. He lifted the goat on to Matu's back and cried : "Let the thahu be like a load on the back that is cast off as I cast off this goat." A boy who was looking on seized the animal's hindlegs and stretched it on its back, while Irumu, grasping a knife, slit open its belly and pulled out part of the stomach. This he opened deftly and extracted a handful of the yellow-green, half-digested contents, which he threw into the basin. He peeled and sharpened a small stick and pinned the edges of the severed stomach neatly together with the skewer. Then he tucked the bulging stomach back into the body cavity of the struggling goat, dipped two twisted antelope horns that he drew from his bag into the dark-brown water, and held their tips to Matu's mouth. The boy spat out the liquid many times, to right and left, while Irumu chanted faster and faster : "Vomit out, vomit out, let the thahu be vomited out," until the words were rushing from his mouth like the waters of a river in flood.

"If the thahu came through the arms, if it came through the feet, if it came through the navel, if it came through the anus, if it came through the roof of the hut, let it be vomited out. If it came from a woman, if the milk of woman fell upon him, let it be vomited out. If it came from the hut, if it came from the homestead, from the dung of a hyena left within the fence, let it be vomited out, let it dissolve like mist and go far away to the land of the Wakamba, beyond the mountain Kianjahé."

A pause followed while Irumu squeezed the goat's windpipe until the animal became limp and all but dead, peeled off its skin, and broke its legs. The longer a little life stayed with

the goat, the longer would life also inhabit the patient's body.
He cut strips from the stomach, took out the heart, testes and
eyes, and threw them all into the basin. From the rest of the
stomach he cut two round discs, made a hole in the centre of
each, and slipped them over his two horns so that they became
like little ruffs; and then he hung a strip of intestine over Matu's
shoulders. Once again the horns were dipped into the liquid,
in which the goat's eyes floated like gelatinous islands in a
dark lake thick with decaying weeds, and thrust their tips
into Matu's mouth for him to suck and spit. When this was
done Irumu severed the strips of gut with a quick slash of the
knife and carried them to the bush. Here he buried them in
the undergrowth at the foot of a tree, and with them the thahu,
which had passed into the intestine of the goat. The eyes were
buried separately under another bush, looking upwards in a
perpetual prayer that God might give wealth to Matu's father.
Now the thahu that caused Matu's sickness had been driven
out, but the gates of his body had still to be sealed against its
return. This was done with three fresh medicines—a white
chalk, a black ash, and a red powder—which Irumu mixed with
spittle and smeared on to Matu's nose, neck and navel, and between his toes.

When the meat of the sacrificial goat was roasted Waseru ate
his portion with relish and a sense of peace that he had long
lacked. Now that Matu was cleansed the boy's health would
return and he would grow strong. And no doubt Waseru's
own luck would change, too, so that he would be able to repay
the heavy debt he owed his father.

7

WASERU and his family returned to their own shamba next
morning. Already they had been too long away from the
growing crops. When they entered the shade of the forest it
was as though they had passed suddenly into nightfall. The
white sunlight was stained a clear green, the air was soft and

cool as mountain mists. Straight-boled trees stood motionless as long-legged cranes waiting patiently for the darting of a fish in the still pool at their feet; but all was movement and bustle in the world above. Long-tailed Colobus monkeys leaped in flashes of black and white, bending the creaking branches as they landed gently on the next-door tree; wood-pigeons called in a melancholy cadence and plaintain-eaters emitted their loud unbirdlike croak. In crevices of the bark, in dark safe holes in the trunks, hunched furry hyraxes slept, betraying their presence to none. On the ground below small fragile-ankled dikdiks picked their way fastidiously among fallen twigs, their round, deep-purple eyes bright with vigilance, fearful of the sleeping leopard; bushbuck and the wary bongo drowsed in thickets, and the giant forest-hog slumbered with his tusks hung low, black as a shadow.

Muthengi hated the forest. It was lonely and dark, and full of ogres. He wanted the light, the laughter, the campanion-ship of cultivated ridges; the tinkle of goat-bells, the song of cultivators were sweet in his ears. But Matu lifted his head when they entered the shadows, and looked about him with pleasure. Outside the sun hurt his head and the incessant herding of goats tired his legs. Here was peace and freedom, and time to dream.

The distance to Waseru's shamba was short, but the path was slippery and steep. Three elephants had used it the night before; a row of watery craters showed where their feet had trod. It was hard, slow going for burdened women; but Wanjeri braced her thick muscles and heaved herself and her heavy sacks out of the muddy pits. The family crossed the swift-flowing Ragati river by a felled log bridge, and saw a roughly built shelter and a small clearing above them on the slope of the hill. Unburnt logs lay across the ground like fallen warriors, and in the gap that their felling had left the sun streamed down on to the rich broken earth and on to the green leaves of the millet that was sprouting with vigour among the charred stumps.

Waseru paused a moment at the foot of the hill to look at it with satisfaction in his heart. It was the work of his hands. Soon the millet would fill the ear. There had been rain, and the earth was moist beneath his feet, the sun on his shoulder warmer than glowing embers. Now surely God would be good, and the crops heavy. "Truly, the soil is fat," he thought, "as fat as the tail of a ram ready for the feast." But he could not show arrogance by voicing such thoughts aloud. He spat and said to his wife : "Now come, and store the food, and go quickly to work with your hoe in the shamba, for the weeds will have grown high in your absence and there is much to be done."

"Ee, you talk always of work," she replied.

She jerked the load farther forward on her shoulders and plodded with bent knees up the slope to her forest home.

CHAPTER IV

The Forest Shamba

I

BIRDS came in twittering excited clouds, later in the season, to peck ripening millet out of the ear. Waseru built a platform in the centre of the shamba and one of the boys was always on duty there, hurling stones from a leather sling on his arm and shouting until his voice grew hoarse. Many fat wood-pigeons came, strutting arrogantly in their green-and-grey plumage; and big dark-blue starlings, gleaming like metal in the sun; and small unobtrusive waxbills with delicate red beaks, who fluttered like fastidious bees among the stiff fingers of the ripening crop.

Muthengi and Matu resorted to cunning as well as to direct attack. From the moist banks of the river they plucked fruits of the glossy-leaved mwerere bush, and these they cut open with a knife. The centre of the fruit was filled with a thick white latex. Into this they dipped sticks, twisting the glutinous latex round and round the points, and then they placed the sticky-ended twigs in bushes and trees all around the shamba. Sometimes a bird would settle on a stick, and then its feet would become hopelessly trapped. There it would flutter, beating its small wings against the air and bursting its throat with frantic screeches, until gradually its wing-beats slackened, a film spread over its eyes, and thirst and starvation put out the spark of life.

At night there were other enemies to be repulsed. By the side of the platform Waseru built a little shelter of branches. Here he shivered, night after night, his club by his side, guarding his crop against the ravages of wild pigs and porcupines. He would wake in the stillness of midnight to see the moon, pale as a shield, behind the moving branches of trees, and to hear a faint rustling in the millet. Sometimes a soft, contented grunt betrayed the presence of a pig digging out the roots of the precious crop with its tusks and trampling the millet-heads underfoot. Waseru would dart out of his shelter with a shout that echoed through the silent trees and hurl his club swiftly at the sound. Then there would be a snort, the tattoo of stampeding feet, and a dark streak of waving millet-heads across the lonely moon-flooded field.

Sometimes he would prowl along the edges of the shamba, a cold moon-shadow flickering mistily by his side, to scare away the silent soft-coated bushbuck and the mild-eyed dikdiks that came to nibble at the grain. The bushbuck, when they felt the earth shake under his footfall, would stand like black rocks among the white-stalked millet, their heads thrown back and their twisted horns pointing to the moon; and then in a single bound they would vanish into the shadows and become dissolved in night.

Strange rustles came sometimes from behind the threatening forest wall that hemmed in the little shamba, a wall beyond which no moonlight penetrated. The sound of the ears of millet singing very softly to each other as they swayed like dancers to the music of a gentle wind was reassuring to Waseru. The millet was his, and he knew its language. Soon it would be singing lightly to him in the moonlight, "I am ripe, I am ready, deliver me now of my children, for they are heavy within me," and he would know that the ears cried for the knife. But beyond the leafy wall were things that spoke soundless language, things that crawled in darkness and were foes of men. The forest itself was an enemy, and sheltered enemies; there were ogres in it, and evil spirits, and—it was said—a monster that sucked the blood of men.

The wind-rippled sea on which the two boys gazed down every day from their platform changed from green to pale brown and then to gold; and when the moon began to wane it was ripe for harvest. To cut the heads with a knife and carry them to the homestead was woman's work; but since the shamba was a large one, Waseru worked side by side with his wife and told Muthengi to help also. Muthengi said nothing, but in his heart he resented the order. Because Wanjeri had no daughters and Waseru no unmarried sisters, he had to perform many women's tasks that were undignified for boys—carrying water, for instance, and firewood, even stirring the gruel when Wanjeri was busy elsewhere.

2

THE time had come, Waseru decided, to build a proper house; and for this, beer must be brewed. He owned no cane plantations, but honey made a stronger brew than sugar juice. Before the rains he had fixed several barrels in the forks of trees. Now, when the pale purple, sweet-scented blossoms of the muthakwa bush were beginning to fade, was the honey-gathering season. Waseru called on his half-brother Ngarariga and two of his companions to help; and one evening, when the sun was low in the sky, they set out with leather pouches slung over their shoulders.

The forest was too dense to penetrate except along paths made by elephants. Soon they came to an ageing tree with a hollow cavity in its trunk. The men gazed up into the tangled branches until they were satisfied that many small black specks, like dust-motes in a sunbeam, were darting to and fro against the blue sky.

Working swiftly and silently, they pulled and hacked at tough, twisted lianas dangling from the tree tops like long whiskers from the beard of the sun, and wound several tendrils together into a rope. Ngarariga, who was young and agile, fastened a strip of liana to his ankles, hugged the tree with both arms, and levered his body upwards with his manacled feet. It was a trick the Kikuyu had learned many generations ago from the Agumba, the pit-dwelling dwarfs. He tied the liana rope to a branch and descended, and the party waited until nightfall for the bees to go to sleep. Grey-eyed dusk came swiftly as a leopard from the thicket; his icy breath chilled the flesh of the waiting men. They drew their skin cloaks around their knees and watched the shadows dissolve and then the early stars spring out of a soft blue sky, like white flowers of forest creepers opening in the thickets. When the stars had grown hard and brilliant behind the roof of leaves and the air was cold as a rock beneath a waterfall, Waseru took his fire-sticks and some dried grass from his leather pouch and spun the hard stick against the soft between the palms of his hands. Soon a spark flew out and took root in the little pile of sawdust that the stick had ground out of the soft wood; and in a moment small flames were dancing in the brushwood. Ngarariga made and lit a torch of sticks and led the way up the liana rope into the tree. Waseru followed, his leather bag over his shoulder.

The bees' retreat was in a hollow of the trunk. Ngarariga thrust his burning torch deep into the tree's heart and thick, acrid smoke curled into the crannies of the wood. The bees rose suddenly out of the trunk in a body, with a communal scream of anger and dismay. They fled into the smokeless air above, too taken aback to assault the men who clung like hyraxes to the tree. Ngarariga held the torch aloft while Waseru plunged his arm into the cavity and scooped handful after handful of thick, glutinous honey into his leather bag. When the store was exhausted the two slid down to the ground, unstung, well satisfied with the harvest of the bees.

3

THE building of a hut was not a task that could be performed by one man's family alone. The help of clansmen and neighbours was expected and freely given. Three days before the appointed time, on the first day of the new moon, a number of Waseru's relatives arrived in a party to cut poles for the walls and roof. Next day a long file of women wound up the path with loads of reeds for thatch on their backs. By the third day Wanjeri had ground a quantity of millet, and honey-beer had been well fermented in two big gourds. When all was ready she went down to her father-in-law's homestead and pulled from the roof of her cousin's hut—which had been hers—a handful of thatch from above the door, and another from the back. This she carried home and put on one side, ready to fix into the new roof next day.

The young men arrived early, singing light-hearted songs about each other's love affairs; the married men, who followed after, talked and joked with more restraint, and worked with greater concentration. When all was ready Waseru stepped forward and drew a circle on the ground to mark the circumference of the walls. Then, taking an axe in one hand and a calabash of uncooked millet gruel in the other, he walked around the circle, chopping at the ground with the axe, and pouring libations of gruel into the shallow furrow. As he went he prayed aloud to the spirits of his ancestors to bless the house and to bring him good fortune.

Then the building began. Holes were dug for the wall-posts, and nineteen stout poles with forked tops were planted firmly in them. In the meantime another group of men was at work on the framework of the roof, lashing branches to a hoop of twisted wands at one end and to a stout axial stake at the other. A skeleton roof shaped like a big convolvulus blossom grew under their hands in a few hours. The spaces between the poles of the wall were filled by roughly hewn planks cemented by clay; the roof was lifted on and secured; and before noon the framework of the hut stood ready for thatching.

When the men had finished and refreshed themselves with cooked food and soured millet gruel, they returned together to their own villages, singing as they went, leaving the women to their share of the task.

Several of the older wives climbed on to the roof with the agility of monkeys, and soon the air was full of flying bundles of reeds thrown up to them by women on the ground, caught neatly in one hand, and secured in tight-packed rows to the roof's framework. Waseru watched contentedly while he put the finishing touches to the woven wicker door. Wanjeri carefully fixed the bundle of reeds from her old hut over the door and above the eaves at the back of her new dwelling, so that the continuity of her life should not be broken. Before sunset the hut was ready—bad fortune would come to the man whose dwelling was not completed between sunrise and sunset, for evil spirits might take possession—and the women had departed to their own homes.

Next day a party was held for the elders whose sons and nephews had helped in the building. Waseru first spilled a drinking-horn of beer and a calabash of fat to the ground for the spirits of his ancestors, and then poured all day for the old men; but he himself drank nothing, for he was a young man not yet entitled to drink beer. It was long past nightfall when the last of the elders, walking jerkily and conversing garrulously with himself, stumbled down the path towards his homestead.

4

BEFORE the rains the bite of the sun grew sharper and heat at midday lay heavily over the dusty cultivation. The weeders, doubled over their work like bent pins, their damp foreheads almost resting on the ground, grew listless; and in the heat of the day they would rest in the thin shade of yam vines or castor-oil bushes, drowsily suckling their babies or talking in soft rippling voices. Down towards the edge of the great plain Laikipia cattle swam in the heat-haze by the salt-lick; the grass was pale and brittle, dry as the chewed-out fibre of cane.

Rains were due once in each season, but in alternate seasons they were heavy: these were called the rains of the beans; the lighter downfall, rains of the millet. The reason for this was that after the heavier rains a period of cold, cloudy weather often followed. Then millet and sorghum would not ripen well, and might even rot in the ear. But beans, sweet potatoes and pigeon peas did not mind the sunless months and so could be safely planted in the heavier rainy season. But they, in their turn, would seldom flourish if planted in the lighter millet rains, for they grew slowly, and needed as much moisture as they could get during their growth.

The rains delayed, this season; eyes were raised continually towards the depthless sky. Every morning the sun flooded those hard and empty spaces without impediment; no mists, hinting at moisture, softened the dawn. In the afternoons fat-bellied clouds drifted along the horizon, patterning the land beneath with shadows as though giant birds of grotesque shapes were sailing overhead; but there was no rain in them. As the processes of the earth slowed almost to a standstill, eyes were turned more often towards Kerinyagga, where dwelt God who sent or withheld the rain according to his pleasure. Waseru's heart grew heavier with anxiety every day. He wondered why God, to whom Kerinyagga was no bigger than a stool, did not stretch out his arms to seize handfuls of the sky and squeeze it, as men squeezed juice from shredded cane, so as to wring the rain out of its formless fibres.

Misgivings deepened as the old moon waned, and the elders debated whether a sacrifice should be made to God. For three days the moon died, and nothing could be done; but then soldier ants emerged from underground to wind their way in purposeful columns through the shambas, along their own walled highways; and the old men nodded their heads and said that rain, the bridegroom who never tired of bringing gifts, was near.

It came in the afternoon, after a day of heat and flies. A huge dark cloud rolled like a line of black-plumed warriors from behind the hills and broke with a crash of thunder, loud as the sound of a thousand warriors' clubs against the shields of the defenders. The storm hurled its countless spears of plenty with steady fury on the thirsty earth, and a solid sheet of water spilled from the eaves of huts. By sunset it was spent. People came out of the low doors of their houses like insects emerging from the earth, laughing and talking because rain had swept away the fear of famine like dust from the leaves of shrubs. Next morning the women left their homesteads early with planting-sticks in their hands and woven sacks of seed on their backs. The ground had been turned, broken and weeded clean, and a fine tilth was waiting for the seed.

Waseru had obtained from the market seeds of the new crop, maize, that was so well spoken of by those who had grown it. It was bird-resistant, and its flavour was excellent when boiled with leaves and nettles: it could be easily stored and yields were good. Wanjeri was suspicious; she did not like the idea of these big new beans that were of many different colours. However, her husband ordered her to plant them, and it was not worth a beating to refuse. She planted the grains in pairs in the shamba where the millet had been, together with two kinds of bean. Down by the river, where the soil was always moist and black with leaf-mould, she made a small clearing and planted arum-lily roots. They took a long time to cook and Waseru complained if she gave them to him often; but then arum roots ignored droughts, and the time might come when the family would be thankful for their thick and rather tasteless tubers.

5

WITH the coming of the rains Waseru hoped that his troubles were buried like the seed of the new crop. But the maize had barely sprouted before bad omens began to appear. One evening Wanjeri found that her big cooking-pot had cracked, without reason, across the base. It was thrown out immediately—a cracked pot was like a broken-bodied man, and to eat out of it would bring deadly sickness—but Waseru knew that bad magic could have caused the fracture. That very day the shadow of a kite had passed over the homestead; and next morning, while Wanjeri was weeding, the baby almost fell from the sling on its mother's back.

E

No doubt of it, Waseru concluded: an evil magic still pursued him. Someone, some unknown enemy, must be scheming secretly to direct the vicious forces of magic upon him. Only the charms he wore had kept at bay evils that were still seeking a rift in his defences.

Wanjeri, also, was in a bad humour. Two wives, an old saying had it, were like two pots of poison; it seemed to Waseru that one was bad enough. When he spoke of visiting Irumu to get protection for the new crops she threw back her chin and said: "Perhaps Irumu has a charm to stop holes coming in very old dresses, or a magic to make cloaks out of leaves."

"Silence, wife!" Waseru said sternly. "Do you not know that you will bring ill luck upon me, if you speak disrespectfully of the mundu-mugu?"

"You speak of respect," she answered. "What respect do you show to your father—you who force me to go to his homestead in an old dress torn and barely decent? Does your father wish to see his daughter-in-law naked?"

"Woman, do not speak so!" Waseru exclaimed, deeply shocked. "Be silent, or I will beat you."

"Then I will run away to my father, who knows what a bad husband you are," Wanjeri retorted. "My brothers, who are rich and strong, will protect me."

Waseru's anger began to sing in his ears; he had half a mind to beat Wanjeri for her insolence. But he thought better of it, and strode off along the winding path that led out of the forest and to the mundu-mugu's.

There were two strangers at Irumu's. One was having his fortune told, but he did not seem to be taking it very seriously. He was laughing and joking with the mundu-mugu, and appeared to be well satisfied with his fortune as it was. Waseru soon learnt from the conversation that the two men were on their way home from a long and adventurous journey undertaken to exchange tobacco for goats with the people of Embu, who lived on the mountain's eastern slopes. Hearing news of famine farther on, they had trekked northwards until they had reached to the first villages of the Meru, a savage and barbaric people who held the last outposts of the known world. Beyond them, and below, stretched immensities of waterless plain that no man had crossed; and somewhere beyond that plain roamed the dreaded, wild-haired Somalis who had once fallen like locusts on the people of the mountain and destroyed their villages and flocks.

The Meru were not true Kikuyu but their tongue, although rough and uncouth, could be understood. They were known as a treacherous people who liked to trade with their neighbours, but often ambushed peaceful expeditions in order to steal their goods. In spite of that, Meru was an attractive country for trade; goats thrived exceedingly on the rich well-watered pastures and the men were on the whole a dull-witted lot, clumsy in the art of bargaining. When Irumu's kinsmen had reached Meru they had found the grain exhausted and the people existing on arum roots and a few bananas. They had sold some millet they had obtained in Embu for fabulous prices in goats.

6

At last the two strangers rose and, after accepting a gift of snuff and some food wrapped in a banana leaf, went on their way. Waseru took his place opposite the mundu-mugu and said:

"Irumu, the magic beans told you where I should put my hut, and I obeyed, and fortune has not been adverse. Now there is another thing that I should like to know. I am a poor man, with no goats to pay for the circumcision of my son, and perhaps, therefore, I may decide to go on a long journey for trade. Therefore, ask of the beans whether the omens are propitious, and whether I may undertake such a journey in safety, and by it increase my wealth."

Irumu rubbed his hooked nose and gave his visitor a long look with his shrewd light eyes. He shook the beans slowly in the gourd, asked them several questions, and read the answers in silence. Then he said:

" Waseru, the design of the future is shown by these beans as the design of a Masai warrior's clan upon his painted shield. I have asked your question, and the beans have answered. You may undertake this journey, although it will not be without danger. There will be rhinos on the path and you will need a magic to make them look away. Hostile warriors will shake their spears and you will require a charm to bind those spears to the warriors' hands. But if you take care to protect yourself with magic, in the end God shall be willing for you to increase your wealth."

Waseru heard these words with deep excitement, although he made no outward sign. He decided at once on the greatest enterprise of his life : he would go to Meru to trade in goats. If Irumu would make a charm to join good fortune to his shadow then wealth would return before him in the fat of Meru goats, and his debt would be redeemed.

Keeping his eyes fixed on the red earth at his feet he asked, in as steady tones as he could muster, for a charm to ensure his safe return. Irumu brought a small cylinder of wood cut from a fallen tree-trunk lying across a stream, and hollowed it out with his knife. Then he poured into it some burnt earth and ashes mixed with chalk—earth taken from seven different paths, and therefore including dust from all the paths on which the feet of man had trod—and hung it around Waseru's neck. Now Waseru knew that he could walk in safety, for he carried on his person the essence of all the roads that led about the world, the sting of their hostility extracted by the mundu-mugu's magic.

But, at first, it seemed impossible to raise a party for the expedition. Wives were too busy to leave their weeding, and of course the journey could not be made without women to carry the grain. Soon, however, word of Waseru's plan spread over the ridges and circumcised girls volunteered eagerly for the trip. They had heard tales of Meru, especially of the wild good looks, the boldness and the strength of the young warriors. But Waseru had to reckon with their fathers, who at first refused point-blank to let their daughters go. The married men's council was convened and a fluent address by Waseru on the big profits to be expected from the venture swayed the meeting just enough to get the project through.

7

ON the morning of his departure Waseru gave his elder son a sharpened stick and small club, and said:

"Now, father, you are to become a warrior; and you must remember to do a warrior's duty while I am away. You must protect the homestead and the crops, and your mother and your young brother, from all harm. If elephants come, or leopards, or if any evil befalls, you must run like a rock that tumbles downhill to the homestead of your grandfather, to give the alarm."

"I understand, father," Muthengi said. "I shall run faster than a reedbuck when it is frightened by a hunter's arrow."

"You must not stop," Waseru added, "for anything at all. You must remember how the chameleon was sent by God with a message to the first man to say that there was to be no such thing as death upon the earth. Because this chameleon walked slowly, and stuttered foolishly on his arrival, a bird which God had also dispatched with the news of death delivered his message first; and therefore the evil of death is entirely the fault of the lazy chameleon, which is now shunned and cursed above all other beasts."

Muthengi promised, and watched his father stride confidently down the path, his freshly greased pigtails swinging gaily, with feelings of pride and importance; but when, in the evening, his mother called him to help her draw water from the river, he was angry and offended.

"That is woman's work," he said. "Now I am like a warrior; my father told me I was to protect the hut and the crops; I will no longer carry water like a girl."

Wanjeri put down the stick with which she was stirring the pot, threw her head back, and burst into a torrent of laughter.

"Ho ho, ho ho, you are a warrior," she gasped. "A stick cut from the bush is your spear, a root from the forest your sword. You have captured many cattle, and they are forest rats, and killed many warriors, and they are francolins. Go, then, and show the warriors your circumcision wounds! Do you not know that young sugar cane cannot make beer?" She went on stirring the pot, chuckling to herself.

Muthengi clenched his fists and was convulsed with anger.

"I will go to my grandfather, he will not treat me so!" he shouted: and indeed he started to run away down the path that led to Mahenia's. But then he remembered his father's last instructions. Reluctantly he turned, and walked slowly back. His mother said nothing, but took her two big water-gourds and went to the river. He followed, and although he did not carry either of them, he helped to load them on to her back when they were full. Later, he went into the forest with a knife to cut some firewood. That, too, was women's work, and he was glad that no one could see him at such an effeminate task.

8

IN his heart Muthengi hid a secret contempt for his brother because the younger boy was willing to perform menial tasks without complaint. Matu's health had steadily improved since the thahu had been vomited out, but he was still a grave, quiet, undersized boy. He had a strange habit of wandering by himself in the forest. At such times he would stare with large, calm eyes at the bright, purposeful waters of the Ragati as they hurried towards the Sagana, at tall tree-ferns that rose in green cascades from mossy trunks, at brilliant-winged butterflies flitting in and out of shadows like fragments escaped from the rainbow that God had once chained under the waterfall. In his mother's shamba he worked hard, and he had an inborn respect for growing things that made him a careful cultivator. Although he was younger than Muthengi and half the size, Wanjeri could trust him better to weed a bean-patch cleanly, to plant seeds neither too deep nor too shallow, or to dig arum roots without hurting the tubers. He had started a little shamba of his own just outside the compound, by the heap of middens. He weeded this himself every morning before following his mother to work, and looked at it several times a day in silence with expressionless eyes that screened an inarticulate delight.

Wanjeri was pleased that he should display so early the instincts of a cultivator. As he grew older he would help her more. He would not despise the work of the shamba and think only of warrior's pigtails, as Muthengi did. The warrior's spear, she thought, had emptied many men's bellies, but she had never known it fill them.

Waseru's homestead was protected against wild animals by a fence of woven sticks, and against sorcerers by a small log, buried under the entrance, filled with three kinds of powder having the property of depriving a sorcerer's poisons of their potency when he stepped over the magic. Yet, in spite of all precautions, Waseru's enemies found a way to direct the powers of evil through his barricade of magical defences.

Early one morning, only a few days after Waseru had left, Wanjeri heard an ominous crack of breaking timber as she gathered herself together on the bed and prepared to rise. One of the poles supporting the bed had broken in two. The cold hand of fear clutched at her breasts; this was a certain sign of evil. Death was the fracture of the branch of life, causing the flesh to wither and rot; breaking was the symbol of death, whether it came to pole or cooking-pot, to gourd or hearthstone. Somewhere an enemy was scheming to break her bones in two, as the pole had been broken; evil was all around her, had destroyed her bed. Now the hut had become thahu. It would not be safe to sleep there again until a goat had been slaughtered and the contents of its stomach sprinkled around the poles and the walls.

The day had started badly enough; but there was worse to come. After Wanjeri had swept out the hut, washed the baby and wiped it dry with leaves, and made up a fire, she pulled aside the brushwood which sealed the compound's entrance at night; and there, immediately between the posts, were the droppings of a hyena. She stared for several minutes in round-eyed, fascinated immobility, while the clutch of fear tightened around her heart. It was true the hyena had not entered; but there it had stood and waited, no doubt trying to get in; and there it had left its dung, in the path of all who passed through the gateway.

This was an omen of the worst possible kind. The hyena, consumer of corpses, was wholly evil, a very part of death itself. If ever a hyena should enter a compound and leave its dung inside the fence, the huts must be destroyed completely and new ones built elsewhere. Last night the maggots of death had crawled into the homestead, into the hut, even into Wanjeri's own bed; the sorcerer who had summoned them had left his warning at the gateway. An enemy, thwarted by Irumu's protective magic in his attempt to destroy Waseru, was striking at Waseru's home and family.

In Wanjeri's ears the sound of sorcery filled the air like the whine of angry bees. The forest shamba had become unsafe. Later in the day she gathered together some skins and pots, filled a small sack of millet from the granary, and called to her sons to follow her down to their grandfather's homestead. Until Waseru returned, until the hut could be purified and the thahu driven away, she would not sleep alone behind such weak defences.

CHAPTER V

The Hunters

I

MUTHENGI was delighted with this twist of fortune, for it meant that he could spend his days herding goats. He refused to help his mother any further in the shamba. She pleaded with him, but he would not listen; and when she asked for Mahenia's help the old man chuckled and said:

"The boy is strong and will soon become a warrior. Why do you ask him to do woman's work? He has no love for the shamba; already his feet tread in the dust of the cattle. Leave him alone, and let him look after my goats." Wanjeri looked sulky, but she could say no more.

Every morning she would go back into the forest with Matu, the baby on her back, to weed her own shamba. The earth was moist and the sprouting maize spread over it a soft film of green like the moss on a fallen tree-trunk. But every morning she shook her head and grumbled under her breath at the damage done over-night by bushbuck and dikdik. They nibbled the shoots and trampled the young plants with sharp hoofs, for there was no one now to scare them away.

Round the edge of the field stood some poles with bunches of leaves on top, to protect the crop against bewitchments.

"And what is the use of such charms?" Wanjeri complained. "What does it matter that evil magic is averted if my crops are destroyed by the feet and teeth of wild animals?"

"I will make a bow and arrow and shoot the bushbuck," Matu suggested.

"And become like an Athi," Wanjeri retorted, "contaminated by the flesh of wild beasts. Your father is not a rich man, but he has not come to that. Nevertheless I should have done

65

better to have married an Athi, it seems, for then I should have lived in the forest as I do now, but at least my husband would have kept the bushbuck away."

A few days later an Athi hunter came to the shamba for the first time. It was early in the morning, when earth and leaves were still cold with dew and shafts of sunlight, soft as a note from a distant herdsman's flute, slanted through the trees. Matu, who was weeding beans, heard no sound, yet suddenly he looked up, conscious that eyes were upon him. There, standing motionless in the shadow of a tree, was a little, wizen-faced man, who stared for a long time in silence. The man was small, no taller than Muthengi; his hair was cropped and dusted with white, and his eyes were as bright as those of a mongoose. He carried a long bow in one hand, and from his belt hung a leather quiver full of arrows. He wore a thick cloak of monkey skin, and the specks of dew that quivered on the tip of each hair were lit by sunlight streaming into the clearing, so that when he moved he glistened like a fish.

When he had gazed for some time at Matu he stepped forward and said:

"Greetings, my grandson."

Matu, still squatting on the ground, stared back in silence. He felt afraid. This apparition was undoubtedly a spirit, come out of the mists of Kerinyagga. He said nothing.

The monkey-like face of the old man puckered in a grin, and he laughed: a very low, almost inaudible sound.

"Do not be afraid," he went on, "I am not a spirit. I am the brother of Mahenia, your father's father, and you are my grandson. I have come to visit my son, your father."

"My father is not here," Matu replied. He was reassured by the old man's explanation, but still not quite convinced. He remembered now that he had heard how one of his grandfathers, called Masheria, had gone to seek food in the forest during a famine and become a hunter who ate the flesh of wild beasts. Matu looked at him with round, awed eyes. He could hardly believe that he was really face to face with an Athi. This man looked exactly like a Kikuyu, except that he was small, and wore unusual costume.

"Have you no mother?" the old man asked. "Surely you do not cultivate here alone?"

Matu shook his head, sprang to his feet, and ran as fast as he could to the compound to tell his mother the news. She came out and greeted the stranger respectfully, addressing him as husband's father; and they talked in the shade of the trees. Matu observed that the old man's face was not properly plucked and that tough, scraggy hairs grew from his chin. A long, shiny scar ran up the calf of one muscular leg, perhaps where an elephant or buffalo had gored him.

After a little he came gradually to the point of his visit. He owned a flock of goats, he would not say how many. Since goats could not thrive in the forest, they were tended by a relative and kept on the land belonging to his clan. But lately a dispute between him and the man who looked after them had arisen, and he was thinking of transferring the care of the goats to another relative. Waseru, who ranked as his son, was a possibility, and he had come to discuss the proposition. Waseru would, of course, get some reward for his trouble in the form of a small share in the natural increase. But since Waseru was absent, he would return some other time to talk it over. His own home was not very far distant; a little deeper in the forest, he said.

2

Matu was fascinated by the queer old man. He did not speak because no uncircumcised boy might address an elder; but he followed the visitor a little way along the path, until Masheria turned and smiled at him, and said:

"I see you walking behind me: do you wish then to come with me, and learn how to trap bushbuck and to spear elephants, and to become a hunter?"

Matu shook his head dumbly.

"Then you must return to your mother," Masheria added. "Only boys who are very brave can become hunters. I see that buck are coming every night to eat your mother's beans. Do you know how to set a snare to catch them?"

Matu shook his head again.

"You have a lot to learn, then," the old man remarked. "Go home now, or your mother will be anxious."

Matu's fear was evaporating like dew before the sun, for Masheria spoke and walked like an ordinary man and not a spirit; and he was not annoyed at being followed by a boy. At last he found his tongue.

"It is true that the bushbuck come every night to the shamba," he said. "They are eating all my mother's crops. Can you make a magic that will keep them away?"

Masheria chuckled again in a curious silent way, and his face was cobwebbed with laughter. "Ho, now you wish to know the secrets of the Athi," he said. "For indeed we know many secrets. We have seen the saltlicks to which the black bongo come, and the copulation of the elephant; we have heard the talk of bees within the hollow tree, and the songs of spirits who hold circumcision ceremonies upon the mountain above the bamboos. Well, my grandson, perhaps I will return, and teach you to trap the buck that feed in your mother's shamba."

He turned and walked with long, bent-kneed strides into the green shadows, his feet soundless on the twig-crossed floor. In a very short time his slight form had dissolved into the sun-flecked darkness.

When Matu returned to the shamba his mother was angry. She reproached him both for his bad manners in standing openly before an elder, and for speaking to an Athi, one who was held in mingled contempt and dread by all respectable people.

"If he comes here again you should stay in the hut," she told him. "Do you not know that you must always hide yourself from the sight of a senior elder? Besides, an Athi might offer you the meat of wild animals, and if you eat it, do you know what will befall? The flesh of your limbs will turn pale and

soft and will slough away, and you will die; that is the conse-
quence of eating the flesh of game."

"But you spoke to him politely, mother," Matu said. "You
asked him to come back when my father is here."

"That is another matter—father," Wanjeri said. "He wishes
to talk of business affairs. Besides, although I warn you not to
associate with these hunters, you must always be polite to them.
You must offer an Athi traveller food, and step from the path to
make way for him, and treat him with great civility. For these
people know a very deadly curse, as deadly as that of a smith. If
a person insults one of them, that Athi will take a wild animal
and he will break each of its bones, saying, 'May the bones of
the person who insulted me be broken as the bones of this
animal.' Then the man will fall sick and he will die. It is
hard for a mundu-mugu to remove such a curse, for the Athi
utters it in secret and no one knows that he has done so. For
this reason beware of the Athi and always be courteous to
them, so that you may escape their curse."

"Yes, mother," Matu said obediently. His fear of the old
man returned and he marvelled that so friendly a person should
possess such awful powers. He took his small knife and
followed his mother to the shamba. The dangers which
crowded around the feet, he thought, were truly as numerous
as soldier ants.

3

Every night bushbuck and wild pig robbed the shamba, until
Wanjeri was in despair. She complained loudly of her husband's neglect, that he should desert her while the crop was
in the ground. And rats had found their way into the granaries;
they were devouring the millet; they would multiply until all
the grain was eaten. She raised no objection when Matu made
himself a bow from the wood of the mugiti shrub and strung it
with the dried sinews of a bushbuck. He practised his aim by
shooting at the fat-breasted pigeons that strutted among the

young plants. And all the time that he was weeding he watched for the small, long-striding figure of the Athi to materialise out of the forest, like a flower springing fully grown from a bush, or an eagle swooping from the rocks.

And then the old man came again. At one moment the shamba was empty save for many birds; at the next he stood there blinking in the sunlight, exactly as Matu remembered him, except that on this occasion his head was covered with a soft, ochre-dyed helmet made from the stomach lining of a goat. He stood before Matu and smiled just as before, and said :

"Greetings, my grandchild. Did I not say that I would come to teach you to make snares? And do you still wish to learn?"

Matu looked nervously around. His mother had gone into the forest to strip the shrub mugeo of bark for twine. He stood up from politeness, and nodded his head.

"Yes, grandfather," he said nervously, "but I do not think that my mother will let me. She says that you . . . that I . . . that it is dangerous. I do not know . . ."

His voice tailed off in doubt. The vision of a buck with broken, dangling legs came into his mind.

Masheria laughed again. "Do not be afraid of me," he said. "Am I not your grandfather, an elder of the clan into which you were born? Should I then wish to hurt you? Come with me, and I will teach you how to make snares in a place where she cannot find you. Then you shall set traps around her shamba; and when she sees how you protect her crops she will be delighted and praise you with trills, as if you were a warrior fresh from triumphs in battle."

Matu hesitated, glancing first towards Masheria, then towards the forest where his mother was. He knew that he was doing wrong. But had not his mother, only that day, been bewailing the ravages of bushbuck? And if he could protect the crops, would she not be pleased, as the old man said, and praise him for his resource—praise him, for once, instead of his brother Muthengi, whom everyone extolled for his strength and courage?

" Come, follow me," Masheria said. " It is not far, and before nightfall you shall return home to your mother."

Matu took a sudden decision. A great curiosity about the life of the old man filled him and mingled with the desire to display resource and to merit praise. The old man turned and strode into the forest, moving as swiftly as a bongo; and Matu padded after him, clutching his small weeding-knife tightly in one hand, his heart pounding like the beat of a mortar against a hollowed tree-trunk when the old women ground sorghum into flour.

Matu was amazed at the manner in which the old man made his way through the forest. The undergrowth appeared to open before him as water yields before the swimming fish. It seemed as if the forest moved with them, that no world existed save this small circle of towering trunks, thick undergrowth, slim hanging lianas and dappled sunlight. They twisted and turned continuously, following faint game-tracks, until Matu had no idea of their direction. He walked in a sort of daze in the old man's footsteps, ducking under branches, scrambling over logs, and trying to place his feet silently among the fallen twigs. Suddenly he became aware of light on his eyes, and a moment later they stepped into an open glade. Unmasked sunlight struck into his face like a sword.

"We have arrived," Masheria said.

4

Matu looked round and could see nothing save brown tufted grass bent sadly towards the west, as though the weight of the sunlight lay too heavily upon it. Masheria chuckled and strode on a little farther; then he bent down and dived into the undergrowth, his follower at his heels. When Matu straightened his back he found himself standing by the door of a round hut, built like his mother's. In front was a little clearing flooded with sunlight, and a granary, and a second hut; and all around was a low woven fence.

He gave an exclamation of surprise and pleasure. The huts had been invisible ten yards away; yet here they were, substantial enough, compressed editions of his own home.

Two women were busy in the compound. One was old and wrinkled with flat, shrivelled breasts; the other was about his mother's age. She was grinding millet on a stone and the older woman was tending a cooking-pot. Two small children were playing around the compound in the sun.

Matu stared at them silently while Masheria explained his presence. The women were delighted. The younger one— who was, it transpired, the wife of Masheria's son Watengu— came over to welcome him and opened her granary to give him food. He shrank away in terror, thinking that she would offer him the flesh of game; but to his immense relief she took out a familiar-looking calabash and handed him a chunk of bean paste and some cold sweet potato. This restored his confidence at once. Everything seemed normal, just as it was at home— the huts, the granary, the food. The women's clothes were the same, and their ornaments and speech; and this woman was, after all, a sort of mother.

He did not return to his own mother that night. He stayed the next day and the next, looking about him with wondering eyes, entranced by a way of life so different from his own in its essentials and yet so alike in its details.

He learnt that there were several families of Athi living close at hand. All were Kikuyu who had left their shambas, as Masheria had done, during times of famine, and gone to live by hunting in the forest. Once they had eaten game they could not go back to the life of cultivators. Long ago, Masheria told him, the ancestors of the Athi had put a curse upon them that they must not leave the forest, nor stop eating game; if ever a man should do so, his legs would wither and flake away and leprosy would consume him.

The days passed as smoothly as clouds moving across the sky. Matu went everywhere with Watengu and his eldest son, a cheerful, friendly boy of about Muthengi's age. Together they set snares—loops of wire on the end of whippy sticks—for the little dikdik in the game paths. They followed with cautious feet the tracks of bushbuck from the shambas which most Athi women cultivated (in a rather slapdash manner) in the forest glades, until the dark chestnut gleam of the antelope's coat flashed for a second in a thicket, and a swift arrow skimmed through the air with silent precision to bury its poisoned tip in the victim's flank. Matu learnt how to boil down the roots, branches and bark of the murico tree (which did not grow in the forest, but below, where the Athi went to strip it) into a thick, glutinous paste, highly charged with poison, into which arrowheads were dipped. Watengu showed him the tall creeper whose roots were dug by elephants to sniff through their trunks when they suffered from colds in the head, and the shrub whose roots were boiled down by the Athi to cure the same complaint in humans. But he knew of no way to keep off the big, savage buffalo-flies that settled noiselessly on Matu's limbs and neck, burying their sharp fangs in his unprotected skin.

5

Luck seemed to have turned against the Athi. For almost a month their skill and patience brought no harvest save a few bushbuck to their arrows. Then, one day at noon, a man came to Masheria's homestead with exciting news: elephants had been sighted in the forest near at hand. They were feeding, travelling slowly along the mountain slopes, and were not yet aware of the presence of men.

This time Matu was told to stay at home, for boys had no part in an elephant hunt. But the tang of excitement in the air was too much for his obedience. He slipped into the forest when no eyes were on him and followed a faint game-path (a month ago he could not have recognised it) until he heard voices ahead. With a fast-beating heart he practised the art of noiseless movement that the Athi had taught him. He drew closer, and heard the hunters discussing a plan of attack.

F

Often they dug big pits in the paths the elephants would take, but now there was no time for that. They decided to organise a hunt.

All the able-bodied men of the community, young and old, were soon gathered in the glade. Each man brought a weapon called a thia : a heavy wooden pole made from the mugiti tree. At one end was a knob and at the other a sharp tapering knife with barbed sides, freshly dipped in poison. Watengu selected seven young men and led them cautiously towards the feeding elephants. Excitement as tense as a tautened bowstring was in the air. The young men spoke in low voices and moved as silently as shadows among the trees. The loud squawk of a monkey checked them in their tracks. They stared upwards, waiting with frozen patience for the aerial spy to swing on to another tree, or to forget its interest in the moving figures below. They moved on in a wide circle, keeping down-wind, until a crackle of undergrowth across a ravine paralysed them again. More crashes followed, and on the far bank they saw a tree-top wave as if shaken by a gust of wind. They listened in utter stillness while the sun climbed a little higher above the trees. The elephants, unsuspecting, were feeding steadily as they ambled down the side of the ravine.

Watengu gave the sign to advance and the party moved forward again, making a wide sweep to cut across the line of their quarry's advance. They made their way down and across the ravine and halted on the same side as the elephants, a little way in front of them. Four or five faint game-tracks, barely discernible, coiled among the thick undergrowth and creepers. At the first such path they came to, Watengu halted. He gazed towards the hidden elephants with all the deadly concentration of a hunting leopard tautening its muscles for a spring. The tall trees grew thickly here. Selecting one whose branches swept across and above the track he handed his thia to the man behind him, grasped a hanging liana, and in an instant ran up the trunk, nimble-footed as a monkey. The dark glossy leaves above him did not stir. He clambered out on to a branch until he was poised above the game-track, and reached down for his thia. He lay down at full length on his belly along the branch, his dark skin and cloak invisible in the sheltering foliage, his thia ready by his side.

The other seven hunters moved on. Each man concealed himself in a similar way on a branch that stretched above a game-track, so that the hunters formed a line strung out across the bank of the ravine. Each man gripped his thia, that held death in its barbed tip, and relaxed his muscles until he seemed to blend in shape and colour with the branch. The furry hyraxes sleeping in the crevices of the trunk did not know of his presence and the bright-eyed parrots, at first disturbed by his arrival, returned to their perches among the leaves.

6

Without warning the web of bated sound spun over the tree-tops was scattered by a sudden roll of drums. The noise surged like distant thunder over the forest, obliterating the faint protests of startled creatures. It ceased, to give way to shouts; and then began again, insistent and undisciplined. Only the eight motionless figures on the branches were undisturbed, knowing that their colleagues had begun the drive. Spread out in a crescent moon formation behind the elephants and beating with clubs upon stiff, dried cows' hides as they marched, they were driving the startled beasts along the side of the ravine.

As the crashing of heavy feet grew closer, the men on the branches gathered themselves together and raised their right arms, gripping their thias, so that each point was poised above a path. The noise approached until it filled their ears and flowed in waves along their quivering nerve-threads. The foliage of trees in the throat of the ravine shook violently; and in another moment a big stone-grey shape burst through a thicket, dodging swiftly towards Watengu's tree. The hunter saw its huge, outstretched, stiff ears, its waving trunk, its small roving eye, and in another instant its broad wrinkled neck was beneath him.

The crashing, suddenly, was all around; the elephant seemed to be making directly for him, an enormous engine of vengeance, bearing down on his flimsy shelter to trample and destroy.

At the moment that it slid beneath the branch he thrust downwards with all his strength, like a strong man breaking ground with the digging-stick, and sunk the head of the thia between the elephant's shoulders. It gave one mighty squeal of anger and plunged forward along the narrow track. Behind it followed four other elephants, three cows and a calf. They passed so swiftly that they were gone before Watengu had recovered his balance on the bough.

He dropped quickly to the earth and stood immobile, listening. The beaters had ceased to belabour their cow-hides and there was a moment of silence, as if all the animals of the forest waited without drawing breath for the verdict of fate upon the elephant. Then it came—a long, shattering scream that tore the silence from the hillsides and echoed faintly from indifferent hills beyond: the last futile protest of a living creature against the uncomprehended finality of death.

As the scream faded the hunters' muscles relaxed and voices called backwards and forwards among the trees. The forest was suddenly filled with people running, shouting, and laughing with joy. The elephant was dead before they reached him. He lay on his side like a mighty boulder, his legs thrust out stiffly, one of his long white tusks half buried in the soft ground. The haft of Watengu's thia was gone, but its barbed iron point was deeply embedded in the elephant's neck. The hunter's aim had been true, his arm strong; and the poison, freshly brewed, had done its work.

7

Within a few moments of its discovery, figures were swarming over the dead beast like ants over a scrap of fat. The death of an elephant was an occasion of ecstasy among the Athi. A mountain of exquisite food had appeared; in an instant seed-time, cultivation and harvest had flashed by and left a lavish crop, ready for the eating, of the greatest delicacy that the stomach of man could savour.

Hunters and beaters joined together in a dance of triumph around the fallen prey. A song was raised in praise of Watengu, whose thia had found its mark; of the hunters who had known where the elephants would pass; of the beaters who had driven them to the right spot, the smith who had made the thia-head sharp and true, and the Athi in general, who were so brave and skilful that even elephants, chiefs of the forest, were brought low.

All the men of the Athi homesteads were soon gathered around, the elders laughing and rubbing their stomachs in anticipation. Their impatience curtailed the dance. Masheria shouted to the young men that he was hungry and could not wait. Watengu thereupon leapt with a great spring on to the back of the elephant and plunged his sword into the flesh of the loin. Then the others drew their swords and knives and fell upon the warm, bleeding flesh with the lust of soldiers wild with victory and loot. Hunks of raw flesh were hacked away and soon, from eyes to toes, the Athi men were red and sticky with blood. Each man carved his chunk, ran to one side, and cut off smaller portions with his sword, plunging his face into the warm flesh and tearing with his teeth at the juicy tissues.

Matu, who stood with the other boys watching the scene, felt great amazement and some disgust. Meat was always roasted brown on the end of sticks, or grilled over a fire. It was unknown, obscene, to eat it in any other way. Here were men who behaved like animals—like vultures, or the unclean hyena. He understood now why the Athi were at once despised and feared by other men.

In a few hours the orgy of greed was over. The gorged men sheathed their swords and wiped blood from their bodies with leaves. The next step was to build shelters around the carcase to sleep in, for no one would leave the spot, except to take meat to his wife, until the last scrap of elephant was eaten. By nightfall, low shelters of sticks had been erected all around the trampled circle, and a ring of fires surrounded the carcase. Everyone was in the highest spirits. Such good fortune had not come to the Athi for a long while.

Matu lingered on, unable to bring himself to return to his temporary home. The proceedings repelled and yet fascinated him. When the sun dipped over the black tree-tops and cold stole down from the mountain he crouched by a fire next to Masheria, and watched great slabs of flesh roasting on the grid above the flames. This, at least, had more decency about it. The meat was being cooked as if it had come from a ram. All around stood calabashes in which thick yellow fat had been collected.

The smell of roasting meat tickled Matu's stomach and brought water into his mouth. He had eaten nothing all day, and his stomach cried out for food. He watched Masheria spear a particularly succulent hunk with the tip of his sword, and chop off a big mouthful. He could hardly bear it; his hands twitched with anxiety to reach out for a scrap. Presently Watengu's son came up, carrying a sac of blood made from the elephant's intestine, as thick as a man's thigh.

"I return now to our homestead, brother," he said to Matu. "It is nearly dark and I am hungry. Come with me."

Masheria looked up at the boy and handed him a small piece of meat.

"Eat this, then, if you are hungry, grandson," he said.

Watengu's son ate the meat greedily. Masheria's twinkling eyes came to rest on Matu's pinched face. He saw the boy swallow twice and lick his lips hungrily. He took another piece of meat off the grid and handed it over.

"Satisfy your hunger, also, grandson," he said. "He who is in need is not shy."

Matu could resist no longer. He buried his teeth in the delicious hot meat, chewed it eagerly, and gave himself over to enjoyment of the strong, unfamiliar flavour. It was not until later, after the evening meal in the hut of Watengu's wife, that thoughts of shame and dread for the thing he had done swarmed into his mind, like rats in a granary, to torment him.

The Athi men stayed for seven days by the elephant, eating, on and off, from sunrise to sunset, and beyond. Vultures hovered continuously overhead and flies settled in dense buzzing clouds over the putrefying flesh. Matu went there once, but the stench of the decaying meat was too much for him. Gradually white bones appeared as the flesh, seething with maggots, fell away. The elephant became like a leaf attacked by caterpillars, with spine and ribs alone intact, and the rotting substance between hanging in shreds from the framework. The Athi grew bloated and sodden, their bellies were full to bursting like over-ripe fruit, and their eyes were dull and heavy. From time to time they took meat to their wives, who stewed it in the big pots. Watengu's wife ground no millet and sorghum and there was nothing else to eat, so Matu had perforce to take the meat every day. Although it was full of flavour and after the first day no longer tough, he ate it with reluctance, and it tasted like earth in his mouth; for he feared that what he was doing would bring a thahu from which he would sicken and perhaps die.

8

After the elephant hunt Matu's thoughts returned more and more to his own mother, and to Mahenia's homestead. The open, sun-flooded shambas, the song of the cultivators, the sound of banana fronds creaking softly in the valleys beneath deep clouds, the dry, friendly smell of goats—all seemed suddenly desirable to him; and fears that he would never see them again began to gnaw like borer-beetles in his heart. Gradually he came to hate the forest, with its cold dark dampness, its vast mysterious depths where no sunlight penetrated, and the moaning of winds in its branches. Often, at night, he dreamt of his mother; and then he awoke cold with panic, thinking of

trapped animals he had seen caught in pits and struggling hopelessly to escape back to their native thickets.

Watengu's wife heard him crying in the night, and when the
men came back from the elephant feast, gorged and smelling
of corruption, she told Masheria. The old man nodded his
head gravely and said :

"He shall go back to his father, for I can tell that he has no
wish to become like us, to join the Athi."

Soon after that an Athi who had been down to Karatina
market to sell a buffalo hide—much sought after for making
shields—returned with an exciting piece of news. A party of
the tall bearded strangers known as Wathukumu had come from
the south-east and made a camp two days' journey away. They
had many people with them, and animals carrying loads on their
backs. They had sent messages ahead to say that if any men
had elephant tusks, they would buy them for goats, beads, wire,
and a soft material for making clothes.

As soon as this news arrived, a council of the Athi was held to
debate whether any tusks should be offered to the strangers.
Although Wathukumu had visited the country before, little
was known of them, save that they were very rich. The object
of their visits was always the same : to buy elephant tusks.
These they carried away on the backs of men, none knew where,
or for what purpose; some said they were used as drinking-
horns by a race of giants. The arrival of the ivory traders
heralded an influx of alluring beads and bright wire, and so was
usually welcomed; but on this occasion it was rumoured that a
party of cannibals had disguised themselves as Wathukumu and
sent false messages to entice the Athi out of the forest in order
to kill and roast them for food. Masheria doubted this, and
offered to go first by himself, accompanied only by his son and
by two women who would carry down a single tusk. If he
was not killed, but given goats, they would know that the Wathukumu were genuine and would take down the other tusks
that had from time to time been buried in the forest.

The Athi agreed to this plan. A few days later Masheria

and Watengu started out with a tusk carried on the shoulders of their wives. Matu went with them; but he felt no elation. He was not sure whether he was to be taken home or to be given to these people called Wathukumu, perhaps to be killed and eaten like a ram. Still, it was no good worrying, and perhaps when they reached the shambas and left behind the forest with all its evils he would be able to escape.

The birds of excitement sang in Matu's head when he stepped out of the forest and stood at last on the borders of the land he knew. The pastures, starred with white clover, glowed with a vigour and a freshness that he had never seen in the sombre forest. There, on the steep hillside beyond, was the familiar red of turned earth, the tender green of sprouting plants, and the pale glow of a hut's roof, like a golden crest on the head of a crane. To his ears came the gentle sound of goats' bells and the distant rattle of empty gourds on the back of a woman going to draw water.

Wanjeri dropped an armful of sweet potato tops when she saw him, screaming in shrill terror that she had seen a spirit; for she believed that a leopard had taken her son, and she had mourned for him as dead. When she realised that he was not a spirit at all she was so delighted that she forgot to rebuke him for his behaviour. She was so angry with Masheria, however, that she threatened to take Matu to her own father's that very night, and refuse to return to her husband, if the old Athi was given hospitality in his brother's homestead. Mahenia was worried, for he could not refuse to shelter his own brother, and he feared the Athi curse; but old Masheria chuckled, nodded, and said that he did not wish to stay. He had heard that the Wathukumu were already camped near at hand, on a tongue of ridge that jutted back into the forest between two streams.

That night he was the guest of the tall, bearded strangers, who wore soft robes as white as the tusk he had brought to sell. Next day the tusk was bartered. Masheria knew the rate, which did not change: ten goats for each length of tusk from finger-tip to elbow. It was a good tusk, and he received sixty goats, which would be divided amongst all the hunters who had slain the elephant.   He drove away his flock in safety, feeling well satisfied with the transaction.   He would claim two extra goats, he decided, as a reward for his courage in going alone to deal with the dangerous Wathukumu.

CHAPTER VI

The Dancers

I

WASERU was away nearly two months. His family began to grow anxious, for Meru was not more than five or six days' journey; and the fathers of the girls who had gone on the expedition came frequently to Mahenia's homestead to ask for news. Some were heard to mutter that the whole project had been ill-advised and foolhardy, and that Mahenia would be to blame if it had met with disaster.

And then, one day, Waseru came, striding ahead of the caravan to bring news of its safe return. He dug his spear into the ground outside the entrance with a flourish of the arm and called loudly to his father and his wife. One glance at his face told them that he had been successful. Mahenia ran forward to greet him with affection and relief and Wanjeri stood there smiling, and said:

"Is all well? Have you brought back many goats to pay for your sons' wives, so that we shall be poor no longer?"

"All is well," Waseru said. "I have travelled far—very far indeed—and I have brought goats: yes, and more. You will see."

There was a great stir along the ridge as the word of the party's approach went round. Young married men left the honey-barrels they were adzing and the granaries they were weaving in the compounds; elders even deserted their beer-drinks; and all converged upon Mahenia's huts to hear the news. Soon the caravan came into sight, climbing slowly up the steep hill from the river. Those assembled to greet it stared with amazement and joy at a great flock of goats that jostled ahead like a river in spate. It was a huge flock, bigger by far than anyone had dared to hope; a positive flood of goats.

83

All eyes were fixed so intently upon them that they barely noted the surprising existence of an extra member of the caravan—a slim young girl, uncircumcised, who walked with downcast head behind Ngarariga, her feet dragging wearily along the road.

A silence fell as the party approached Mahenia's homestead, for the mind of every man was filled, as a lover's with the image of his loved one's features, with the magnificence of the goats.

When greetings were over, Waseru strode up and down in the midst of a ring of listeners, brandishing a club, and recounted his adventures in a loud, ringing voice, with a wealth of detail and many pauses for dramatic effect. This was the moment of his triumph, to be enjoyed to the full. The audience punctuated his tale with cries of astonishment and suspense, and sometimes with shouts of praise for his courage and resource.

The story was a long and stirring one. They had found Meru, as they expected, in a state of famine: the granaries empty as gourds taken by women to the river at evening, the children's bones dry as maize stalks after harvest, and full-fed hyenas prowling boldly round the compounds at night. They had traded their millet for goats at highly advantageous rates; and a leading elder with six wives, at whose village they had slept, had offered one of his uncircumcised daughters for two sacks of grain. "It is indeed more painful for me to hear my children crying out for food and to watch them wither before my eyes like uprooted weeds," he had said, "than to see them depart forever to dwell among strangers. In your country there is much food; that I have seen with my own eyes; your granaries are full as the stomachs of pigeons after a millet sack has broken in the path. Therefore, take one of my daughters, and let her become your own; and when she marries the bride-price will be yours entirely." So Waseru had chosen a thin but shapely girl, nearly ready for circumcision, whose name was Ambui; the Kikuyu women had spoken kindly to her and given her food, and she had returned with them to become Waseru's daughter.

On the way home the expedition had passed through many hardships and adventures. A band of Embu warriors had laid an ambush, but the caution and quick sight of Waseru and his brother Ngarariga had detected the trap in time. They had taken a different route through the forest and avoided the enemy spearmen. They had slept in the open and hyenas and leopards had prowled around their fires; only the courage and wakefulness of Waseru and Ngarariga had saved the goats, and perhaps the women, from the jaws of savage beasts. They had run short of food and dared not approach hostile villages to renew supplies; only the will-power and tirelessness of Waseru and Ngarariga had kept the column from breaking up, and the women from being lost among the Embu. They had marched on through rain and cold, heat and hunger, driving the goats always ahead; and now at last Waseru had brought them back unscathed, with wealth to swell their fathers' flocks.

"All around me I see the faces of my kinsfolk," Waseru concluded, "and I ask you—have we done well? Have we brought goats to enrich our clan? Have we returned your daughters to you in safety, you fathers whose daughters carried millet to Meru? Are you satisfied with all that we have done?"

A great shout went up from the audience as the tale came to an end; a shout of praise. The sound ran through Waseru's body like a draught of warm beer. This was indeed an adequate return for all the fears and hardships of his venture. He lifted his hand to acknowledge the applause. His father's wives burst into the shrill rippling trills of delight and admiration that women made when they wished to praise a man. Other women joined in, until it seemed as if a great concourse of birds was singing in mass exaltation, or as if all the he-goats in Kikuyu were ringing their bells on a distant hill-top. The women started to dance in a circle, waving in the air gourds of gruel and branches hastily plucked from a mukenya bush nearby, and from time to time pouring some of the gruel over their bare, shining heads to express their uncontrollable delight.

"God has been good," Mahenia said to his son, spitting on

his left breast in blessing. "No doubt it was Irumu's charm that protected you from the ambush set by the Embu, and from the rhinos on the path. You should present Irumu with a fattened he-goat, for had it not been for his magic, you would certainly have been killed."

"I will do so, father," Waseru agreed, "for indeed Irumu's magic was very great."

2

The division of the goats was a long and complicated business. It had been arranged that the fathers of the girls who went to carry millet should share one-third of the total, the owners of the millet another third, and that Waseru, Ngarariga and two other young men who had gone with the party should divide up the remainder. But adjustments had to be made because the girl Ambui, who could not be divided, was part of the spoils; and much discussion took place before the matter could be fairly settled. In the end Waseru received the full rights of a father, but surrendered some of his goats. In a few seasons, however, she would be marriageable, and worth thirty goats and several fat rams—property which he could use, when the time came, to secure a wife for his son Muthengi.

Now that he had a little flock, Wanjeri gave him no peace.

"Since you are an owner of goats, why do you not give me skins for new clothing?" she asked. "Are you not ashamed to let me be seen indecently dressed, like the wife of a man who must beg land?"

"The talk of women is like the rattle of dried beans in an empty gourd," Waseru retorted. "No doubt you expect me to kill my few young female goats in order to provide you with dresses. In that way I should soon become as rich as Wangombe, who has ten wives."

"Yet the skin of this goat belongs already to Irumu and I must go clad in holes," Wanjeri complained as she toiled up the steep hillside to her shamba, a heavy load of green banana branches on her stooping back. Her husband walked ahead, driving a young male goat picked for the sacrifice that must be performed before the homestead could be purified of thahu, and Wanjeri's bed fit to sleep in. "No doubt the wives of Irumu are clothed in as many skins as the banana leaves covering an unbaked clay pot that is drying. Am I then to wait until the goats from Meru grow thin with age before I have a new dress?"

Waseru knew that her complaints, although irritating, were not unjust. Her ochre-stained skins were worn as thin as leaves and in places they were torn and ragged.

"The beans are already swelling in their pods," he remarked. As he spoke they reached the entrance to his little compound. Weeds had grown up to the fence and choked the gateway. It was blocked with branches of the murembu shrub in whose leaves resided the power to repel hyenas. " You must harvest them soon. When they are threshed you may take two sacks to Karatina; perhaps I will exchange them there for skins; that is, if skins are not too expensive."

Wanjeri grunted, and slid the bananas off her back. The leather thong had bitten a deep groove into the skin of her flat, shining forehead. Ambui, the Meru girl, trudged behind, the baby swaying in a sling on her back. She was silent and timid, shy as a young antelope, but she treated her new parents with proper respect.

Wanjeri pulled aside the hut's wicker-plaited door and kindled a fire. The logs, stacked on a wooden platform supported by four poles above the hearth-stones, were dry, and soon thick swirls of smoke were pushing upwards through the thatch. All at once the roof became alive with rustlings and the busy scurrying of invisible feet. The rats, who had found in this dark, dry dwelling an ideal refuge, were deeply offended at being thus disturbed.

"All day I work in the shamba to fill the granary," Wanjeri exclaimed, her voice shrill with complaint, "and all night the rats work as hard to empty it. Surely the bodies of these animals must be possessed by spirits, for they are very small, and yet they eat as if they were giants."

And, indeed, when she opened the granary she saw that rats had devoured completely her small remaining store of yams and sorghum. Now the family would have little to eat but bananas until a new harvest was in.

3

The maize, from which so much had been expected, was a failure. The sharp teeth of antelopes had nipped its tender shoots and wild pigs, destructive as falling boulders, had torn up the shamba. The surviving plants had grown to a great height, taller than a man; but then the cold, sunless weather had come and the grain had failed to ripen. Waseru shook his head sadly when he saw the wizened cobs, half suspecting magic; but he resolved to try again in the millet rains, when there would be more sun at the time of harvest. But the bean crop was heavy, and now that Wanjeri had the adopted Meru girl to help her, the harvest was quickly gathered. The beans, of three different sizes and colours—black, red, and white— were threshed with sticks on a stiff ox-hide in the compound, and then set out to dry. They made slow progress because of cold mornings when the sky was stained the sombre black of iron-sand, and all colour fled from a land without shadows. But after the turn of the noon the black heavy clouds began to crack like a worn-out calabash, to let streams of warm sunlight through; and then one day a clear blue morning dawned. The sun came up again in splendour over the mountain's shaggy shoulder like a well-greased warrior, gleaming with red ochre, striding out to war.

For several seasons Waseru had put off the operation of piercing his sons' ears because, before it could be performed, the permission of his wife's eldest brother had, by custom, to be given. In the leisure that followed the bean harvest he decided that the event could be no longer postponed. His eldest brother-in-law, Karue, was liked by none; and, worse still, ugly rumours of sorcery were abroad. Waseru feared that he would demand an unfairly heavy payment of goats before he gave his consent. Such payments were generally looked on as goodwill presents from the father's clan to the mother's, but Karue would no doubt regard the goats as a debt to be paid to the last hair of the last goat's tail.

Unpleasant as it was, however, the situation had to be faced. Waseru did not dare to go himself, for he still owed Ndolia nine goats and several brews of beer, and he was afraid he would be poisoned; but Ngarariga agreed to carry through the negotiations. He drove over a good female goat and a partially fattened ram and returned with a demand for three more goats and another ram. Waseru was so angry that he vowed never to send another goat; but in a few days he had to send Ngarariga back with two more. He dared not jeopardise his sons' safety, and the ear-piercing could not be further postponed. Then, at last, Karue sent a grudging permission, and a discourteous reminder of the rest of the debt.

Matu tried not to cry out when a sharpened stick was thrust through the flesh of his ear-lobe, and then of the upper cartilage, and twisted about until the hole was big enough to take a small plug of wood. But he could not suppress a whimper, and his father rebuked him with looks of shame. His brother's face remained calm as a cloud and gave no sign that he had even felt the pain.

4

In these days Muthengi lived a life of freedom and yet of discontent. Early in the morning he would disappear for the day. Sometimes he would return late at night for the evening meal and sometimes he would not come home at all, but would sleep in the huts of his companions. There were days when he herded his father's goats conscientiously, guarding them from hyenas and pulling down tendrils of a tall creeper with red, trumpet-shaped flowers which they particularly favoured. There were other days when, the goats forgotten, he would roam the ridges with a band of other boys and do no work at all, but shout jests and boasts to girls working in the fields, or hold banana feasts in the bush, or badger the mothers of his companions for food.

He paid little attention to anything his own mother said. As soon as the beans were harvested she was able to dig clay— to have done so while a crop was in the ground would have brought a curse upon the harvest—and to make cooking-pots. She mixed the clay with water in a hollowed tree-trunk, moulded the fat-bellied pots with her hand, dried them under banana leaves in the shade, and finally set them to bake around a slow fire. When they were hardened she loaded them on to her back and set off on a three-day journey to Ndia and back, for there the best market lay. She asked Muthengi to go with her to help carry pots, but he refused scornfully and did not conceal his contempt when Matu agreed to go. To do girls' work, and without protest, was the sign of a weakling and a fool. What young warrior would weigh down with burdens a back that should be erect and muscled only for the throwing of spears?

Although Muthengi taunted his brother, Matu's grave, pinched face showed no expression, and he did not reply. But in the evening, while the family sat around the fire waiting for the food to cook, it was Matu who shamed his elder brother, while Muthengi sat sulkily by the wall, ready to avenge the first sign of contempt. Waseru had a fondness for riddles, of which there were a great many, and all with answers that were well known. He liked to test his sons' memories and the quickness of their minds. When a lull came in the conversation he said:

"I saw an eagle standing on three trees."

In the silence that followed Matu's small voice cried:

"The cooking-pot!"

Waseru nodded his approval, and said again:

"My field is large, but only one plant grows there."

Again Matu's excited voice said:

"The sun!"

"Is your tongue silent, Muthengi, like that of a giraffe?" Waseru asked. "Here is a riddle for you: My son stands amid spears, but is not harmed."

Although his father had given him the clue, Muthengi could not recall the answer. He scowled from the shadows in sullen silence. Matu's usual gravity crumbled; he sniggered, and whispered to a white kid held in his arms:

"The tongue!"

5

After harvest came the season of dances. Every evening young men with rattles on their legs and serval-cat skins dangling over their buttocks sang their way to the appointed spot, their faces and chests white with lime. They spent many hours before the dance arranging their plaited hair in the smartest possible way and decorating it with white feathers. But the heads of the girls were shaven; to spend overmuch time decorating their persons would have been both immodest and unduly frivolous. Far into the night the rhythmic voices of the dancers floated down sleeping valleys and over silent ridges that lay like the pale, still shoulders of giants bent in obeisance before the luminous beauty of the moon.

Muthengi longed with all his spirit to join these dances, but they were not for boys. Several times he crept up to the level, grassy field where they were held and gazed entranced at the leaping figures of the warriors, at the tempestuous swirling of Colobus tails and blackpocked serval pelts, and at the tongues of firelight flickering like golden lightning over glossy skins. But when he reached the circle's edge, sucked in by the rhythm of the dance, one of the njamas * in charge made a quick dash towards him waving a bundle of burning sticks and shouting abuse, and Muthengi fled in shame and fright.

* Senior warriors, members of the warriors' council, responsible for enforcing law and order.

There were dances, however, for the uncircumcised, boys and girls alike. When the moon was half grown a decision was reached among the boys to fetch lime with which to paint their bodies for the dance Kibaata. They carried with them small bows and arrows, sharpened sticks for spears, and shields made from the bark of a tree; and as they marched they chanted a song in imitation of the warriors. In each boy's mind the lumps of lime were cattle, and the pit from which they dug it an army of Masai.

Long before darkness fell on the following evening they were ready. Lime coated their legs beneath the knee and a white pattern decorated cheeks, backs and arms. Over their buttocks dangled skins neatly sewn with cowrie shells, and over their fuzzy heads was passed a thong into which the long wing-feathers of guinea-fowl and cranes were fastened. Several of the boys had small iron rattles tied to their legs below the knee. Envy stabbed Muthengi like spear-thrusts when he saw these rattles, for all the world like those on a warrior's leg, and his mind returned continually to the problem of how he could get some for his own adornment.

6

At sunset the dancers, lads and girls together, gathered on an even, springy stretch of turf, their whitened faces grotesque in the last golden rays of the sun. When it had sunk and the first pale star hovered like a silver humming-bird in the east, the dance began. The children formed a ring, arms on shoulders, and began to rotate very slowly around the leader of the chorus, who stood alone in the centre.

Muthengi was the nucleus of the ring. He began his song slowly, swaying gently on his feet. At sudden intervals he jumped high into the air with heels close together, jerking his head violently back and forth on a rigid neck. A full-throated chorus took up the last line of each verse and chanted it over and over again to a quickening tempo. Soon the circle was rotating swiftly and boys and girls were stamping vigorously with the rhythm of the beat. Muthengi sprang higher and higher as he chanted, and as the speed quickened he seemed to return to earth more and more often opposite his adopted sister Ambui, who had slipped off from the forest shamba to attend the dance.

Ambui was maturing quickly, and Muthengi often found his eyes upon her. With her long-stemmed neck and smooth, sloping forehead she had grown into a girl of beauty. Ample food had filled her spidery limbs and rounded out her once-hollow belly. With plumpness had come a new independence which annoyed Wanjeri, but added to her charms.

When Muthengi grew tired of leading the chorus he yielded to another and joined the circle next to Ambui. Her shoulder was warm and slippery to his touch, and he felt his blood tingle as he watched her young breasts thrown up and down by the vigour of her movements like leaping fishes in a smooth, dark pool. Her body was filled with rhythm and her throat with song; she quivered like cane-stalks in the wind, and the rippling trills of applause for the singers burst from her throat like foam racing down a waterfall.

Hitherto he had thought of her only as a sister, one who helped his mother to cook food, bring firewood, and sweep the hut; now his body felt drawn towards her as the tongue of a thirsty man is drawn towards a spring. He knew, at the same time, that such thoughts were evil, perhaps sent to him by sorcerers, because she was his sister and the crime of incest a serious one. It would be possible, theoretically at least, for her to undergo a ceremony making her the daughter of a tree, so leaving her free to marry into his clan; but the time for thoughts of marriage was not yet. In any case it was highly unlikely that Waseru would agree. Muthengi tried to think only of the dance, and leapt again into the centre to improvise more verses of the song.

After the dance was over, half-way through the night, Muthengi and Ambui returned to Mahenia's along paths winding through the shambas, skirting stockades of silent slumbering homesteads and whispering clumps of trees. In the distance the deep, melodious voices of the young warriors echoed the rhythm that still pounded in Muthengi's head. His blood was hot and his breath came quickly, for he knew that he had danced well and that girls would be speaking of his prowess as they sauntered home.

He did not glance round at Ambui, but he could hear her light footfall on the path behind him, and he knew that moonlight was flowing in a silver film over the smooth greased skin of her bare arms and shoulders, and that her eyes were soft as a gazelle's. Mahenia's homestead was dark and silent, save for a faint rustling in the thatched roofs that lay white as mushrooms under the moon. No one stirred when Ambui quietly pulled aside the woven door of Wanjiku's hut. Muthengi looked quickly round him and encircled her waist with his arm, fumbling at the cord that secured her apron. The blood was pounding in his ears like a mortar. She tried to pull his hand away, but suddenly the strength of a lion flooded his limbs and he tightened his grip. Her hands plucked unavailingly at his arm. She was trembling, but whether with terror or desire he did not know. He pushed her forward into the hut and pulled the door to behind him.

7

THEY danced every night until the moon rose too late for dances and misty shadows no longer leaped behind them on the sweet-scented grass. Muthengi's springs grew higher and lighter; when he came to earth his feet beat on the ground with the hollow sound of a porcupine's stamp. Although he could no longer dance with Ambui nor touch her in public—that would have been indecent, now that they were lovers—all the time his song and his dance were for her, the long-necked and slender; he could feel her eyes glowing like hot charcoal upon him. A wild recklessness filled him, an exaltation that he had never known before. Strange fancies flew unbidden into his head, like weird-plumaged birds darting into a tree that was sometimes as tall as a mountain and at other times as small as a toadstool. For the first time he became conscious that his body had a life of its own; he could feel it itching and twitching quite independently, as though it were an animal and had nothing to do with him. Once he gazed at his hand in amaze-. ment, as if seeing it for the first time. He immediately realised that the hand was calling for the haft of a spear, as Ambui's body now called for his after the dances, and he knew that the time had come for him to enter the warriors' ranks.

One matter was as bitter to him as the taste of the fruit ngaita, the medicine used against tapeworm: he, the most skilful dancer, the leader in song, was without rattles on his shapely legs, whilst other boys, worthless francolins fit only to scuttle away under his feet, came to the dance with these clattering ornaments strapped to their thighs by strips of hide decorated with beads and shells. In particular Irumu's son Kabero, a vain, impertinent boy, aroused in Muthengi's heart feelings of intense disdain and envy. Kabero was a slight, insignificant little creature to look at; but because his father was a rich man and could afford to give him expensive ornaments, he strutted about like a fat pigeon. His wit was nimble and his words darted like bee-eaters in and out of people's ears.

Muthengi knew him to be stupid and vain, so it was all the more annoying when girls sought his companionship and giggled at his sallies. No doubt they were fascinated by Kabero's handsome rattles, by his expensively beaded belts and flashy bangles—girls were all fools, as easily dazzled as moles. Once Muthengi lost his temper with Ambui because she went off into gusts of laughter at some whispered remark of Kabero's which Muthengi knew to be a thrust at him; and he beat her over the shoulders until she cried. That night she stayed in the forest homestead and refused to come to the dance. The rhythm seemed slow and ragged to Muthengi and when he jumped into the centre of the ring he danced so listlessly that a

group of girls, friends of Kabero's, laughed and taunted him
with insults.

"You sing of your manhood," one of the girls called out,
"but now we see that manhood only makes you tired. When
we are circumcised we shall seek out warriors whose penis is
not made of words."

"Perhaps Muthengi is a hyena, a hermaphrodite who copu-
lates with himself," Kabero shouted. His sally was greeted
with a roar of laughter, and a flood of fury surged up in
Muthengi's throat. There was no more deadly insult than to
be called a hyena, and to be openly taunted with the charge of
self-abuse was almost as bad. He put his head down and
charged blindly at Kabero, his arms whirling like flails. Several
boys seized his arms and held him; three or four others came
to his aid. Girls ran, screaming, out of danger. Several of
the older boys started to belabour writhing backs with bundles
of smouldering brushwood snatched from the fire. Kabero
watched from the shadow of a bush, his teeth gleaming white
as doves' eggs in the moonlight. It was delightful to know
that the swaggering, conceited bully Muthengi was at the
bottom of the struggling heap. But soon three young warriors
came striding along the path towards their own dance, and
stepped aside to put an end to the brawl.

8

ALL that night Muthengi's mind was filled with dark ideas concerning the vengeance he wanted to take upon Kabero. His
legs were aching with bruises and a swollen cut over his eye
throbbed steadily. It was all Kabero's fault. Kabero was
trying to outwit, to torment, perhaps to kill him. Kabero, with
his rich, powerful father, his rattles, and all his finery. Shortly
before dawn a plan came into his head, and then at last he slept.

The following evening he walked down to join the group of
boys who were painting themselves for the dance. When no
eyes were on him he slipped away and hid himself in a clump of

bushes by the path leading to Irumu's homestead, a heavy club-headed stick ready by his side. The stars were hard as spear-points before he heard the sound for which he waited: the clattering of rattles approaching down the path. He waited until Kabero had almost passed him and then, with a low-pitched shout, flung himself on to the back of his enemy. Kabero flattened out without a sound. Muthengi lifted his club and thrashed the prostrate boy with all his strength; then he threw the club aside and kicked until his toes were bruised; but Kabero was limp and silent on the ground.

Muthengi dropped to his knees and unfastened the straps that fixed the rattles to Kabero's thighs and ankles. Although the pounding blood was clouding his eyes so that he could barely see, he managed to fasten the rattles to his own legs. Still Kabero did not stir. Panic began to curdle Muthengi's mind. He ran down the path towards the dance at his topmost speed, the rattles clattering wildly on his legs. He had expected that their long-coveted music would be sweet in his ears, but instead the sound was full of menace, like the curses from a thousand sorcerers' tongues.

Next morning the sky was thick and overcast and all through the forenoon, while he hoed the forest shamba, Muthengi's consternation grew. Why should the sun not shine to-day of all days, unless it was ashamed to look upon the evil that had been done? At last he could bear the suspense and guilt no longer. He wandered off, like a sick animal, to find a dark and lonely place to hide. Here Waseru found him, squatting on his heels by the stream.

" You, my son, speak to me," Waseru said. His voice was high, and Muthengi saw that his arms were shaking with anger. "Is there truth in what they are saying in the homesteads of Irumu's clan? Have you poured shame over the heads of the men of your clan? Have you indeed struck down one of your own age-grade as if he had been a wild pig, and drawn his blood?"

Muthengi's shame was such that he could not raise his eyes

to his father's face. Waseru's self-control dropped from him like a lizard's tail; he spoke as no father should ever speak to his son.

"Answer, you boy," he shouted. "Tell me, are you indeed my son, or some monster sent to humiliate my clan?"

Still Muthengi was unable to speak.

" Your silence has tongues," Waseru said, his voice quivering with anger. " I know now that you are a thief, and one who has drawn the blood of an elder's son."

He lifted his arm and slapped Muthengi twice across the face with an open palm as hard as he was able. The blows sent the boy reeling, and as his shoulders hit the ground a red wave of anger surged over him like the bore of a river in spate. He leapt to his feet and shouted:

"Yes, I am a thief, and how can I be otherwise, when my father denies me what all fathers give their sons? Kabero has rattles on his legs and finery when he goes to dances, while I have nothing—nothing! Now I am a grown man, strong as a warrior, why am I not circumcised? Why do you treat me as if I were a boy like Matu, when I am a man?"

"How can you speak thus to your father?" Waseru cried. "How can a boy who knows nothing of good behaviour talk of circumcision?" His anger burst out from his blood; he wrenched a whippy branch from the bush and started to belabour his son over the head and shoulders. Muthengi covered his face with his arms and stood his ground until his father's anger wore itself out. Then Waseru threw the stick away and walked back without another word to the homestead.

Muthengi stayed alone in the forest until sunset. When he came home, driven by cold and hunger, he went straight to the thingira and drew Kabero's rattles out of the folds of an ox-hide. The skin of a freshly-slain he-goat was pegged out to dry in the compound. Waseru had already made a sacrifice, pouring blood and fat to appease the spirits of his ancestors for the serious crime of having struck his own son. For the son and the grandfather were as one person; Muthengi and Mahenia were mystically the same. In time Muthengi would himself have sons, who would perpetuate the spirit of Waseru; and to beat him was to insult a person who would one day be in the position of Waseru's own father.

Muthengi laid the rattles at his father's feet without a word. Waseru was plaiting thin peeled sticks to make the walls of a new granary. Without looking at Muthengi he said:

"Tomorrow I shall return the rattles to Irumu. I shall have to pay five goats, perhaps more. Kabero is injured in the head. Five goats gone as if a hyena had taken them, because of the foolishness of one of my clan, a thief."

Still Muthengi said nothing, but he did not go away.

"I shall speak to Irumu to-morrow," Waseru went on. "We shall discuss the amount of compensation. It is hard to talk of circumcision when I must pay all my goats away in fines."

Still Muthengi stood still, his eyes on the ground, his tongue silent.

"I shall see Irumu to-morrow," Waseru repeated. " This is no case for the council of elders; private matters are not taken to the public meeting-place. It may be that we shall discuss other matters also, and that after the millet harvest a circumcision ceremony will be held."

CHAPTER VII

The Circumcision

I

WHEN young millet dusted the earth with green the candidates for circumcision banded together to practise, in twos and threes, the steps of the traditional kuhura; and when the grain was knee-high they started to dance.

Muthengi adorned himself under the expert eye of his uncle, Ngarariga, who, as a young man, naturally knew more of the latest fashion than Waseru. His chest, back and legs were coated with lime in traditional zig-zag patterns which, it was said, had been shown to the first Kikuyu man when he talked with God upon the peak of Kerinyagga. His thick, fuzzy hair was shaved and the shining pate painted with lime and decorated with a strip of monkey fur. Waseru had traded honey and tobacco at the market for a rattle like Kabero's, and a serval-cat skin which hung down over the buttocks like a woman's apron. Muthengi wore a cape of black and white Colobus monkey pelt, and strips of colobus fur were tied below his knees and ankles. Waseru had shaped him a wooden shield cut from a muringa tree, and on it he painted in red and white, with lime and ochre, a dog's-tooth design belonging to his tribal group, one which his father had painted on his own shield when he, as a young man, had danced before his circumcision.

For three months the candidates roamed the countryside in their finery, pausing to sing and to dance the kuhura whenever they reached an open and convenient space. They danced on the outskirts of markets, and women applauded loudly with trills. They danced before the homesteads of rich men of their father's age-grade, whose wives brought them out food on platters. Wherever they went people greeted them with shouts of welcome and gave them hospitality, for they were privileged people : the young men soon to gain full membership of the tribe, the youths whose bravery would repulse attack and whose fertility would ensure the future of the race.

At last the millet was gathered in and a meeting of fathers was held to fix the circumcision day. The ceremony would set Waseru's feet, no less than those of his son, upon a new path. Now he must cease to be a warrior, a young man, to wear his hair in greased and ochred plaits. His head must be shaved, and with the shorn hair he must bury his youth and gaiety, the privilege of dancing with the warriors, the duty of springing to arms when the war-horn sounded. He must pay two goats to join the senior elders' council whose members ordered ceremonies, judged cases, and kept the peace; he would be privileged, for the first time, to drink beer. Into his keeping would pass many closely guarded secrets, and as a sign of his rank he would carry a polished mungirima staff and a fan of leaves and wear spiral metal ornaments in his ears.

2

THE fathers' meeting elected Irumu as master of ceremonies, the mathanjuki. He fixed his eyes upon the sun, calling to memory the position of the moon—a young moon threw harmful influences over such an event—and said :

"My son Kabero shall be circumcised in eight days. On the day before, the mambura festival shall be held by the sacred fig-tree on the slope above the stream at Wathakumu. Let all whose sons and daughters are candidates see that the youths and maidens are prepared."

The next few days were busy with preparations for great feasts to be held at Irumu's, to be presided over by the mathanjuki and his senior wife, the circumcision-mother. Gourds of beer, millet gruel, and bunches of bananas were brought to the homestead, together with communally purchased fattened he-goats. For each candidate a sponsor was chosen, and for ever afterwards this man and his wives would stand in the relationship of parents to the boy concerned. Waseru chose for Muthengi the muramati's son Gacheche, a steady-going, reliable man likely to be a faithful ally in case of trouble. Over the entrance to Irumu's homestead an arch of poles and branches was built, surmounted with a bundle of sugar-canes. No one could enter the homestead without walking through this arch, and it was so constructed that if a sorcerer should pass beneath it, his medicines would immediately lose their evil power.

In a hut built for the candidates in the bush, nervous tension grew as taut as the head of a drum. The boys roamed the bush with dry throats and burning eyes, knowing that the last days of childhood were falling away one by one, like stones dropped into a deep pool. A new life, bright as a sword and wide as the sky, was opening in front of them. Very soon they would be men, with all the powers and joys of war and killing, of sex and procreation, laid open to their grasping.

On the third day, and every day after that, Irumu came to instruct them in things that must be known to men; and at the same time his wife, the circumcision-mother, fulfilled the same office for the girls.

3

IRUMU taught them the history of their people and the behaviour which each tribal group must observe or shun. He recited the long list of things which brought thahu, and explained how the sickness which followed could only be averted by the slaughter of a goat. He talked of the virtues with which a man should be invested, of how he should be at all times dignified and quiet, disdaining to raise his voice in anger like a child, or to display the foolish emotions of impatience, rowdiness or fright. To assert a claim or an opinion stridently was to insult the listener by assuming him to be unjust or stupid. While quick to avenge a deliberate slight, he should be ready always to forgive an injury that did not arise from malice. If a man offended him and, realising his error, proffered in silence a bead torn from his cloak, or a small ornament from his person, the gift should be at once accepted as a sign of pardon.

Above all, the virtue most to be cultivated was that of industry, for without industry no person could become rich. A man should be industrious in husbandry, clearing bush and breaking new land, protecting crops from wild animals, caring for livestock so that it would increase. He should be industrious in war, keeping his body trained to hardships and his weapons keen and bright. He should be industrious in observance of the law and in respect for custom, so that the continuity of the tribe might flow from generation to generation and the spirits of ancestors be at peace.

The duties of manhood, Irumu continued, were many; but supreme among them were the defence of the country and the procreation of children. If ever there came a generation who failed to carry out these duties, the Kikuyu people would perish like a plant which bears no seed and which is choked by weeds of greater strength. Warfare was like an axe, of which courage was the iron head and cunning the wooden handle. Just as the head of an axe was useless without a handle to wield it, so bravery was of no avail without strategy and wit; but as a handle without a head could fell no trees, so a cunning plan would fail unless it was joined to an army of fearless men obedient to their leader.

4

As to the other responsibility, Irumu continued, it was the duty of every man to beget as large a number of children as the fertility of his wives would permit, so that his clan might multiply and his ancestors continue their earthly existence in another shape. In marriage the woman's duty was to obey her husband at all times, to cultivate the land, and to cook and brew; but the husband, also, had duties towards his wife. He

must find her land to cultivate, break it for seed, provide her
with a dwelling, see that she was well clad and protect her from
magic. Should he fail in these duties his wife might return
to her father, and if the council upheld her complaints the undutiful husband would lose entirely the bride-price that he had
paid.

He must satisfy, also, her sexual desires, or else his wife
would leave him for another man. In this she would very
likely be upheld by the council; moreover, a man clumsy in
love would be derided by his contemporaries and become the
constant butt of jokes. Such technique, like all others, had to
be learnt; and Irumu gave the candidates detailed instructions.
After a child was born no man must lie with his wife until she
had ceased to suckle the baby, four seasons after its birth, for
no woman's strength could suffice to nourish at one time a
child in the womb and a child at the breast. If a man lay with
his wife too early, and her milk fell upon him, he would fall
sick and sterility would afflict his cows and she-goats. Nor
must he lie with her when the thahu of death lay on the homestead, nor when a cow was about to calve (lest the woman beget
a calf instead of a human baby), nor when food was cooking
in the pot, nor on many other prescribed occasions.

He warned them further that union between unmarried boys
and girls was forbidden. If a child was born out of wedlock
both would suffer disgrace and ridicule; all the youths must
avoid the girl at dances, lest her milk contaminate them. Each
girl to be circumcised with them would be given an under-
apron by her mother, who would say: "Remember now that
this apron is for your protection, as a boy's shield is for his.
Keep it tied always around your waist. If a young man tries to
remove it he is an evil youth to be avoided, for you are the
wealth of your father and he who would plunder you is like a
thief." No youth must force his love upon one who was unwilling, but he might lie with the girl of his fancy in her bed and
do all that was necessary to excite her passions and satisfy his
own provided that he did not untie the apron that her mother

had given her. In this way young men would learn how to bring pleasure to women and would gauge also the depth of their love before goats were paid; for it was wise to remember, Irumu said, the truth of the saying: "It is only when the spear is forged that it has notches."

Lastly, he adjured them, the ceremony in which they were about to take part would unite all those who were circumcised together with a tie that nothing in their future lives could break.

"Such men," Irumu said, "will be as brothers. Each youth must give help to anyone of his circumcision-age who is in need; and he must do none of his fellows an injury. If a man of your circumcision-age comes to your homestead, you must welcome him as you would welcome a son of your own mother; and should he wish to lie with his circumcision-brother's wife, you must yield him your place in her bed. A man may be compared to a strand of silk within a spider's web. No thread can hang alone; each is linked with its fellows to make a whole. Thus some threads link a man to his father, to his father's clan and to his ancestors; and others bind him to his circumcision-brothers. Different ties unite him to the elders who rule the country and administer the law. All these threads came together to form a web, and that web is the Kikuyu people. So long as all the threads hold together, the web is strong and serves its purpose; but whenever a strand snaps, the web is weakened. Therefore, although the strength of every man comes from his unity with his people, yet also the people draws its strength from every individual. So a man must fulfil his obligations as readily as he uses his privileges; so he must fight with courage and labour with devotion; so he must beget children and respect the elders; and in all things he must act with justice and obey the law."

5

ON the flattened crest of a soft-sloping ridge stood a small fig-tree whose trunk forked not far above the ground; and here, on the seventh day, a great crowd assembled for the mambura. Warriors whose heavy pig-tails pulled back their heads until their chins were tilted forward rubbed shoulders with quiet, shaven-headed elders and with chattering women so excited that they could not keep still. Loud-voiced njamas kept the spectators back by brandishing long canes. Soon the clattering of rattles was heard and the candidates appeared in a body, painted and hung about with ornaments, resplendent in tall head-dresses made of feathers.

In the circle kept clear by the njamas they started to dance. As the sun mounted the sky the pace quickened until the ground shook beneath stamping feet and the air vibrated with rhythmic song. Women applauded with continuous trills, sometimes bursting into song in praise of sons and clans. Within the same circle, but in a separate group, Ambui and the girl candidates danced, hung about with beads and shells like the boys, and with rattles on their legs.

When signs of exhaustion began to appear, the sponsors came forward and gave to each candidate a stick to which the tail of a Colobus monkey was tied. The dance resumed its frenzy and then, at a sign from Irumu, the boys drew back a little from the sacred fig-tree and one by one hurled their sticks between the forked branches. With a shout they fell upon the tree as if it had been an enemy. Like monkeys they clambered into its branches and tore down handfulls of twigs and leaves which they handed to their mothers, sisters and aunts, who leaped like klipspringers around the tree. Instead of stakes the girls threw rough belts of bark which were picked up by a small girl at the other side of the tree and broken in two, lest a sorcerer should use them to injure the owners.

That evening a great feast was held at Irumu's homestead for the parents and relations of the candidates. Gourd after gourd of hot, sour beer was drunk, platters loaded with food were handed round, and loud-voiced rejoicing proceeded far into the night.

6

MUTHENGI and his fellows danced until late in front of their temporary hut. When their parents came to call them before dawn they were waiting, taut-nerved, for the great ordeal. First their fathers blessed them by sprinkling beer over their bodies with a branch of the mukenya bush. Then, taking a mouthful of the beer, they spat out with the liquid all the insults and disrespect that, unwittingly or in angry moments, they had offered to their sons since birth. The procession set out in the darkness, singing with great bravado, to the river that ran below Irumu's homestead. On the bank they halted while all their clothes, their ornaments, their rattles, and everything that they wore were stripped from them. Then, naked in the pale starlight, they ran swiftly into the river and waded out until the water clasped their waists. Although its grip was icy they felt nothing, for inside them a great fire burnt, and their heads were dizzy as if with honey-beer. They splashed water over their bodies with stiffened arms, chanting in unison the circumcision song. The sound echoed down the valley to scare shy duikers from night-shrouded shambas and waken the startled birds.

Dawn had blunted the fine points of the stars when they marched in single file up the hillside, singing with a rhythm steady as the beat of a tranquil heart. Behind them pressed a crowd of eager spectators. Everyone halted on an open pasture on the crest of the ridge, and presently shouts and trills heralded the arrival of the girls. They took up their position a little way off. Suddenly the first arm of sunlight touched the bush-cloaked hillside across the river, and every shrub and tree sprang into the sharp outline of light and shade. The grave-faced Gacheche stepped out of the crowd and took his stand behind his ward. Muthengi sat down on the ground with his legs stretched out in front. Gacheche handed him the bunch of leaves torn from the fig-tree on the previous day and he seated himself upon them in a position where they would catch the blood. His face was taut and set, as expressionless as a mask. Ranged in a line beside him were the other boys and, after a gap, the girl candidates, who were seated between the supporting legs of their women sponsors.

A few moments later a shout went up from the spectators and the boys' circumcisor came into view. He was an old, wizened man, famous for his skill in operations. He was dressed in full regalia, with many rattles on his shrivelled legs, his face framed in a tall head-dress of ostrich plumes. A deep expectant silence fell upon the crowd. The candidates gazed steadily ahead, seeing nothing. The circumcisor walked slowly up to the first boy and drew a knife from a leather bag on his arm. Without further preliminaries he bent over, cut the foreskin with a few deft slashes, and pinned it back with a thin skewer. Blood spurted, but the boy did not wince; his face, closely watched by peering spectators for a twitch of pain, remained impassive. His sponsor quickly threw the boy's cloak over his head and body, and the circumcisor passed on.

Muthengi's turn came quickly and by no sign did he betray the pain of the knife. But the boy after him was less brave. His face contorted as the knife slashed and a low whimper escaped his throat. A deep derisive groan went up from the crowd. One of the warriors laughed loudly and called out an insult. He was silenced by a njama, and a cloak was thrown quickly over the boy's head. But no cloak could hide his humiliation, or protect him from the future ridicule of his fellows. He had publicly displayed cowardice and his shame would pursue him for the rest of his life.

At the same time an old woman operated upon the girls. The arms and legs of the candidates were pinned down by their sponsors so that they could not move, but they, like the boys, bore without flinching the pain that seared their nerves when the circumcisor, with a flick of the knife, amputated the clitoris and then, with two more slashes, the lips of flesh on either side. A convulsive shiver passed through Ambui's body when she felt the knife, but she did not cry out nor lose control of the muscles of her face. Blood spurted from the wound, and the woman circumcisor quickly plugged it with a small strip of greased leather. Then a crowd of chattering women gathered round to praise her loudly for her courage. Now they welcomed her unreservedly into Waseru's clan and she, a stranger, was no longer without kin.

7

THE ceremonies that followed lasted many days. The boys retreated into a shelter specially built for them, and the girls to their mothers' huts; but fathers and sponsors met at Irumu's on the morning after the operation to drink the beer for the eating of the fat ram. Next day came the beer for the shaving of the candidates, and a ceremonial shaving was performed under the direction of the circumcision-mother. The boys' heads were scraped as smooth as eggshells, care being taken to burn every scrap of hair as a precaution against witchcraft, and Irumu blessed the youths by sprinkling on their heads and navels a mixture of the stomach contents of a goat and honey-beer.

He had barely finished when the peel of bells was heard approaching, and two men came into sight. One, an elder, wore an iron bell fixed to each leg and a ring of smaller bells around his ankles. Behind walked a tall youth carrying a long yellow gourd, encircled with strings of shells and covered with pictures and designs. A shout of welcome went up when the crowd saw the old man, for the bells proclaimed him to be a wandering troubadour, and the object in the young man's hand was the gechande, a rattle inscribed with a key to the verses of the troubadour's song. Irumu spat upon his hand and offered it to the troubadour, thus signifying his trust; for by giving to another a fragment of his body, the spittle, he placed himself at the stranger's mercy. The visitors were given meat and beer and then the troubadour took his rattle and started to sing. Many of the verses were meaningless to his listeners, yet the rhythm held them enthralled. The words were mainly traditional; each troubadour spent many years in learning them from a fellow-singer. Other verses were topical, invented by the minstrel as he roamed the country over, singing at markets and circumcision feasts, carrying news and stories over the ridges from one end of the land to another, and back again. The elders shook their heads when this troubadour sang of the coming of locusts, in great brown swarms, to devour the millet, and of how the leader of warriors Kaheri had called out his men to resist them, but in vain. Because boys had helped to fight the insect invaders, the troubadour sang that the new circumcision-age had been called Ngege, meaning locusts; and it was by this name that Muthengi's age became known.

On the last day of feasting the beer for the breaking of the branches was drunk. Next morning the arch of shrubs and sugar-cane fixed over the entrance to Irumu's homestead was destroyed. That same day the boys returned to their fathers' homesteads and their temporary hut was burnt down by the elders. Muthengi's sponsor led him home, and his parents came out to greet him. Waseru marked his nose, chest and feet with white chalk and Wanjeri smeared him all over with castor oil. A small goat was presented to him as a compounded fine for all the occasions when Waseru had spoken roughly to him as a boy. That night he slept in the thingira, for he had become a man.

CHAPTER VIII

The Notched Spear

I

WHEN Muthengi's wound was healed he begged from his mother a gourd of beer and from his father a small goat. Now that he was a warrior a set of weapons must be made, and for this he must buy iron at the market. As soon as Wanjeri had made a small brew of beer she carried it over to a smith who lived near the iron workings on the Chania river, and Muthengi broached the matter of a sword and spear.

The smith was a squat man with broad shoulders and a sullen look. There were many bangles on his arms and fine chains of his own making on his ankles. He started by asking such a ridiculous amount of iron and charcoal for the job that Mutheng knew he was trying to cheat. Bargaining went on until the sun was overhead, and at last Muthengi succeeded in beating him down to a reasonable amount. He felt well satisfied; no doubt about it, he was a shrewd man of business as well as a fearless warrior.

"I wish to have the weapons," he demanded, "before the moon, which was full two days ago, is dead."

Before the smith could answer, Wanjeri, who had been sitting quietly against a wall of the hut apparently asleep, intervened. Her voice was shrill and indignant.

"On no account agree to such a ridiculous bargain!" she commanded her son. "Do you not see that this smith is taking advantage of your youth and ignorance?"

Muthengi was furious at her interruption; but because she was his mother he could not speak sharply to her. The smith looked at her sourly and asked:

"Can it be that among your clan women sit on the council of justice while men suckle infants?"

"Can it be that in your forge the iron for five spears makes only one?" Wanjeri retorted.

The smith's looks grew even more sullen, for he hesitated to insult an elder's wife. Muthengi's nervousness increased. All that he had heard of the potency of smiths' curses came into his head.

"I shall bring half the quantity you mention," he announced, "and you shall make the spear first. If there is sufficient iron over, the sword shall be forged at once. If not, I will bring more."

The smith agreed reluctantly to the compromise and sealed the contract by accepting the beer. In the next few days Muthengi exchanged a small goat from his father's flock for several lumps of iron and then, with Waseru's help, felled a mukoiigo tree from the forest, chopped it into lengths and burnt it into charcoal in a roughly built clay kiln. Another brew of beer was made, and on the appointed morning he set out for the smith's dwelling followed by Wanjeri with a full gourd of beer; Ambui, crouching like a frog under a heavy load of charcoal; and his circumcision-mother, who bore lumps of iron ore wrapped in banana leaves.

2

THE smith's forge was a round hut without walls. In the centre was a hollow where a small fire of charcoal glowed, kept hot by the smith's son, who worked the bellows. He raised each arm in turn to fill two goatskin lungs whose ends were united in a single clay nozzle. The bellows' song was like the breathing of a sick sheep. The visitors sat down outside the forge to watch the forging, for Wanjeri had warned her son to see the whole process performed under his eye. Smiths were notoriously sharp; if they were not closely supervised they would claim that the iron had been poorly smelted, that half of it was sand and that fresh supplies were needed.

No member of Muthengi's tribal group might work in iron, and he observed the process a little nervously. Iron was a dangerous and unpredictable thing : half alive, half dead. On haft or handle it lay inert and rigid, but under the hand of a smith it would grow supple and steal colour from the heart of the fire. Iron alone could burn without destruction, and he had heard it talking angrily with water. Just as it could command life or death within itself at will, so could it wield powers of life and death over its users. A thrust of the spear could drive life from the body, yet as man's servant the knife tilled the soil and gave him sustenance. Smiths, who knew the secret of controlling iron, possessed a magic derived from its mysterious power which they could direct against their enemies. They were men with whom it was best not to quarrel.

By evening the spear was finished. Its haft was smooth and slender and its grooved blade wide and sharp. Muthengi weighed it in his hand, balanced it above his head and made as if to hurl it many times before he was satisfied. A spear was like a wife; it must wear for many seasons and do its work well. There was iron enough over for a sword, so he arranged to bring another gourd of beer the following day for its forging. He led the three women home in silence, but his heart was singing with the joy of handling, for the first time, his own spear.

3

Now that he was a young man a great change came over Muthengi's life. He was concerned no longer with his father's goats. His task was to herd the cattle of richer men, to protect them from lions and raids, and to keep himself in constant readiness for battle if ever the horn of war should sound over the ridges.

Senior warriors, seasoned in battle, held the office of njama. These men formed the council of war, which was in charge of the defence of the district and which alone could send parties of warriors out to raid. The chief of this council, elected by his fellows, was a warrior called Nduini. He was known as a steady, upright man of common sense, a careful general, and one who never lost his head. There were some who said that his caution was greater than his courage. The newly-circumcised considered that age had deprived him of his dash and that a younger man should take his place; but youths of the newest age-grades could not sit on the council of war.

Only the richer men owned cattle. Their herds were driven to the edge of the plain for grazing—unless, of course, the Masai were reported within a day's journey of the Amboni river. The cattle must also be driven frequently to a salt-lick, of which there were three within reach: Iruri, Gethwini and Wamurogi (so called because it was near the homestead of a poisoner who, after conviction for several murders, had been tied up in banana leaves and burnt to death). The largest salt-lick, Iruri, lay at the foot of the hill Niana, where the green hilly forests of the Kikuyu flattened out into the brown treeless plain of the nomad Masai. Iruri was a somewhat risky place to take the cattle, but of late there had been no Masai on the plain and Kikuyu stock were grazing right down to the Amboni, which lay definitely within the Masai sphere. The council of war aimed at keeping half the available force of warriors on guard over the cattle and half off duty in their homes, ready to assemble at the sound of the war-horn to repulse a raid.

Soon after Muthengi had obtained his weapons he was called by an njama to take his turn of duty with the cattle herds. Pride and excitement filled his heart; now at last he would take his place as the defender of his clan among his fellows. He went down to Iruri in the early morning, swinging lightly over dew-soaked turf. The rains had started. The sweet scent of new shoots was everywhere and the earth was dark with growth and moisture. Birds were darting self-importantly across the soft sky with twigs and moss trailing from their beaks. The earth, like the young warriors, had put on its bright bead ornaments: flecks of blue and orange, red and purple, the delicate petals of wild flowers shining out of the wet, sweet-stemmed grasses and the swiftly-growing shrubs.

Muthengi's own skin glowed in the morning sunshine no less brightly. He wore, for the first time, the warrior's coat of ochre and fat. Rattles clanked merrily on his ankles and feathers waved in his hair. Suspended from his neck was a pair of tweezers for pulling out all the hairs on his body, and a small horn containing a charm. A bead belt around his waist supported a club and his new sword in its ox-hide scabbard that he had dyed vermilion with the powdered root of the mugaka shrub, mixed with cane juice and a little soda. Muthengi filled his lungs and laughed aloud, for the day was new-born and the world was young. He knew that it was good to be alive, and a warrior on his way to the plain.

4

EACH day the young herders arose before the sun, when the sky was white as polished metal behind the black crest of Kerinyagga, and pulled aside the thorny branches blocking the entrance to the cattle enclosures. Cows and calves slept in separate bomas. The calves lolloped quickly towards their hump-backed mothers, but they were held back by one herdsman while another crouched on his three-legged stool and milked the mother with one hand into an open calabash. Only when this was over were the bleating calves allowed to suck their breakfasts. Milk from the calabashes was poured into long, thin-necked gourds, already prepared by rinsing with cows' urine and filling with smoke, and put aside until evening, when the milk would have turned into a delicious sour junket.

The no less delicious breakfast food was easily obtained. A heifer's legs were roped with leather thongs and she was thrown on her side. One herdsman seized her horns and half twisted her head over his knee, so that the neck was laid bare, while another fitted to his bow an arrow that had been blocked by winding a thick roll of twine just below the point. He aimed carefully and fired into the cow's jugular vein. The arrow was jerked out and a jet of blood sprang from the wound, to be caught in an open calabash. When the measure was full, the skin around the wound was pinched together and the heifer released; the blood was poured, frothing, into two gourds, already half filled with milk. The gourds were passed from hand to hand and each young herdsman took a long draught of the warm, satisfying fluid.

After the cattle had visited the salt-lick they were driven far afield in search of pasture. At this time of year herding was easy. Before the rains the long, dry grass, as high as a man's shoulder, had been burnt off, and already the stiff, blackened stumps were bright with new growth. Below Iruri the great plain Laikipia stretched into space, as green and pleasing as an endless field of young millet, and thickly dotted with big herds of hartebeeste and zebra, gnu, oryx and gazelle. Later in the year, when the game migrated and sap lay dormant and a cloud of pink blossom covered the Cape chestnuts, it was a different story. Then weary cattle, stark as dead trees, plodded long miles in search of pasture through grass whose dry stems slashed like knives at the herders' legs and feet. Then the shrill, unchanging song of grasshoppers was like a flame that never flickered in the ears of the young men, and a mist of fine dust from the cattle's hooves rose into their thirsty throats.

But such hardships lay in the future. Now the new grass was sweet and luscious and the ground springy beneath the herdsmen's feet. Muthengi soon learnt the Masai trick of standing for long stretches of time on one foot, resting the other against the inside of his rigid thigh and leaning on his spear. All day long he guarded cattle on the level plain, dozing sometimes in the sun, moving sometimes with a long, loping stride to head off a straying beast. Overhead, fat multi-coloured clouds grew gradually out of a blue sky, deeper than the wisdom of God, as sheets of purple muthakwa blossom unfold from buds small as dust-motes to shroud the hillsides after rain.

Before the sun sank to rest the herdsmen drove the cattle back towards the bomas and watered them at a spring.   As night fell beasts and men found shelter in their separate enclosures, and the herdsmen told each other valorous stories over their evening meal around the fire.

5

THE peace of the district was shattered abruptly one morning, a little before noon.

All along the ridges women were weeding in the shambas and men, for the most part, lounging in the shade or intent on the game giuthi, which was played with counters of beans in two rows of shallow holes dug in the ground.   Suddenly the sleepy silence was pierced by a distant high-pitched shout.   It had an instantaneous effect. Women dropped their knives and straightened their backs with consternation on their faces.   Men jumped to their feet and stood listening, their heads cocked to one side. The shouting came again quite plainly, a sort of wail, long and high, from a distant ridge.

In a moment people were scurrying in all directions like winged termites rising out of the earth after a shower of rain. Warriors dived into their huts to extract their head-dresses, their rattles and their weapons of war.   In the compounds their womenfolk helped them to strap on swords and quivers and handed them spear, club and shield.   Boys herding in the bush drove the goats with all speed towards the forest.   The air was full of shouting.   Nduini brought out the war-horn, the horn of a kudu, and ran to the top of a hill to send its warning on to the western ridges, towards Wangombe's and the distant cattle.   Two ridges over the signal was taken up by the next horn, and soon its clear note was floating down from the hills to salt-lick and plain.

There the herders heard it, and sprang into action.   First, runners spread out on the flanks of the herds to bring them together and drive them towards the Amboni, away from danger.

All the rest of the warriors, Muthengi among them, assembled by the salt-lick ready to charge into the battle wherever they might be needed, and if possible to cut off the enemy's retreat. Black balls of ostrich feather were lifted off the tips of spears and swords loosened in the sheaths. Presently a low, throbbing chant began, deep in the chests of the warriors, and soon the war song was rising up to the ridges above, while feet stamped in unison and flashing spears quivered under the sun.

Matu was herding goats near his grandfather's homestead when the shouting started. With terror itching in his legs he drove them helter-skelter to Mahenia's, where his grandmothers were dressing Ngarariga for the fight. Mahenia was nowhere to be seen.

"Fly quickly to the forest," Ngarariga ordered. " Go first to Waseru's, and he will tell you what to do. You should be safe enough there; the enemy will never get as far as that."

Two njamas ran by, calling to Ngarariga to join them.

"Masai have seized our cattle at the salt-lick of Gethwini," one shouted. "They are driving them now towards the plain behind the hill Mawé; our warriors were taken unawares. I carry Nduini's orders ! Run to the ford below Mawé, where the path crosses the river. Here the Masai must pass on their retreat, here Nduini will fall upon them to recapture the cattle. Run on, like the whirlwind that races over the plain !"

The njamas hurried on, pausing at each compound to summon all able-bodied men of the warrior classes. Columns of smoke standing up above the ridge behind them showed that the victorious Masai, not content with carrying off cattle, were firing the huts. The hillside glittered like quartz as the spearheads of converging warriors hurrying to the ford caught the sun. An njama blew steadily on the war-horn and the air was full of shouts.

In Mahenia's homestead his two wives quickly collected a few calabashes of cooked food and some water-gourds, gathered up the terrified small children and set off up the path that led into the forest and to Waseru's shamba. Soon they joined a stream of women, children and old men hurrying in the same direction. The elders were shaking their heads dolefully and many of the women were in tears. The refugees moved for the most part in dispirited silence, save for the bleating of agitated goats and the whimpering of babies. The silence of the forest was broken only by the harsh screech of monkeys and the fluting of wood-pigeons; distant shouts of triumph or defeat were muffled by a wall of trees. They halted at the swampy glade below Waseru's shamba and sat in an uneasy silence, listening with the intensity of hunted animals. Waseru searched among the crowd for his father, but without success. Several distracted mothers failed to account for all their children, and most of the elders missed some of their goats.

6

A TALL warrior, his head-dress waving like a storm-tossed tree, came panting to the salt-licks at Iruri with Nduini's urgent orders.

"Go to the ford below the hill Mawé," he shouted. "Run like the eland, there is no time to lose ! The Masai have split their ranks; some have turned back towards the forest and seek a way behind the hill Kiamucheru with most of the cattle; Nduini has gone to cut them off, if he can. The others are making for the Mawé ford. Run, warriors, with feet like arrows and the hearts of lions; the lives and wealth of your fathers are yours to save !"

With a great shout the column set off at a fast loping run up the slope ahead, dodging through thick grass to avoid pits dug to trap hostile invaders. They were shaking with excitement, their eyes were burning and their throats dry. When they reached the ford it seemed as if the grass on the hillside opposite had turned to black feathers, so thick were the moving plumes. Muthengi had barely recovered his breath when a deep groan came from the warriors and over the edge of the hill ahead, a shoulder of Mawé, the tawny crest of a Masai lion head-dress appeared. The tall, long-legged enemies, each with a narrow white shield on his forearm painted in red and blue, poured over the horizon. When they saw the Kikuyu ahead a low rumble came out of their throats, like the growl of a lioness getting ready to charge. They halted on the opposite slope, closing their ranks for a charge.

Muthengi gazed at them in exhilaration, lust of battle mingling with fear and admiration in his heart. They were taller than any men he had seen before. Their thighs were straight as saplings, their features sharp as axes, their skins lighter than honey. His limbs began to quiver like the wings of a sunbird when its beak sucks honey from a red-hot-poker bloom, and his blood raced wildly in his veins.

The Kikuyu army was marshalled by njamas in three ranks. In front was a line of warriors crouching on their heels, hidden behind broad shields, with clubs ready in their hands. Behind were the bowmen, whose arrows had been newly dipped in the poison which the Athi had taught them to brew; and behind them, a line of spearmen. Although they were outnumbered by perhaps four to one the Masai, to whom fear was unknown, lined up in a double rank and couched their spears for the attack. At a word from the commander a great shout filled the air, and simultaneously the Masai rolled down the hill in a compact red wave and with the speed of rushing water. They crossed the shallow stream without breaking ranks and surged up the hill to throw themselves against the shields of the Kikuyu.

As they started up the slope the first line of the defenders hurled their clubs at the advancing phalanx. There was a sound of thunder as the clubs rattled against the flashing shields of the Masai. But the shields were narrow, and some of the clubs, glancing off, struck the heads of the warriors and felled a few of them to the ground. The club-throwers then leapt to their feet, scattered, and ran around, drawing their swords, to form a line behind the spearmen.

A volley of arrows sped like a swarm of bees straight into the faces of the Masai. Many hung quivering in shields, but others bit into legs, arms and feet. The Masai kept on and did not waver; but barely had they engaged the first line of the Kikuyu when many of them jerked their limbs, spun around with queer motions, sank squirming to their knees and finally toppled over and lay still.

The Kikuyu spearmen crouched to the ground as the Masai fell upon them, thrusting upwards and sideways at their opponents' legs and faces. The ranks of attackers and attacked dissolved into a seething whirlpool of warriors fighting hand to hand. The Masai, although so heavily out-numbered, fought as if possessed by devils. Warriors with arrows deep in their thighs lunged about them with their spears until poison congealed their blood and weapons dropped from their helpless hands.

Muthengi had not imagined that men could fight with such ferocity. He crouched low behind his shield, and when the line of Kikuyu bowmen scattered, the onrushing giants loomed ahead. One came directly at him, spear poised high to strike. Muthengi leapt like a frog to one side and the spear plunged into the ground beside his heel. He swivelled around and lunged, but the Masai's slim body bent like a reed and the blow glanced off his long shield. Before Muthengi could recover his opponent plucked out the spear, jumped back and struck again. Muthengi caught the blow on his shield. The spear-point pierced the hide and quivered a finger's breadth above his heart. The blow knocked him backwards, but with a twist he pulled his arm from the loop of the shield, rolled over and jumped to his feet, his sword already out of its sheath.

For a few moments they eyed each other, swords in hand, their feet dancing on the turf. The shouts and blows all around them rolled unheard over their ears. Muthengi saw the bared teeth of the Masai widen in a grin of triumph; the shieldless man was at his mercy. He stepped back and half turned as if to fly. The Masai lunged, and, at the same moment, Muthengi leapt forward and heard iron cut air behind his head. His arm swung and his sword crashed like a falling tree on the Masai's

I

shoulder. A bone cracked, the Masai's knees crumpled and the proud, steel-sinewed body folded up at his feet.

The odds against the invaders were too great. When the Kikuyu line stood firm the Masai knew that they were doomed, but they fought on until the end. None surrendered and none fled. When the fight was over fifty Masai and as many Kikuyu corpses lay on the blood-soaked ground.

The victors, many of them bleeding, some in great pain with deep gaping wounds, stripped the dying men of their weapons and gathered up the spears. Muthengi wrenched the spear of his dead adversary from his own shield and carried it proudly home. There was no trophy more prized than the spear of a Masai warrior killed in single-handed combat.

7

FOR several days hyenas howled in satisfaction over the ridges and the sky was full of vultures, for corpses defiled the land. When only whitening bones remained, those whose huts had been burnt set to work to make good their losses. The forest rang with axes, and columns of women wound their way to a swamp near Karatina to return like moving reed-beds, weighed down with thatch. Warriors laid aside their spears and helped their fathers to weave wicker doors and the round walls of granaries. Within six days, smoke was rising from new roofs wherever an old one had stood, fences were being built around the compounds, and goat-bells sounded again from the bush.

But the damage had been heavy, for Nduini and his section of the warriors had failed to cut off the retreat of the main body of the raiders, and the Masai had succeeded in driving away most of their captured booty. So nearly half the cattle of the district had gone and several families, once rich, were ruined; while those whose homesteads had been fired had lost their whole season's store of beans and maize.

Waseru, the fortunate, had lost nothing, for Matu had saved all the goats. But his luck would not make much difference to his welfare, except that Wanjeri would be certain of next season's seed. He was bound to share all the food in his granaries with his father's family, with his more distant kinsfolk and even with men of his age-grade, if they were in need.

And, in the general confusion, a sickness had found its way into old Mahenia's body. He had been over on Irumu's ridge with a small group of elders when the disaster happened and had only just reached the forest in time. They had spent all night in the open, on the cold damp earth, not daring to emerge until news reached them of the outcome of the fight. And because there had been no women amongst them, there had also been nothing to eat.

It soon became apparent that Mahenia was very ill. His breath rattled in his throat, his mind rambled and his flesh was hot. Waseru sent for Irumu, who came with his bag of medicines and entered the old man's hut. When he emerged his face was grave.

"Mahenia is very sick," he announced. "A goat should be sacrificed immediately, but even so I do not know if it will save him. Mahenia has enemies, and this has been the hour of their opportunity."

Waseru heard this news with the utmost distress. A he-goat was quickly brought and suffocated, and Irumu sprinkled the stomach contents mixed with medicines around the old man's bed and over his person, uttering magic spells; but Mahenia failed to rally. For a long time Waseru and his two step-mothers sat by the old man's side listening to his quick, uneven breathing. Later, the muramati arrived and took his place by the bedside with the dying man's two sons.

At last, towards evening, Waseru heard his name called faintly from the bed. He knelt down and put his ear close to his father's mouth. The muramati also bent down to listen, for he was to witness his kinsman's will.

"It is time for you to go," the old man gasped. "My wealth is yours, my son. The goats that sleep in the hut of Ngara-riga's mother and the land that she cultivates are for him. The land that Wanjiku cultivates and the goats in her hut are for her sons. Cherish my children as if they were yours, and husband the wealth of my goats. Trust in Irumu, my friend : beware of all who belong to the clan of Ndolia, for they wish ill to our clan, particularly Ndolia's son Karue, who is a sorcerer. Arrange the marriage of my daughters and my uncircumcised sons. From the suitor of my eldest daughter take thirty goats . . ." His voice tailed off as a paroxysm shook him and his body was rent by gasps.

Waseru leapt up, alarmed, and called for Ngarariga. Together they lifted Mahenia from his bed. His skinny body was as light as an empty gourd. They carried him quickly a little way into the glade below the huts. Here, out of sight of the path, they laid him on a level piece of grass well screened by bushes. By his side Waseru cleared a patch of grass and kindled a small fire. Mahenia's wives gathered logs in silence. Sorrow flattened the features of Ngarariga's mother, and towards the end a few tears trickled down her cheeks.

The sun had fallen behind the trees and the air was cold and grey as the dying man's face. Waseru, conquering his fear of death, bent over his father to tuck the old man's cloak around his skinny knees, rose quickly, and walked away into the thickening shadows. The others followed, and no one looked back.

Next morning the fire had gone out in that part of the glade. Waseru and his family kept their eyes averted when they passed along the path, and no one mentioned Mahenia's name. In the night they had heard a hyena calling to its unclean fellows close at hand, and they knew that Mahenia's spirit had taken its place among the ancestors of his clan.

8

MUTHENGI had little time for sorrow at his grandfather's death. The minds of warriors were not concerned with such things. His blood ran quicker whenever thoughts of battle flitted into his head, and supple-skinned warriors tossed and swayed to-

gether unceasingly in his dreams. At night he would sometimes recount his battle adventures to an excited audience sitting
around a fire outside the huts.

One evening his father passed by in the midst of such a recital,
and paused to listen. His stomach felt warm as if with beer
when he heard again of his son's courage and strength. One
day, perhaps, he will become the warriors' leader, Waseru
thought, and keep the first share of all captured cattle for himself. It was a pity that the trophies of the last raid were only
spears and swords instead of cows.

He picked up the spear Muthengi had won from his Masai
foe, and as he felt along the haft his fingers came to a fault in the
smooth iron. He examined this in the firelight and saw that it
was a small notch.

The discovery aroused a puzzling memory in his mind. At
first it evaded him, but later in the evening recollection leapt,
like a leader in full regalia into the dancers' circle, on to his
tongue.

"Muthengi," he called out, "a great thing has happened—it is
a sign, perhaps, from God."

Everyone fell silent immediately, since he was an elder and
must be listened to with respect.

"Many seasons ago when Matu fell sick," he continued,
"Irumu the mundu-mugu made a prophecy. 'One day your
son Muthengi,' he said, 'shall slay a Masai in battle and bring
back as his trophy a spear with a notched haft. That shall be
known as a sign that he is to win great renown as a warrior, and
become a leader.' Now, bear witness: this spear that Muthengi
captured from a Masai has a notched haft. The prophecy is
fulfilled!"

There was a murmur of excitement and wonder, and people
were heard to remark that Irumu was indeed a great magician
who could see visions of what the future would hold. Muthengi
lifted his arrogant chin a little higher, and his lips smiled. Now
he was certain that in due season he would become the leader of
the warriors, and bring great wealth and honour to his clan.

CHAPTER IX

The Raiders

I

AFTER the Masai foray Nduini and his warriors were blamed for having failed in their duty to protect the cattle; nor had they retrieved their honour by overtaking the retreating enemy and recapturing the bulk of the stock. The girls taunted them, saying: "You warriors, you ran after the Masai just like chameleons, your bones were soft as fat, you were afraid." The young men grew so angry that they refused to speak to the girls. They went to live by themselves in a hut in the bush, feeding on two bulls presented to them by Wangombe, whose cattle they had saved.

But Muthengi and others of the Ngege age-grade were praised for their courage in destroying the detachment of Masai at the Mawé ford. Because of this they grew conceited, and began to grumble at Nduini's leadership. He was too old for his position, they said; he did not take the initiative, but waited for others to attack. "The goats with a lame leader," they quoted, "do not reach good grass."

A few months after the fight Muthengi, restless for battle, put forward a new idea: to raid the Ndia, who lived two days' journey to the east. Their leader in war was a man called Kutu. These people had some cattle and a lot of goats; they had lived in peace now for many seasons and their livestock would have multiplied. The idea was eagerly taken up by the young enthusiasts and adopted by several warriors on the council. Nduini himself, anxious to retrieve his reputation, agreed that the proposal had merit, and eight scouts were chosen to go to Ndia and spy out the land. Because Muthengi had first urged the expedition he was included, although this was unusual, for youths of the newest age-grade were not generally entrusted with responsible tasks.

Early on the morning of their departure the eight scouts gathered at the mundu-mugu's for the sacrifice of a ram. Irumu, whose beans had foretold success, led them to the river below his homestead and mixed the ram's stomach contents in running water, together with medicine which would give speed to the warriors' feet. Then he blew over the scouts a little yellow powder to make them invisible to their enemies. The ram's meat was roasted on a grid and half of it given to the scouts; and when they had eaten they started off by a forest path to spy upon Ndia.

They came back on the eighth day, carrying dried cows' dung in their food-bags to prove that they had indeed approached the Ndia herds. There were about two hundred cattle, they said, at a salt-lick they had visited, and many goats, so sleek that their coats shone like a woman's head. Irumu mixed the cows' dung with medicines, tied it up in leaves and buried it by the entrance to his compound, so as to prevent the cattle from moving away from the salt-lick for eight days.

2

FOR two days the warriors prepared. They plaited their hair with twine, rubbed it with ochre and tied it up in pigtails. They greased their spears and put on ornaments and rattles. They painted their bodies on the right side with ochre and fat and their right legs with lime; but the left side remained bare so that friend and foe could be distinguished in the fight.

Early on the third day they gathered below Irumu's homestead. The mundu-mugu came out dressed in a Colobus cloak and many ornaments, driving before him two he-goats and a ram. A strip of goatskin was tied around the middle finger of each warrior's right hand and powdered lime marked on his forehead. Irumu mixed lime with saliva in his mouth and spat lightly into the warriors' faces to bless them. At such times, if a man was destined to be killed, tears would flow from his eyes. Then each warrior drank a sip of the blood of a he-goat mixed with honey and with three separate medicines which caused arrows, spears, and swords to glance aside. As an extra precaution Irumu scooped out the root of an itoka lily, filled it with a rare and especially potent medicine and thrust it down the hole of an ant-bear, thus burying the evil powers of the spears which the men of Ndia would hurl at Nduini's army.

At sunrise on the morning of their departure all the warriors gathered on a level stretch of pasture and formed a circle bisected by the path that led along the ridge. There were about a hundred young men, dressed for battle in black ostrich-feather head-dresses, heavy painted shields and anklets of Colobus skin. They waited in silence until two njamas came into sight. The first carried a flaming torch in one hand and a black ants' nest of dried mud—the githembo—in the other. The second bore the great secret war-charm that only the warriors and the mundu-mugu, who kept it buried under his hut, had ever seen.

The two njamas took up their positions at the two intersections of the path and the circle of warriors. He who held the githembo set alight to it, threw away the torch, and ran swiftly around outside the circle, while the other njama ran with the charm held aloft in the opposite direction. A third njama jumped into the centre of the circle with a bundle of sticks and hurled them about him at the warriors, who ducked and twisted to avoid being hit. Then the circle wavered and broke, and the men marched off along the path to war. Each one trod, as he departed, upon the githembo's ashes, and passed beneath the great charm held high above its guardian's head. Now the vulnerable body of each warrior was wrapped in a hard chrysalis of magic which could not fail to deflect the enemy's weapons. Now they would burn the villages of the Ndia as they had burnt the githembo and crush the men of Kutu underfoot as they had crushed its ashes, be their enemy as numerous as the swarming ants whose nest they had thus destroyed.

3

THE rattles on the warriors' legs were stuffed with leaves, and the raiders moved so silently through the forest that they barely disturbed the monkeys in the trees.

They marched in four sections. In the van went a company of seasoned warriors, the Gitangutu. Then came the Butu, for the most part older men and inexperienced boys whose job was to look as formidable as possible and, if the raid was successful, to drive away the booty. On the two flanks marched the Thari and in the rear the njamas, the pick of the army, whose task was to cover the retreat. Nduini's place was at the head of the Gitangutu, whence he would drop back, after the charge, to lead the njamas.

The raiders slept two nights in the forest. On the third morning trees showed the wounds of axes, and they knew that cultivation was close. They moved with leopard's caution, skirting glades where sunlight would strike their weapons. Soon, turning a corner, they came upon a small boy herding goats. He stood for a few seconds rigid as a startled hare at dusk, gazing at them with terror-widened eyes, and then turned and fled down the path, his small cloak flapping like a bird's broken wing. Two spears flashed together through the air. One, perfectly aimed, transfixed him between the shoulders. He fell without a sound, writhed like a skewered insect, and lay still. The scout pulled out his spear and wiped the blade on a leaf, and the column moved on.

By noon they were close behind the salt-lick. The cattle were still there, guarded by only ten or fifteen men. With great caution the warriors took up their positions for the charge. They pulled the leaves out of their rattles, gripped their spears, and crouched ready for the charge.

With a high-pitched yell Nduini leapt from the forest's shelter and led his men forward over a field of beans. A hundred warriors catapulted after him, as if that shattering shout had released them out of the earth. As they charged they gave great leaps into the air with stiffened legs, covering the length of a man with each jump. The herdsmen turned their heads, saw, and flung themselves upon the cattle, driving them with frantic shouts towards the shambas. They were outnumbered ten to one. Nduini's men thundered down upon them like a landslide of rocks from the mountain. The spears of the raiders buried their heads in backs, limbs, heads, like swift hawks dropping with outstretched beaks upon their prey. In a few moments all was over; only two herdsmen escaped.

Hurriedly the Butu rounded up the cattle and drove them into the shelter of the trees. Warriors ranged up and down the cultivated land in search of smaller stock. Women darted, screaming, from their huts, and boys scurried like porcupines into the bush. Herds of goats were sighted, rounded up, and driven away.

Group by group the raiders reached shelter with their booty, until all were assembled in a glade. Nduini and his njamas strove to sort out the jumbled army and to start the flocks and herds on their way. Time was their enemy, for frightened livestock could only be driven slowly and with many checks along the narrow overgrown game-paths by which they had come.

Gradually the glade emptied of its milling mass of animals. The Gitangutu went ahead lest an ambush had been laid, the njamas under Nduini formed ranks in the rear. In the distance they could hear shrill shouts and the summons of Kutu's war-horn; the Ndia were gathering for the counter-attack.

But the delay in starting enabled a party of Ndia to reach the path ahead of the raiders. Concealed behind trees and undergrowth, they waited for the leaders of the enemy's column to appear. Then, at a signal from their leader, they pulled their bows. Suddenly the shadows became full of arrows darting as silently as buffalo flies and settling with deadlier sting on unprotected flesh.

For a moment the ambushed Gitangutu wavered, throwing up their shields, half turning to run. Then Muthengi, who was near the lead, charged forward, hurling his spear at a flash of brown in the undergrowth. A man cried out, threw up his arms and toppled over. Muthengi drew his sword and crashed through the undergrowth towards the bowmen, followed by his shouting companions. The Ndia loosed a final flight of arrows which rattled harmlessly against advancing shields, threw down their bows, and drew their swords. In and out of the shadows crouching men, red with paint or blood, moved like crabs, in thrust and parry.

Gradually the Gitangutu drove back the bowmen until the Ndia turned and dodged through the trees, pursued by a hail of flying clubs. The way was clear, and the long line of stock moved slowly forward. At the rear Kutu counter-attacked fiercely, but Nduini and his njamas, fighting with great ferocity and courage, formed a wall of iron which the Ndia could not overthrow to reach their stock beyond. Nduini's men drew slowly away, until at last Kutu no longer followed. The bulk of the captured stock was safe; the raiders had triumphed.

4

NDUINI'S warriors returned chanting a song of victory, driving before them a big herd of sheep, goats and cattle. Workers in the shambas threw down their tools and ran to the path to see them pass. The joyful trilling of the girls was sweet as cane-juice to the young men. Women pranced like wydah-birds in the mating season when they saw that their sons were safe; but there were a few who cried, "Where is my son?" and, "Why does my husband linger?" Then the warriors looked straight ahead, and one answered: "He does not leave Ndia," or "He will not come." At the tail of the army a group of young men walked slowly, with deep gashes in their legs, arms and ribs.

The mind of everyone but the bereaved was on the distribution of stock. This was in the hands of Nduini. He rewarded each man according to his rank and to his conduct in the fight. Muthengi received as his share one cow in calf, and two goats.

This made him very angry; he considered himself entitled to three cows, the portion of the bravest njamas.

"Did I not head the Gitangutu's charge when the leaders wavered and would have fled?" he cried. "Was not my spear the first to kill? Nduini is a mean and evil porcupine! He is jealous because I am braver than he is, and because other warriors have remarked upon it."

"Do you not know that such boastful words are unfit for the mouths of men?" Waseru rebuked him. "Remember that the fluttering bird only wastes its feathers! Why do you complain when you have a cow and a calf? Your good fortune is indeed great."

"It is no good fortune," Muthengi replied sullenly. "I won the cow by my prowess in war."

That day each warrior took some trophy of the raid—a small goat, or a captured weapon—to Irumu, whose magic had protected the survivors from death and brought them victory. The mundu-mugu told them to return in eight days for the purification of all those who had killed men. Until then, warriors who were polluted with blood might not eat food with their family, for they had touched death and were unclean.

5

AFTER Muthengi was circumcised Waseru had paid two he-goats and six gourds of beer to the junior council of elders, all married men, and taken his seat. They met under the big fig-tree at Karatina on the mornings when no market was held, and sat all day to determine guilt and mete out punishment. The penalties for theft followed a regular scale based on the return of the stolen property and a two-goat fine—one to go to the plaintiff and one to the council—for every goat stolen. The difficulty was to fix the guilt. If an accused man, haled before the council, denied his guilt, certain tests were used. A pair of oxhide sandals might be marked with chalk by a mundu-mugu in a special way and the accused might be required to jump over them. If he was in fact a thief he nearly always refused, for a guilty man who took the jump was certain to fall sick. Or a bead might be inserted between the eyeball and the lid of the accused, who was then ordered to shake his head. If he was innocent the bead would fall out, but if he was guilty only tears would come.

Should both parties persist in their accusations and denials, they might be required to take the oath on the gethathi stone; or the accused man might be ordered to beat a goat to death in the presence of the elders, saying at the same time: "If I lie, may I die as this goat dies; may all my bones be broken if I lie." A thief always confessed his crime and accepted the lesser evil of a fine rather than face the ordeal of the goat and the certain death that would follow a breach of the oath.

Waseru's experience on the council soon taught him the truth of the saying: The hungry person will eat cane protected by magic. Many shambas were guarded by charms which brought injury to anyone who stole the crops. Theft led inevitably to sickness, as when men broke out in sores; this might be accepted as corroborative evidence if the sufferer had been openly accused. Sometimes the magic passed through the actual thief to his wives or children or near kin. Because of their relatives' crimes, many children came out in running sores; others grew listless and skinny, and suffered from diarrhœa, or from twitching of the limbs.

6

WASERU had not been long on the council before the time came for his own generation, Mwangi, to take over the government of the land. Men of his father's generation, Maina, were growing old and tired, and beginning to lose their keenness in judgment and debate. Their sons said among themselves that they had reached their prime and should shoulder responsibility for protecting the country from pestilence and famine, for controlling ceremonies, and for administering law. Before the change could be brought about, every man of the incoming generation, throughout the land, had to pay a three-goat fee to the retiring elders. Such payments were spread over a long period, and not until the last one was complete in all Kikuyu could the handing over of the secrets of power take place.

A season was fixed for the ceremony, called Itwika, and in each district a hut was built large enough to hold all the men of the Mwangi age from the ridges it served. Here, when all was ready, the horn of war was carried. Here, also, came Waseru and all married men of the Mwangi generation, sons of Maina, to live together for six months and prepare to receive from the older generation the right to rule. From each Itwika hut twelve delegates were chosen to represent their group of ridges at a central building, where men from all districts north of the Chania river gathered to live together for several months and to be instructed by elders of the retiring age.

At last the first day of the great ceremony came. The deputies of the Mwangi age dressed in their finery of paint, feathers and shells, and gathered on an open space near the central Itwika hut. Grass and bush all around had been cleared to make room for a great crowd. Work was forgotten; women and babies, children and old men, converged on the green field bringing beer, gruel and platters of cooked food for the feast. A goat was sacrificed, and twelve elders from each generation shared the roasted meat. While the younger men of the Mwangi age blew on war-horns and performed a strenuous dance, cheered by the trills of excited women, the twelve chosen Mwangi delegates were taken by those of the Maina age who kept the secrets into the bush, away from the noisy crowd. Here, hidden from sight, certain parts of the great secret were passed from the old keepers to the new. No one, save those who were present, knew, or would ever know, what had taken place. They only knew that the key to the unity and strength of their people had been given into the keeping of fresh guardians, who in their turn would hand it on to another generation, so that the continuity of the Kikuyu people would never be broken. How these secrets had originated none could say.

They were the hidden seed within the fruit that was the people, the seed from which new fruit would always spring.

The elders of both ages returned to the meeting-place, mask-faced and solemn; and the dancing ceased. Full in the public gaze, and with many fluent speeches, the Maina elders transferred to their successors symbols of the power that the new rulers would wield. They handed over a razor, to show that the Mwangi age would now lawfully control the circumcision of youths and maidens; a red stick, to symbolise the rule of law; a trumpet, for the power to call to dances and public meetings; a string of blue beads, for the right to decide on the proper ornaments and decorations; and other things.

Next day the twelve chosen Mwangi elders, who would become the office-holders of their age, set off with their Maina mentors for a sacred place on the Chania river's banks, held by tradition to be the spot where the nine daughters of Mumbi once had lived. Here they met twelve delegates from the country lying south of the Chania. None but these twenty-four delegates and the elders who instructed them knew what followed next. The secrets were too deep and too sacred ever to be revealed. A few scraps of information, half-spoken hints, had leaked out. Waseru had heard, for instance, that in the dark of night a trumpeter would blow his war-horn, the Maina elders would speak a summons, and the fearful monster Ndamathia would uncoil its snake-like body from the black waters of a pool. None save the office-holders of each generation had seen it, but sometimes, people said, its head came into the homesteads at night seeking a meal of offal, although its tail could never leave the pool. Others believed that it was tempted from its hiding-place with the bait of a virgin, decorated as if for circumcision, with which it copulated by the water's edge. Then the new Mwangi elders, their courage steadfast as a tree, would give it beer, and when it was drunk each one would pluck a hair from its slimy tail.

Next morning the delegates dispersed and the hairs of Ndamathia's tail were placed separately on the roofs of the

Itwika huts. The holders of the secret removed them a few
days later and buried them under a fig-tree. The Itwika huts
were pulled down, and a mundu-mugu wrapped a strip of skin
from a sacrificed goat around a finger of each member of the
new ruling age. Thus the transference of power was completed, and the senior elders of the Mwangi generation took up
the duties of government, according to the custom of their
ancestors and with the sanction of the tribe.

CHAPTER X

The Bride

I

THE rule of the new generation began with a disaster. For some time it had been known that a plague had struck the Masai cattle. Scouts sent down to the plain came back with reports of rotting carcasses, whitening bones and a sky black with vultures. This was bad news, for, as Irumu remarked, birds lacking in figs will go to the fig-tree. But a disaster worse than a Masai raid fell upon the ridges. The curse that was striking down the Masai cattle turned to the Kikuyu herds. Animals broke out in sores like those of a man bewitched. Their heads hung low on their necks like heavy fruits at the end of slender branches; their eyes became dull and staring; they folded their legs beneath them, and in a few days they died. The plague swept through the herds like a hailstorm over ripening grain, annihilating beasts, fortunes, hopes.

Muthengi guarded his cow and its new-born calf day and night, believing that his vigilance could protect her from the enemy's magic. She was mild-eyed, sleek and healthy, and would have many other calves to found his longed-for herd. Irumu gave him a charm to shield her from sorcery, but shook his head when Muthengi pressed for an assurance that it was proof against the plague. "There is no medicine for misfortune," the mundu-mugu said.

One morning Muthengi saw that her head was heavy and her eye dull. By evening her nose was streaming and her mouth full of small sores, and on the next evening she was dead.

Muthengi refused food that night and sat silently in the thingira, his cloak over his head. Waseru eyed his son compassionately. He took a deep pinch of snuff and said :

"Grieve not, my son, for what the fire has burnt cannot be recovered. The calves which this cow would have borne filled your mind, but they were dreams; the heart eats what it wishes. You are young, and success is the fire in the hut at the end of a long journey."

"All that I had is no more," Muthengi lamented. "How can I help but grieve? Where shall I replace my cow, or gain the wealth to get a wife?"

"The dung-heap grows by the straws that are cast upon it," Waseru answered.

Only one force could have brought about so great a disaster, and that was the wrath of God. No sorcerer could have wrought such havoc. And only one hope remained: that God could be persuaded, by means of a sacrifice, to relent of his anger.

On top of Niana hill stood a sacred fig-tree of great age, and around it lay a green pasture dedicated to God. Above the dark crown of the lofty tree arose the crest of Kerinyagga, pale and soft as a petal, and opposite, beyond a falling cascade of violet hills, a three-humped spine of mountains stood up black against the sky. Below stretched the long patient plain Laikipia, brown now with drought and naked to the sun. To this tree, on the appointed day, eight senior elders of the ruling generation, men whose first wives had passed the age of child-bearing, drove a ram and a he-goat to the sacrifice. Both animals were black as burnt trees, fat, and without speck or blemish. They had reached as near to perfection as any beasts of their kind that could be found in the land, for nothing less was worthy of God. When the he-goat had been suffocated and its flesh roasted, one of the elders poured fat over the trunk of the tree and on to the ground and, lifting his arms towards the mountain, prayed:

"God, the possessor of whiteness, who dwells alone in the hill of whiteness, send rain to fertilise our fields, and withdraw from our land the plague that has poisoned the blood of our cattle. We have suffered much, we have borne enough, and we ask for freedom. We bring you now a he-goat and a ram, a very fine he-goat and a most excellent ram, the best that we have in all our flocks, O God! These we give to you as gladly as you will give us deliverance. Send down to accept our gifts through these roots that grew out of the sky, and draw out of the earth the evil that afflicts us."

The black ram was killed and roasted and its fat smeared over the sacred fig-tree and the bodies of the suppliants. Half the meat was left under the tree, the heads pointing towards the east and covered with branches of mukenya, the shrub of good fortune. When all was finished the deputies to God turned and walked downhill without looking back, lest they should see a messenger, perhaps in the form of an animal, descending the trunk to carry the offerings back to his master.

2

IT was no surprise to see the Masai again invade the ridges; but no one had expected them to come with grass, the symbol of peace, in their hands.

Those who lived at the foot of Niana were the first to see them. The tall, graceful forms, walking with the loose ease of leopards, were unmistakable; but they carried sandals instead of shields. They gripped plucked grass in fists and mouths and carried long bows smeared with sour cream. They walked naked, waving short leather cloaks above their heads. Without glancing to right or to left—they might have been walking through an empty desert, so oblivious were they of curious and hostile stares—they strode on until they reached Irumu's homestead. There, placing a little grass on their plaited heads, they waited in silence for the mundu-mugu.

When Irumu came they spoke to him through an interpreter, a Masai who had gone to hunt game in the forest and there learned the tongue and customs of the Kikuyu from other Athi.

"Our cattle have been destroyed like dry grass before a great fire," this man said. "Once the plain was brown under the feet of Masai cattle, now it is white under their bones. Babies cry for nourishment, but their mothers' breasts hang like withered leaves from a dead tree. All are weak from hunger, and their bodies are parched. Therefore we come as envoys, to ask whether you, the Kikuyu, whose fields the vultures cannot devour, will send your women to trade food with women of the manyattas."

Irumu saw that their bones stood up beneath the skin and that their cheeks, the colour of copper, were gaunt. He could not look at them unmoved, any more than a ram could stare at a leopard with unconcern. In the very lines of their taut bodies, clean as the sweep of far-off hills, he sensed danger. Their eyes, long and slender as the leaf of a lily, were watchful and hard. Their faces were arrogant as the plain; as if the same proud spirit of indifferent tranquillity that kept Laikipia had clothed fragments of itself in flesh.

"I hear your words," Irumu answered. "How can we be sure that they are not bait with which to set a trap? For between Masai and Kikuyu there is always war."

"The Masai fight with spears, face to face, and not with cunning," came the answer. "Only the coward digs pits to trap the feet of his enemy in the path."

At this a stir ran through the silent watchful audience that had gathered outside Irumu's homestead, like the shadow of a cloud passing over a sun-drenched hillside.

"Only the fool comes to beg with insults," Irumu said.

A light groan escaped from the onlookers' throats, and when the interpreter had spoken an utter silence fell. The fingers of the Kikuyu stiffened as they gripped their swords. The Masai neither stirred nor spoke. It was as if they had closed their ears and Irumu's insult had bounced back and floated off into space.

"There is little food on these ridges," Irumu continued. "God has withheld the rain, crops have been poor, and many of our own people are weak from hunger. There is a Kikuyu saying: 'In a year of many hyenas it is useless to ask for help.'"

"If there is no grain, still there are bananas, yams, potatoes," the Masai answered. "The starving man does not reject porridge because it is sour."

"If we send our women to the plain with yams and bananas," Irumu persisted, "what will they bring back in return?"

"Our sheep are big and sturdy," the Masai replied. "Our women have copper wire and blue beads of great beauty, brought by strangers from a country far away."

An excited chattering broke out at this from a group of women listeners; and the young men, also, stirred with interest.

Still Irumu was not convinced. The Masai made no attempt to elaborate their request, to sit down to a long discussion, to engage in the fascinating exercise of wits required to strike a bargain, as any Kikuyu would have done. They were as cold as a rock under a waterfall, as deep as the sky, and as unpredictable.

"I will answer when the sun is overhead," Irumu said at last. "There is food in the granary; my wives will serve you."

The Masai answered with expressionless faces:

"We will not eat. We will await the answer."

"We do not fight with poison," Irumu retorted; but the Masai turned and strode to the shelter of a tree a little way off. There they lay upon the ground and waited, long ochre-dressed hair hanging around their narrow rock-hewn faces. They came to beg, and yet arrogance was stamped like a brand upon their faces.

Irumu summoned all the elders of the senior council within reach, others of the ruling generation, and Nduini to represent the warriors, and told them of the Masai's request. Several elders counselled its rejection, suspecting a trap; but Irumu said: "The way of the leopard is not that of the bushpig, nor of the zebra; yet all are animals. So the way of the Masai is not our way, although they too are men. The Masai trample others before them like a herd of zebra stampeding over the plain; but we, who have homes to protect, fight with cunning like the leopardess. But we must not think that because we use our intelligence, others do so also. I do not believe this is a trap. If we send women to the plain to trade they will get very good terms, because the Masai are hungry and therefore in no position to bargain. Let us, therefore, agree to their request."

3

FOR three days women were busy cooking porridge and roasting bananas and yams. Excitement was great. Masai had long been a word of terror, meaning burnt-out homes and the loss of husbands, sons, riches; but now every woman seemed determined to visit the homesteads of these hostile savages.

"Masai warriors are taller than a tall maize plant, more savage than lions, and without any self-restraint," Muthengi told his sister Ambui. "It is said that they live openly with girls in a big house, all under one roof, without shame. Why do you wish to go? One of them may seize and rape you, and I, or any of our warriors, will not be able to save you."

Ambui burst into a peal of laughter. "You see now how much braver girls are than warriors," she said, "only they make less noise about it."

"You will make enough noise if a dozen warriors rape you," Muthengi remarked.

"What must happen, will happen," Ambui said. "The tree that bends before the gale does not get hurt."

"Sister, your attitude is entirely shameless," Muthengi exclaimed, deeply shocked. "It is time that you were married, and learned modest behaviour."

Next day the women set off, burdened with food in woven fibre sacks. They took their loads right up to the Masai manyattas, curiosity stronger than fear. The two groups of women stared at each other for a long time with intense interest, taking in every detail of dress, ornament and looks. The Kikuyu were amazed at the tall straight backs, the erect carriage, the long necks of the Masai; above all at the great coils of copper wire which swathed their limbs from ankle or wrist to knee or shoulder, and which stood out like huge metal ruffs around their necks.

"They are tall like men," Ambui said to her mother in wonder, "and their riches must be great, for their ornaments are many."

The Masai, for their part, were no less amazed at the bent backs of the Kikuyu, at their crouching gait, and the lines across their shiny foreheads where leather straps had left their mark.

"These people are like burdened donkeys," they said, "and they are fat with much eating. They crouch like baboons, and their legs are naked. Yet they have wire in their ears as we have, and their cloaks are sewn deftly with beads and shells."

By arrangement, no warriors from either side were present or even close at hand. When the food had been exchanged, with the help of Athi interpreters, the women compared their babies, ornaments, and household equipment, and by both parties the market was voted a great success. Subsequently, and for several seasons, Kikuyu women made frequent trips to the manyattas on the plain. They took grain, tubers and tobacco, and returned with brown Masai sheep, skins, and copper wire. After a little the men welcomed these expeditions, for they were able to add sheep to their flocks at a price less than half that prevailing at Karatina. Peace with the Masai, they agreed, was a great deal more profitable than war.

4

WASERU did so well out of the Masai trade that he decided, two seasons later, that he could at last afford a second wife. The first payments had been made for Ngarariga's bride, and although Mahenia's two widows were now living in his homestead under his care, Wanjeri was constantly urging him to marry a young girl so that her work would be lightened.

And he had found a girl who appealed to his fancy. Her name was Hiuko; she was one of Irumu's daughters.

Waseru called on the mundu-mugu and spoke, in general terms, of his intention to secure a second wife.

"You would be wise to do so," Irumu said. "Every man should take a young wife when he begins to feel the approach of age."

"I have a girl in mind," Waseru ventured.

"Her father will be fortunate to acquire so dutiful a son-in-law," Irumu said politely.

"I have not mentioned the matter to her yet; first I shall speak to her father."

Irumu said nothing, but took a deep pinch of snuff and handed the bottle to his companion.

"She does not know of my intentions," Waseru repeated, "but I should like to know whether you think she would agree."

"Is she a girl from near at hand?"

"She is a girl from this homestead, even. My eyes have followed your daughter Hiuko in the fields when she digs, at the river when she draws water, and when she goes to the dance. There are others who work harder in the shamba, and many more beautiful than she; but still I am ready to speak of marriage, if her father agrees."

Irumu turned his head aside, and Waseru knew that he was laughing. Anger threatened, and he rose to leave.

"Do not be offended," Irumu said. "It is not that I would reject you as a son-in-law; I laughed because she already has another suitor. He has not yet brought beer to me to broach the matter, but I know through Hiuko's mother that she loves him and that he means to ask for her as his bride."

Waseru felt pangs of anger like the stings of hornets stabbing at his heart.

"Is this suitor a young man?" he asked.

"A young man of her own age-grade, one with whom she dances until half the night has gone at the season of full moon."

"He is young to marry, then, this suitor; no older than my son, Muthengi. She would do well to consider that her work would be lighter and her position greater if she married an elder; nor would her husband be likely to be killed in battle."

Irumu laughed again, and Waseru, who could see no humour in the situation, frowned.

"Perhaps it would be best," the mundu-mugu said, "if you were to settle the matter privately with this suitor I speak of; for he is none other than your son."

Waseru stared at his friend in amazement, forgetting his jealousy in surprise.

"Muthengi! But he has said nothing of this to me."

"He is waiting, no doubt, until he is old enough to think of marriage; he must serve his seasons as a warrior first. Do not grieve, Waseru. Girls will turn to young men as the bee to sweet clover, the bird to millet, the rain to earth. We are old men now, and girls will no longer look at us with eyes of desire. No doubt I could say to my daughter: 'You are to marry my friend, Waseru; I have accepted his beer and two fat rams.' Perhaps she would agree, for she is a dutiful girl. But of what use would that be? Would she not run away and leave you grieving, and should I not then be obliged to return your goats? She loves another whose blood is full of youth. Your marriage would crumble like dry earth, the moisture of affection being absent; remember that hearts do not lead into each other like the tunnels of moles."

Waseru was silent for a little while, applying himself to his horn of snuff.

"I see that your words are true," he said at last, "and I see also that I shall soon be paying goats to you for your daughter Hiuko in order that she may sleep in another's bed. No doubt I shall have to do so, for no man can refuse to give his son the girl he desires, lest he offend the spirit of his father and other ancestors of his clan."

"You speak as a man of wisdom," Irumu said. "Search for your bride among those whose suitors have been killed in war, or whose lovers were impetuous in bed but laggard in paying goats for a girl big with their child. The tree loses its blossom when it bears fruit, and the foolish eyes of young men turn away; then old men, who know that trees flower again in due season, may step in and take what they desire."

5

WHEN the crops had ripened and been reaped food was plentiful again, and there was a season of peace. With the full moon came the dances, and every night the ridges shook with song.

Muthengi had won fame in dance no less than in battle; his leaps were higher, his voice lustier than any of his fellows. He was surrounded always with soft-voiced maidens whose firm brown skins, smooth as water flowing over rounded stones, shone with the lustre of flower-petals in the light of the flames. When he danced with a girl who stood stiff-kneed on his toes, her hands on his shoulders and his under her elbows, he watched her long, supple neck, her tossing breasts and her deep, laughing eyes with mounting excitement; but discipline was strict and njamas patrolled the ground with bundles of sticks ready to belabour anyone who broke the circle.

Girls had their own dances, especially one in which they imitated the motions and rhythm of grinding millet between two stones, swaying their bodies in perfect unison to the swinging tune. At such times they would stir the blood of the young men by their lilting words, which praised the brave and pricked with contempt the weakling and the coward.

SONG OF THE GIRLS

Maidens, will you trill for a coward, one who
Fears to strip the bark from a mugaithiu?
One who dares not bring us the bark of trees, who
    Flees from Laikipia?

Hard, oh hard to scale the tall Kerinyagga,
Are they eagles? Why do they climb the mountain?
They will bring back wealth for their eager sweethearts,
    Ornaments, bracelets.

We who bear the logs are like warriors, we who
Bear the greatest loads are the Gitangutu,
Those whose loads are light as a leaf are Butu,
    Weak as the coward !

Let us sing to praise the brave fighter; he will
Reach the mountain Thimbui; he will pass through
Smoking homesteads, villages black and ruined—
    Trill for the valiant !

Waiyu, son of black woman, what to call him?
When he comes we trill for him, call him victor;
Greet the brave man joyfully; do not tell us:
    Trill for the coward.

After the dance Muthengi would often walk home with a girl
in the cool moonlight, past the whispering canes and the grey
shadowy shambas, to her mother's hut; and there he would
creep into its warm smoke-filled depths and lie in her bed till
dawn. Then he would remember what he had been told at
his circumcision: that the sunbird hovers with quivering wings
outside the flower's mouth, sipping its fragrance, but does not
break a way into its honey-store.

The choice of brides was difficult, for many attractive girls
looked at him with favour and his father, although not rich,
was regarded as a trustworthy man. Finally he decided on
Hiuko, who, although not beautiful—her neck was too short,
her legs too skinny for that—was strong and healthy and worked
hard in her mother's shamba. At the dances her eyes followed
the leapings of his whip-muscled body with unquestioning
devotion. He knew that she admired him above all others and
was flattered by his choice; and at night, in her mother's hut, she
responded so eagerly to his caresses that he could hardly wait
for marriage to complete the consummation of his love.

6

His father, although scarcely enthusiastic, did not condemn
his choice, so he went to his mother and asked her to brew some

beer. Early next morning he set off with Ambui and Ngara-riga's young wife at his heels, each bearing a full gourd. He found Irumu in his compound under the shade of a tree, with his four wives and their daughters and a number of kinsmen gathered around. Muthengi greeted him with deep respect and presently, after an interval of conversation, he said:

"I have seen your daughter Hiuko at work in the fields; I would like her to cultivate a shamba for me."

Irumu looked at his daughter and asked:

"Are you willing to cultivate the shamba of the son of Waseru?" and she answered, "Yes, I am willing."

Then her mother poured beer into a horn and handed it to Irumu. Looking again at Hiuko he said: "Daughter, if you do not like this man, I will not drink." But she said, "Drink." After he had done so he refilled the horn and handed it to Hiuko's mother, and then to his other wives and to his kinsmen. For the rest of the morning details of the bride-price were discussed. Irumu asked the usual thirty goats and, in addition, four fat rams and fifteen gourds of beer, and ten more goats on the birth of the first child.

That evening, when the goats were driven in, Muthengi and his father picked out twenty from the flock. With two friends of his own age-grade he drove them to Irumu's. The mundu-mugu examined each one carefully as it was brought before him, and after the last had been approved he accepted the payment. On the next evening ten more goats and two rams that had been fattening in the pen in Wanjeri's hut were driven over. Their paddle-shaped tails, weighed down with fat, dragged behind like heavy logs; their fat-filled dewlaps brushed the ground. Irumu accepted these also, though not without remarking that they were thin as starving rats.

Next morning all the women of Waseru's household carried full gourds of beer over to Irumu's, where the bride's family and kinsmen were gathered to receive the gifts. One of the fat rams was killed and roasted on a grid; and all day long Irumu's family and Waseru's feasted together, and drank. That evening the women of both families, warmed with beer and excited by rejoicing, performed the women's dance, the Getiro, in the compound. As a sign of great delight Wanjeri poured gruel, presented to her by Hiuko's mother, over her own head, and over the heads of her husband's kinswomen. At the end of the day Hiuko's mother put grass in the mouths of Wanjeri's empty gourds as a sign of peace between the two clans, and the visitors returned home well content.

That same day Muthengi went to the muramati of his clan with a small offering of beer and asked permission to take land for cultivation from the forest next to his father's shamba. The muramati agreed, for that part of the forest belonged to the clan and no one else had laid claim to the land.

7

NEXT day a group of young men of Muthengi's age-grade appeared early in the morning and worked with him all day on the new shamba, breaking ground in readiness for the bride. The women of the household were busy once more pounding cane for beer, the brew known as the beer for the washing down of the meat. Two more beer-drinks followed, both at Waseru's homestead : the beer for the knowing of the bride's new home, and the beer for the laying of the stools. At last came the final brew : the beer for asking the bride to cultivate the young man's garden. In the evening Irumu gave his consent to his daughter's marriage, and next day Muthengi was free to take her.

From sunrise that morning he and friends of his age-grade worked at the building of a hut immediately behind his mother's, in Waseru's homestead. In the afternoon his mother and her friends thatched it, and before nightfall all was ready. That evening four young men of Muthengi's age-grade, in full-dress regalia, sprang upon Hiuko from the bush with wild cries as she was leaving her mother's shamba. She struggled and cried out, as was the custom; but they bore her off to the new hut in her father-in-law's homestead.

Here she lay for four days, face-down on the bed, moaning and weeping and chanting melancholy songs which extolled the virtues of the clan from whose friendly shelter she had been snatched away. Her husband did not once approach nor speak to her. Ambui and Ngarariga's wife brought her cooked food, and friends of her age-grade paid her visits to bring her comfort. But Hiuko wailed and moaned like a neglected spirit, using the words and songs that she had been taught at her circumcision.

After four days Wanjeri entered her hut for the first time, bringing a calabash of fat. The bride smeared the fat over her head and, attended by Ambui, emerged from the hut to pay a short visit to her own mother. That night she returned and slept for the first time with her husband. The following day he took to Irumu's the brew of beer for the stealing of the daughter.

For the next month Hiuko did no cooking, but ate food prepared by her mother-in-law. When a month had elapsed her head was shaved and she paid a final visit to her father's homestead. Irumu came to the entrance to welcome her with a present of a small she-goat. Many children ran out to greet her, but she held a bunch of leaves over her face. Now was her last chance to break the marriage. If she told her father of deep unhappiness, he might consent to return the bride-price and take his daughter back. But Hiuko had no such sorrows. Irumu smeared fat over her head; her mother gave her a gourd of gruel to take to her husband; and at nightfall she returned to her new home.

Next morning Wanjeri took her into the forest to gather firewood, and then to the river to pick out three big stones for her hearth. These stones, once chosen, would become so closely bound up with her existence that they could never be abandoned or exchanged. That day Wanjeri gave her also a cooking-pot, a digging-knife and a freshly smoked gourd. Wanjeri cooked the first meal, of the black beans njahé, in the new pot, making pretence to show her daughter-in-law the method. Muthengi and his young wife ate this meal alone. So Hiuko crossed the river of marriage spanned by no bridge of returning; and Muthengi left behind his boyhood and became a full member of his clan, no longer a vassal in his father's homestead.

CHAPTER XI

The Red Strangers

I

AFTER the good seasons, a series of grave calamities fell upon the land.

First, the millet rains failed completely, and then long hot days of biting sun continued far into the season when the bean rains should have come. Irumu gathered the elders and sacrificed a black ram, but the ears of God were sealed against all entreaties. The land grew parched and powdery until the deepest digging-knife could turn up no moisture. Streams dwindled into listless trickles; the young bean crop wilted and died when it had barely sprouted; even the leaves of sweet potatoes and climbing yams turned yellow with drought.

A second sacrifice was made, and still God's anger remained unappeased. Shambas waited for rain like a young bride for her husband, but the millet rains failed a second time. Cattle grew dry as stubble; bones rubbed holes in flesh so that sores came; goats bleated unavailingly in the harsh, withered bush. Throughout the land there was desperate hunger. Grain and beans alike were long since finished, yams and potatoes shrivelled, and the young bananas failed to fill and grow. Boiled leaves, the roots of arum lily and sometimes the stringy flesh of goats who had lain down in hopelessness to die, kept families barely alive. Men and women whose bodies were already weakened by age perished as withered fruit drops from the boughs when strong winds blow.

The newly-broken forest soil kept its moisture longer than most, so that Wanjeri and Hiuko were able to raise small crops of black beans. But Wanjeri's small girl-child cried all day, and Matu once again fell sick. He had been circumcised with the age-grade Thunguya (so called because a scented flower much sought after by bees had flowered that year) and had grown into a weedy, spike-limbed youth with a wide, patient face and deepset eyes that were wiser than his years. Suffering had taught him a restraint not always found even in elders, and shyness in the presence of other youths had made him quiet, observant and self-contained.

2

THREE young men who took goats to Kaheri's country in search of food came back with a curious story. A strange man, they said, had come into Kaheri's from Masai land; but he was not like a Masai at all. His companions carried sticks which made a loud noise like bamboos cracking in a fire, yet they did not break. These sticks were a sort of magic; they seemed to possess some peculiar power of killing at a distance.

This man, they said, had gone to live with Kaheri. He had built a house with angles; he wore strange clothes and kept his legs covered; and he carried a charm which made a noise like water dripping from a roof. On its surface were two small sticks that moved as slowly as chameleons, and of their own accord. As soon as this charm was brought into Kaheri's country the rainclouds had dispersed and none had gathered since. It was therefore believed by many that he was a sorcerer who was keeping away the rain with his charm.

At first he had caused a great deal of amusement by his freakish liking for the small black bean njahé, the food of pregnant women, and Kaheri's people called him by a name meaning the eater-of-njahé. But when disquieting news came from Wyaki's district of the arrival of other strangers of the same kind, the elders began to regard him as less of a joke. It was said that these newcomers had made a big camp near a place called Dagoretti and had killed several warriors who had disputed their right to draw water from a spring belonging to a certain clan. A mundu-mugu had prophesied evil if they were

L

allowed to stay, and so the elders' council in Kaheri's district had decided that the eater-of-njahé must be expelled. But Kaheri, the head of the council of war, had opposed them, and without his agreement the warriors could not be called out.

As the drought continued, the elders became more than ever convinced that the sorcerer's magic was to blame. They believed that he had won over Kaheri, an ambitious and self-seeking man, by flattery or perhaps by magic. Again they appealed to Kaheri to expel the stranger with his warriors, but again Kaheri refused. In this dilemma they appealed to Karuri, a powerful mundu-mugu living some distance away. He was a man of wealth and great influence on the council of elders, and the warriors of his district always consulted him as to the wisdom or folly of a raid. Karuri pronounced in favour of the elders, and against Kaheri. The sorcerer, he said, must be driven out.

The warriors of Karuri's district were called and paraded in full force. At dawn they attacked Kaheri's homestead, where the sorcerer lived. At first victory seemed certain, but then the sorcerer invoked his magic against the attackers and men fell dead without wounds from spear, sword or arrow. Terrified, Karuri's men fled. The sorcerer continued to live at Kaheri's, and drought continued to ravage the land.

That, at least, was the story, listened to with misgivings mixed with scepticism. It was hard to believe that any individual could possess so powerful a magic as to influence rain, which was sent or withheld according to the will of God.

3

THE matter was soon forgotten in distress over a new calamity which swept the land—a disaster even greater than the drought.

It started when one of the young men who had visited Karuri's fell sick. In a few days his body was covered with running pimples, and the stench of evil arose from it. At first he rolled on the floor of his hut, maddened by irritation and then by pain, for the pimples grew into rotting sores. A mundu-mugu was sent for; but although he sacrificed a goat and rubbed cow-dung into the sores, before nightfall the man was dead.

Within a few days the pestilence had spread to several homesteads round about. In one, four small children took sick and died within as many days. All had the same symptoms: fever, an outbreak of pimples exuding an evil-smelling pus; delirium; and death.

Alarm spread quickly, and every mundu-mugu was besieged for charms. People awoke with terror in their hearts, searching in themselves for the first signs of the deadly fever. Old men recalled a similar outbreak in their youth, when half the people had been destroyed; its name was mothuro, the all-finishing disease. Only one cause could be ascribed to a misfortune of such magnitude: the anger of God. And the cause of divine wrath was not far to seek. Old men of the fourth and most venerable grade, who were at once consulted, had no doubts: it was the continued presence in the country of a stranger of unclean habits and evil intentions towards the Kikuyu people.

The old men recalled also details of a method used before to cleanse the country from disease. Njamas were despatched to all the homesteads in the district carrying orders that every man, woman and child was to catch one fly and bring it in his hand to a central place near Karatina market. Next morning people streamed towards the meeting-place from every ridge and valley, like red ants on the march before rain. They were gaunt and bony with long hunger and many dragged their legs painfully, stopping every few yards to gain breath. Each person held out a clenched fist, and in it buzzed a captive fly. They gathered in a great ring around Irumu, who awaited them under a sacred fig-tree with eight chosen elders and a boy holding a young brown ewe.

Irumu slit open the ewe's belly, pegged back the flaps of skin, and rubbed several medicines into a hole made in the stomach. At his signal the circle around him broke and the people filed past one by one, each person pausing to thrust his fly into the ewe's belly.

When the stomach was stuffed with all the living flies the flaps of skin were replaced and Irumu sewed them together with twine. The ewe was hoisted on to a young man's shoulders and the procession set off along a path leading towards Karuri's, in the direction from which the pestilence had come, until it reached a spring that bubbled up from under a moss-coated rock on the side of a hill. A deep hole was dug above it and there the young ewe, now a mere barrel of flies, was buried. In this way the pestilence, driven by magic into the bodies of flies, was trapped in the belly of the ewe and buried deep beneath the spring, under the sources of life which flowed on above.

4

IT soon became clear that some mistake in a detail of the cere-mony had been made. The pestilence spread, destroying youths and maidens as the knife of the harvester cuts ripe millet, carrying off babies and children and with them the wealth and hopes of their clans. Everywhere tortured bodies pullulated and stank with running sores, and groans of pain and desperation arose from dark huts. Hyenas slunk about in the open by day, their ugly jaws grinning loosely, nor did they wait for life's ex-tinction to begin their meal; the air was flecked with bald-necked, fattening vultures and heavy with the sickly stench of putrefaction. People scarcely dared to venture off the path, for corpses rotted in every stretch of bush. Men feared their wives and boys their fathers, lest pimples should sprout like buds of death on the bodies of those who shared their beds and meals; they feared to sleep and to awake, lest the pestilence should strike them; above all they feared the fingers of death brushing against their faces, like bats' wings invisible in the blackness of a clouded night.

A few recovered, although the marks of the disease never left their faces. Irumu called these fortunate ones together and told them that a charm could be made to bring protection to others, but he needed, as one of its ingredients, the ground-up pimples of a recovered man. They were asked if they would agree to give part of their bodies to Irumu, to be used for the benefit of their clansmen and friends. When their consent had been obtained Irumu scraped off the withered pustules, mixed them with certain medicines, and called those who had not yet been attacked. He cut their arms with a knife so that a little blood flowed, rubbed in some of the mixture, and marked them with ochre and lime. A few of those who were given this magic did not escape, but many were protected and lived safely through the months of plague.

Waseru gave strict orders that none of his household was to venture out of the forest until the pestilence had passed.

"If a man eats with one who is thahu," he said, "he becomes unclean. So, too, with this pestilence; if I eat with a man into whose homestead it has come, I am in danger. Therefore no one must leave these shambas or eat from another's pot, and perhaps then we shall escape the pestilence, for we are well protected by charms."

Waseru, it proved, was right. For three months the members of his household did not leave the forest, nor did they allow anyone to pass through their own gate. Tobacco ran out, but Waseru went without snuff; beer-drinks, games of giuthi and meetings of the council were ignored. All stayed at home and cultivated the shambas, and not one of them did the pestilence attack.

It vanished as it had come, without warning or cause. A month went by without a new case, and hope strengthened that God had relented at last. Then, a little before the bean rains were due, the long drought broke in a violent cloudburst and they knew for certain that God's anger was done. For three months it rained heavily, almost every day. As swiftly as a chameleon the country turned from brown to green. Weeds sprang up in the shambas, the dusty bush was washed clean, leaves stood up again upon the branches like the hairs on a wild pig's back. The throats of birds quivered with song; frogs croaked in the swamps, and women sang as they carried digging-knives and the little seed they had saved to the shambas.

About this time it was heard that the sorcerer had left Ka-heri's, and the elders were convinced that it was he, with his mysterious charms, who had brought the drought and then the pestilence upon them. Only Irumu scouted this idea.

"No man is strong enough to bring about such things," he said. "Do I not know the secrets of all the magic that has been handed down to us by our ancestors? There is no charm to make the clouds shed their moisture, nor to slay with pestilence; these things are the affairs of God. For to God the wiliest sorcerer is like a man so foolish he will slaughter his young she-goat; the clouds are his cattle, that are driven out to pasture at his will; and pestilence is the poison that he keeps secretly within his stoppered gourd."

The other elders agreed, but added: "It was the presence of this stranger in our country that angered God, and he sent these disasters upon us because he was displeased."

5

AFTER the next harvest there was talk of another stranger, be-longing to the same tribe as Kaheri's eater-of-njahé, who had come to live at a place called Tetu, by the foot of Nyeri hill. It was said that his face appeared to have been coloured by red ochre, yet it was not so painted; and that he had companions with him who were digging a deep ditch. What the purpose of this ditch might be none could tell.

A prophecy made in the rule of the last generation was re-called: that men with bells in their ears—that was, seemingly deaf, since they would understand nothing of ordinary speech—would come walking like the small frog kiangere, whose skin was a pale ochrish tinge. No doubt about it, the elders said; the prophecy of the old mundu-mugu had been fulfilled.

Then news came that Wyaki's warriors, to the south-east, had attempted to drive these strangers away but had been crushed by the magic of killing at a distance with fire. Wyaki himsel had been captured and taken away to the Wakamba's country, where he had disappeared.

Muthengi, now at last elected the leader of warriors as Irumu had foretold, was inclined to treat the matter lightly.

"These Wathukumu have often come before, my father," he said to Irumu. His wife was pregnant, and he had taken a brew of beer to his father-in-law. "They buy the tusks of elephants from the Athi and pay for them well; then they return to their own country. They come in peace. Why should we need to fear them?"

Irumu shook his head doubtfully and filled his nostrils with snuff. He had aged greatly in the last few gruelling seasons. His hair, not recently shaved, was grey as ashes and his face deeply lined, although his light, darting eyes were still unclouded. But his limbs were stiff and skinny. Only with difficulty could he clamber into bed or lower himself slowly on to his three-legged stool. His hand shook so much that he could no longer hold the pincers steady to pull out his hairs, and one of his sons had to pluck his chin.

"Never before have Wathukumu stayed to build houses," he said. "Nor can I understand why they are digging ditches. And why have they not come before the elders' council to explain their purpose, nor sent envoys to the council of war to ask permission to pass through the country? I do not like it; the omens are bad."

"Why must you worry?" Muthengi asked. "We can drive them out at any time we wish. Our warriors can resist even the onslaughts of the Masai ; how then should we fear these Wathukumu, who are only a few?"

"They have a strong magic," Irumu said. "Karuri's warriors are brave too, but they were defeated. And now we are ravaged by disease and greatly reduced in numbers."

"There is no magic greater than yours," Muthengi replied. "If this stranger enters our country he shall be driven out with

spear and sword. We who have repulsed the Masai of Laikipia can have nothing to fear."

"Your words are brave, my son," Irumu said, "and your
heart also ; but sometimes words are like gourds : going to the
river they make much noise, coming back they are silent. I am
a very old man, but I do not remember that anything like this
has happened before."

Muthengi smiled in his mind, but said nothing. Old men,
he thought, always shake their heads when something that they
have not been consulted about occurs.

6

WHEN the young bean shoots began to dust the earth with green,
one of the red strangers came into the country at the head of a
small column of men. A few of these were dressed alike in
cloth that fitted them closely—tall, broad warriors with strange
flattened faces, speaking a barbaric tongue. They marched together and slapped their feet down loudly on the ground, so that
they could be heard a long way off. The others were young
Kikuyu, men from Wyaki's country, and they carried loads, like
women, on their heads and backs.

The stranger camped at Wathukumu, where the ivory-
traders always stayed. The Athi came down from the forest
carrying tusks and the stranger bought them, paying the usual
price. Women came in the evening to sell milk and food, and
were well received. But when all the ivory had been bought
the stranger did not go. Instead, he sent word by one of the
men from Wyaki's that he wished to talk to the ruler of the district. This message was taken to Irumu, to Muthengi, and to
several members of the senior elders' council. The messengers
did not know who was meant by the ruler of the country, since
there was none ; but meetings of the warriors' and of both the
elders' councils were summoned.

Muthengi addressed the young men in great anger. No
message, he said, had been received asking permission from the

warriors to pass through the country. No envoys had come holding grass. The stranger's arrival was therefore an act of war.

"Go home to paint your bodies and bring out your weapons," he exhorted them. "Let us drive these invaders from our country, sparing none. This stranger has only twelve warriors, and we shall overwhelm them like a flood."

The njamas agreed at once, but before they could disperse a message came from the senior elders' council to say that a deputation was going to the stranger's camp to ask the purpose of his visit. The elders wished no warlike action to be taken until the deputation had returned.

Four members of the senior elders' council presented themselves at the camp that evening, driving a small goat before them as a gift to show that they came in friendship. The red stranger met them; he had been painted, they thought, with ochre; his body was covered in cloth, like all Wathukumu, and his hair was smooth, flat and short. He neither squatted nor stood, but rested his buttocks against a piece of wood secured in place by four poles. He addressed them through an interpreter who was a Swahili, and whose Kikuyu words were hard to understand.

The elders returned late that night to their homesteads with bewildered minds.

"He spoke words which we cannot have heard aright," the senior envoy reported to the council. "This we understood: that the stranger does not wish to go away. He says that he has come here to live, and that others like him will follow. At first I thought that he must wish to beg land; but he did not enquire for the muramati of my clan, nor did he make offerings of beer. He says that he belongs to a very powerful ruler who lives a long way off and who has conquered our country; and that he, the servant of this ruler, has come here to settle lawsuits and to collect tribute. I thought that the interpreter must have made a mistake, but I asked him to repeat this part, and he said the same thing again.

"Personally I think that the stranger is mad. Since we know that no one has conquered our country, how then can this distant ruler, who has never been here, send a servant to collect tribute ? And how can a stranger talk of administering justice in another land ? We did not know what to reply, for we thought that his words were the ravings of a lunatic, so we left him alone."

This report was greeted with incredulity and a good deal of laughter; but Muthengi was annoyed. Next day he summoned the warriors' council again and declared :

"This stranger says that he comes from a distant ruler to govern our land. Warriors ! Have you yet been conquered by strangers ?"

The warriors, with one voice, shouted "No !"

"He says also that he comes to collect tribute for his master, our conqueror. Warriors ! Are you ready to pay him tribute ?"

The sound of their denial startled the cultivators in the valley.

"What, then, is your wish ? Shall we let this boastful stranger dwell amongst us, or shall we drive him out as we have driven out the Masai ?"

The cry was like a peal of thunder over the mountain :

"He shall go !"

7

NJAMAS hurried from homestead to homestead to warn the warriors, and soon the young men, freshly painted and fully clad for war, converged on the level meeting-ground close to Irumu's. Muthengi and eight njamas went to the mundu-mugu's hut and told him of the decision. There was no time now to consult the beans.

Irumu rubbed his chin uneasily. He knew that the disease mothuro had reduced the available force of warriors by more than half, and that many of the survivors were still weak from famine. But when he saw that the limbs of the young men were already beginning to shake with desire for battle, he agreed to give them protection. A goat was quickly slaughtered and the warriors blessed with stomach contents mixed with honey, and their fingers bound with strips of flesh.

Before the ceremony was over two scouts ran up to say that peculiar preparations were being made in the stranger's camp. A fence of branches was being built and the men were being herded within like cattle. It seemed clear that the stranger meant to resist, yet his followers had no spears or shields.

Muthengi laughed when he heard this, and brandished his spear. His body shone in the sunlight like the burnished bronze feathers of a sunbird, and ostrich feathers danced above his head.

"Indeed these men are cattle," he cried, "and we young lions who sniff them from afar. Warriors, forward! Fall upon them like lions, let none escape alive!"

A shouting, excited body of some eighty warriors—all that survived out of over two hundred—marched down into the valley to the ford below the stranger's camp. Here they formed into three ranks—club-throwers, archers and spearmen—and stamped their feet to make the rattles speak. Then the war-song started, slowly at first, gaining speed and vigour as the voices swelled. The stamping quickened and the noise of rattles shook the leaves. When the limbs of every warrior were quivering in frenzy Muthengi, with a great shout, led the charge up the slope towards the camp above, hidden behind a belt of trees.

Long-limbed warriors sped up the slope at his heels and through the trees to see a wall of thorns across the green pasture ahead. As they leapt into the open a noise of loud crackles, like the sound of elephants stamping through bamboos, filled their ears, and simultaneously four warriors, who led the charge behind Muthengi, pitched headlong to the ground. Several others halted in mid-stride and clapped hands to ribs or shoulders. The men behind checked their stride. No spears or arrows had been thrown, yet their companions were spurting blood.

The first line, the club-men, crouched down behind their shields and approached the fence in crab-like bounds, Muthengi at their head. The big shields covered the whole of their bodies; they knew they were safe. They could see no one ahead; the enemy was hidden behind the wall.

Another crackle of noises exploded in their ears and, without reason, five more warriors flung up their shields and toppled over, as though a violent blow had knocked them off their feet. An njama just behind Muthengi lay there in convulsions, his legs flaying the ground. Muthengi turned and saw blood staining the ground. Next to him lay Gacheche's son, one of his own age-grade and kin, with a trickle of blood and froth oozing from his mouth.

Yet there were no spears, no arrows; nothing but a noise.

Another crack sounded and something kicked a little spurt of dust out of the ground at Muthengi's feet. He looked down, and there was nothing there. Something invisible and deadly was trying to kill him from the air.

Terror clutched at his bowels in a fearful grip and seemed to wrench them from his body. For a moment his legs were paralysed and his feet seemed pegged to the ground. With a yell of panic his warriors leapt into the air like grasshoppers and flung themselves in a wild wave of flying heels, skins and feathers into the shelter of the forest.

Muthengi stood erect and held his heels to the ground with the last dregs of willpower, waiting for the crackle that somehow killed. None came. He turned and walked slowly across the pasture after his fleeing warriors, the spear steady in his hand. Behind him nine dead and seven wounded lay still upon the blood-soaked grass.

8

THAT night the council of war decided upon submission.

"He kills us with fire at a distance," an njama said. "He slays without weapons, out of the air. How can we fight against a noise?"

"He has a magic more powerful than anything we know,"

another said. " It is something so strong that Irumu, the greatest mundu-mugu in the land, has no antidote. It is best to submit, or we shall all be killed."

" It is better that he should take our cattle than our lives," a third agreed. " Then he will go, and we will raid Kutu's and Karuri's again to replenish our herds."

" If we submit at once he will return quickly to his own country," a fourth said, " and leave us again in peace. Men go far to capture wealth, but what man fails to return to his home when he has found it ?"

Muthengi sat in silence, his face like a dark cloud over the sun. His council was against him; he alone urged war and derided admission of defeat. Nduini was sent in his stead to lead the deputation of surrender. Muthengi sat all day in his father's homestead refusing to eat or to speak, his eyes on the ground and rage deep in his heart.

Two days later the stranger departed, taking with him no cattle or goats. He told Nduini that twenty young men must go at once to Tetu, at the foot of Nyeri hill, to dig a ditch.

The whole performance was so mystifying that no one could put forward an explanation. For a day the senior elders' council discussed it. How could a man conquer an enemy and take no cattle ? The very lack of purpose in such an action made them uneasy. The wisest course, it was decided, was to send the warriors to Tetu, although it was feared that they would never return. Besides, the seven who were wounded in the fight had been taken there, and their relatives wished to find out what had become of them.

So twenty warriors were selected to go. None wanted to, for they were afraid, but they could not disobey the council. Muthengi refused sullenly to lead them and Nduini was appointed in his place. To everyone's surprise, Matu, who had proved reluctant and self-effacing as a warrior, volunteered. Before they went Irumu blessed them with mukenya sprigs and beer and gave them especially potent charms.

The warriors were away for two months. Their relations

knew that they were still alive, for at intervals scouts were sent to Tetu and reported that the young men were digging together in a ditch with peculiar implements of iron belonging to the stranger.

The twenty youths returned in good health, but as mystified as ever. Each carried in his hand two round and shining objects, made of metal, presented to him by the stranger. They were clearly some form of magic, but the stranger had not explained from what evil they gave protection. Irumu was unable to make any suggestions ; he had never seen such things before. A few wore them in leather pouches around their necks ; some buried them under the hut in case their use should be made clear later ; but most threw them away in the bush, thinking them useless and possibly charged with danger.

"This stranger asked us, by means of his interpreter, who was the ruler of our district," Nduini said. "We told him : no one man, but the generation called Mwangi rules the country. The stranger asked again : who among these elders is the greatest ? We replied : none, but Irumu the mundu-mugu is full of wisdom and president of the senior elders' council ; and Muthengi, son of Waseru, is our leader in war.

"The stranger told us : 'Say to Irumu and to Muthengi that I wish to see them here. I do not ask them to dig a ditch, but to talk. If they come in peace they shall become rulers and rich men, but if they lead the warriors against me again, as they did before, I will kill them all by burning them at a distance so that none remains alive."

"How can this madman talk as if his warriors had conquered us ?" Muthengi asked hotly. "What is it to him who rules the country ? And why does he not take our cattle and goats, and then go ?"

"He does not say," Nduini answered, "but he is certainly mad."

Irumu said : "It would be best to go to him, or he will come again with his magic. Perhaps he waits for the harvest, and then he will return to his own country."

9

WHEN Muthengi received the message he said nothing, but went silently to his hut. He rubbed fat and ochre on his limbs and painted his legs with chalk. He tied Colobus skin ruffs to his ankles and rattles to his thighs; he put on an apron of serval skins and tied monkey tails to his elbows, and wound strings of beads and cowrie shells around his chest. He arranged his hair with great care in ochred plaits and three pigtails, and surmounted it with his ostrich-feather head-dress. On his hip he strapped his red-sheathed sword and in his hands he took his spear, his club and his big white-faced shield with its red and black design. In full battle attire, and with no attendants, he strode alone along the path to Tetu.

There he saw a strange sight before him. At the foot of Nyeri hill was a level place, and here rows of huts had been built as if by a man with a fantastic number of wives. A little way off, under some trees, stood a big house of poles and grass, but with four angles, and a pole jutting out of its thatched roof. A piece of coloured cloth was tied on to the pole. All around the flat space and the houses was a big ditch, as deep as a man was tall.

He crossed it by a bridge of planks and walked directly to the big house of angles where he knew the red stranger would be. At the door a man stood before him and spoke words which he did not understand, but he paid no attention and walked on through a door which required no stooping to pass. There were holes in the walls which let in much light, and there was no fire.

He saw the stranger opposite in the attitude which had been described to him, with a flat board between his body and the floor. His face was pale as if from leprosy and his nose sharp like an axe; it seemed that he wore a piece of smooth black skin over his head.

"You summoned me," Muthengi said. " I have come."

He stood still, filling the room, spear and shield in hand.

The stranger rose to his feet and for a moment the narrow, light eyes of one stared into the hate-filled eyes of the other across the room. Then the stranger shouted an order and a man came running.

"Who are you, warrior ?" this man asked. "What do you want with the white-skinned ruler ?"

"This man sent for me," Muthengi answered. "I am the son of Waseru. I am here."

Through the interpreter the stranger asked: "Do you not know that it is forbidden to come with spears and swords into this place ?"

Muthengi answered : "How can it be forbidden for warriors to carry weapons ? And who should forbid them but I, their leader ? But tell the stranger that he need not be afraid ; I shall not kill him."

The stranger laughed at this, and questioned Muthengi about the number of his warriors and other things. Then he said :

"I have come in peace and not in war ; nor shall I take away your cattle and goats. I have come to govern the country with justice on behalf of my leader, who is a very great ruler indeed and has conquered many people besides you. I therefore say : if you will keep peace between your warriors and me, I will make you a leader in your own country and you shall help me to rule. But if you resist, then I shall bring followers who kill as you saw your warriors killed, and there will be much bloodshed and suffering, and you yourself will be captured and sent far away from your own people to live alone in poverty. Which, then, shall it be between us : peace or war ?"

Muthengi did not answer. He did not know what to say. He had come to talk of the number of cattle that were to be seized, but this man spoke of rule and justice and things which had nothing to do with the matter at all.

The stranger gave an order and two tall men came from behind and seized his arms roughly. He did not struggle, although his heart leapt within him like a prisoned bird. They took him to a hut, thrust him inside and barred the door ; and they took away his spear, sword and shield. Anger choked him with such bitterness that he sat upon the floor and shook all over; a red cloak enveloped his eyes and a noise of thunder drummed in his ears.

10

TOWARDS evening the interpreter came into the hut with a smouldering log and kindled the fire. He greeted the prisoner with friendliness, but Muthengi would not speak. Presently he cooked maize in an open pot and roasted bananas in the ashes, but Muthengi would not eat.

"Why are you angry ?" the interpreter asked. "This stranger has not come here to take your cattle or your goats. He comes in peace, and will protect your people from the Masai."

"What protection do we need ?" Muthengi demanded. "Is not that the daily business of my warriors ? And when did we send for help from strangers ?"

"You did not send for them, but they have come," the interpreter said. "There are very many of them, and their power is great. They will not go away, for I have seen them come across the water and I understand their ways. If you do what they tell you, they will reward you well with position and with riches, but if you fight you will be killed. Only a fool would hesitate in his decision."

"I do not understand what he says," Muthengi continued. "He talks of ruling the country. How can one man rule a country ? Now it is ruled by the generation Mwangi, to whom the generation Maina told the secrets of power ; and after them the generation Muirungu will rule."

"He will see that justice is done," the Swahili said. "He is a very wise judge."

"Justice is done by the council of elders and by the council of aramati, the old men," Muthengi said. "It has always been so, and their wisdom is never in doubt. Did they not learn the law from their predecessors, who were in turn taught to govern by their fathers ? What does he, a stranger, know of justice ?

M

Has he no justice in his own country, that he comes to seek ours?"

"He knows a better justice than that of your councils," the interpreter replied, growing a little impatient. "He knows also of a new God, who is very powerful; and he can cure men who are sick."

"There is no God more powerful than God, who dwells on Kerinyagga," Muthengi answered, "and who can cure sickness except a mundu-mugu?"

The interpreter picked a roast banana out of the ashes and handed it to Muthengi without answering. "Many strange things exist in this ruler's country," he continued. "His people have laid two ropes of iron side by side from the edge of Wyaki's country to that great water of which you know nothing, because you are an ignorant savage; it is from beyond this water that his people come. They travel on the iron ropes in something which I cannot describe, but it snorts like a rhino, and it runs so quickly that it can travel in a night and a day a distance which it will take a man three months to walk."

"That I do not believe," Muthengi said.

"It is true, nevertheless. If you are wise you will make friends with these strangers. Be warned by the fate of Wyaki, who fought them, and has been taken away to a distant country; and another man, whose mother was an Athi, has been put into his place by these strangers."

"They could not do that," Muthengi said. "I am the leader of the warriors, and no one but the council of war could elect another in my place. I think that you tell me many lies. No doubt this man will soon return to his own people and leave our country alone."

"You are a fool, then. He will stay."

"Why?" Muthengi demanded. "Has he then no country of his own? Why does he not return to it when he has taken our cattle and goats, as the Masai do?"

"I do not know," the interpreter said.

All next day Muthengi waited in the hut, while his anger

slowly mounted. To treat him in such a manner was as gross an insult as could be offered to a warrior, a young man called a piece of God. Towards evening he was taken out, but when he asked for his spear and shield they were refused. Anger came over him until his limbs shook as they did when he was ready to fight. Seeing this, his captors pushed him back into the hut and left him, alone and impotent in the dark.

That night the interpreter came again to share his hut, and spoke of the same things : of the power of the strangers and of the wisdom of becoming their friend.

By the time he was fetched again on the next afternoon Muthengi was weak with hunger and grief. His rage had fled, leaving only a cold pain in his heart. He was led again before the stranger, and saw the interpreter standing by his side. After the stranger had spoken, the Swahili said :

"This man repeats again the things I have already told you. If you will do as he says you will be sent back at once to your homestead and become like a chief njama to this ruler, who will consult you on all matters to do with the country. Also, because of your importance, you will acquire many cattle and become rich. What is your answer ? Is it war or peace ?"

Muthengi looked at the stranger's sharp, graceless face, which he could not read, and at the big warriors ; and when he thought of all that the interpreter had said a feeling of hopeless entanglement weighed him down. He was like a mole struggling helplessly in a trap. The red stranger had a magic that was too strong.

"It is peace," he said. "I do not know how this has happened, but I will do as he says."

At a word of command the warriors dropped his arms, and the stranger stepped forward and took his hand.

"Now there is peace between you," the interpreter said.

BOOK II: MATU
1902—1919

CHAPTER I

Tribute

I

FOR two seasons Irumu's magic bound the stranger's feet so that they could not return; but then, one morning, he came again. With him were many young men carrying loads. People were amazed to see warriors behaving like women; surely, they exclaimed, these men must be ashamed to bend their backs under loads and lean their foreheads against leather straps.

The stranger sent for Muthengi and tor the elders who carried the mungirima staffs of the senior council. Through the Swahili interpreter he said:

"Now you must know that all fighting is finished, either between you and me or between you and the Masai. I have come to promise you peace, which is my gift to you, and justice; but in return for this I demand a tribute. Therefore each married man amongst you must give me one rupee for each woman in his homestead."

The elders, to whom the word was strange, asked: "What is a rupee?"

"It is the round metal object which was given by this stranger to those who dug the ditch at Tetu," the interpreter said.

"How can we give this person such things?" the elders asked. "Only those who went to Tetu received them, and since they appeared to serve no purpose, most of them have been thrown away."

"That is very foolish," the interpreter replied. "Do you not know that such things can be exchanged for food and goats?"

"It is you who are foolish," the elders rejoined, "to think that any man would exchange a good goat for such objects.

Can you eat them, or use them for ornament ? Perhaps, however, our smiths could learn to make them, and then we could give them to the strangers."

"That is not allowed," the interpreter said. "You talk like ignorant men ; because you have never travelled, you think that the world ends at the Sagana river. If you took these rupees to Maranga, or beyond to a new place called by the Masai word Nairobi, you would be able to exchange them for food and skins. However, that is beside the point. Those who received these objects when they dug the ditch at Tetu are now to give them back. Those who do not possess any must take one goat each to Tetu, and give it to the servants of this stranger."

2

At this a tremor of alarm passed through the group and the elders spoke to each other in low tones. Now, it seemed, the dreaded confiscation of stock was to begin. They withdrew at once to continue the discussion in private ; but Muthengi was ordered to remain.

"Between you and the stranger a pact has been made," the interpreter said. "You are to obey him, and he will give you protection. Now he has decided to make you into a ruler, greater than anyone else on these ridges. All shall obey your orders. If anyone fails to do so, you are to come to Tetu, and if the stranger is satisfied that you have spoken the truth he will send his warriors to enforce your word. But if you lie to him your power will be taken away and you will become dishonoured and poor."

Muthengi kept his eyes on the ground and said nothing. Deep thoughts were stirring in his mind. He knew that what the interpreter had said was quite impossible. Only in matters of war would warriors obey the orders of the warriors' leader, just as in matters of law people obeyed the senior elders' council, in matters of land the muramati of their clan, and in matters of magic the mundu-mugu. He knew, too, that no man of his generation could presume to rule, since all were still ignorant as children of law and custom. The suggestion that the elders, to whom one of his age-grade must pay the deepest respect, would obey a young man of the warrior class was too fantastic for consideration. It was clear, however, that this stranger was an ignorant and stupid man who understood none of these things. Since, as the proverb said, the fool roasts bananas for others to eat, it might be that something profitable would emerge from all this talk of friendship and ruling.

"The orders that you are to give your people," the interpreter continued, "will come from this stranger, and from him alone. He is now the ruler of the country and you are to be his chief njama. For this work he will give you—so long as you perform it faithfully—generous payment. He will pay you five of these rupees every month."

"I do not want these metal objects," Muthengi answered. "What can I do with them? Why does he not give me goats?"

"It is the same as if he gave you goats," the interpreter said. "You can exchange rupees for goats."

This was obviously an even greater lie than the stranger's previous statements. "How many are needed to obtain a goat?" he asked.

"One rupee will buy one goat."

Muthengi could conceal his incredulity no longer. It was impossible to believe that the world held anyone so foolish as a man who would surrender a goat for a useless piece of metal possessed, it seemed, of no magical powers.

But the thought of five goats a month burrowed like a mole underneath Muthengi's mind. It seemed incredible, yet what if it could be true? Five goats a month, thirty goats a season, two hundred and ten goats in four seasons with the increase of one to each female in a season . . . it was impossible to encompass so many goats with the mind's eye. He decided to agree to all that the interpreter said. It could do no harm, and no one could be certain that everything the stranger said was lies.

"It is good, you are appointed a chief njama," the interpreter said. "As a sign of his goodwill, this ruler has brought you a present."

Muthengi was given a large supple cloak made of a material he had never seen before. It was thick and soft and coloured a brilliant red like leather dyed for a scabbard. He fingered it with astonishment and delight, thinking that it would shelter the stomach from cold winds and keep the body warm at night.

3

The interpreter, whose name was Ali, was left behind with his two attendants. Muthengi had taken a liking to him, and presented him with a he-goat. The next morning Ali arrived at his hut and said :

"Summon now three of the njamas, for we must count the number of huts on the two ridges over which you have been given authority."

Ali told the njamas to cut a number of long sticks from the bush. He led the way along the narrow paths which criss-crossed the ridges and at each homestead he counted the number of thatched roofs within. He broke off a piece of stick to represent each hut and handed it to one of the njamas, telling him to carry the short sticks carefully and to drop none.

Muthengi grew alarmed and uneasy as the day advanced. Openly to count a herd of cattle, a family of children, a group of huts, or anything else, was well known to invite disaster. This Ali, who seemed so wise in some things, was strangely ignorant in others. Fortunately many of the homesteads had been well concealed in patches of thick forest in order to escape the eye of the Masai, and paths wound so tortuously that Ali soon grew confused. Muthengi guided him away from as many hidden clumps of huts as he was able, so that when the count was finished it was by no means complete.

The njamas threw down their armfuls of sticks and Ali

drew from among his clothes a small red object with something that was white and possibly alive entrapped within it. He produced also a small stick which he rubbed against the white, not as hard as if he was making fire. Muthengi observed that black marks appeared on the white after the stick had passed, as if burning had occurred. His nervousness increased. Here was another kind of magic, but he did not know what it was intended to do.

When Ali had finished he said : "My master, now your ruler, wishes to know the number of all the huts on the ridges in the land of the Kikuyu this side of the Chania river. I have counted the huts on these two ridges, and tomorrow I must do the same elsewhere. How could I remember the numbers to tell him ? This device in my hand remembers them for me. A month later, if necessary, it will tell him where I have been, what words I have heard, and all that I have done."

"Will it tell this frog-skinned stranger what words have been spoken ?" Muthengi asked incredulously.

"Yes, if I desire it to, and if you lie he will hear of it and have you beaten."

"I am a warrior," Muthengi said. "Only women and some-times children are beaten." He looked at the magic apprehen-sively, but he did not believe the interpreter's words.

"To-morrow I must leave," Ali continued, "and for every one of these sticks you are to bring to Tetu one rupee, which you must obtain from the owner of each hut that we counted. If the owner has no rupees he is to give you a goat instead. If you keep any goats the stranger cannot fail to find out, because he will know the total number of huts and therefore the total num-ber of rupees and goats that you should bring to Tetu."

"And out of all these goats," Muthengi asked, "he will only give me five ?"

"They are not for him. He will exchange them for rupees, and send the rupees away to another country to his ruler."

"Even these strangers you call white-skinned, mad though they appear to be, cannot be such fools as that," Muthengi said. "And what if my kinsmen, and Irumu's, refuse to bring me goats?"

"Then you are to send njamas to take those who refuse to Tetu, where the stranger will judge them. And if any man living on these ridges kills another, or steals his property, or injures him in a dispute, you are to send that man to Tetu also; for now the white man's law is yours, and he will judge all wrong-doers and all serious disputes."

"This stranger must be rich beyond all counting," Muthengi said, "if he takes a goat from each litigant and judges every case alone. I am sure that the council of elders will not agree to that."

"The choice is no longer theirs," Ali answered.

When Ali had departed, Muthengi set about the task of collecting goats from all the married men on his ridges. At first the opposition was adamant. For two days the matter was debated by the senior elders' council. Many maintained that payment would be foolish; the stranger had left and would not return; who had ever heard of goats being taken except in war? The defeat of the warriors by strange magic, however, was fresh in the minds of others who, fearing that even more potent magic might be at the stranger's command, advised payment of the goats. The council of caution at last prevailed. With great reluctance the elders agreed to pay the goats, and the young men drove them into Tetu in batches. When all who could be persuaded to contribute to the levy had done so—there were many dissenters—Muthengi put on his war attire and went a second time to Tetu, eight ochred and befeathered njamas at his heels. They passed without molestation across the bridge and were welcomed by the stranger. Muthengi was given five glittering rupees, and that evening he exchanged them without difficulty in the stranger's camp for five good goats. Then he realised that the red stranger had indeed something to offer as the price of friendship.

4

MATU had kept the coins he had received for ditch-digging under the floor of the thingira in his father's homestead, where he slept. Now, hearing that the owner wanted them back, he dug them up and gave them to an njama who was going to Tetu. His interest in the behaviour of the strangers had been eclipsed by his interest in a girl of his age-grade whom he had met soon after harvest at the dances. She was one of Wangombe's many daughters: as tall as he was, with strong shoulders and full breasts, quick of wit and alight with laughter. She was a graceful dancer, but he was clumsy, and when he jumped the muscles of his spindly legs, bearing the scars of many sores, never jerked him far enough towards the stars. Sometimes she had let him dance opposite her, however, and they had spoken together in the moonlight when his blood was hot with leaping and the path dew-cold beneath his feet. She had several suitors, but she did not seem to favour any of them unless it was Kabero, Irumu's son, who had grown into a tall, merry-featured young man with a quick tongue that could stab as deep as a sword. Kabero was known as a wit; he was popular with the young women. Although he was only a youth he had already attained such skill at the game giuthi* that he had defeated several elders on his ridge, and was spoken of as the coming district champion.

During the season of dancing Matu looked for her every night. Sometimes he thought that she threw her glances towards him like arrows in the dance. Perhaps, after all, he looked as well as any other youth, with a white-painted chest, flying white monkey tails and a white feather in his ochred hair. Shyness, he told himself, was a fool's sponsor. His leaps rose higher and his voice grew full with song. When a chance came he sprang

---

* A game played with round counters, such as beans, and two rows of holes in the ground. It is widespread throughout Africa, and involves such complicated feats of mental arithmetic that few Europeans can play it.

into the centre of the ring and led the song with a verse extolling his courage and the good name of his clan.

> " Hark, you girls, the bamboo I broke, that grew so
> High, so high above on the mountain's shoulder
> Now is withered : high will I climb to fetch it,
>   Far will I travel !
>
> When the cows go down to the water, herders,
> Drive them down below where the cows of my clan
> Go ; my cows must drink of the pure clear water,
>   Water unsullied ! "

The men moved around him in a circle, stamping their legs, and took up the chorus :

> " Go, my cows must drink of the pure clear water,
>   Water unsullied ! "

When Matu had done he leapt back into the circle feeling flushed and bold.   Now he had come forth as a young man should, with raised voice, to lead the chorus of his fellows ; surely the blood of Wangombe's daughter must have quickened to the rhythm of his song.

Kabero landed with a graceful leap in the centre of the circle. His limbs were long and muscular and bright as clouds, as he stamped his feet to the rhythm.   In a full voice he led the song :

> " Hawk who tried to sit on my head,
>   why did you
> Fly away ?   I flew to the forest,
>   there I
> Found a youth who feeds on the wild
>   beasts, there I
> Perched on his sore legs."

The sound of high-pitched giggling shook Matu's ears as the girls took up the chorus and chanted :

> " Found a youth who feeds on the wild
>   beasts, there I
> Perched on his sore legs."

Matu's eyes burned with anger and rage blotted out the stars. All around him were white-toothed faces, hideous with ridicule; he felt himself ringed by spears. He kept his face impassive and danced on as if unhearing. When the dancers broke off for a rest he slunk into the shadows and walked home, the yellow-flecked leopard of hatred at his heels. All night he lay sleepless on his bed planning the curses he would call down upon Kabero and upon the foolish, disdainful girl who no doubt was lying by Kabero's side.

5

WHEN he heard gossip that Kabero had taken beer to Wangombe, he knew what he must do. He went again to the dances, and one night when he placed his hands on the girl's shoulder— she was openly contemptuous of him now—with his finger-nails he scraped off a little of the ochre and castor oil on her skin. This he wrapped carefully in a leaf and took it next day to a mundu-mugu along the ridge: a man of less renown that Irumu, but still competent in magic. When the mundu-mugu heard what was needed he took the scrapings from the skin of Wangombe's daughter and mixed them with medicines from two of his gourds.

"Hang this in concealment in a tree which stands by running water," he said, "on land belonging to Wangombe's clan. Then, as the stream will flow and cannot stop, so will her menses flow and she will be unable to conceive. Nothing can release her from this curse of barrenness until you are sorry for her, and throw away the charm."

Matu paid him a fee of one goatskin; and when the moon was dead he fixed the charm secretly in the branches of a tree by the river below Wangombe's homestead. He walked back through the cold darkness with the exaltation of revenge in his heart. Through the girl who had humiliated him he would reach his vain, complacent rival. The curse of no increase would fall on Kabero and his clan, and the shame of sterility upon his wife.

After the curse was laid Matu's head felt light as a butterfly and empty as a new gourd, but his feet were heavy and slow. Sometimes his mind would fill with visions as though torrents of water were rushing into an empty pool; then suddenly it would be drained dry of thought. Strange fancies danced across his eyeballs. Sometimes he saw blood and dying men, and old women with half-eaten leper faces, or shambas seething under a sheet of yellow locusts; at other times the quiet faces of sleeping girls, and flaming trees of strange colours, and fat black goats moving slowly over a green pasture.

He worked often in his mother's shamba, even now that he was a grown man. Somehow the crops he helped to cultivate were nearly always heavier than those on other shambas. He knew the ways of wild plants and animals as others knew the steps of dances and the tactics of war. He spoke little, but his eyes were never clouded or his ears closed, and often in the evenings he could let fall some piece of news that neither Muthengi nor Ngarariga knew, although they had been to the market or sauntered all day about the ridges.

When a message came from Irumu Matu put down the iron scraper with which he was felling a goatskin for a woman's dress without a word and went at once to the mundu-mugu's homestead. He had known within him that the summons would come. The interview was long and strange. Irumu had heard of the curse; how, Matu could not tell. Rumours had reached the girl and she was frightened; her father was willing to pay a fat ram to Matu if he would remove the spell.

Matu said nothing until Irumu, who did not press for a reply, asked him whether visions often came into his head. Then Matu opened his mind to the mundu-mugu and laid out before him the fancies that troubled it. Deep in his heart hid the fear, so long a living part of him, that a curse derived from eating the flesh of wild animals—even though he had not been circumcised at the time—was closing in upon him.

Three times Irumu threw the beans to probe the cause of

Matu's visions and of his failing health. With eyes still gazing at the beans he said:

"The thing that troubles you is here; it is not a thahu. It is something that comes from God. It is a sign that within you are powers of magic and powers to see into the future. You will be married soon, to another who will work well for you although you do not desire her as you desire Wangombe's daughter. Later, when you are married and have children, you are to become a mundu-mugu, to learn the secrets of magic and of medicine and of foretelling the future. Visions have come because these powers are already stirring within."

Matu was silent for a long time after Irumu had spoken. He was frightened of the powers that moved already as a child moves in the womb; he did not know whether the life of a mundu-mugu would bring him happiness. But, if God had so decided, it would have to be.

"How can I marry?" he asked. "The girls here look only at warriors brave in war and skilled in dancing. As for me, the spear is heavy, it does not spring from my hand like a bird taking flight; and because there was sickness in my legs when I was little I cannot dance."

"You speak thus because of one girl who has been chosen by another," Irumu said. "It is not one ridge only that has bananas on it; you must cut your bunch from another plantation."

6

THE land cultivated by Wanjeri and Waseru's second wife, and by the wives of Ngarariga and Muthengi, had, in some eight seasons, grown tired and unproductive. The time had come for new land to be cleared. Muthengi and his uncle Ngarariga took beer to the muramati of the clan and asked for fresh strips of land. Because of famine and pestilence many shambas had been claimed by choking bush and weeds, the inheritance of the goats, and the muramati had no difficulty in showing the two young men strips of bush where their wives might cultivate.

Before the move could take place a most unwelcome visitor arrived : Karue, the mundu-mugu, brother of Wanjeri and son of Ndolia. He came one evening at sunset when the meal was cooking in the pot. His body seemed more crouched, his keen eyes more evil, than ever before. It was clear that he had suffered from a severe sickness, for he had let his hair grow long, and it stood up around his head in a black cloud.

Waseru, returning from a council meeting, greeted him politely but with dread in his heart. He had been expecting the visit for so long that he had half hoped to escape it. He should have known Ndolia better. There was a debt to pay, that was admitted; but the amount was again in dispute. He agreed to seven goats, and would have paid them long ago had it not been that Ndolia now demanded seventeen, and five brews of beer. Waseru had rejected Ndolia's fantastic claims, and so the matter was still in abeyance. Now he almost wished that he had swallowed the injustice and paid the claim.

Karue was silent all the evening. He greeted his sister and his nephews, to whom he should have been as a second mother, with the barest courtesy. After the meal in the thingira an incident occurred which left no doubt as to the enmity that lay like an unsheathed sword between Ndolia's kin and Waseru's. Karue went into the hut where his sister and her daughter were eating, and sat by her fire. Waseru followed uneasily; he could not stop Karue and yet he felt the air to be heavy with threats. Then Karue deliberately lifted his feet and placed them squarely on Wanjeri's hearthstones.

This was an open and cold-blooded affront. To place the feet on a woman's hearthstones was to curse her by saying : I will trample you and your children underfoot as your hearthstones, the very core of your life, are now beneath my heel. There could be no greater insult.

Now Waseru knew that there was undisguised hostility between the two clans. Next morning he refused to pay Ndolia any part of the debt. He felt Karue's eyes, hard as stones, striking through into his head and warnings of disaster whistled in his ears. Ndolia would bring a case before the council of aramati, Karue said; because it was a dispute between men of two districts, a joint meeting of the two councils would be called. Waseru watched him until he had passed out of sight in the forest. No one could tell what evil spells might now be laid upon the household.

7

WASERU'S fears were fully justified. The day after Karue's visit a fat green caterpillar, called thatu, was seen within the compound, crawling rapidly towards Wanjeri's hut. With cries of consternation Waseru was summoned from his tree-cutting and Wanjeri from her cultivation. They came running, and stared at the caterpillar with dismay. Taking two small sticks, Waseru lifted it with great care and carried it into the bush. A half-fattened ram was quickly snatched from its perpetual meal of sweet-potato tops in Wanjeri's hut and slaughtered. Waseru poured a calabash of its fat in front of the caterpillar thatu, praying that it would be satisfied and bless the household, and go away.

The caterpillar crawled out of sight, but Waseru was still profoundly disturbed. Such insects housed the spirits of ancestors who had grown hungry for fat, or angry with their living kin, or who wished, for some other reason, to visit the homesteads of their descendants. In normal times such a visit was not unduly disquieting; once fat and beer had been poured the caterpillar-spirit was usually satisfied. But in this case the confluence of the two visits, Karue's and the spirit's, could hardly be due to chance. Waseru remembered well his father's last warning against Ndolia's clan. He had even mentioned Karue by name. Now, angry because Karue had eaten food in the homestead whilst he himself, a cold spirit living underground, went hungry, he had returned in a caterpillar's skin. Or perhaps, Waseru thought, he was tying to bring a warning of some evil that menaced his clan.

In a few days Waseru knew that this had indeed been so.

First, Wanjeri's daughter—a sturdy obedient girl whose circumcision was to take place within the season—fell sick. Then the youngest child, newly weaned, developed acute pains in her stomach, vomited, and within two days was dead. The elder daughter grew steadily worse; her strength fled and her eyes were glazed. Irumu's diagnosis left no doubt as to the cause of illness. She had been poisoned; and Karue was to blame.

Irumu ringed the homestead around with protective magic and used all his wiles to drive the poison out. But it was too late. The girl sank into a coma and her limbs grew rigid. On the eighth day she was carried out of the hut and into the bush to die. Wanjeri, dumb with misery, stayed with her until the end. She never rallied, and by nightfall she was dead.

The loss to Waseru was great. His affection for his round-limbed, laughing daughter had been deep. And within a few seasons, very likely, the bride-price would have been paid. Now he was the poorer by thirty goats and all their increase and by three he-goats slaughtered in a vain attempt to save her; and a life had been lost to his clan.

8

KARUE's vengeance had not yet run its course.

Waseru's new wife was pregnant, and her time was near. One evening, as she was returning with full water-gourds from the river, Karue's sorcery caused her feet to slip on the hill; and she fell heavily on to a stone.

Labour started immediately. She was carried into her hut and placed on the stool of childbirth, and a woman skilled in midwifery, one of Waseru's clan, was called. Night fell and the time for eating was long passed, yet still the pains continued and the birth delayed. Waseru took a he-goat from his flock, climbed with it on to the roof of her hut and cut its throat, so that its blood dripped down on to the roof to appease the angry spirits that had found their way to the hut and lodged perhaps in the roof. But still his wife's labour continued while her strength waned, and her groans grew hollow as a hornbill's cry. Karue's magic had successfully bound the baby within her womb. A desperate summons was sent for Irumu, who came at dawn and sacrificed another goat. Then he took long thongs of ox-hide and bound them as tightly as he was able round the hut, to prevent the return of the spirits that he had driven out.

At last, soon after sunrise, the baby came; but it was not a normal child. It was born feet-foremost. No baby that entered the world in such a monstrous manner could grow into a healthy member of its clan. The midwife quickly stuffed its mouth and nostrils with grass and laid it on one side on a skin. All night long Waseru had waited to hear women's trills coming from the hut—five for a boy, four for a girl—to proclaim his wife's safe delivery; and he had looked forward to going in the morning to the plantations to cut the canes—five for a boy, four for a girl—whose juice would be the child's first nourishment; but when he saw a silent woman hurry from the hut with a bundle in her hands, he knew that no trills of joy would set his fears at rest.

All day the evil which had entered into his wife fought with her life, and with Irumu's magic; and gradually evil stifled life. Towards evening her body, tormented all day with pain, grew still, and in shuddering gasps her spirit came out of her mouth. Karue had triumphed for the third time.

Waseru was distracted with grief and rage. There was no end to the disasters that were falling upon him. As soon as the midwives left he barred the door of the contaminated hut. Before nightfall he broke down the mud plaster at the hut's rear and hacked away posts to make an opening, and opposite this hole he made a gap in the compound fence. All night in the thingira he could not sleep; his ears listened for the scuffling and yowling of hyenas. The smell of death was in the compound, and hyenas came; and in the morning he fired his dead wife's hut and watched it smoulder to the ground.

CHAPTER II

Justice

I

WASERU'S triple loss was catastrophic, and his rage against Karue too deep to be suppressed. He took the case to court. He accused Karue of poisoning his two daughters and killing his wife by witchcraft; and he claimed blood-money from Karue's clan. For a man the blood-money was one hundred and ten goats and seven for the anger of the victim, but for a woman it was only thirty goats, the price of her replacement. Waseru claimed two payments of thirty goats, and one of eighteen goats for his young daughter.

Waseru grew more and more nervous as the day fixed for the hearing approached. Although he knew that his case was just, he did not see how he could prove his accusations. Ndolia was a rich and important man; Waseru was of little account. The elders would never decide against Karue; some of them probably would be his kin. And for each day the council sat, he must pay a fat ram as fee. Perhaps it would have been wiser to have invoked sorcery to fight sorcery: to have uttered seven deadly curses on the seven holes of the githathi, an object of such dreadful potency that no human eyes had ever seen it. But to curse Karue on the githathi would involve a journey into Karuri's country and a heavy payment to the clan who kept it buried in the ground; and although it would bring certain destruction to his enemy, it would not enable him to collect blood-money from Ndolia's clan.

Waseru could think of only one way to improve his chances: to put so keen an edge on his own eloquence that the elders, in spite of themselves, would be carried away by his appeals. Fortunately, there was one method by which this might be done.

For several days he searched bush and shamba for a certain small black-backed beetle carrying within it magical powers to loosen the tongues of nervous orators. When at last he found one he made a hole in a banana, inserted the beetle and roasted the banana in the ashes of a fire. On the evening before the trial he ate the banana in secret, with the beetle inside it. Then all his anxieties began to fade. Even before he slept he could feel great thoughts, irrefutable arguments, crowding into his brain. The magic beetle could not fail to endow him with oratory before which even the poisoner Karue, who wore hyena's jaws in place of a heart, would quail.

2

WHEN he found himself seated on his low stool under a big fig-tree close to Ndolia's homestead, the wisest among the elders in a semi-circle in front of him and a great crowd behind, only the thought of the beetle's powers within him kept his purpose constant. Now was no time to stammer and feel afraid; now was the time to stand up among his fellows and demand his rights. He repeated to himself the saying: the eyes of the frogs do not prevent the cattle drinking.

He, the plaintiff, was the first to speak. Holding a little bundle of sticks in his hand to prompt his memory, he told how enmity had grown between the clans; how Karue's discourtesy had swelled like the rotten stomach of a cow until it culminated in a grave and open insult; of Karue's reputation as a poisoner; of Karue's visit, and how the two children had died of poison afterwards; and of the death by witchcraft of his pregnant wife. He claimed full blood-money, for Karue had taken all that he had, save one wife who would soon be too old for child-bearing. When at last he ended there was a murmur from the elders and he knew that his fluent oratory had won their sympathy to his side.

Irumu stepped out of the semi-circle and gave his support to part of Waseru's testimony. There was no doubt at all, he

said, that Waseru's two daughters had been killed by poison,
and his wife by a magic of exceptional power, so strong that it
would yield to no ordinary treatment.

Then Karue spoke. He, too, told of Waseru's dispute with
his own clan, and of the dishonesty of an undutiful son-in-law
who had for half a lifetime evaded his just debts. For many
seasons Ndolia had been trying to collect the final payments
which even Waseru admitted, but in vain; and now the debt
had grown to thirty-two goats. His own visit to Waseru's had
been the highly distasteful call of a debt-collector. Because
Waseru could no longer avoid payment in any other way,
he had invented this absurd story of poisoning and sorcery,
which everyone acquainted with the speaker, Karue, knew to be
a malicious lie. Waseru had no proof; his words were like
wood-ash floating in water; he had flung them out in futile anger
and they drifted without purpose or strength. Karue denied
the accusations utterly and counter-claimed on behalf of his
father, now a very old man, for thirty-two goats.

The council sat for two days, hearing many witnesses on
both sides. When it became clear that the elders were divided
in opinion, it was decided to put the question of Karue's guilt
to the test of an ordeal.

A fat ram was killed and over its fragrant roasting meat the
choice of a reliable ordeal was discussed. Most of the elders
favoured the licking of a red-hot knife; but the mundu-mugu
who was called to conduct the ceremony had a better idea. He
held a small wooden box in his hand. Curiosity ran high; no
one could guess its contents. Waseru and Karue were told to
stand in the centre of a ring, facing the elders, side by side.
The mundu-mugu unstoppered several of his gourds, mixed
three kinds of powder in his palm and rubbed the medicine into
the nostrils of the two litigants. They waited in silence, their
faces blank and stolid. Waseru knew that from any test he
must emerge triumphant, his innocence proved; but still his
throat and mouth were dry and his heart pounded as quickly as
the feet of young men at a dance.

The mundu-mugu opened his box and pulled out a small, grey wriggling animal. It was recognised at once as the gituyu, a sharp-fanged forest rodent of a ferocity quite out of keeping with its size.

Grasping it behind the neck, the mundu-mugu held it up to Waseru's nose. Without hesitation it buried its pointed teeth in his nostrils. With all his willpower he forced himself not to flinch, but he could not conceal a trickle of blood that flowed from his nose. There was a low murmur from the crowd. With a contracting heart Waseru knew that the gituyu, no doubt bewitched, had turned against him.

The mundu-mugu jerked the beast from Waseru's face and held it up in front of Karue. The critical moment had come. If it turned away, Karue's innocence would be proclaimed.

The gituyu buried its fangs deeply in Karue's nose, biting so viciously that the mundu-mugu had to pinch its head before it would let go. This time a louder exclamation went up from the crowd. It had bitten both men, so clearly there were lies on both sides; but of the two it had bitten Karue with greater ferocity.

The ordeal was over, and the leader of the council announced that the case was finished. The council would adjourn to eat another fat ram, and would proclaim its findings when the sun was low.

3

THE verdict, after all, was indecisive. Neither party, members of the council agreed, had proved his honesty to the elders' satisfaction. Waseru had lied in regard to the bride-price and behaved undutifully to his father-in-law and his wife's brother, but the death of his wife and daughters was clearly due to poisoning and sorcery. Karue had been guilty of ill-mannered and unjustified behaviour, but the more serious charges had not been definitely proved.

Both parties, the judges concluded, must face another ordeal:

that of the beating of the goat. If either lied, he would be well advised to confess before he raised the club in his hand. When the life of the goat had been beaten out, it would be too late. Then, if a man had lied, certain death would come to him within a single season.

The elders' spokesman paused, hoping for a confession in face of such a threat; but none came. If Karue, having beaten the goat, died within a season (the elder continued), or even if he fell sick, this would be taken as proof of his guilt; and then his clan must pay blood-money in full to Waseru. But if he did not die or fall sick, then it would be known that Waseru's accusations were false. Waseru, in the meantime, must pay Ndolia the balance of his debt, computed by the council at twelve goats; and to atone for his insulting behaviour, Karue must pay Waseru two fat rams.

Next morning the ceremony of the beating of the goat took place. The legs of a he-goat were tied and the mundu-mugu put medicine in its eyes, nostrils and ears. Then he laid a special spell upon it, and Karue and Waseru were given clubs and told to take the oath.

" May I die," each man vowed in a strong voice, "as this goat dies, may I be broken in pieces, if I have lied in anything that I have said." Repeating the oath again and again each man in turn brought his club down on the goat's ribs. The sharp crack of bones followed the thud of clubs and soon the animal had become a lifeless pulp at their feet. Its broken body was thrown into the bush, unflayed. Then the case was over and the elders, staffs of office and fans of leaves in hand, made their leisured way on bent and skinny legs to their own homesteads.

4

WASERU was away on a short trading expedition when Karue's son, a newly-circumcised youth, came to collect the last batch of goats due under the judgment of the elders' council. It was in itself almost an insult to send someone so young and unimportant to collect the debt. The boy was conceited and badly behaved. He greeted Wanjeri pertly, failing to lower his voice in respect, and omitted to use those forms of address to Muthengi and Ngarariga due from a youth to his superiors in rank. " It is easy to see," Matu said in a low voice to his brother, "that the child of the leopard will claw like its mother."

The youth had to stay the night, however; and, as the weather was warm, the evening meal was eaten outside, by a fire lit in the compound. Distant thunder rumbling behind the mountain pressed heavily on the temples of the young men. They ate in silence, resenting the presence of a member of the clan that had poisoned three women of their family.

The visitor suffered from no embarrassments. He ate too fast for good manners and before the meal was over he committed a breach of courtesy almost as bad as his father's insult to Wanjeri. While the gruel-gourd was being passed from hand to hand he put one foot deliberately on top of Muthengi's foot. For a moment Muthengi sat rigid, his skin tightening over his bones, waiting for the gesture of apology to come. But the youth did not remove his foot.

Muthengi leapt up with an exclamation of anger. Others might keep silent under such a deliberate insult from a junior in rank, but not he, a chief njama of great renown.

"You ignorant scrap of hyena's droppings," he cried. "Did your father teach you only the manners of wild beasts? Did your mother nourish you on the dung of kites?"

Karue's son had also jumped to his feet. "Those are foolish words for a coward to use !" he said. "You run away like a francolin, your father is a rogue who evades his debts. Your clan is despised by all other clans for its poverty and cowardice !"

With a grunt of fury Muthengi seized a piece of firewood and brought it down on the head of Karue's son. The youth staggered backwards, recovered, and with the speed of a striking snake he whipped his sword from its sheath. As he raised it to lunge at Muthengi the blade's tip struck Matu, who had jumped back into the shadows to avoid the brawl, on the shoulder, and gashed the flesh.

Muthengi's hand leapt to his right side and an instant later a sword cut a flashing arc through the air. Muthengi's blow was hard and true. A rib snapped like a branch as his blade bit through into his enemy's chest. Then the boy's slim body was lying like a plucked flower on the ground, limp and lifeless.

5

WASERU returned to a homestead of strange silences and averted eyes. Not until evening did Muthengi come, ashamed and sullen, to relate the news.

Waseru was almost stupefied by the disaster. No greater misfortune could befall a person than that one of his family should kill a man. He had felt before he went away that nothing more could happen, that the limit had been reached. But even the life of Karue's son had become an instrument of Karue's vengeance.

"All my goats," he lamented in his own mind. "All, all will go. The huts will be empty as a bee-box when the swarm has left." To his son he said : "There can be no avoiding payment of the blood-price. We cannot deny the youth's death. Truly the wealth of our clan will vanish like a pool of water in the rocks on a day of fierce sun."

"The elephant is not overburdened by its tusks," Muthengi said, moved with pity for his father's distress. "Seasons have been good, and goats have increased; all the married men of our clan will contribute. Besides, these strangers pay me rupees which I can exchange for goats at Tetu, and now that I am a chief njama I can take goats from others. It is a disaster, certainly, but not one from which we shall be unable to recover."

The collection of contributions towards the blood-price—one hundred and seventeen goats—from all the property-owners of the clan was a long, tedious affair. Before it had been completed, the stranger from Tetu came again to camp at Wathukumu's. He summoned Muthengi and several of the elders and asked if all was well in the country; they replied that it was, except that the bean rains were too heavy and the young plants were being drowned by unending torrents. The stranger replied that this was the will of God, and that he had come to collect tribute again, which he would do once in every two seasons. This time no one was to pay in goats, but in rupees, and at the rate of two for every hut. The elders asked him where rupees could be obtained and he said that young men could get them by working in Tetu at tasks in which they would be instructed.

"I do not understand the purpose of these rupees," one of the elders complained. "If the stranger already has great quantities stored at Tetu, why does he give them to us and then ask for them back again? How will this make him any richer?"

The interpreter explained that the rupees were like sticks to show how much work a man had done; for every month's labour he received two rupees. It was therefore a device by which the newcomers could get young men to do the work that they required. "It is the stranger's custom," he added. "In his country everything is done with rupees. You must do as he says, or he will be very angry."

Next day a message summoned Matu to the camp. He found the stranger outside his tent in the attitude peculiar to him, perched on his long-legged stool, with the magic stick that burnt marks on strips of thin white bark in front of him. Matu saw that Kabero, smiling and at ease, stood beside the stranger under the shade of a tree.

"The stranger has heard," the interpreter said, "that your father is paying blood-price to a man called Karue, because you killed his son in a fight."

"It is true that our clan is paying blood-price," Matu said. "It is most unjust, because Karue killed a woman and two uncircumcised girls of our family; but his son insulted us, and so he was slain at our homestead, and we cannot dispute the claim."

The interpreter spoke to the stranger and then he said :

"It is against the stranger's law to kill another person.   You must come to Tetu, where he will sit in judgment on you for having killed Karue's son."

Greatly to Matu's surprise, two iron bracelets joined by a chain were fixed around his wrists, so that he could not move his hands freely.   Then he was given to a warrior and roughly treated, and made to walk all the way to Tetu with his hands tied.   When he arrived he was put into a hut whose door was kept shut as if it were night and given food so finely ground that he could not eat it.   He was too bewildered to protest, for the matter had passed altogether beyond anything he could understand.

6

A FEW days later he was taken to the stranger's square light house and made to stand behind a wooden barrier.   He was delighted, however, to see that Muthengi had come, and Kabero and Ngarariga also.   But his pleasure was spoilt by the presence of Karue, who sat apart, his sharp eyes flicking over the room like the tongue of a lizard.

The stranger kept his eyes fixed on the magic object where, Matu had been told, words had in some way taken shape and could be seen by the eye.   He spoke for a long time, and then the interpreter tried to explain his meaning.   But the interpreter was a newcomer belonging to some strange race; his tongue was clumsy and confused and he made many mistakes. Matu could not understand much of what he was trying to say. So far as he could make out, the stranger had been told by Kabero that he, Matu, had killed Karue's son, and wished to know whether this was true.

Matu replied by telling the story in detail : how Karue had killed his two sisters and his father's wife, the judgment of the elders, and the insults of Karue's son.

"It was Muthengi who killed the youth, not I," he concluded.

"Muthengi's sword is swifter than mine, and he is braver. But I do not understand the purpose of this, since our clan has not denied the liability. Tell Karue that the blood-price will be paid, so there is no need to bring a case, even though he owes my father seventy-eight goats."

The interpreter translated this and then said : "This stranger is saying blood-price no exists. Blood-price will not your father pay. No blood-price but the man who is killing dies. Nor is poisoning possible now strangers come. They have no magic, therefore you have no magic. That is stranger's will."

As Matu could not unravel this at all he made no reply. Muthengi, however, said : "I do not understand. Does this stranger say that our clan need pay no blood-price for Karue's son?"

After the interpreter had spoken to his master he said : "Yes. No blood-price need pay. Man die instead."

"Then this stranger is a most clever and wise man," Muthengi said with enthusiasm. "He can see into the hearts of others, and he knows that Karue is a liar and a poisoner and a thief. It is certainly unjust to pay blood-price to such a man. Tell the stranger that now I know he is a man of great wisdom, and that I will always come to him for judgment."

The interpreter translated, and then replied :"Stranger being pleased you like good law." The stranger made more marks of burning with his stick on the white bark.

Karue, in whose face bewilderment and rage had mingled, broke into a tirade of indignation, but he was silenced by a loud shout from the stranger.

"Leave alone words, you go," the interpreter said. Karue relapsed into a bewildered silence.

"The stranger wants," the interpreter continued, "where is sword from above your shoulder?"

Matu puzzled over this for a little, and then found the meaning. "You ask me about the wound on my shoulder? The sword of Karue's son cut me as he struck."

Then Kabero was called and questioned. Matu was amazed

to hear him tell a great number of lies. First he said that he had been present at the fireside with Karue's son; then he described a fight which he had never seen; and then he swore that the sword of Matu had been the sword that killed. Matu tried to interrupt him, but was silenced roughly. Then he realised what had occurred. Kabero had heard of the charm that had been hung in the tree to bring barrenness to his young wife; he was angry with Matu and was seeking revenge by making trouble between him and the stranger. It was a subtle way to conduct a quarrel, typical of Irumu's crafty and self-confident son.

When the young man had finished the interpreter said: "You hear words by Kabero. What you saying?"

"He is lying," Matu replied indignantly. "He was not there, and it was Muthengi, not I, who killed Karue's son. But what does it matter? Are not Muthengi and I brothers? Whichever it was that held the sword, our father Waseru and other members of our clan must still pay the blood-price."

7

DURING Kabero's speech Muthengi had been deeply absorbed in thought. Now he looked up at the stranger and asked if he might address his brother. The man assented, and he said:

"This stranger appears to be our friend. He has made a pact of brotherhood with me and now I think that he wants to help us, as a brother should. He sees that Karue is a poisoner, and says that our clan need pay no blood-price for the death of the youth. Therefore we ought to help him, as he is our friend. It is evident that for some reason he wishes you to say that your sword killed Karue's son. It does not matter which of us did it, and as he seems anxious for you to agree to what he says, perhaps it would be best for you to do so."

Matu thought this over while the interpreter spoke with the stranger. There appeared to be good sense in what Muthengi said. The matter was a detail, and if it would please the

stranger, who was clearly on their side against Karue, it could
do no harm.

"Very well," he replied. "If he says that the sword was
mine, I will not disagree."

The interpreter was clearly puzzled by the exchange and uncertain of the meaning of all the words.

"The stranger likes to understand," he said, "if your sword
was sword of kill?"

"Tell him yes, if that is his will," Matu replied.

The stranger burnt marks with his stick for a long time, and
then spoke at great length. The interpreter looked at Matu
and said:

"Judgment against you, you killed. Men are themselves being killed because their anger speaks with swords. They are to
be strangled by this stranger until dead. You lucky, you will
not be dead, because the sword of Karue's son hit above your
shoulder. You will stay here in Tetu for six seasons to belong
to the stranger, you now his."

Matu said nothing, for the words did not seem to make sense.
He supposed that the interpreter had made a mistake. Muthengi, however, asked: "But why is Matu to stay here in Tetu?
The affair of the young man's death is between Karue and my
father Waseru. What has the stranger to do with it?"

"That is stranger's law. Matu killed, he evil man. Therefore he stays with stranger."

"Does the stranger give him to Karue?" Muthengi persisted.

"No. He stays here."

"Who gives him food?"

"The stranger gives him food."

"Then what does Karue receive in compensation for his son,
who is dead?"

"He not receive anything."

"That I cannot understand!" Muthengi exclaimed. "If a
man loses his son, or a child his father, must not his family be
given compensation for their loss? How else can justice be
done?"

"Stranger's justice different," the interpreter said. "Matu must stay here."

"Then the stranger gets something for Karue's loss, and Karue's clan gets nothing at all," Muthengi said. "This seems to me a very peculiar law, and one with no justice in it at all. Now I understand how these strangers have become so exceedingly rich; when they sit in judgment they award nothing to the injured person, but everything to themselves."

"That is the law nevertheless," the interpreter said. The stranger spoke sharply to his njamas, who drew their feet together with a loud noise; and Matu, too confused to make a protest, was led away.

Contact

I

MATU was now compelled to lead a strange, comfortless life whose purpose he could not divine. At sunset he was herded like an ox into a fireless house with men of many age-grades and clans and given a paste of maize ground fine like millet to eat. At first he dared not touch it, since he did not know who had cooked it nor what poisons it might contain. Hunger compelled him to take the risk; then he found it was badly cooked and tasteless, and clogged his bowels.

By day he and his fellows marched out together to work, guarded always by a man who would kill them, so they were told, if they ran away. Once two young men did make off when the guard was not looking, but they were not killed. They were, however, captured and brought back to Tetu, and here they were badly beaten, as if they had been disobedient women. When Matu saw the weals on their backs he decided that it was not worth trying to escape. He expected Muthengi to come to fetch him any day, for he knew that there had been some mistake and that his brother would put it right.

As day after day went by and Muthengi did not appear his misery grew. He began to fear that he would never again return to his own country. Muthengi, his father, his whole family had cast him aside like the squeezed-out pulp of cane : perhaps they had even betrayed him for a bribe of goats. Death would creep upon him among all these strangers—some of them, perhaps, unclean—while he was sleeping in this cold, empty house, or working senselessly under the hot sun clearing a shamba in which nothing was ever planted.

Daily he grew more listless, and often the guards spoke

fiercely to him in a foreign tongue. His axe fell with blows as light as those of a woodpecker's beak on the gravel that they were digging from a pit. Then sores returned to his legs until he could barely walk, and a black, buzzing cloud of flies followed wherever he went, fattening on the oozing pus.

One day a black-bearded, light-skinned man whom he later learnt to call an Indian came and examined his legs and took him to a separate house, where he rubbed the sores with a sort of fat and then wrapped white cloth around them. This was evidently a kind of medicine, but since no goat was slain nor prayers offered, Matu had no faith that his sores would be cured. They were very painful, and he was glad that death was near.

When his companions were taken out to work early next morning Matu was told to stay behind. The chief of the guards, a rough-mannered Swahili with a face full of little pits as if it had been half-eaten by ants, said :

"Come with me, you. Because you are as feeble as a girl, and a fool as well, you are to be given easier work to do—work suitable for weaklings and half-wits."

Matu scarcely listened to what was said. He moved on his bandaged legs slowly because of their weakness, and followed the Swahili to the stranger's house.

2

IN his new work Matu learnt much about the inexplicable habits of the red strangers. Every morning his sores were treated by the Indian, who seemed to be a sort of mundu-mugu, and then he went to the stranger's house and was given work. Sometimes he dug in a small shamba and planted seeds. When they came up they were different from any plants that he had seen before. Some had big leaves which were plucked and, so he was informed, cooked and eaten like the spinach which grew behind his mother's hut; but others were not eaten at all. They produced flowers in great quantities, and of bright colours.

When he asked what was done with them he was told nothing, that the stranger liked to see them there; but this was impossible to believe. One day he looked through the open door of the stranger's house and saw them inside, and then he understood that they were needed for some ceremony, doubtless connected with the stranger's magic and too secret to be mentioned by name.

He enjoyed planting and tending them, and as time went on he grew familiar with the strange plants and could recognise them all. He began to discover a pleasure in watching them bud and unfold their brilliant petals. He could see that, massed in small clumps or in long strips, the flowers produced a sort of pattern like the design on a shield or on a belt of beads, and he sometimes imagined that he was making a living belt around the waist of a young warrior whose ochred body was the red earth, with green hair of grass.

This work made him happier, and he thought less often of his family and home. He seemed to be under the charge of a man called Karanja, who worked in the stranger's house. Karanja was a Kikuyu of his own tribal group and age-grade, though from a distant part of the country; and these bonds united them at once. He was generous by nature and always ready with a joke. Matu found it hard to believe that the stranger was given food by men, but this apparently was so. There were no women in his household; even his room was swept by men. Matu began to wonder if he were indeed some sort of god, since God alone had no wife or children.

When he asked about this Karanja laughed and told him that in the stranger's country there were many frog-skinned women, and that perhaps this one (who was called Kichui because he wore a ring) had six or seven wives. Karanja added that these strangers seemed to be normal in regard to sex, although overhasty in their technique, and lacking in subtlety. Some had married Kikuyu girls, but they did not eat with them. They ate many strange things, Karanja added, including large birds. Matu was shocked to hear this; such a depraved diet would cer-

tainly make them unclean, and he was afraid that the stranger
would pass on the infection. There was no mundu-mugu
among his companions and if he contracted a thahu he did not
know how he could be cleansed.

3

IN front of the stranger's house was a flat, open sward of excellent grass. When Matu first came there were no goats or cattle
on it, and he concluded that it must have been set aside for some
very highly valued herd. This idea was confirmed when, during the long dry period before the bean-rains, Kichui ordered
six men to carry large cans of water from the river and to pour
the contents on to the ground through a vessel fitted with a
clever device that turned the water into raindrops. Matu was
much impressed and wondered with growing interest what
manner of beast could be worthy of such preparations.

One day, when he arrived for work, he found a strange con-
traption with two long horns of wood standing on the pasture.
It was moving backwards, and a man gripping it by the horns
followed behind. As it moved it made a loud noise, like countless grasshoppers singing by a high waterfall.

At first he thought that it must be alive. It appeared to be
devouring the grass at an astonishing rate as it moved. In front
was a thick sward, ankle-high; where it had passed only level
turf, smooth as a grinding-stone, was left. He gazed at it
dumbfounded, and would have run away if the guard who took
him to work every morning had not been there. Surely, he
thought, only a beast of enormous magical powers could eat at
such a pace.

The creature stopped, and the man with it; the noise ceased.
"Come here," the man said. "You are to take this cord and
pull. And do not let the string grow slack, or I shall know that
you are lazy."

Matu approached cautiously, eyeing the grass-eater with ap-
prehension. He did not know whether it might charge, like a

rhino, although it was small. He took hold of the cord but still it made no move.

"Pull," said the man behind, "you are very slow."

"I am afraid," Matu answered. "Does this beast bite?"

The man turned away his head and laughed loudly, shaking all over.

"I can see you know nothing," he said. "This thing is not alive. It contains many knives which go round and round and cut the grass, like many women together cutting millet."

Matu could scarcely belive this to be possible, but he pulled on the string and felt the object move behind him. Very nervously, and using all his willpower to control his shaking knees, he walked forward. The creature sprang into life and followed with a loud clatter at his heels. Sweating with terror, he increased his pace, but the creature only came on faster. He dared not look round to see whether it was gaining on him. He broke into a jog, his red blanket flapping around his wobbling knees.

"Slowly, slowly," the man behind shouted, laughing above the noise. "Do you think the Masai are after you? Don't you know how to walk?"

Matu, with a great effort, slowed down, and the grass-eater also slackened speed. As the morning went on he grew more used to it and realised before noon that, as the man in charge had said, it was not alive. Later in the day he was told to sweep up the grass which it had cut and not, apparently, eaten.

He puzzled over the purpose of this device all day. Before he returned to his sleeping-quarters he decided to ask Karanja what it was for.

"Outside the stranger's house is excellent pasture," he said, "yet no cows have come to eat it. Now the grass has been cut as if it were ripe grain. What is the grass for? Who is to eat it?"

"No one," Karanja said, "it is to be thrown away."

"But that is impossible!" Matu exclaimed. "The stranger has taken great trouble to secure a wonderful pasture. I have never seen such rich grass.   In the dry weather I and five others carried water to it every day, it grew thick as the finest sorghum, green as young maize.   There could be no better grass in all Kikuyu.   You cannot tell me that all this trouble was taken in order that the grass should be thrown away !   Does the woman burn the millet she has weeded many times and guarded from birds for many months?   Does a man kill his healthy young she-goat?"

"Nevertheless," Karanja said, "Kichui has ordered all the grass to be thrown away."

"Can it be for a sacrifice to God?" Matu asked.

Karanja shook his head.   "I have never seen him sacrifice anything to God," he said.   "It is just that he likes grass to be short, instead of long."

"Then why does he have water sprinkled on it to make it grow long?" Matu asked.

Karanja shrugged his shoulders.   "I do not know," he said. "If you work for these strangers it is useless to ask : 'Why must I do this?'   They have no sense, and do many foolish things without reason."

4

THE territory within the ditch at Tetu was like an ant-heap from which people were constantly going out and coming in. Gradually Matu became aware that beyond the world which he knew lay another world, altogether different, and full of things and creatures of which he had never heard or even seen in dreams. Sometimes little pieces of this other world were broken off and came drifting into his world, as pieces of a fallen tree a long way upstream may be washed by the torrent into a pool below. He felt as if he were back in childhood, when everything was curious and unpredictable, and the correct behaviour in each new situation had to be cautiously learnt.

There were many warriors inside the ditch : strange, wide-faced, dark-skinned men who shaved their heads like elders and wore high red coverings of cloth upon them. They spoke in harsh foreign tongues and ate huge quantities of meat. Sometimes they would march out over the bridge, their legs moving together as if they had been one man, and when they returned wild rumours would fly about of the many Kikuyu they had massacred and the homesteads they had burnt; but Matu had never met anyone who had seen this happen. On one occasion young men came back with them driving many cattle and goats, and a market was held within the boma at which those who could bring rupees took away the beasts in exchange.

On this occasion Matu saw his brother, who brought rupees and returned with goats.

"I have told Kichui that you must return to Waseru's," Muthengi said, "but he will not agree. At first I did not like to insist, because he helped our clan against Karue. But on this occasion I brought a message which, I thought, would oblige him to let you go. The message is from Kabero, the son of Irumu. He has married Wangombe's daughter but she has not conceived, and the mundu-mugu has seen that this is because of the charm which you hung in a tree. Kabero offers you a fat ram if you will remove it, and asks you to return immediately."

"You must speak to Kichui, then," Matu answered. "Until he gives me permission I must stay here, otherwise his warriors will kill me."

"He will not give permission for you to go. I cannot understand it. I asked him: 'What have you, then, against Kabero, the son of Irumu?' and he replied, 'I have nothing against him.' I said: 'Then you must let Matu return, for until he does so, Kabero's wife cannot conceive.' He replied that it was no affair of Matu's whether another's wife conceived. He did not understand. Sometimes he is so stupid I do not know what I can do!"

"There is a reason, I think," Matu suggested. "He keeps near his house some large brown birds—larger than a francolin, but not so big as a crane. They run along the ground and are very noisy, but I have never seen them fly. He cooks these in a

pot and eats them; and not only that, but Karanja says that he
eats their eggs. Can you wonder that he is stupid, since he eats
the flesh and the unborn young of the most stupid of all
creatures, a bird?"

"Perhaps that is why his skin is smooth and pink, like an
eggshell," Muthengi suggested. "No doubt it will cause him
to fall ill of a thahu and die. Although I do not think that I
wish him to die now," he added thoughtfully. "It seems that
he has as many rupees as there are lice in a sick man's hair, and
now I am able to exchange them easily for goats. Perhaps, if I
offer this stranger an ox, he will let you go."

5

BUT Matu was still forced to remain at Tetu. A path wide
enough for six men to walk abreast was built down the Sagana
valley and a huge bridge thrown over the river. Many messengers came by this path from the world beyond, bringing
tales of a place called Nairobi, in Masai territory, where there
were huge houses that shone in the sun like new rupees, and
thousands of men of all tribes and ages, and a stranger who
claimed to rule over the whole land. There were tales, too, of
boxes made of iron that moved on ropes of wire laid on the
ground, and of people who sat in these and were drawn about
by a huge black animal that breathed loudly and was always on
fire, with smoke coming out of its mouth. Matu did not,
however, believe much of what he was told.

One day a strange apparition appeared from the east. At
first it seemed to be a herd of cattle, and behind it rose a tall
column of red dust. Then it was seen that the cattle were bound
to each other with leather thongs. They walked two by two
with a wooden pole across their shoulders; there were sixteen,
and all bulls that, unaccountably, had been castrated. They
dragged a large wooden object which, instead of scraping along
the ground, seemed to be suspended in mid-air on four iron
hoops criss-crossed with poles. Men walked beside the cattle,

sweat streaking their dust-caked faces, uttering sharp, loud cries and swinging a thong attached to a stick over their heads.

It was a strange sight and a little shocking; never before had cattle been bound together and so roughly handled. It was surely indecorous to beat so valuable an object as a bull, a symbol of great wealth, in such a summary fashion. One of them might fall and break its leg, or die on the road. Kichui—for evidently the cattle were his—must indeed be rich to risk his wealth in such a reckless way. The wooden platform proved to contain a large number of things belonging to Kichui, and no one could understand why they came in such a cumbrous way when the backs of women would have borne them, with more speed and far less trouble and expense, in the normal manner.

A few days later, when his labours in the shamba were over for the day, Matu heard a noise coming from the house. Kichui was sitting outside with a small box by his side. He called to Matu, with whom he was by now on friendly terms, and pointed to it with delight. He was laughing, and Matu could see that he was in a state of great joy. A sort of trumpet stuck out of the box and peculiar sounds were emerging from the hole. At first Matu thought the noise might be that of singing, but it did not have the rhythm of song and struck on his ears as a series of ugly and discordant noises. However, he could see that Kichui was very pleased, so he looked impressed and gazed at the box for some time and then said "very good" in the Swahili tongue which he was learning from Karanja. (He had already learnt that strangers were insulted if they did not receive open praise, even though this was known to be in the highest degree unlucky, and normally would only be given with deliberate intent to harm.)

Kichui had in his mouth a stick which Karanja said was not a charm but a piece of tobacco, and Matu watched him light it with a very small fire-stick which worked instantaneously, and without any effort. He could not think why Kichui should bother with useless objects like this box of noises when he knew how to make such excellent appliances as these small sticks that could instantly produce a fire. But there was no accounting for his behaviour, as Matu and Karanja had often agreed. A man as rich as he could have ten wives and a hundred cattle and squash his enemies as a man squashes a louse; he could spend his days hearing cases and drinking beer, his wives' granaries would never be empty of food, nor their wombs of children. Yet with so many delights in his grasp he opened his hand and lived without wives, or flocks, or herds of cattle. It was so senseless that Matu dismissed the whole matter from his mind.

6

KICHUI displayed his madness in its most ludicrous form when he tried to lay a curse upon his own cattle. He had bought three cows, which were herded in a small boma at night. One day he gave orders that dung from the boma was to be carried to the front of the house and buried in a part of the shamba that had been dug for seeding.

Matu could not believe his ears. To bury the dung of a cow was to bring death upon it, just as death, or at any rate severe sickness, would come to a man whose excreta were covered with earth. If Kichui's cows died, Matu knew that he himself would be blamed. He refused emphatically to obey the order.

Kichui told him a second time and then, when he refused again, grew angry and shouted loudly and raucously, like a badly behaved child. Still Matu did not dare to risk the accusation of making magic against Kichui's cows. Karanja came out, hearing the angry words, to ask what the trouble was. When he heard he said to Matu:

"Kichui is very ignorant and does not realise that he may kill his own cows. But he gets very angry if people do not do what he says; he is like a child whose upbringing has been badly neglected. You had better bury the dung as he says, and I will tell him that if the cows die he must not allow any blame to fall on you."

Karanja talked to Kichui, and Matu, with great reluctance, buried the dung. The cows were fine big ones, sleek and fat, and he hated to do them wanton harm in this way. Besides, he had become quite attached to Kichui, in spite of his foolishness, his frequent noisiness, and a lack of courtesy which led him to abuse the people nearest to him in a loud voice when any misfortune occurred, or when they had not understood his words. He once so far forgot his self-control as to strike Matu in a temper when the knives in the belly of the grass-eater were broken against a stone, which had doubtless been put in the way by some enemy. Still, it was a pity that Kichui's cows should die through his own ignorance and stupidity.

Matu's worst fears were realised. Less than a month later one of the cows fell ill, weakened, and in due course died. Kichui gave it medicine, but to no avail. Not long afterwards another fell into a hole being dug for a latrine and broke its leg, and Kichui killed it. The third remained alive, but it did not flourish.

Matu hoped that this would teach Kichui sense, but it did not appear to. He told Karanja that he wished to buy dung from the owners of cattle near at hand. Even Karanja, who had learnt to stand a good many shocks was upset.

"No one would let the dung of their cattle be buried," he told Kichui; "for the cows would surely die, as yours have done."

"You are a fool like the rest of them," Kichui said.

"The fool cannot see himself," Matu remarked, when he heard the story. "He sleeps when the house is burning and then blames others for not waking him up."

7

WHEN six seasons were over Matu was called to the house of an Indian and given a piece of the magical white bark, with designs burnt upon it. He was told that he might go away, and keep his blanket.

"I shall no longer be killed if I leave?" he asked doubtfully.

"No," the Indian said. Matu could now carry on a conversation in Swahili. "But if you kill anyone again, or steal, or do not pay taxes, you will be brought back."

Matu was sorry to leave Karanja, of whom he had become fond. His friend gave him two of Kichui's birds, a male and a female, to take back for his wife when he married; for although no man would eat one, it was believed that its eggs would do no harm to women and small children and that the white fluid inside them was a good medicine for burns. Matu also took a few round tubers of a new kind, smaller and whiter than a sweet potato; some seeds of vegetables; and two handsome shining jars which he put in the lobes of his ears. The greatest prize of all was given him as a parting gift by Kichui. This was a tin of pure white salt, ten times as strong in flavour as the ash of papyrus normally used. Kichui seemed to possess a depthless supply, and Matu thought that his country must be a fine one to contain so much excellent salt, as well, according to Kichui, as giant cows which gave prodigious quantities of milk.

As Matu walked back along the red, winding path between tall grass and bush, he wondered if he was visiting a country seen in dreams. All was as he remembered, yet subtle differences were there. The limbs of the young men were still glossy with fat and ochre and their hair dressed and plaited, but many of them wore lengths of red-dyed cloth knotted over their shoulders and a few had blankets such as his own. For the most part they were without spears, and many had even left their red-sheathed swords at home. He noticed, too, that homesteads were being built out in the open, away from the patches of forest which had hitherto concealed them, where a raiding party could find them easily and approach without fear of hidden pits. At a market, where he paused to trade a little of his salt for ochre, he found that the cents of rupees were everywhere accepted. There was also a square hut near the market where an Indian sold blankets, salt, bangles and ornaments of wire, small shining mirrors, and vivid coloured beads.

On the way he stayed a night with his sister Ambui, who had

married a man of a clan which owned a ridge three rivers from his own. She seemed contented enough, although it was clear that some enemy had laid a curse upon her, for her legs had swollen up enormously and her feet had become like those of an elephant. There was a great deal of dissatisfaction among the young men, Matu learnt. Before the strangers had come the warriors had herded cattle and gone to war, as God had intended them to do; now the country was quiet and raids forbidden by the elders. The warriors were taken off to carry loads as if they had been girls, to walk with bent backs and aching necks up steep paths, straps pressing on foreheads that were meant for the plumed head-dresses of war. In return for this they were given coins which they could now exchange for blankets and also goats, but they resented deeply the degradation of the work of the hide strips, as this task was called.

Why then, Matu asked, did they not refuse to go?

Because the njamas were thorn-in-ear with the strangers, Ambui explained. In each district the strangers had picked out one man for their favoured friend. (Muthengi had been so selected on his ridge.) Each chosen man was given rupees, which he could trade for goats, and called a ruler, although of course he was not one at all. The njamas were friends and kinsmen of this so-called ruler, and obeyed him. If a man refused to go when he was called for the work of the hide strips, several njamas would come when he was away from home and seize his cattle or his goats. Of course he could bring a charge of theft before the council and the njamas would then be ordered to repay the stolen stock, and fined; but they paid no attention to the council's commands. In the old days their fathers would have paid the goats. Now the old men repudiated all responsibility, saying that their sons were only doing what the strangers told them.

And then, if the aggrieved person made himself too unpleasant, the njamas would make some private arrangement with their foreign ally, and the unfortunate man would find himself brought before a stranger on some charge which he could not understand. The result, at any rate, was always the same : he lost his stock. It was best, therefore, to do what the njamas said and to discharge these unpleasant menial tasks for the strangers ; though why they did not get women to carry their loads, no one could understand.

Ambui's hut was in the homestead of her father-in-law Mturi, and several of her husband's younger brothers and sisters were there. Among them Matu noticed in particular a young girl with a newly shaven head and a graceful, although perhaps over-skinny, body, somewhat marred by thick scar-tissue on one thigh and shoulder. Ambui said that she was a cousin whose mother was dead, and that the marks came from a fall into the fire when young. Her name was Wanja. She turned her face away whenever Matu approached and seemed shy and quiet and well-brought-up, and her body looked strong. Matu asked if she had a suitor, and was told that no one had as yet brought beer to her father. He looked at her with interest and tried to carry away her image in his mind. A great longing for a shamba and a flock of goats, for a wife and his own hearthstones, filled his heart.

8

WHEN at last he stood on the ridge opposite his own and gazed across at the land belonging to his clan, it seemed as though a light wind dissolved the seasons between the present and the day of his departure as if they had been a wisp of smoke. The sap-heavy, drooping leaves of bananas still darkened the valley bottom, their red cones pointing to earth ; weaver-birds bent the reeds in the river-bed and smoke drifted slowly from gleaming thatches towards the ponderous clouds. The tinkle of goat-bells and the voices of children sounded, as of old, from the sharp-scented bush, and the three clear notes of the gai-ky-ngu dropped like pebbles into a still pool from a fig-tree's crown.

His father's homestead was in the place where he had left it, and he found his mother in the shamba. She threw down her knife and danced around him, flapping her arms and trilling with delight. Others came running, and soon he was surrounded with laughing, shrill-voiced women and girls, all talking at once, questioning him about his adventures, telling him of their joy at his safe return. They led him home, singing a song in his honour; his mother gave him food and smeared him with castor oil in welcome. Soon Waseru appeared, more dignified but no less delighted, and that night a fat ram was killed in Matu's honour.

He found his family little changed, except that Waseru had acquired a new wife. The blood-price to Karue had never been paid. Several people had died after Karue had visited them, and the conclusion that he was a poisoner could no longer be resisted. The elders of his own clan had met together and decided that the case against him was proved; then they had killed a ram and made a public declaration that the clan would make no claim for blood-price should Karue be killed. After that it was only a matter of time. Karue went everywhere armed and guarded by his sons; but one night he was speared in the back. No enquiry into his death was made. A poisoner was like a porcupine, a pest whose only treatment was extermination.

"I passed many goats and cattle on the path," Matu remarked. "Can all these be the property of our clan?"

"They belong, for the most part, to Muthengi," Waseru replied. "He is now a very rich man."

"Can he become so rich on Kichui's five rupees a month?" Matu asked.

Waseru laughed, and tipped snuff into his palm. "Courage is found in him who holds a weapon," he said. "It is true that he receives only five rupees a month directly, but a river has more than one bridge over it. Very frequently the strangers send to Muthengi for youths to go to the work of the hide strips. Muthengi tells njamas to fetch them from their homes. They have no wish to go, and if a young man can pay Muthengi a goat, or perhaps a fat ram, he is left alone, and another is taken in his place. In this way Muthengi has acquired many cattle and three wives, although he is only a young man."

"These strangers keep the Masai away, and that is good," Matu observed, "but although I have lived at Tetu for six seasons I do not yet understand their customs, or why they are here."

"I do not understand their law," Waseru remarked. "Things have become very bad in our country, so bad that I think God will be angry and send another drought. Now that the young men no longer have to defend the country they do nothing all day but walk about in their finery and steal food from the shambas. Worse than that, some of the young men have started to drink beer."

"Surely that is not possible!" Matu exclaimed, deeply shocked.

"For the most part they are checked by shame, and the elders refuse to give it to them. But there have been cases where they have stolen beer. And cattle, even, too. We of the elders' council were hearing such a case only a few months ago. Nduini —you remember him?—lost two bulls. He sent his sons to investigate, and they found that a group of young men from Wangombe's clan had driven them away and eaten them in the bush. Nduini brought a case, of course, and the council ordered the youths to repay the two bulls and to pay a fine of ten bulls for each one taken. But their fathers refused to pay. In the old days that would never have happened, but now people who are in the wrong ignore the councils' judgment and take their cases to the stranger's court.

"Muthengi heard of the dispute, and told Nduini to go before the stranger at Tetu. This he did. Then the fathers of the thieves came and told many lies. They claimed that the two bulls had belonged to Wangombe, and had been lent by him to Nduini to herd. Any sensible man would have known this to be a lie, for the fathers could not describe the bulls, nor the circumstances of the handing over. But the stranger grew confused—he does not understand the truth of the saying that a council of law does not jump over a stream—and so he dismissed the case.

"Then the elders' council met again, and decided that Nduini had a right to capture the cattle owing to him from Wangombe's clan. He sent his sons and they drove away four bulls and nine cows. The elders of Wangombe's clan complained to the stranger, and men with killing-sticks were sent to capture Nduini's sons. They took the young men to Tetu and have kept them there ever since. I do not understand it at all. Nduini was within his rights; the council had told him what to do. Now many people who have broken the law take their cases to Tetu, because often the strangers support them and because they do not have to pay a goat for fees.

"Once the authority of the elders' council was like a big tree; those who had been wronged could find shelter in its shade. Now it is like a dead tree that has lost leaves and branches; and the young men ignore it. How can a country flourish when the tree of justice is dead and the elders' authority is trodden like ants underfoot?"

"The laws of the stranger are surely beyond comprehension," Matu agreed.

CHAPTER IV

Road of Snakes

I

BEFORE he went to Tetu, Matu had been a nonentity whom the girls despised; now he was a hero. No other young man had lived for six seasons in daily contact with these stupid and yet powerful strangers. Matu was respected for his courage in daring to remain, and for his good fortune in returning alive. He had come back with a very potent charm. People constantly asked to see it, and inspected it with interest and awe. It was the piece of bark with designs upon it. He tried to explain that these were words which could be seen instead of being heard. Few people could believe this, but it was thought that the charm would protect him in his dealings with the strangers and bring success in cases taken before them.

The girls, he found, no longer ridiculed or ignored him; they gave him inviting glances and spoke in admiration of his looks and bravery. Not only was he a friend of these powerful strangers, but his clan had now become rich. He realised that he could choose a bride with little fear of the girl's refusal.

He had been back about a season when a messenger summoned him, one morning, to Muthengi's homestead. There he found a group of young men sitting under a tree. Presently Muthengi came out to them and said:

" The stranger has sent for young men to go to a place near Wangombe's old homestead by the Sagana river. You, whom I have summoned, are to go there to-morrow; an njama will take you."

Muthengi had grown into a man as quiet and cold as a forest pool, and without laughter. His look was arrogant and he had the dignity of an elder, although, as a member of the junior council, he carried no staff. The young men had learnt, of late, to be afraid of him. Then one said :

"Two seasons ago I was taken for the work of the hide strips; · I went very far, and the heavy loads hurt my neck so that I was unable to turn my head. Now I am taking beer to the father· of a girl I wish to marry. I cannot go."

Others followed him in protest, until everyone had proffered some excuse.

" To complain is to pound water with the mortar," Muthengi replied. " Twenty men must go; there can be no excuses. If any one of you can find another to go in his place, and if he can pay me a fine of a fat ram, he may stay with his father. If he cannot do this, he must obey."

A heavy silence fell. Matu could feel hostility towards his brother rising like porcupine's quills among the young men. One by one they rose, without another word, and stalked away. They knew that they could not resist. Their fathers were unable to pay the fine; and if they disobeyed, Muthengi would send njamas to seize their fathers' goats.

Matu had thought himself safe from interference because of his relationship, but Muthengi had changed. It seemed as if the stranger, and not Waseru, was his father. Every day his flocks and herds grew. He had paid goats and beer to the muramati of Wangombe's clan for land, and his wives were cultivating many shambas.

Next morning Matu started off with a party of twenty young men. His uncle, Ngarariga, was in charge. They left their spears and swords behind and carried cooked food in leather bags slung over their shoulders.

They found a great gathering of people by the Sagana river, and an extraordinary number of grass huts. An overseer gave them three huts, and each man received a blanket, an iron cooking-pot and a ration of ground maize-flour and salt. Matu was used to this food, but the others complained; in their homes maize was boiled whole, and here the fine flour made an indigestible paste.

Their work, it soon appeared, was to build a wide road with many bridges; wide and flat enough for ox-drawn wagons to pass. It was called the road of snakes, for the frog-skinned man in charge had eyes with peculiar lids and a long thin body, and was known as the Snake.

2

EARLY in the morning the clamorous call of iron against iron rang up the valley and echoed among the creeper-covered rocks. Sleepy men rolled over in their blankets and broke off lumps of cold porridge from the remains of the evening meal. When they went to work the air was sharp-toothed and the sky a brittle blue, but later on a haze of heat eddied about the hill-side and the sky's colour deepened like slowly drying blood. Then they looked with longing towards the drowsy shade of trees and banana groves, where small goat-herds dozed and soft-breasted doves slowly digested castor-oil beans; but they had to go on labouring in the sun. Sometimes women working in the shambas offered them sticks of cold refreshing cane or cooked yams, and at midday they paused to eat cold food they had brought with them wrapped in banana leaves. The sun was low in the sky before they shouldered their picks or kerais * and strolled back to camp, often singing a chorus in praise of their strength and virility, to sit around the cooking fires and gossip while the maize-flour porridge simmered in the pot.

Matu did not dislike the life, although he missed the leisure and friendliness of his home and hot afternoons of pick-axe labour tired his back and shoulders. He learnt many new things. One was that stone, the intractable, could be split and shaped as if it had been timber. At one place on the road they came to a rocky outcrop which could not be avoided. The Snake ordered many fires to be lit on top of the rock, and to be piled high with banana trash and dry branches. They blazed

* Large shallow iron bowls, shaped like basins, and often used for carrying earth.

up hotly and then were quickly beaten out, and water poured over the blackened rock. The water sizzled angrily and the rock split with sharp, startling explosions. Into the big fissures which appeared men pushed long iron bars, and these they twisted around until the rock broke into pieces and fell away.

Such things were of interest to Matu, but others considered them of no importance. The young men grew restive as day succeeded day and still they were made to work with kerai and pick. Why, they asked, should they build a road nobody wanted—and one, moreover, highly dangerous, since it was broad and straight and could be used by enemies from Kaheri's or Kutu's as an avenue of attack—at the stranger's bidding? They were being treated like cattle, who have no choice as to whether they graze near the boma or are driven to the plain; they were being made to do the work of women, digging and carrying soil. In their absence others would be dancing with the girls of their choice, making love to them and going to their fathers with offers of goats and beer. Many tasks that should be done in their homesteads, too, were going undone; land needed clearing, honey collecting, help giving to those of their age-grade or kin who were getting married, starting shambas, or planting bananas or cane.

At last several of the young men could bear it no longer. They decided to run away.

They left one night, when the evening meal was over, stealing out of the fire-ringed camp before the moon had risen. Next morning, when the overseer saw that they were gone, he was very angry; but for some time nothing more occurred. Others, encouraged by this success, ran away to their homes.

One day a band of the stranger's warriors came driving those who had escaped in front of them like sheep. The young men of Matu's group were there. Njamas had come to fetch them, they said, and Muthengi had fined each of their fathers a goat. They were very bitter against Muthengi. After that they stayed at the camp, but a man from another district who ran away three times was beaten so severely that he could not work for several days. The young men were indignant, but there was nothing they could do. "Now we will ask our mothers to sew us aprons," one remarked, "for we are like women who obey when their husbands say : 'Bring food and fetch sweet potato tops for my goats'—women who are afraid that they will be beaten if they disobey."

3

ONE day two strange monsters appeared on the road of snakes.

Matu was on his way to fetch earth in his kerai when he heard shouts and looked around to see a large animal of extraordinary shape racing towards him. Its long neck was outstretched and its feet were drumming on the road. He dropped his kerai with a screech of fright and tumbled down the bank. When he recovered the animal had halted, and he saw that its peculiar shape was due to a man sitting on top of it. The animal was white, with a long tail, and it snorted in a most savage manner through a red-pitted nose. Matu gazed at it in terror; he had never seen anything like it before, even in dreams. At first he thought it might be the monster Ndamathia that lived in the Chania river, but now he saw that it was nothing like a snake. Then a second monster appeared, with another stranger sitting on top of it, one leg hanging down on each side. This person was dressed in a long apron and had much fine hair, unshaven, gathered on top of the head; on closer inspection he recognised a woman's shape. He wondered why she was so covered up that no one could see whether she was a well developed woman or an ugly skinny one.

Some time after that another animal came shaped like a small house that moved. It made a loud noise—so many of the strangers' things made noises that he thought they must use some magic connected with sound—and gave out an evil smell, and he could not understand how it went forward, unless it was propelled by spirits. It did not obey its owner so well as the animal which he later learnt to call a horse. It refused to climb a hill above the camp, and ran away backwards. Many people were called, Matu among them, to push it from behind as if it had been an obstinate cow; but although they were giving it help it roared angrily at them all the way up. That night heavy rain fell. The road became ankle-deep in red mud and the roaring object could not move forward. In the end it had to be lifted up and carried, and Matu thought it was dead, for the stranger who came in it spent a lot of time bending over its inside. Eventually it came to life again and went away, but Matu did not consider it nearly so remarkable as the horse. Walking, he thought, would be less trouble.

4

AFTER he had worked on the road for four months he was given twelve rupees and told to go home. He was surprised to receive the rupees, as he had not been given any at Tetu. Soon after he got back the stranger who had taken Kichui's place at Tetu visited Muthengi and said that everyone must pay three rupees, or six if they had two wives. This was a bigger sum than had been demanded the previous season, and it made the elders angry. But Matu was able to pay at once, and the rest of the coins he buried under the floor of the thingira.

For many months after his return Matu walked about the ridges watching the girls at work in the shambas and talking to them at sunset when they filled their water-gourds at the river, or on their way home from expeditions to the forest to collect firewood or bark for twine. At night he often joined in the small impromptu dances that took place in between the proper seasons. He saw several girls that were beautiful; but often he learnt, on discreet enquiry, that the one who had taken his fancy was lazy in the shamba, or sulky-tempered, or pert, or too willing to allow young men to sleep with her. More and more often he found his feet pointed towards the homestead of his sister Ambui, where her husband's quiet, self-effacing cousin lived.

Wanja, the daughter of Mturi, was not a girl who was always ready with a quick, apt reply to a boy's joke, and she was shy in the dances. But, save for the defacement of the scar tissue, she was not ugly; she had the big umbilicus that was a true mark of beauty. She was strong and a hard, steady worker. Her fingers were deft at plaiting fibre bags and at stitching the seams of goatskin cloaks. He knew that she admired him, and was flattered at the attentions of Muthengi's brother. On several occasions his resolve to ask her to cultivate his shamba failed and his tongue went dry; but at last, one evening, he gathered up his courage and put the question. Wanja giggled and looked at her feet, and answered : "There is plenty of food at my father's; but when I have finished cultivating his shamba, perhaps I will find time for yours." A warm flood of joy swept over Matu's mind, for he knew that his suit was accepted, and that now he might take beer to Ambui's husband to beg her as his bride.

5

THE rains came soon after Matu's marriage, and then he gave Wanja seed and showed her where to plant it, and how deep. She laughed at him, asking him how he knew the work of women; but he did not rebuke her. She planted maize and sorghum and beans, and also the small white potatoes he had taken from Kichui's shamba at Tetu. He instructed her how to cultivate the strange vegetables he had tended at Kichui's, whose seed he had brought. Behind her hut he told her to dig a patch for gourds. His mother had given him the custody of a number of banana trees in the valley, inherited from Waseru's father; and in between these trees, yam vines grew on the mukongogo trees. He had a section, also, of a cane plantation by the river. He trailed a wild vine on posts around his shambá to protect it from thieves, who would be seized with pains in the back if they passed beneath the long tendrils.

His only remaining problem was to acquire goats. Fortunately, Muthengi now had so many that one man could not possibly supervise their care; and so he distributed the surplus for safe keeping among his kin. A flock of thirty was handed over to Matu to look after, together with two rams for Wanja to fatten. The recognised fee for these services was two kids out of every ten born, and one goat for the fattened rams. In this way Matu hoped slowly to assemble the nucleus of a flock of his own.

He gave Kichui's birds to Wanja and she built them a small cage on legs next to her granary. Here they slept at night, safe from hyenas, gennets and mongooses. The female had so little sense that she did not make a nest, but laid her eggs in different places, generally on the refuse heap, in the most improvident way. Because of their homelessness Wanja called them the beggars. She collected the eggs, however, and put them in the birds' cage, and in due course a number of fluffy yellow chicks were hatched. Wanja grew quite attached to these and fed them with a handful of grain now and then; but she could not bring herself to eat a bird. For a long time, therefore, the beggars were quite useless.

When the young plants sprouted, Matu felt at last a deep satisfaction; for now the crops which his wife tended would be his to reap and the smoke which filled his lungs in the evening came from his own fire.

6

Soon after his marriage he paid a visit to Irumu, to find the mundu-mugu shrunken and wasted with age. His eyes were blurred and a few white whiskers straggled from his chin. Skin was stretched as taut as drying cow-hide over his bones.

He listened with nodding head to all that Matu told him of Tetu and the road of snakes, and said;

"At first I thought that these strangers would go, but now I know that they intend to stay, and that because of their magic we cannot drive them away. It is the will of God. Now the power of the elders is broken like the bones of a goat beaten before the council. Men steal and evade punishment, for thieves need no longer pay compensation. Instead, they are taken to Tetu to work for the strangers. What sort of justice is this, where the judge receives something and the injured one nothing? Is it not in itself a kind of theft? The country is like a swarm of bees when the queen is dead. Soon I shall die, for I have seen enough."

Then Irumu asked Matu if he still saw visions when he slept. Matu replied that he did. Sometimes he saw the rainbow, in the form of a snake, taking sheep from a hut; he saw a giant with cattle coming out of his knee, and goats being driven to a sacrifice, and the faces of the dead; once a lion had spoken to him in a high voice like a woman's, and once he had travelled to the top of Kerinyagga and seen the feet of God, which were as big as mountains and had long claws that gripped the rock in many directions like the roots of a gigantic fig-tree.

Irumu nodded; all this, he said, was a sign from God that Matu was to become a mundu-mugu. He told Matu to go away, to spend one night alone in the forest, and then to return with a pure-white goat, white as the petals of the flower kangei, without a single black hair. He must bring also the skins of eighteen goats and a gourd in which the two kinds of beer were mixed; and then he would be initiated into the lowest grade. There were many secrets that he could not learn until his eldest children were circumcised.

7

MATU collected the eighteen skins with difficulty, and on the appointed day he drove the white goat to Irumu's. Here were gathered Irumu and seven of his colleagues in magic, with many of Matu's kinsfolk who had brought gruel, cooked food and beer. When Irumu had asked a blessing from God and wisdom from the sun, the white goat was suffocated. Some of its blood was mixed with beer in the long narrow-necked gourd which was to contain Matu's fortune-telling beans, and sipped by

Matu and all the magicians. Irumu then led Matu into the bush to collect beans from the mubagé bush and strips of the creeper mwimba. Each mundu-mugu contributed a handful of beans from his gourd, including several objects of special significance; two cowrie shells joined together, the sign that a woman would bear twins; a piece of ear-ring from a Masai warrior, the sign of victory in battle; the head of an arrow; the horn of a goat; the tooth of a lion killed by a herder on the plain.

Irumu then took his pupil to one side and read his fortune, showing him how future events might be divined. Next, the old mundu-mugu gave him nine small gourds and the appropriate medicine to go into each. One powder made youths attractive to girls, another enabled girls to fascinate young men; a third conferred bravery, a fourth removed obstacles from the path, a fifth brought peace between enemies. Three different medicines brought good luck and riches, and one averted evil magic. Ten little ruffs were cut from the skin of the goat's right leg and slipped over the necks of the ten gourds; other strips were tied around Matu's wrists and fingers. A feast followed, and the white goat's flesh was shared among the magicians. Matu stoppered the gourds with cows' tails and put them in the magic bag by which all would know him for a mundu-mugu.

Next morning he learnt the secrets of his tutor's medicines. He was shown the tree whose burnt bark, rubbed on the throat and navel, cured gonorrhœa, and the bush whose root expelled spirits causing stomach sickness. He was told how the root of a milky-sapped tree revived a man who had fainted, how the seeds of another drive out a cold in the head, how the fruit of a third, infused in water, cured diarrhœa, and how the ashes of the feathers of the tick-bird, rubbed on the body, cured impotency in men or sterility in women. He was given a little of the fine yellow earth which, blown over a man, would make him invisible, and some powder which, buried in the ground, would cure madness. Irumu also showed him a rare shrub whose root and bark, ground to a fine powder and sprinkled over food, would kill the man who ate it slowly and without fuss, and he pointed out other shrubs whose ashes, rubbed on to forehead, fingers and toes, were antidotes to poisons.

8

MATU'S first child was a boy. When it was safely delivered, he went to the river and cut five sticks of cane. Wanja chewed some of the pulp and spat the juice into the infant's mouth, so that in after life its nature should be sweet and its temper mild. For five days no one but midwives entered the hut. On the fifth Wanja was washed, her head shaved and the hut swept out with leaves. A goat was killed and she was purified and then a feast of rejoicing was held among the men of Matu's clan. He was so delighted that he gave Wanja a small fat ram for herself to make her strong.

The skin of the goat was carefully felled with an iron scraper and sewn with a thorn-spike needle into a sling. In this the baby passed most of its infancy, going with its mother every day to the shamba. From this swaying, sun-hot eminence it grew to know the world through a flickering veil of flies. Matu named it Karanja after his friend at Tetu, because he hoped that it would grow up to be as clever.

He was kept busy telling fortunes and making charms, for there were many quarrels. Young men who had not been taken by the stranger's men to Tetu, or made to labour on the road of snakes, had little to do. They no longer needed to train themselves for war, or to protect the cattle against Masai raiders. They danced a great deal, and dressed their hair; they played the game giuthi, and sometimes demanded beer when their mothers were brewing, although this made their fathers deeply angry. But now, if an elder of the council saw a young man drinking and threatened him with a stick the young man would complain to the stranger, and the elder would be taken to Tetu and perhaps fined three or four rupees. People who had been wronged, knowing that they would get no satisfaction from the elders' council as of old, would often resort to magic to bring sterility on their enemy's wives or cows, and illness to his goats and children. Matu gave many such medicines to his clients, and found a great deal of sickness to cure.

9

WITH every season that passed Irumu grew more gaunt and bony, his eyes more rheumy and his limbs feebler. He spent long days in the shade of granary or hut, half asleep. A morning came when he could not leave his bed. He sent for his surviving brothers and all his sons and told them how his property was to be divided. He charged his sons to bury his body, as befitted an important man, and then in a low but urgent voice he said :

"My kinsmen, you have seen a more powerful magic than mine come into the land. Your feet are set on strange paths; they travel away from the knowledge that has been handed down to us from our ancestors, generation by generation, from all that the spirits of our forefathers guard, towards wild cold places of which we can know nothing at all. Against this new magic the wisdom of our ancestors is as dust blown against a rock, or as a twig carried down by a river in flood.

"Lately I have seen visions of a land in which there are no trees, but only pestilence and famine, and the cries of women whose sons and husbands will not return. As a young girl's apron protects her from men of evil intention, so trees protect us from our enemies. When women walk all day to seek firewood, then shall evil come, and when the cultivation lies naked under the sun. But you must be patient; one day the pestilence will be driven out, and on the day when trees again darken the ridges, then shall good fortune return. Then evil spirits will fly underground, and young boys will herd cattle, and the hair of the warriors will be cut short.

" Remember, therefore, be patient under your sufferings; do

not try to drive away the strangers with spears or with magic, for they have deadlier spears and a stronger magic than we. Why they have come I know not, but they have come in peace, and perhaps one day God will send them sense, so that they will be able to understand our customs and our law."

The long speech exhausted the old man, and at nightfall life left his body quietly in the hut. Irumu's importance justified his burial, and he had sons to perform the task. When the grave was dug four sons wrapped his body in an ox-hide and laid it on its side with the knees drawn up and the head towards the west. His hut was pulled down and the materials scattered over the grave. Among them was his bag of medicine gourds, whose magic had exorcised so many spirits and brought comfort to the bewildered and the sick. No other hand could touch the gourds that had been his. They were left for gradual dissolution before slow attacks of sun, rain and all-devouring insects. In a few seasons a young mununga tree, from whose spikes charms were made, sprouted from among the rotted timbers. This was kept inviolate, even to its smaller branches, from axe or fire. It was recognised as the special resting-place of Irumu's spirit.

CHAPTER V

Men of God

I

ONE day Matu heard that two strangers had started to build a house on a hill called Tumu-Tumu, beyond Karatina. His chickens were now laying many eggs and he decided to take some over to see if he could make a sale. He found four large houses of grass, built on the flat crest of the hill. But no ditch had been dug, nor could he see any warriors, although he looked for them by the doors of all the houses.

Finally he found the person who cooked for the stranger and sold him the eggs. Presently a man who wore a long white robe like a Wathukumu, but who was in fact a Kikuyu from Kiambu, came into the kitchen, and Matu was able to question him.

These strangers, he learnt, were not the same as Kichui, although they spoke the same tongue. He was surprised to hear that they did not collect rupees or goats. He was even more surprised to be told that they had something to do with God. They brought a message, the man from Kiambu said, from God, which they wished to give to the Kikuyu people. Matu asked if they had been to the top of Kerinyagga to talk to God and his informant said no, because this was the God of the strangers who did not live on Kerinyagga at all, but very high up in the sky.

He was interested in these strangers, and stayed on next day to see what they were like. He saw a young man who was evidently sick, since he wore a beard. Matu assumed that this must be a son of the elder who had spoken with God; but Kamau, his informant, told him that this young man was the chief stranger. He had with him one wife, and a friend. Matu thought that Kamau must be mistaken, for only old men could talk with God; these people were far too young for such a sacred function.

The chief stranger, hearing of Matu's presence, came up and greeted him in Kikuyu. The words were so badly pronounced that Matu wanted to laugh, but he managed to avoid such a breach of manners. The stranger asked if he would like to work in the garden. Matu accepted, for although he did not need rupees and had his own shamba, he was interested in this place, so different from Tetu, and wanted to find out what it was for.

2

HE worked for a month at Tumu-Tumu and discovered many curious things. The biggest building of all, made of mud and poles with a pole sticking up out of the roof, seemed always to be empty; and he asked Kamau the reason for this.

"That is a place where people go to talk to God," Kamau said.

Matu was very surprised. "Why do they not go to a fig-tree?" he asked. "The fig is sacred to God, because its roots have grown from the sky, and God sends spirits there to eat sacrifices."

"This God does not eat sacrifices," Kamau replied. "He does not like them."

"How can God fail to like a good fat ram without blemish, the pick of the flock?" Matu asked, even more amazed. "And why should God listen to a prayer which is not considered to be worth a sacrifice by those who pray?"

"All the same, the strangers do not sacrifice rams or he-goats," Kamau said. "They talk to God in a loud voice and sing, and then he listens to them."

"God listens to a song?" Matu asked incredulously. "Surely he does not attend to such trifles as that!"

"This God does not mind; but when people disobey him he uses a very strong magic to turn them into salt, and he sends cattle plagues and diseases. But he loves everyone, and when a small bird, such as an njigi, dies, he can hear it fall."

"That is absurd," Matu said. "Birds are senseless things which eat millet; God cannot possibly be interested in them."

"The strangers say he is, nevertheless. He has a very big bird in the sky which he sends with messages, and it helps him to rule. It can fly from here to the big water, called in Swahili the sea, without rest. He also has a son, who was born in the country of the strangers, but was killed there a long time ago."

"That is quite impossible," Matu said. "God has no children, nor wives, nor goats. He is quite alone. Everyone knows that."

"This God had a son," Kamau insisted, "who was killed by very wicked men who did not listen to what he said. All this is recorded in signs, and those who can understand them know exactly what happened, although it occurred many generations ago."

"Has this God, then, a wife?"

"No, there is no wife. God chose a virgin and she became the mother of his child."

"But that is a very shocking thing indeed!" Matu protested. "If a girl conceives before she is married, everyone ridicules her, and the man is fined ten goats. That story cannot possibly be true."

"It was magic," Kamau explained. "She did not lie with any one, yet she conceived."

"Now I know that this is all untrue!" Matu exclaimed. "Can a plant sprout from the earth without a seed, or a child grow in its mother's womb without the intervention of a man? All this has nothing whatever to do with God."

"You are very ignorant," Kamau retorted angrily. "You do not know anything, and for that reason when you are dead you will go to a place where there is a very big fire and there you will roast like a yam for many, many seasons."

"Now I see that your sense has flown off like a bee," Matu said. "That is quite impossible."

"You think so because you are ignorant. I have become a follower of this stranger's God, who is very much more powerful than any other and protects me from illness without my going to a mundu-mugu to get charms. When I die my spirit will go into the sky, where I shall find many companions, women as well as men, and be very well content."

"Are there any cattle and goats in this place as well?"

"No, I do not think so, but there is much singing, and a kind of musical instrument, bigger than a flute."

"I do not think it sounds a very good place," Matu said.

3

THOSE who were working for the strangers at Tumu-Tumu had been asked to bring their children for the white man to see. Many refused, fearing that he might have an evil eye. A few brave fathers took the risk. Their children were taken to one of the grass houses and kept there all the morning. The stranger, whose name was Sasi because his hair was the colour of ochre, said that he intended to teach them to speak to God. The startled parents explained that only elders could understand such matters, and that it was both useless and disrespectful to teach children to address God; but Sasi replied that the children must come every day for a month. A rumour arose that he intended to fatten and eat them, and at first their mothers refused to let them go. But in time the scare blew over, and a small number returned to Tumu-Tumu to hear stories about the foreign God.

It soon appeared that Sasi intended to teach them the magic from whose secret so much of the strangers' power was drawn: the magic by which words could be made visible.

When Matu heard this, he could not believe it to be true. No one in his senses would impart the secrets of so strong a magic to uncircumcised children: creatures of no knowledge or experience, unable to understand magic, to cast out spirits, to administer medicines or charms. It was so absurd that Matu dismissed these strangers at Tumu-Tumu as even more lacking in sense than the others he had encountered. This liking for children, members of the age furthest of all away from God, must be due, he thought, to the childishness of their minds; in children they could see their own reflection.

All the same, the magic of making words visible fascinated him, and one day when he was taking flowers to the house—for Sasi, like Kichui, indulged in some secret ceremonial connected with flowers—he asked whether he could learn the magic too. Sasi said yes, but it would take him a long time—two seasons, perhaps three or four.

"It is not a magic at all," he added. "It is a piece of work, like making an ear-ring or a bead belt. It must be taught slowly; no person can learn in a month."

"A bee does not start with the honey-comb," Matu agreed. "All things must be learnt by degrees. But if this thing requires skill, why do you teach children, who are not wise like elders and have no knowledge of magic and ceremonial and the law?"

"Because children are quick to learn new ways," Sasi replied, "and God loves them."

"But a great many children die," Matu objected, "and then the teaching is wasted, like seed thrown into a stream."

4

THE other stranger, Sasi's brother, appeared to be a sort of mundu-mugu, but Matu could not believe that his methods were sound. Sickness, as was well-known, came from a thahu which only purification could remove, or from the malignant activities of spirits of the dead. Until the basic cause was known, the spirit responsible could not be appeased or driven out. Sasi's mundu-mugu gave his patients medicines to swallow or to rub on their wounds, but he made no attempt to find the true cause of their illnesses. He did not even make use of lime or of the stomach contents of goats, without which there could be little control over supernatural forces. A mundu-mugu who used such superficial methods was like a cultivator who cut the stems of weeds with a harvesting knife, leaving the roots to sprout again.

Matu decided to test the mundu-mugu's powers for himself. He complained of pains in the stomach and in his legs and arms. The doctor did not consult the beans to discover the cause; all he did was to give Matu a white powder dissolved in water, which turned out to be a purgative. Matu could not find that it had any other effect. He went to Sasi and asked:

"Is this medicine of your brother's able to free a man from the attacks of spirits?"

"Spirits are not the cause of sickness," Sasi said.

Matu smiled at Sasi's ignorance, and, to humour him, asked: "What, then, is the cause of sickness?"

"Sickness comes when the body is unable to do its work, perhaps because it is tired or has been given the wrong food, and sometimes because of very small animals which get into the blood."

"It is troubled by spirits, not small animals," Matu informed him. "Among our people there are men who can drive away these spirits with magic. Can your mundu-mugu drive away these small animals you talk of?"

"Sometimes he can, but not always. A man can only be cured of his illness if God wishes him to live."

"God likes men, and always wishes them to live, unless he is angry at something and sends a pestilence. It is only spirits whose intentions are evil. Has your mundu-mugu a magic to make barren women conceive?"

"No; it is God who decides whether a woman shall conceive."

"How could God wish a woman to be barren?" Matu protested "Only her enemies, or her husband's enemies, or malicious spirits, would bring such an evil thing upon her. Can this mundu-mugu, then, cure impotence in men?"

"Sometimes, if God wishes it."

"I have a sister, Ambui, who has been cursed, and her legs

have swollen up until they are the shape of an elephant's.   Can he remove the curse and make her legs thin as they were before?"

"That is impossible; there is an evil in her blood which no one can drive out."

"Can he restore life to the body of a man who has been poisoned?" Matu persisted.   "Or, if a man's finger is cut off, can he cause another one to grow?"

"Such things can only be done by God."

"Then I do not think that your mundu-mugu will be very much use to us," Matu said.   "Many people go to a mundu-mugu to get protection against poison, or because their wives are barren, or because their legs swell up.   A wise mundu-mugu is able to deal with such things."

Nevertheless Matu observed that the mundu-mugu knew of a neat way to sew up cuts with a bent iron needle, and had a black medicine that stung like hornets and that seemed to heal wounds better than cowdung.   The children said that he had given them a strong powder to drive out worms, and had a medicine to soothe the pain of burns.   But apart from these things Matu could not see that the mundu-mugu, as a fellow practitioner, had anything to teach.

5

MATU went one morning to the ceremony of offering prayers to God, and was deeply puzzled as to its purpose.   The rains had been fair, there had been no raids or pestilence and Sasi appeared to ask nothing of God that was worthy of his attention. Uncircumcised children joined without understanding in song, no sacrifice or tribute was offered, and Sasi mumbled his prayers into the earth instead of lifting his face to speak to God. The whole ceremony was so irreverently conducted that God would certainly pay no attention.

A sight that he witnessed a few days later confirmed his opinion that Sasi was quite unfit to intercede with God.   Sasi's wife was being sent away in a wagon because she had been ill, and before she left Sasi put his arms around her and embraced her openly, in front of the ox-drivers and many others. Matu turned his head away for fear some further indecency should assault his eyes. It was worse than a breach of good manners; it was obscene. To put a man with so little sense of decency in charge of religious ceremonies would be an insult to God.

When he went to receive rupees for his month's work, he asked Sasi to explain a statement that Kamau had made, but which he could not possibly believe.

"I have heard," he said, "that your God, who lives in the sky, does not wish a man to have more than one wife. Surely this cannot be so?"

"It is indeed so," Sasi replied. "To have many wives is a very great sin."

"But this cannot be true!" Matu again persisted. "Only poor men have one wife, and God does not like poor men."

"Nevertheless God forbids more than one wife," Sasi said. "A man and a woman should be together always, and when they are dead their spirits become as one."

"But why is this?" Matu asked.

"It is the law of God."

"And in your country, does everyone obey such a law?"

"Yes, everyone. There is no man with two wives."

"That is the most remarkable thing that I have ever heard," Matu exclaimed. "What, then, does a man do when he is rich? And if he cannot marry many wives, what is the object of wealth? Does not God, then, wish his people to increase?"

"Yes, if they keep the law."

"Then he must wish them to have many wives, who will bear children to increase their clans," Matu said. "One woman cannot bear many children; but the clan of a man with ten wives increases greatly. This God of the strangers is not like ours. No doubt it is best for every people to have their own God."

"There is only one God," Sasi said. "I have come to teach this to the Kikuyu, who live in an ignorance as dark as night. If you work here for two years, I will explain to you all these things."

"I cannot do that," Matu said. "I have a wife, and goats, and a shamba; but I will bring you more eggs."

Matu went home deep in thought and more confused than ever before. But a solution of the greatest of all the mysteries concerning the strangers, the mystery of why they had left their own homes, began to appear. They had rebelled, perhaps, against the cruel and senseless law forbidding a man to take more than one wife; they had come to a place where God desired them to have as many wives as they could afford.

6

ABOUT the time that Matu's first child was weaned, Muthengi sent for him and ordered him to take a number of young men to a place in the Masai's country called Nanyuki. They were to carry loads for the strangers, but Matu was to be an overseer; he would not have to carry anything himself. He offered to pay a young bull to escape the task, but Muthengi refused, and so he was obliged to set off for Nanyuki with food and blankets and a charm for protection against lions, a group of thirty youths under his command.

At Nanyuki the camp of the stranger, whose name was Kiberenge, was like a white rock in the midst of a brown swirling pool of Masai cattle. The air quivered with bleats and lowings, like the string of an archer's bow when the arrow is shot. Above the camp hung a grey mist of dust and over the cattle a wavering cloud of flies. The great bush-speckled plain Laikipia was sun-sodden and weary of waiting for rain, but in the afternoon the thick, coloured clouds of hot weather were still massed heavily over a knife-edged horizon.

A deep silence fell on Matu and his men as they approached the camp. They could not walk at ease among so many Masai, any more than a man could stare unflinching at the noonday sun. Unconsciously their muscles tautened as if to grip the spear and their feet itched for flight. They passed close to a group of warriors who were driving a herd of cattle into the enclosures for the night. The sun was in their red wild faces and on the blades of their spears, and it seemed as if they shone with blood. The two groups passed in silence, but the air between was brittle as a dead twig

From Kiberenge's servants Matu learnt that the Masai were about to leave Laikipia with their cattle and their goats and all their possessions.

"The grasses of Laikipia are kept low by the cows of the Masai," Matu said. "How is it that the warriors have agreed to go?"

"It is the orders of the Serkali," his informant answered; "that is, the ruler whom the strangers obey."

They started from Nanyuki early in the morning, when the sky was white behind Kerinyagga and the sides of the mountain the iridescent purple of a grain of maize. First went the mobs of Masai cattle, lowing protests to the morning and leaving a darkened track in the spear-white dew. Masai warriors swooped like lean darting birds on their flanks, pigtails and short cloaks flying in a steady wind. Behind them came sheep in brown bleating waves and then the women, driving donkeys half-submerged in hides, cooking-pots, water-gourds, blankets and other gear. Small children trotted by their side with fly-sealed eyes, and the sullen elders, carrying light spears, brought up the Masai rear. Then marched a short column of soldiers, their red caps burning like scarlet flowers on the grey-white plain, and after them a long file of Kikuyu porters, two hundred in number. Some carried bits of Kiberenge's many possessions —his tent, his soft bed, many sharp-edged boxes of peculiar foods that were found inside metal vessels, and various bundles of extremely awkward shapes—and others bore many sacks

of maize, ground very fine for the soldiers to eat. At the end
walked the stranger's servants and behind them, at the rear,
Kiberenge himself, on a brown horse.

Matu walked among the porters to see that they did not lag
behind or throw away their loads. He swung from his hands
two objects containing fat and small captive flames to light
Kiberenge's tent at night. He was impressed with them
because of the piece of plaited cord which burnt perpetually
without being consumed; as soon as possible he intended to
buy one for himself.

7

THEY marched for five days across the plain, camping each
night by a small thorn-margined river, and for three more over
the cold tufted shoulder of the high mountain Sattima and
past a lonely reed-fringed lake called Ol Bolossat. The Masai
slept by their cattle around their own fires, aloof from the
Kikuyu and the soldiers. Their hearts burnt with anger like
a blazing tree, but they would not allow the flames to break.
through their flesh. They were leaving forever the pastures
that their cattle had found sweet, the plain that they, the Purko,
had taken away from the extinguished Laikipia section of their
own tribe.

On the afternoon of the eighth day they came suddenly to
the edge of a great valley, the like of which Matu had never
imagined. It was so deep that cattle beneath would appear
smaller than woodlice crawling over stones at a man's feet.
It was so wide that no one could see whether any rivers flowed
down the blue hazy escarpment that formed the far wall; and
the forest that clothed that distant mountain-side was like the
fur of an animal's pelt. Below, in the valley, lay a big lake,
blue as a wild delphinium, enfolded by a rib of dark trees.
Although Matu stared for a long time at the valley's grey-green
floor dancing beneath him under a haze of heat, he could see
no shambas at all. Everywhere there was only grass, grey

before the coming of the rains, flecked like a brindled cow with trees and belts of bush.

"Can all this belong to the Masai?" he asked in amazement. "Can this, also, be their cattle's pasture?"

"The Masai once called it theirs," one of Kiberenge's servants answered. "But their manyattas lay far to the south, near the lake they call Naivasha. These pastures in front of us are bad, and when cattle are grazed here they grow thin and die. Now the strangers have built a road of iron in this valley. They have brought along it their own cattle and sheep, and driven the Masai away. Their sheep are white all over and very fat, with wool as thick as thatch on a well-roofed hut."

The descent into the valley was long and steep. They dropped down through bamboos and forest trees, leaving the cold thin air of the heights for the valley's warmth. That night they camped at the hill's foot and next day they came to the shores of a big lake.

Here Matu saw the iron road, like two endless snakes twisting along the white-floored valley. They camped by its side, and after dark a huge black fire-breathing beast went by, making a great noise. Matu was disappointed, for he had been told that it breathed out long shafts of fire and this one did no such thing. But he saw many sights that were strange and new : huge flocks of long-legged red birds standing in the lake; big-nostrilled cows that lived under water; great quantities of food being taken from the iron wagons; an instrument that was held between the lips and made a shrill noise like a bird. Above all he was impressed with the long strands of wire, so long that the end was not in sight, stretched between poles by the side of the road.

Some of this wire ran overhead and some at the height of a man's waist; this, he was told, was for keeping cows in one place. Such prodigality was almost beyond belief. A short length of wire, enough to encircle a woman's arm five or six times, was worth a goat. The wire along the road must represent the value of a number of goats too great to be encompassed in one man's mind. For the first time he began to realise dimly the incalculable wealth of the strangers. This was borne in on him again when he went to an Indian shop to buy a new blanket. He had seen several of the wagons that moved by themselves advancing before a column of white dust along the road. He decided that he would buy one, for he was tired of walking about at the orders of the servants of the Serkali. The Indian laughed and said it was impossible, so much did these wagons cost.

"I am working for the Serkali," Matu persisted. "Kiberenge will certainly give me a large number of rupees when my task is over. The sum might, perhaps, be sufficient."

The Indian laughed again. "Do you think that you, a Kikuyu porter, could buy one of these things, which are called motor-cars?" he asked. "Even among the strangers it is only the richest who can do so."

"How many rupees, then, do they cost?"

"I do not know," the Indian answered, "but at least a thousand goats."

Matu was astounded, but he believed the Indian—he had seen at least a thousand goats' worth of wire already—and went sadly away.

8

AT the camp by the lakeside, called Nakuru, Masai sheep died in large numbers. In a few days the column moved on to the valley's far edge, where the steep wall which enclosed it began to rise. This wall, like the one they had descended, was thick with forest, but the trees were different from any that Matu knew.

They entered this forest the next morning. There was no track. A few short, squirrel-eyed hunters clad in grey monkey-pelts came down to guide them along faint winding elephant paths. The Masai warriors were told to stack their spears and help the porters to cut a track along the hunters' path wide enough for cattle to tread. The porters followed, crawling like a column of ants through tough, interlacing undergrowth, under rough-barked junipers whose branches were festooned with light green Spanish moss as if a thousand feathery waterfalls had been arrested as they fell.

The Masai murmured savagely among themselves when they were told to cut the path. Before they had led the way two hundred paces they threw down their knives, turned, and stalked back in a body to where Kiberenge was sitting on his horse.

They would not drive their cattle any further, they said. In the forest the cattle would certainly die; already many beasts were sickening from cold.

"We wish to return to Laikipia," they continued. "That is our country; in the blood of our cattle we have eaten the grass of the plain. Turn your feet, then, and lead us back."

Kiberenge argued with them for a long time. Matu watched their faces and was afraid. He did not understand the Masai tongue, but their words were like the bite of spears. At last Kiberenge shouted an order and the waiting soldiers sprang into life. They took their rifles in their hands, spread out in a crescent behind the cattle and drove them into the forest without waiting to see what the owners were going to do.

The Masai gathered together angrily, like swarming bees. But there were elders with them, and women driving donkeys, and vast flocks of ailing sheep; they were like hawks trapped with birdlime on their feet.

Soon the Masai cluster broke and a tall warrior led his fellows along the path in the cattle's wake. Once he stopped and thrust his spear deep into the ground as if he was transfixing an enemy's heart. He passed close to Matu, who looked with terror at his face. His chin was tilted upwards but his eyes did not see the treetops. His look was prouder than a lion's, blacker than an eagle's. Only when all the warriors had driven their sheep into the forest did Matu feel safe. Now at last the plundering Masai, he thought, would leave him and his clan in peace. Now the pastures of Laikipia, and all the world that lay beyond, would be open to his own people. It was sweet to see the humiliation of the Masai and the downfall of their pride, to know with certainty that they would not return. The strangers were clearly the allies of the Kikuyu, for they had driven away the ancient foe.

9

It took four days for all the Masai sheep and cattle to enter the forest, so great were their numbers. At the summit of the steep, tree-clad range, was a wide brown plateau, boggy underfoot, and full of little springs. Here were no trees; only the lonely tall lobelia and a giant heather three times as big as a man. After nightfall Matu saw stars beneath his feet, pricking the still waters of pools in the flat rocks. The cold was greater than anything he had imagined before. When he awoke in the morning he was terrified to find that the water had been bewitched. It had turned into a white brittle stone that bit the hand. It was clear that these mountains were inhabited by strange, evil spirits. He shivered continually with misery and fear, and all the Kikuyu fell as silent as birds at roost. Masai sheep died in hundreds all along the path.

At the top, where rivers rose, they found another stranger's camp. Here they left the sullen Masai and in the frosty morning turned their backs upon the herds and marched down the trampled, dung-strewn track into the warmth of the valley below.

On their return they camped in a glade among a forest of olives, just above the plain. Here, in the evening, Matu found a small cluster of Kikuyu shambas hidden among the trees. That night he ate well-cooked and flavoured food instead of tasteless, clogging maize flour at the homestead of a man called Kagama, who had come from Kiambu to settle in this wild land.

Matu asked many questions about the country. He learnt that the soil was rich and gave excellent crops of maize, bigger than at Kiambu, although millet and sorghum had been overcome by weeds. There was firewood in great quantities, and timber for houses, and the pasture was excellent for goats.

Kagama explained that all the land belonged to strangers, but he did not know who they were. Sometimes one of them would arrive with tents and porters and order the men who were there to cut down trees or dig up stumps; but as a rule no one came to worry them, and they were never called upon to do the hated work of the hide strips.

The column started on its way next morning and at last, weary of loads, reached the shores of the lake Naivasha, that lay in a cup of purple hills. Here Kiberenge left them. An Indian gave Matu a blanket and twenty rupees, and another man told him of a path by which he might return that scaled the mountains behind Naivasha and led to Tetu. Three days later he reached his homestead, footsore and thin, but full of joy to hear the glad trills of his wife and cousins and to see his small son staggering over the fresh-turned shamba to welcome him home.

CHAPTER VI

Emigrants

I

SOME seasons later, Matu's maize began to grow light of cob and his sorghum short of stem and his beans suffered from a yellowing of the leaf. He took a gourd of beer to Gacheche, now the muramati, and said that he was going to cultivate lower down the ridge, on land that had belonged to his grandfather Mahenia. Gacheche took a pinch of snuff and answered :

"That land has already been claimed by Muthengi."

"But his wives are not digging there," Matu said in surprise. "No one can claim land which he does not use, if another wants it. That has always been the law."

"I know that," Gacheche said, "for am I not guardian of the land of our clan? But Muthengi now has many wives and innumerable goats, and he claims that piece of land as pasture for his flocks. If I tell him to take his goats farther away because the land is needed by another of his clan, will he then obey? And if not, can I, or the council, make him do so?"

Matu remained silent for a little, struggling with his resentment.

"Had such a thing happened when my father was young I could have taken a case before the council," he said at last, "and they would have awarded me the land. But Muthengi takes such cases before his friends, the strangers; and if I fight him I shall lose my own goats. I will go, therefore, to cultivate in the forest, although it is very hard work to cut down trees and millet no longer flourishes there because of the cold."

"Have you not heard that we are not allowed to cultivate in the forest?" Gacheche asked. "We may not clear the trees for shambas, or even fell them for firewood, any more. While you were away a stranger came from Tetu with soldiers and drove out all those who had cleared shambas inside the forest, as your father Waseru did when he was young. He drew a line, and said : 'Below this line you may cultivate, but above there is to be forest always, and it belongs to the Serkali. If any man cuts down trees he will be fined fifty goats, and if he does it a second time he will be taken to Tetu.' Some of our clan refused to go, but the soldiers came and burnt their homesteads. You must, therefore, seek land elsewhere. Perhaps you will have to take a goat and some beer and ask for land from the muramati of another clan."

"Must I then become a beggar, using the land of others?" Matu said indignantly.

"I do not know what else you can do," Gacheche replied. "Muthengi has taken nearly all the land of our clan, and our numbers have increased. Even now the fallow is insufficient for the goats and many have been taken a long way off for pasture. But I will speak to Muthengi, and perhaps, as you are his own brother, he will relent."

2

MATU's heart was bitter, and he was puzzled as to what he should do. Everywhere he heard complaints against Muthengi's rapacity and his monopoly of land. As he brooded over his troubles, his mind turned again and again to the country he had passed through with Kiberenge when they had driven the Masai of Laikipia over the Mau. He thought of the deep soil, untouched beneath red-stemmed oat grasses, and the black forest stretching into unfathomed distance. Here axe and fire could creep unchecked up long tree-deep ridges; here a man could clear a shamba and his wife could cultivate with no one to stand in his way; here was grazing enough for all the livestock of his clan. And here goats were far cheaper than at Tetu or Karatina.

Matu thought a great deal about this land, and about moving

his homestead there; but he put off a decision from day to day. He could not bear to leave his clan. Waseru was getting old, and now sat on the aramati's council. Matu often conducted business transactions for him and helped Wanjeri with the shamba. The old people would not understand his departure; they would be saddened by their loss. His ancestors, too, would grow angry, seeing that one who should give them fat and beer was no longer there to carry out his duties. And what was a man, Matu reflected, without his clan? He was like a finger severed from the hand or a rock broken off from a hillside. Who would help him to break his shamba and build new huts? With whom would his sons be circumcised? Who would pay the blood-price, if by some act of his a man was killed? Or avenge his own life if he was murdered? If his crops should fail and his goats die, no one would be bound to give him food and shelter.

He decided that the break would be too final and too deep and he made up his mind to ask Muthengi directly for land. His own brother, he felt certain, could not refuse such a request. But Muthengi was angry because his cattle were dying, and because two of his wives and several children had fallen sick.

"Why do you come to me?" he demanded. "You have many goats and skins brought to you in payment for your magic; why do you not take land from Irumu's ridge, or from Wangombe's? Those clans have more than they need; but I have not enough to feed my own goats. I cannot spare any."

Matu rose without a word and stalked home through the shambas, trembling with rage. That night he could not bear to speak a word to his wife. When his anger died a heavy weight remained in his heart. It was as though his own brother had thrust a spear into his breast. Sometimes he thought he must be dreaming, for surely no grandson of Mahenia could have spoken such words. Now it seemed that Muthengi was like a great kite whose wings obscured the sun, and that all the people of the district were tormented by his shadow.

The following evening he broke his long silence to address his wife:

"Prepare yourself, daughter of Mturi, for a long journey," he said. "God has spoken to me in a dream. I am to leave these ridges, for surely an evil spirit has gained control of my brother Muthengi's body. Gather together all your pots and skins, gourds and calabashes, and exchange all your grain and other foodstuffs at the market for rupees; for when this moon is dead and the new moon is eight days old, you must be ready to start upon a long journey."

3

THE path climbed steeply from Tetu over the blue mountains of Nyandarua, beneath Sattima's clouded peak. It was a broad track made by the feet of the Masai who had used it, since time began, to raid over the mountains, and by the cattle they had driven back before them when the blood had dried on their spears. Few Kikuyu had been along it; to them it was an artery down whose channel death had poured. But now that the Masai were gone they had lost no time in making use of it. Over the mountain lay Naivasha, where the railway ran; and from Naivasha a man could travel now to far strange lands, to the sea whence the strangers had come or to a great lake of crocodiles where a race of naked people lived.

Matu led the way at sunrise up the path. It was the track by which he had returned from Naivasha; it was cold, but he knew that it was safe. Behind came Wanja, her back heaped high with water-gourds, heavy grinding-stones, a roll of goat-skins, a sack of maize seed, a winnowing platter, and bananas and cooked food. Her son Karanja trotted by her side. Wanja could not manage everything, and Ngarariga had lent them a sturdy circumcised daughter as a carrier. She bore the baby in a sling on her back and took charge of the cooking-pots and more woven sacks of grain and beans. The goats had been left, for the time being, with Ngarariga. Matu drove two he-goats in front of him in case they should be needed for sacrifice, and carried on his belt a small leather sack full of coins. He had sold all his skins and many live goats and had brought with him a capital of more than two hundred rupees. Over his shoulder was slung his bag of medicines. Once he would not have travelled without sword and spear, but now he carried only a panga* in his hand.

In a little while they came to the bamboos. They plunged into a deep moss-green tunnel where the air itself seemed like a distillation of greenery; it hung motionless, as thick as liquid honey. On either hand the slender curved bamboos rose like rigid tapering fingers to clasp each other overhead. The roof was a tracery of grass-white stems and feathery branches, and the floor a mat of fallen sword-shaped leaves. The little party plodded wearily up the slippery path, disturbed by strange noises from the bamboos, which groaned and creaked like old men in the midst of painful death.

It grew colder as they mounted, and the sun seemed farther away. Once, at a turn of the path, they caught a glimpse of Kerinyagga with a narrow band of pure white cloud lying across it, like a long flight of egrets locked together wing to wing. The great mountain was shrinking now, as the form of a brother shrinks into the distance when he walks away to war. Towards evening they emerged from the tunnel as suddenly as they had entered it and stood upon a rolling plateau where the grass grew in waist-high tufts. They slept little that night, because of the cold and the spirits that could be heard crying amongst the bamboos. The clear liquid whistles of a bird woke them in the mist-swirled dawn, and after a little food they moved on over the moorland through a cold dew. On each side of the path were giant heaths, and the air was sharp and tangy in the nostrils. To the right arose the peak of Sattima, frowning with its forest brows. Often they crossed small hurrying streams, for they had come to the birthplace of the rivers, and the ground was soggy underfoot.

Next day they slid down a steep slope through a sweet-

---

* A large, lance-shaped knife, introduced by Europeans and widely used for digging, weeding, cutting and other purposes.

scented forest of junipers and tall mukurue trees. They emerged on to a flat plateau, densely coated with tall grass, and plodded wearily across it, slipping in the black greasy mud. At the end of the fourth day they saw a great cleft lying in the purple haze of evening far below their feet. The waters of Lake Naivasha sucked the last blue from the sky and held it there until the swift darkness stole all colour from the day.

That night they reached Naivasha, and Matu decided upon a great adventure. He would travel, with his wife and Ngara-riga's daughter, in the wagon pulled by the fire-swallowing beast which was known as Karamati.

4

IT needed all his courage to carry through the confusing negotiations necessary before he and his two women could clamber into one of Karamati's wagons and sit, European fashion, on wooden planks amid a close-packed, chattering crowd. He had not realised that the women also would have to take up this awkward posture, and before they could do so the household goods had to be taken off their backs. People jostled them in an ill-mannered, insulting way, and Matu grew hot, angry and afraid. He had never seen so many people of such different kinds. Some of the men were dressed in cloth, like Europeans. He saw outlandish foreign women wrapped in coloured cloth, their hair cut and combed into elaborate patterns as if they had been young men. He was shocked and fascinated at the same time. Suddenly something hit them in the back and threw them forward. Shrill screams came from the women and Wanja's eyes began to roll with terror. When they sat up they saw that the earth was moving away. They covered their faces with their hands and waited rigidly for the end. The seat beneath them began to sway, and then to jerk like the limbs of a dying cow. Wanja moaned softly in her agony of soul. There was a loud, rushing, clanking noise in her ears: the sound made by spirits coming to seize her by the neck. Then she heard Matu's voice shouting at her above the tumult:

"Daughter of Mturi, have you no sense at all? Do you want to disgrace me in front of all these people? Take your hands away from your face and hold on to your water-gourds."

She obeyed, but the earth was still going away and the trees were running by one after another, like sheep hurrying behind their leader. Her loads were rolling about over her feet. When she had brought them under control she realised that she was not going to die, but that by some unheard-of magic the wagon in which she sat was whirling through the air like a bird in flight.

Matu's terror had been almost as sharp as hers, and now a new fear overcame him. Squeezed against him on either side were two young men, neither of them Kikuyu. They had a musky smell which offended his nostrils. What if one of them, or one of the many people who had touched him, was unclean, and had passed on a thahu? Or what if one was a sorcerer who would lay a curse upon him?

He sweated with anxiety; but at the same time he could not help feeling excited. This Karamati could take him to the fabulous distant waters, up mountains, over the tops of rivers, anywhere he liked, to the very farthest point in the world. He could go to find the country of the strangers, where Karamati had been born. All the time it shook like a warrior going into battle, and roared in his ears. It was indeed a mighty monster. Clouds of sparks flew by, as if a great smith, taller than a camphor tree, were striking on an anvil bigger than a hill.

They passed Nakuru and came to the place where he had camped with the Masai, which was called Njoro. Here they clambered out of the wagon and friendly travellers handed down their household goods. Slowly and methodically the women, too overcome at their safe delivery to speak, began to load their burdens on to their backs.

When the wagon had gone on Matu stood quite still for a few

moments and gazed after it, his wide quiet face expressionless, but a light of triumph in his eyes. Then he turned and looked about him, feeling suddenly uncertain and forlorn. On one side stretched the flat plain, long grass bending in ripples before the wind; on the other rose the Mau. He led the way slowly in that direction, feeling weak and afraid. Now his father's well-built homestead hidden among trees, the comforting faces of his kinsfolk, were gone. Now his very life was like a ripe fruit hanging from an ownerless bush, that any man could pluck and crush between his teeth. Behind him pressed the silent treeless plain, empty and immense, and before him the unfamiliar forest, full of spirits whose demands and fancies he would not know how to meet.

"Hurry, you foolish women," he said irritably to his companions as they adjusted their leather straps. "Do you want night to overtake you on the path, and lions to eat you?"

5

THEY slept that night in Kagama's homestead, on a forest-clad hill high above the plain.

The land belonged to a stranger, Kagama said, who had given him a shamba for his wives. Sometimes this man sent for him and told him to join with others in felling big trees and hauling them away with oxen, or in making fences for cows, or in some other work; and then he was given rupees. There was so much empty land that to take a shamba from the forest was as if a fly should eat its fill of a fat ram.

One day he heard that the owner of all this land had come. He found him in a camp near the river Njoro, and asked for land to cultivate and grazing for his goats. The stranger agreed, and showed him a place in a bend of the river where the ground was fairly flat and the forest not quite so thick as elsewhere. He found that he did not have to pay any goats.

The next day, with a light heart, he started to make himself a home.

First, with Kagama's help, he built a temporary shelter of grass, thatched with branches, where he could live until he was ready to build a hut. Wanja went to the river to get three stones for the fire. Nothing had distressed her more than being forced to leave behind her own. She knew that no good would come of it; but she had not been able to carry three big stones over the mountain path. So she took new ones from the Njoro river, and a burning brand from a neighbour, and her new fire was lit.

For the next month Matu laboured with axe and fire to destroy the trees. His two women followed after to break the clods with clubs and pangas. The rains had started, and they worked against time. Every afternoon black, angry rainclouds rolled over the mountain's crest above and broke over the forested shoulders of the Mau. Each time Matu ran for shelter, but was drenched before he had gone ten paces; and Wanja moaned in despair at the rivulets which poured into the temporary hut.

Before nightfall the storm would pass over. Then long rays of sunshine would stream over the rain-drenched hillside, and on every leaf and grass-blade a drop of water would catch and hold the golden light. The fresh strong smells of rising sap and leaf-mould would surge out of the earth, and nimble-footed bushbuck would step delicately from the thickets to shake the moisture from their chestnut coats. Sometimes a steady rain would return during the night and at dawn the sky would be dyed the angry crimson of a flamingo's wing. Then Matu and Wanja would stay indoors until the sun had climbed over a close-packed wall of cloud to dry a little the tall red-oat grass that stood among the trees high above a man's head, and drenched him as if he had plunged into a river. But as a rule the sun sprang fully armed into a sky the colour of a bead. It seemed as if each day was born afresh, alert with wonder; there was no telling what might happen to it before nightfall; darkness seemed a hundred seasons away.

After the rain the cultivated earth lay black and steaming in

its fecundity, and sap-taut shoots grew rapidly towards the sky.
Matu, seeing the soil's great fertility, gave his son Karanja a
small knife and said :

"My son, remember that the soil is the fat part of a ram, and
a young cow is like a beehive.   Look at the fat and the flesh of a
ram : you will see that the flesh is white and the fat is black.   So
is good soil black, like a ram's fat.   Go now and cultivate it well
with your mother, so that you may learn to become a man."

6

WANJA planted among the stumps all the maize seed she had
brought, two kinds of beans and some sweet potatoes.   Here
and there she put in sticks and planted by them seeds of the
tree-pea njugu.   The millet of three different kinds she left in
the granary, for the time to plant it was not yet.   Finally she
put in a few black beans of the castor oil bush, so that she would
not lack oil for smearing on her body to make her limbs shine in
the sun.

But she soon learnt that the seasons of the Mau were different
from those of her own country.   Heavy rain came when everything should have been dry and the shamba had not been
prepared for planting; and there appeared to be no millet rains
at all.   It was extremely confusing, and she complained loudly
to her husband that the land must be cursed by the displeasure
of God.

"Have you not seen that the goats of the men who live here
are fat," Matu answered, "and that their children are fat also
because there is plenty to eat?   Do not be foolish, but cultivate
well, and God will send us good crops."

To make sure of this, he bought a he-goat for two rupees—
less than half the rate that prevailed at Tetu—and sprinkled the
stomach contents mixed with two spirit-repelling powders
around the boundaries of his new shamba, calling on God to
bless him with heavy crops, many children and fertile goats.
Then he awaited with confidence the harvest of his first crop.

7

Matu was distressed to find that the women did not share his enthusiasm for the new shamba and the pioneer life.

They complained continually of the heavy soil; of the tough-rooted weeds that must be planted at night by spirits, so quickly did they grow again; and of the river's steep banks, so slippery after rain that water-carriers could scarcely clamber up. They grumbled also at the long distances between homesteads, and the lack of neighbours; at the wild animals; and above all at the vast concourse of spirits inhabiting the wild, malignant forest that pressed in upon them all, spirits that could be heard shrieking and moaning angrily among the trees. When a full moon rode high over the tapering beard-hung cedars, and stars swam like silver fishes in and out of their spike-leaved branches, Wanja could not sleep because of these raucous, hostile noises.

One day Wanja fell and dropped the baby by the river, and Matu realised that spirits had indeed tried to hurt his wife. He killed a goat at once and purified her, and decided to delay no longer the building of a proper homestead. He hewed the posts out of a big cedar whose base had been eaten by fire, while Wanja cooked food and brewed beer. All the neighbours were summoned to the site, blessed with gruel; and in a day a stout hut of cedar posts and mud was built.

The maize grew to an extraordinary height. The stems were thicker than Matu's wrist. But the beans were half choked by quick-growing weeds and there was trouble with the tree-peas and sweet potatoes. Although Matu tried to stay awake at night to drive away wild animals he could not prevent bush-buck from eating off the pea shoots, and wild pigs were as numerous in the forest as zebras on the plain. Night after night they ravaged the sweet potatoes. Every morning Wanja gazed at the results with despairing eyes and complained:

"Am I then to cultivate for the benefit of wild animals? Am

I now to be the wife of a forest pig? What did you come here for, leaving the good land of your clan, to live like an Athi or a monkey among trees and beasts? I cannot endure it any longer. I shall run away to my father and tell him that you ill-treat me, and that I must return to my own clan."

"Have you no patience, no sense?" Matu retorted. "Do you expect the tree of wealth to bear fruit in a single season? It is always the clumsy dancer who complains that the ground is stony. Can you not see that the maize is tall and strong and the goats fat and healthy? Learn patience, and do as you are told."

The attacks of wild pigs continued to devastate the sweet potatoes, and after two seasons Matu reluctantly admitted that he could not fight them off. He told Wanja not to plant them any more.

"Soon I shall return to Muthengi's," he told her, "and then I will fetch seeds of the foreign potatoes that I brought from Tetu. I do not think the pigs will find them, for they grow very deep in the ground and each plant produces a great many. And they are very good to eat.

"And how will I fatten he-goats or rams," Wanja demanded, "if I have no sweet potato tops to give them?"

"I do not know," Matu replied. "Perhaps there is no way. Then I shall be without fat rams to eat."

Wanja laughed derisively. "All men are alike," she said. "They want three things: to lie with girls, to drink beer and to eat fat meat. No doubt if you went without fat rams you would lie down and say you were too tired to get up."

"Silence," Matu said angrily. "You are as ill-mannered as a woman who hands food to her husband with her left hand. I shall beat you if you talk in this way."

After that Matu had to pretend not to care about the lack of fattening rams in the pen in his wife's hut, but it made him very sad to know that he could not again eat their juicy, succulent flesh.

8

WANJA was no less disappointed by the failure of the sugar-canes that had been planted by the river. The banks were abrupt and rocky, covered with thick prickly bush and creepers. There were no flat swampy stretches enclosed in bends of the stream, such as those used in Kikuyu for cane, and it had been hard to find a suitable place. They sprouted, but soon afterwards they withered and died. Wanja blamed the dryness of the land and the cold nights, for after sunset the air grew bitter and the skin of travellers tightened over their limbs. She tried again, but with the same result. How, Wanja demanded, lacking sugar-cane, could she make beer?

Around the homestead Matu planted some banana suckers brought from Kikuyu by train, but they refused to establish themselves at all. At Wanja's request Matu killed a goat and sprinkled the land with stomach contents, asking God to bless the bananas and imploring the spirits to leave them alone; but he knew from the first that a sacrifice would be useless, for the land was too cold.

"This place is cursed," Wanja protested bitterly. "God does not like it, and we have little left to eat. Why do you not return to your own clan, where wild animals and spirits can be kept from the seedlings and bananas and canes will grow?"

One night they heard the trampling of hoofs outside the compound, and lay terrified in the darkness of the hut.

"It is the spirits driving their cattle to water," Wanja whispered in an agony of fright.

"It is the buffalo that live in the forest," her husband replied, "and that is very nearly as bad."

Matu was right. A herd of buffalo had marched through the shamba, trampling beans and tall maize plants into the mud. In the morning he gazed at the damage with saddened, patient eyes, mournful as an anvil-bird. Almost he felt that Wanja was right, and that God did not wish him to cultivate on the Mau.

"They have passed on," he remarked hopefully. "They will not come again."

Wanja said nothing, and he felt uneasy, knowing that silence could be a bandage hiding an ugly sore. She went about sullenly, as one who had reached the limit of endurance. They had no food, now, but a little maize bought at the Indian's shop. When the rain started again, however, she planted millet among the remnants of the sweet potatoes and beans, and he decided that her threats had been the fruit of anger, not of intent. "He who goes on a journey," he said to himself, "does not leave bananas to roast in the ashes."

The buffaloes had razed the shambas of others besides himself. Men were afraid to go from one homestead to another along forest paths, and women refused to cut firewood, so frightened were they of the savage black herd. Many people came to Matu for medicines to protect them against meeting buffaloes on the path. Matu took some of the dung, mixed it with different powders, put it in the horns of goats and gave it to his clients to hang around their necks. As a result of this no one was hurt, in spite of the serious damage done to many shambas of ripening maize. Matu made another magic to protect the shambas and after a few discouraging incidents this proved successful, for it brought a young stranger with a rifle to the Mau. He killed several of the buffaloes, and the rest took fright and went away to hide in the bamboos.

9

WHEN the silk of the maize began to shrivel, much rain fell; and then the sun came, so that the plants were the tallest and the cobs the biggest Matu had ever seen. So heavy were the cobs that he wondered that the stems did not break, and in spite of the buffaloes' depredations the crop was good.

"Now, you see," he told Wanja, "this land is fat. Next season you will fill two granaries, and sell besides several sacks of grain at the Indian shop."

"Then I hope you will get another wife," Wanja said. "The weeds here are such that I work until sunset and still they outstrip me."

"I shall go to my father's at the time of the full moon," Matu replied, "to fetch my goats; and then, perhaps, I shall see about another wife."

In the dry season he walked back over Nyandarua to his father's homestead and returned, a month later, driving his goats before him and carrying a long, roughly-woven basket full of chickens. He hoped that Wanja would learn to eat them, and cease her complaints about lack of food. He carried also a sack of small white potatoes, thickly pitted with eyes.

When he reached home he found Wanja more aggrieved than ever. Bushbuck had fattened on the beans. Spirits had thrown sticks at the roof of the hut and danced upon the thatch. Wild pigs, with no one to check them, had done as much damage as a herd of elephants. As for the millet, cold had stunted it in youth, a drought had come just when it needed moisture, and then rain had spoilt it at harvest. The seasons were completely mad, she said.

She planted millet a second time, but the creeping white-flowered weed kangei appeared in the shamba. Wanja went out with her panga when the sun leapt up over Nyandarua above the cloud-packed valley, and returned only when francolins were calling by the river in the evening, but still she could not keep it under control. Rain fell on and off, at scattered intervals, for six months, so that as soon as the shamba was clean another shower came and the weeds sprang up all over again. The weeds choked the millet, which could not grow more than knee-high. As soon as it ripened, the birds arrived. Every morning, soon after sunrise, big flocks of green parrots would rise out of the forest and descend upon the shamba. They returned only when the sun's rays were severed by the black edge of the Mau, squawking as they flew. Pigeons came also, and blue starlings; long-tailed mouse-birds, flycatchers with white spectacles, and golden-breasted weavers flashing like flowers in the sun. They ate all that was left of the millet Wanja had planted with such care, and when the harvest came there was no grain to cut. The whole affair was so discouraging that Wanja did not plant millet any more.

Matu gave her the white potatoes and told her to grind maize instead of millet for gruel. He had noticed that Kagama's wife did this, and flavoured the gruel with a sweet, brown, sticky substance bought from the Indian, and made from cane. Wanja took the potatoes, but said nothing; she had become as sullen as a rainy sky and her face was drained of laughter.

10

ONE day a new stranger arrived : a short man with black hair smooth like leather and the usual sharp features, abrupt jerky ways, harsh voice and incalculable thoughts of his kind. He summoned all the heads of families and told them to clear the land of bush and trees. He himself remained near at hand in a tent to direct the work.

The big trees were attacked with axes, their trunks fastened by chains to oxen, and dragged downhill to the railway station. Then the stumps were dug out with picks and burnt. Matu asked why the stumps must be removed and was told that the strangers, whom he had learnt to call Europeans, tilled the soil with big knives which were dragged through the soil by oxen, and that these would break against the stumps. It was said that a European down on the plain had dug up, by means of these knives, a shamba so vast that it would take a man all day to walk around it, and that he had planted a new crop like millet, but with only one ear on each stalk and with very big grains.

Matu worked for two months at the digging of stumps. On one day in every seven he was told not to come. Much to his disappointment, no knife drawn by oxen was brought, and when the European had built a small mud-and-timber house with an iron roof, and with big iron barrels to catch the rainwater, he paid each man eight rupees and went away for good.

By now, however, other Europeans had come. All along the Mau the sound of voices shouting at ox-teams and the crack of whips could be heard as land was cleared for shambas, and big square houses were built. Always these people called on others to work and did none themselves, but paid out many rupees. They gave orders in Swahili that were extremely hard to understand, the present, past and future being inextricably confused; but when their commands, however obscure, were not immediately grasped, they were apt to grow impatient and abusive, and to behave in a most ill-mannered way. But Matu was well content, for as long as he lived on land belonging to a European he could not be taken for the work of the hide strips. Besides, the land was limitless and the climate perfectly suited to goats, and his own flock grew fat, sleek and fertile.

Wanja gradually became accustomed to the insanity of the seasons. She never gave up complaining about the weeds, the cold and the coarse, monotonous food, but she admitted that her granary was readily filled. When the white potatoes flourished and a fence was built high enough to keep bushbuck out of the beans, she had enough to eat. Near her hut she made a little burrow in the ground which she fitted with a wooden door to keep out gennets and serval cats, and here she shut the chickens by night. In time she grew quite fond of eating eggs, or cockerels stewed with vegetables in a pot. At last her natural cheerfulness returned; and after Matu had negotiated a particularly profitable deal in goats, he bought her some wire ear-rings and a small sheep and gave her five goat-skins for a new dress, to show that he had forgiven her for her ill temper.

I I

By telling fortunes Matu learnt the stories of many of his neighbours' lives. All had come by railway from places near

Nairobi, from Dagoretti or Kiambu; but some had been to distant lands and seen many strange sights before they reached the Mau.

Matu's friend Kagama told such a story. His adventures had started one day when, as a young man, he had gone to the market carrying a spear. At that time Europeans were still rare; but one, belonging to the Serkali, was living at Dagoretti. Kagama laid his spear down with many others before he entered the market, as was the law. The European came, seized the spears, and asked to whom each one belonged. Kagama claimed his, and the European said :

"I see you are a young warrior, strong enough to be a soldier; you must come with me."

Kagama was afraid to refuse. He went with the European to Nairobi, where he lived with many others in a hut, ate food cooked by men, and was taught how to behave like a soldier. After six months had elapsed he and his fellows were put into the train. They travelled for a day and a night, until they reached a place called Nandi. Here several of them who were guarding the railway were killed at night by spear-thrusts in the back. The European officer summoned the Nandi warriors to a house and told them to stack their spears and to go inside, where they would find much food. They did so; the soldiers closed the doors and surrounded the house, and next day the Nandi warriors were bound and sent in three iron wagons to Nairobi, where they worked for twelve months making roads.

Kagama stayed in the Nandi country for a long time, driving back the warriors who came at night to steal the iron ropes on which the train ran. After eight seasons he returned home, bought a wife, and settled down. But the elders did not like him because he had been so far away, learning none knew what evil and dangerous magic from Nandi sorcerers. Several attempts were made by enemies of his father's clan to seize for cultivation the land he had inherited. Friends told him that threats had been made against him and a poisoner consulted; so when he heard from a cousin, who worked as cook, of a white man who was ready to give a shamba to anyone who came, he decided to move to a safer place. Others joined him, and a group of ten went by train to this European's farm, which adjoined that on which Matu had settled. He saw that the land was good, and sent to Dagoretti for his wife; he had prospered, and now owned over a hundred goats and two wives, and was negotiating for a third.

Fear of sorcery and desire to escape from poisoners had driven several others among Matu's neighbours from their homes to cultivate new land on the Mau, where personal quarrels and old feuds between clans could no longer threaten their safety. He heard many such tales of witchcraft, duplicity and adventure, as he squatted over his magic beans in the shade of a tree. He learnt to tell by the tone of voice whether a man was lying or sincere, surly or even-tempered; whether desire for truth or for profit lay behind his visit. Although he was young, men found him easy to talk to and quick in his grasp of situations; his gentle, calm manner drew out their troubles as a skilled hand rubs pain from a cramp-afflicted stomach. Passions, hatreds, ambitions, fears, were spread before him like beans lying on a goatskin. He kept his own counsel, asking help only from the white sun, which was strong and saw all things, and from God, who looked across two lakes from Nyandarua to the Mau.

CHAPTER VII

War

I

MORE Europeans came to live in clearings on the edge of the forests of the Mau. Others brought ox-drawn knives to carve the great plain, which lay glistening in the sun like the pegged-out hide of a mighty cow. Beyond stretched a long line of purple mountains, sometimes as pale and diffident as a light cloud, at other times a dark vivid gash across the sky. On one day the smooth brow of the pale hill called by the Masai Menengai, and the lake's bright lidless eye beneath it, would seem but an hour's journey away; on the next the crater's outline would be blurred by a faint mist of many colours, soft as the beat of a nightjar's wing.

The Europeans put up many wire fences and drove the big zebra herds away. They darkened the plain with their shambas, and cattle bomas arose like the tattoo marks on a warrior's cheeks. Then, just as they seemed to have settled down to cultivate like reasonable men, a day came when suddenly, and without warning, many of them departed almost overnight. They left their cattle and belongings and even their wives behind, their crops halfway to harvest, and disappeared as if to escape a sorcerer who had threatened their lives.

At first no one could offer any explanation for this new form of madness. Later, Matu heard that they had gone to fight in a war against other Europeans who lived a long way to the south. This surprised him, for he had not known that more than one kind of European existed in the world. He listened, however, to conversations at the Indian shops by the railway and heard that, just as there were Masai and Wakamba and Kikuyu, so there were many white tribes, and that these fought among each other in the same way. Matu returned to his homestead quickly and resolved to go no more to the shops until the battle had been fought. He did not want to get caught by the Europeans and made to go to war, as he had been made to build roads or drive away the Masai. He was more than ever pleased that he had left Karatina for a place beyond Muthengi's reach.

2

A SEASON passed, and still the Europeans did not return. He could not understand why the battle had not taken place and one side or the other won a victory. The big houses stood empty, and men were no longer called to work at felling trees or digging out stumps.

On the plains, however, there was much activity. Men were kept hard at work driving long spans of oxen and turning up the land with round knives. In a single day one such implement would do the work of perhaps a hundred women. The elders did not think much of the idea. "What," they asked, "would become of the women, if oxen did all their work in the shamba? There would be nothing for them to do, and then they would certainly get into mischief and commit adultery a great deal. It is much better for women to work. Then they obey their husbands, and cook food properly, and do not answer back." But the younger folk, Matu among them, saw that with this implement a man would be able to cultivate much bigger shambas, and with far less trouble, than by hand.

They did not, however, know how such things might be obtained. So Wanja continued to dig the shamba with a knife, while more and more of Matu's time was spent at his neighbours' homesteads. Although his son was not yet circumcised, he had grown to be fond of beer. At first he bought his wife cane for brewing, but then it was found that stronger beer could be made from the sweet brown substance sold at Indian shops, and known as jagoree. This saved a lot of trouble; there was no longer any need to crush and pound and squeeze. As a result women brewed more often, and hardly a day went by when a beer-drink was not held somewhere within reach. Many fell into bad habits and lurched home every evening dizzy and fuddled in the head. Young men, as well as old, made their wives brew, and the elders shook their heads over their snuff-bottles when they spoke of the breakdown of law and custom, and of the idleness and drunkenness of the youths.

The price of grain at Njoro was very high. Wanja carried down her surplus to sell for rupees, and Matu's hoard under the floor of his hut steadily grew. Within a year of the war's beginning Wanja gave birth to another son, who was called Kaleo; and a season later Matu bought a second wife, a laughing sturdy girl who had come from Kiambu to bring pots and bananas to her brother. He paid fifty goats and three honey-barrels, and Wanja made ten brews of beer. He chose a shamba for her from the forest and cleared it, for now there was no European whose permission need be asked.

3

No one could understand why the war did not end and the Europeans return to their cattle and crops. News came that the enemy had been driven away and were being pursued into a distant country; but no cattle were seen coming back. It appeared that Europeans thought less of capturing cattle, which was the object of war, than of killing their enemy, which brought no advantage at all.

Kagama's eldest son went to Kiambu to look for a man who owed goats to his father, and stayed away for so long that some misfortune was feared. He returned, some months later, with a strange tale. He had found his father's debtor in Nairobi outside an office of the Serkali, waiting in a line with many others. These men were called in, one by one, to see a European with buttons of shining metal on his coat, who sat under a piece of brightly-coloured cloth. This man asked their names and other questions and gave each of them a piece of paper, and they were taken away to a big camp. Kagama's son went in to tell the European about the debt, but he found himself in the camp also. Here he was given food and made to march about with other people, and to dig ditches for a latrine.

One day he passed a house where corpses were being carried out and put into a motor-car waiting outside. Fear seized him, for he knew then that the camp was unclean. That night he and two others climbed over the fence and escaped, and next day he found work with an Indian carrying big stones for house-building. He stayed there two months and then returned home with twelve rupees; but he had not been able to collect his father's debt, for the debtor had gone away to Mombasa in a train. Now he drove a goat to Matu's and asked to be purified, as he had slept in a camp where there had been corpses and was therefore unclean.

After hearing this story, Matu decided that it would not be safe to leave the Mau. He did not do so even when he heard that his father was very ill. The message came with one of Ngara-riga's grown sons, Reri, who walked over the mountains with the news. Although Reri was a young man, still unmarried, tall and strong and at the age of dances, his hair was clipped short like an elder's. He told Matu that all the young men cut their hair now, as Europeans did. They were no longer warriors, so why should they dress it in pigtails and feathers? Besides, dressed hair was heavy and dirty, and took a long time to do. He said that Europeans from the Serkali had taken a levy of cattle and rams from all the richer men. They had also called for volunteers to fight in the war, but nobody had agreed to go because no one had yet seen a friend or relative who had made a safe return.

Reri was a fine dancer. His good looks and ready wit made him popular with all the girls. Several came to Matu coyly, and with much embarrassed laughter, to ask for magic to make the young man come to their mothers' huts at night. In

Matu's opinion no magic was needed for this. He warned his cousin that several fathers were growing suspicious lest he should rob other men's barrels of their honey, but Reri only laughed.

Events followed the course that Matu had foreseen. Two girls who became pregnant named Reri as their lover, and for each girl he was fined ten goats to go to the father, and three to the elders' council. He had no money to buy goats, so the council decreed that his cousin Matu must pay the fine.

Reri, somewhat subdued by this misfortune, promised to get the goats from his father to repay the fine. He left for his home, saying that he would return within two months; but he did not reappear. Matu was not surprised. He bore his loss as stoically as he could, and arranged with the father of one of the pregnant girls to marry her himself, deducting the amount of the fine from the bride-price that he had to pay.

4

MATU heard no more news of his parents for nearly two seasons. Then, late at night, one of Nduini's sons arrived, tired and hungry, wearing tattered clothing that had once belonged to Europeans. He tapped on the door and called, and when Matu went to let him in it seemed as if a hunted animal were waiting for sanctuary outside.

After Wanja had given him food he told his story. One day an njama had come to his homestead, he said, with a message from Muthengi: a big law case was to be held at Karatina and everyone was to attend. When he approached the market-place he saw that a wire fence had been put around it, making it into a big pen. He also saw a number of soldiers ordering people to enter the pen. He hid, waiting to see what would occur. When the pen was full the soldiers shut the gate, and all the people inside were trapped. He himself ran away and hid in the forest for fifteen days, and avoided capture; but since then he had not dared to appear openly on the road or at places where Europeans might be looking for him. So he had fled from his home to escape Muthengi's njamas, who were capturing young men everywhere as if they had been seizing goats for the slaughter.

He heard afterwards that the people in the pen had been divided into three batches. One batch was called Fita, and these were sent to Nairobi with a guard of soldiers. The second, a small batch, was called Shamba, and they went to work for Europeans on farms close to Tetu. The third was called Rotha; these were the old and infirm, and they were allowed to return to their homesteads.

One night, soon after this, another man tapped on the door of Wanja's hut furtively, long after dark, as Nduini's son had done. Matu opened it cautiously and asked the stranger's business. To his great astonishment a European's voice answered him in Swahili; before Matu could recover the man had entered and crouched by the fire. His clothes were tattered and dirty, and he wore a blood-stained bandage around his head. He had no hat. Matu thought that he must be a fugitive, although there was a danger that he might turn out to be a spy.

"I am very hungry," this strange man said, "it is two days since I have eaten. Can you give me food?"

Wanja served him with gruel and maize porridge, which he ate greedily; and he slept that night on skins in Matu's thingira. Next day he thanked his host and said: "Do not tell the Serkali about my visit, for I am running away." Wanja gave him food for the journey, and he vanished into the forest without saying where he intended to go. Matu did not give him away; but he never heard what became of the fugitive European, who also, no doubt, was trying to escape from the war.

5

ON every seventh day a market was held at Njoro. It was not to be compared with that at Karatina, so little was there on sale; still, one could buy Kikuyu food that came by train from Kiambu, food that no one had been able to grow at Njoro in spite of many attempts. Ochre and snuff, wire ornaments and cooking pots, were also on sale. Best of all, visitors to the market could gaze at the alluring wares on sale in the Indian shops : blankets of many colours, shirts and hats, tins in which to bury rupees, lamps and the fat to go in them, and sticks of tobacco that a few of the bolder young men would light and swallow.

Sometimes the train arrived while Matu was at the market, and then he would stand beside it to watch the travellers swarming in and out. It was like an ant-heap with wings. People of more kinds than he had imagined possible were to be seen on their way to distant countries, mixed up in an astonishing manner. Here were young girls seated next to elders, skin to skin, unable to turn their heads away; rich men dressed like Europeans and poor men going without food; poisoners next to pregnant women, and young mothers dripping their milk on to children not their own. The train brought danger and thahu and many improprieties; but it also brought the flavour of adventure and the smell of the unknown. Where were so many people bound for, Matu wondered, and whence had they come? Like a river they travelled onwards, but they never returned. In his youth the world had been a bud and he a beetle in its heart, enfolded by the protective petals of knowledge and truth; the world then had been a place of certitude. Now the petals had opened and floated away; he, the beetle that was left, could not tell what had become of them. On what could the beetle feed, how could it find protection from wind and sun and birds? It swayed uncertainly and dangerously in space; the ground was strewn with the wreckage of the flower that had given it life.

The train brought news as well as troubling thoughts. Matu was at the station when the Indian driver shouted to the platform crowd that the war was finished, that many Europeans were on their way back. He returned home in an excited frame of mind. Now, at last, he could go back to his own country to see his father and mother and all his relatives and friends.

He left his two wives to tend the crops, and walked over the mountain to Tetu and beyond. When he arrived he found such a scene of desolation that his heart became like water and he wanted to turn and run. But he walked on, keeping his eyes on the path before his feet, to Waseru's homestead. The entrance was closed with the shrub of death, and in the fence of the compound a hole had been torn. He turned his head away, grief and shame filling his heart. He had come too late; his father was dead.

6

AT Ngarariga's Matu learnt that his mother had perished too. Ngarariga had grown rib-thin and scrawny and his voice was heavy with despair. His three sons, Reri amongst them, had been taken for the war and had not returned; he scarcely hoped to see them again. Last season's millet rains had failed entirely; the crop had not even germinated. The bean rains had been late and very poor. The crops had grown, although feebly; but just when they had needed warmth and sunshine, the sun had withdrawn behind heavy layers of cloud and a harsh cold had paralysed the crops. Every morning thick mists had swirled about the ridges, wrapping themselves like the spirits of snakes around trees and bush; maize, beans, sweet potatoes had shrivelled in the soil.

A feeling of despair had settled over the ridges. The strong young men were gone, no one knew whither; nor was it believed that they would ever return. At night the land lay silent save for the whisper of leaves and running water and the whistle of spirits, for no dances and no circumcision ceremonies were held.

By day pot-bellied children sprawled listlessly in the shade of empty granaries with misery in their eyes. Women, racked with hunger, sat under the eaves plaiting baskets—there was little to be done in the fields—or ranged already thrice-combed shambas for arum roots or withered sweet potatoes. Some went into the forest and dug up wild roots to stew. Old men grew thinner still, and too weak to move; many of them lay all day in huts which grew odorous and defiled, and when death came there was no one to hear their last instructions.

After several months of hunger three wagon-loads of maize came up the road, watched by eyes dulled with lack of hope. They went to Tetu, and word was spread around that anyone who could follow them would be given gruel. All who came were given a daily ration of maize flour, and Tetu became like a big camp. There was great thankfulness, for although the food was insufficient to satisfy hunger, it was enough to keep away starvation. But those who were too old or sick to walk could not reach salvation.

When more wagon-loads arrived, the European in charge at Tetu said that a road would be built to Embu, and that all who wanted food must work on it. Many of the able-bodied men and women, even some elders, agreed to do so. Ngarariga, although he carried a muramati's staff and had long ago ceased to think of labour, decided to work rather than to face starvation. He carried heavy loads of soil, and was given flour each night for gruel. Slowly he, and others with him, regained their strength. It seemed that at last the worst was over. The Serkali had been able to find maize, and would keep alive all those strong enough to work.

7

BUT before the new crops were harvested a pestilence swept through the country like a flame, leaving the ground strewn with corpses. Its name was Kimiri,* and it took the form of a high

* Spanish 'flu.

fever. People would wake up cool and healthy, and within two
days they would be dead. No man dared go into another's
homestead for fear of entering a hut where a corpse had been.
By every path and roadside lay rotting corpses, their flesh moving slightly, like wind-stirred leaves, with a mass of maggots
finishing work that hyenas had begun. Some lay in the attitude
in which they had fallen, too weak to go on, a water-gourd
or an empty calabash by their side.

It was the pestilence that took Waseru, Ngarariga said. The
old man had escaped the famine, for Muthengi had sent him
food. He was feeble and nearly blind, and sat all day under
the eaves of his hut taking snuff or muttering to himself. He
asked often for his sons. Sometimes Muthengi visited him,
but not often; and he called in vain for Matu. Kimiri killed
him quickly; and within two days Wanjeri also was consumed
by the fever, as a cricket by a swift grass fire.

Throughout the land, Ngarariga continued, hunger and
plague walked like angry lions, and on every ridge half the homesteads were closed with shrubs and stank of death. Never
before had such a double disaster fallen. Three sacrifices had
been made by the elders, but God's ears were stuffed with
cloud. It was thought that he was angry because the young
men had allowed themselves to be taken away to perish in the
Europeans' war.

Waseru's wealth, which had not been great, was divided into
two. One part was shared equally between his adult sons,
Muthengi and Matu; the other part was given to Ngarariga to
hold in trust for Waseru's uncircumcised children by his surviving wife. Muthengi's inheritance would be as a drop of water
in a pool; his homestead was like the camp of the police at Tetu,
so many huts were there, and out of his great wealth he had
hired an Indian to bring food in a wagon from Nairobi so that
his wives and children had escaped famine. Nevertheless, an
equal division of his father's property was the law. The land
that Wanjeri had cultivated was shared equally between her two
sons. Matu knew that in practice his brother would secure it

all; still, half was legally his, and one day his sons might be able to claim it. He resolved to establish his right in the presence of witnesses. He therefore took Muthengi and three senior elders of the clan to the spot and planted itoka lilies, the acknowledged boundary marks of his people, in the corners of his claim. Then a fat ram was slain and eaten by the elders and the two brothers to bind the settlement, and Matu blessed them with its stomach contents mixed with blood.

8

A FEW days later, the first batch of young men returned from the war. Eight came from Tetu, walking in silence along the path with bundles of clothes and cooking-pots strapped to their backs. Their faces were gaunt and their skin tightly stretched over ribs and shoulder-blades. They looked about them with dazed, deep eyes whose glances seemed to brush indifferently over the surface of all they saw, as a mundu-mugu will brush the curse from a man with the cow's-tail stopper of his medicine gourd.

Girls and women rushed to meet the approaching party, trilling loudly with delight. Slowly the men seemed to awake out of a dream. They recognised their relatives and asked for news, but their voices were strange, like the flat note of a hollow tree struck by a club where before they had been like clear goat-bells on the mountain. Those who had left as youths returned as old men, walking slowly. Three wore beards, showing that they had been sick, and their hair was unshaven.

Ngarariga seized his staff and hurried down to see them, hope opening like a flower in his heart. He met them in the path and gazed eagerly into their faces; one at least of his sons must be there; surely Reri could not have failed to return. He recognised several of his kinsmen, but not the faces that he sought.

"Where are my sons?" he said. "Why have they not come?"

The men looked sideways at him, but no one answered. They made as if to move on. Ngarariga stood in their way, and because he was an elder they could not push him to one side.

"Why do you not answer?" Ngarariga said. "My sons went with you from the pen at Karatina. Surely they would not have stayed behind! What has become of them, of my three sons?"

"We do not know," one of them answered.

"Where have you come from?" Ngarariga insisted, "and what have you done, that you stayed so long away from your fathers' homesteads?"

"Do not ask us questions, old man," another said. His voice was loud and rough. "Can you not see that we are tired after a long journey? Stand aside, and let us pass to find our fathers."

Ngarariga was astounded to hear a young man speak with such rudeness to an elder. But his distress was so great that he could not reprimand him. He stepped to one side and leant on his staff, his face stiff with pain, while the silent group filed past him. The women followed, subdued, no longer trilling. Now he was certain that his three sons, all that he had, were dead.

In the houses of the eight who had returned the rejoicing was like matted grass over a swamp, for underneath lay a feeling of bottomless disquiet. The young men were strange and for that reason frightening; so quiet, so numb, as if they carried something dead within them and had left in a distant country their old knowledge of laughter and desire.

Nduini was one of those who welcomed home a son. He slaughtered a goat and asked his kinsmen to a feast of celebration. Although no one lacked food that night, and many young women came to the household after the feast with ochre-smeared bodies, there was no dancing and no song. After he had eaten the young man rose, saying that he was tired and needed sleep.

"Now that you have come back," Nduini said, "and the strangers' war is over, we wait to hear news of the country to which you went, and of all that became of you and the others who were captured at Karatina fifteen months ago."

The young man turned his head away as if he had seen something unclean, and said in a deep voice:

"You must not ask me of such things, for I will not speak of them so long as I live."

The young man slept and rested for many days and sat in the shade by the homestead, doing no work. Sometimes girls who walked along the path stopped to talk to him, and when he saw one that he liked energy began, little by little, to return to his limbs. But Nduini was not satisfied. Something had happened to his son that he could not understand. He went to one of those who had returned with him; and said:

"My son will not tell me anything of the places he has seen, or of what he did there; he is not well, and I think it is because of something that he saw while he was away. You are his friend, and of his age-grade; tell me what is troubling his mind."

The young man said: "Do not ask him about the things that he has seen; they are too terrible to be spoken of."

"There is much that is terrible in war," Nduini replied. "It was very terrible when the Masai fell upon us, and the corpses of our warriors and the ashes of our homes lay about us like dead cattle in a year of plague. But he who goes to a mundu-mugu may be purified, and the evil vomited away."

"Do not ask me," the young man said, "nor your son; for we who have returned have sworn an oath between us never to speak of what we have seen."

9

MATU returned to his own shamba haunted and distressed by all that he had heard; he was more than ever glad that he had come to Njoro and thus escaped both the famine and Europeans' war. The harvest had started, and he watched with satisfaction while Wanja's granaries were filled. Afterwards he sacrificed a goat and placed a little of its stomach contents mixed with fat in the granaries, thanking God for a good harvest.

One day he came back to his homestead in the grey of the

evening, at the hour when the parrots flew back to the forest, to find a strange man seated by the thingira fire. He was tall and gaunt, and under a thin blanket his ribs protruded like the branches of fire-killed trees. A big beard covered his chin and his hair was long; the pus from sores oozed through a piece of cloth bound around his ankle. When Matu entered he looked up quickly and then away again, crouching on a stool over the fire.

Matu greeted him politely and sat down opposite. He glanced at the stranger nervously, and then more closely, for something seemed familiar about his face.

After a long silence the traveller looked up at him and said : "Do you not know me, then, my cousin?"

Matu stared incredulously at the stranger, doubting his ears. The man was bearded like a cedar, his hair was matted and wild. Underneath was the shape of a head that matched another in his memory.

"Reri, son of Ngarariga !" he exclaimed.

"I come to ask food and shelter," Reri said, "for I have been very sick."

Matu reflected that Reri owed him twenty-six goats and would perhaps seduce his youngest wife, who had not forgotten her lover; but there could be no question of turning away his uncle's son.

"Peace be with you," he said. "My wives shall bring you food."

All through the evening his covert glances returned to Reri's face. He could not believe that a man could change so much. The well-preened youth who had danced till the moon was low, who could no more resist flirting with girls than the bee could keep away from the purple muthakwa blossom, was dead. Another had returned, deep-eyed and quiet, and sick in mind and body; one from whom the smooth-limbed girls would shrink nervously, or whom they would ridicule as a sort of ogre at the dances.

Reri stayed in Matu's thingira for three months, growing

T

slowly fatter and resting a great deal. Sometimes a fever would shake him violently as though with cold, and then he would break into a great sweat. At such times he would lie in the darkness of the hut covered with blankets, and Matu's young wife would take him water in a calabash.

One day Matu said to him: "How can you fail to be sick when you are so severely troubled by spirits? I will give you a goat if you will vomit out the thahu and let a mundu-mugu drive the evil away."

"The spirits that cause my sickness are not those which you can understand," Reri answered. "They come from a long way off and trouble me with memories. What I have seen is too deep and too evil to be vomited out. But I will buy a goat, and you shall cleanse me if you wish."

Reri's purification was long and thorough, and Wanja shaved his hair and beard. Matu was greatly relieved when his cousin was again recognisable as a young man. For the first time his own son Karanja was not afraid to sit in the same hut. Reri was pleased at this, and took the boy out next day to look for honey in the forest. Matu made him a charm to ensure good luck and another to bring success with women, and from the day of his purification he grew steadily stronger.

One evening he said to Matu: "Now I shall go back to my father's, since I am strong enough to walk over Nyandarua. When you come to visit me I shall give you a fat ram, for you have been generous and helped me when I was sick."

"That is good," Matu said. "When you return, Ngarariga will ask you what has become of your two brothers who went with you to the war."

"Do not speak to me of that," Reri said, "for I cannot answer."

10

HE left the next day. Matu's curiosity about the things that had occurred during the war was great, but for many years no one who had come back would speak. He never learnt the whole truth; but years afterwards, when Reri had become an elder and in his mind the fire-blackened plain of the past was hidden under fresh grasses, Matu asked if the story might be told.

Even then Reri was unwilling to speak. But Matu urged him and at last he told of how he had been captured with many others in the pen at Karatina, and then he said:

"There were four soldiers to take us, armed with rifles, and they marched us together down the road. The road was dry and the dust strong in our throats, and as we marched the noise that our feet made was ru-tu-tu-tu-tu-tu-tu on the road.

"At Thika we were put into the train and taken to Nairobi, where we were given food and blankets, and then put into another train. Here we slept together in a wagon like cattle, on the hard floor; and the noise of the wheels was tee-chee-chee-chee-chee-chee-chee on the rails.

"We stayed two days at Mombasa, and saw the sea. Wagons were moving about on it without reason, each one following its own purpose, like a bird. We did not know where we were being taken, or for what purpose.

"After two days we were put into this wagon on the sea. We were locked into a small room with iron walls. Then the room began to move about beneath our feet: it was as if we had been in the belly of an animal. We were so frightened that we could not speak. Twice we were taken up out of the room, and that was worse, because we could see nothing but water in any direction and no land anywhere. When we died our spirits would be lost and hungry in the sea, forever unable to return to the land of our own clan. There was one who jumped out, meaning to swim back while there was yet time; but he was drowned.

"But we saw land again at a place called Dar-es-Salaam, and came out of the ship, and were put into a train which went to Morogoro. Here we were told not to drink water from the wells, as the enemy had put poison into them. We were very thirsty and many did not believe that such big springs could be poisoned. They went to drink the water, and all who did so were seized with pains in the stomach and died. They were buried together in a big ditch, but we could not leave that place, and we stayed there carrying very heavy stones to build houses.

"After two months we went by train to Dodoma, and there we were told to walk for ten days to Iringa. No Europeans went with us, and no soldiers, only guides; but we could not run away, for everywhere there was nothing but bush. We were given ten oxen at Dodoma and told to kill one every night, and that on the eleventh day we would reach Iringa. We marched for many days. The sun made our heads like pots of gruel boiling on the fire, and our feet went ru-tu-tu-tu-tu-tu-tu through the bush. On the way many people got diarrhœa. Some could no longer walk, but lay down and were left behind, and the hyenas ate them. I had diarrhœa, but was able to walk, and soon we came to a camp of soldiers and I went with my brother and another man to see a European. Many people were dying under the same roof without being taken away; that building had a dreadful curse; there was death in it, and an evil smell. So I ran away and went to cut firewood; but when I inquired for my brother I was told that he had died.

"We left that place and went on to a big river like a lake, where men took us across in boats. On the other side was a camp. Here a sickness fell upon me again and I was taken to another hospital; but people were dying all around me, and after two days I escaped in the night. Next day I went to work digging ditches, although my limbs were weak.

"A month later we marched on again; we reached some mountains, and then a country as cold as our own. We stayed at a place called the camp of bullets. It was on the top of a hill. We carried bullets down to the bottom, where wounded men were taken, and we carried wounded men back to the top. Sometimes they died on the way, but we still had to carry them, and to defile ourselves with corpses; and at night we were too tired to cook food.

"From the camp of bullets we were taken to a place where we had to dig graves and to bury those who had been killed. We had to lay our hands on corpses. There were two flags, a red one and a white. When the red flag was hoisted we were told to stop work and lie down. When the white flag was put up we had again to bury corpses.

"There was a European in charge. He walked up and down with a stick in his mouth, and this stick was a form of magic, because bullets flew all around his head and over his shoulders, but he was never struck. Some of us were struck, and many more died from sickness. A man who was working close to me was struck in the wrist. He looked at his wrist and his blood gushed over me like a waterfall, and there was blood even in my eyes. He fell down to the ground and died at my feet, away from his own clan.

"I was no longer afraid to touch corpses. I wished to die, and therefore no danger could come to me from thahu. I walked about seeking a bullet that would kill me, but I could not find one. I did not think that I should ever see my home again. Sometimes I dreamt of home, but we did not speak of our own country at all in the camp, because we tried to keep our minds empty of such thoughts that hurt us more than hunger or wounds.

"One day an enemy was captured bringing a letter to the European officer. When the European read it he laughed loudly and said : 'Do not kill the askari, for now there will be no more fighting, either on land or sea.' A soldier told us that we would be taken home, but we did not believe it. We carried many heavy boxes of bullets to a place called the camp of lorries, and then we walked through the bush for ten days, carrying many sick on stretchers, until we reached the railway. My second brother was with me, and he fell sick, and on this journey he died.

"We went to Dar-es-Salaam, and after a month I was put into a ship and told that I was to be taken to Mombasa. But this did not make me happy, for I did not want to live. I saw Mombasa and thought that I was dreaming; but when I reached Nairobi I understood that I had come home. At

Nairobi I was given seventy rupees and told that I would be taken to Tetu. I did not want to see my father then, for my sickness had returned and I feared that he would ask for my two brothers. I left my companions there and came by train to your homestead until I should die, or be rid of my sickness.

" Those of us who returned agreed that we would never speak of the things that had occurred, because they are too evil to be mentioned; and even now I have not told you all of what I saw, for words do not exist to describe such things. Sometimes these things return to me in dreams, and then I wake and I cannot sleep again. Sometimes, when I see a European, they come back to me also, because it was the Europeans who captured me and the evils that swallowed me when they took me for the war were caused by them. But now I have a wife and children, and I do not often think of such things any more."

BOOK III : KARANJA
1919-1937

CHAPTER I

Marafu

I

KARANJA was startled out of his doze in the shade of an acacia by the thump of hooves near his head. He jumped up, clutching his wooden spear, fearful for the safety of his father's goats. He had grown to be a thin, light-skinned boy of an age when the ceremony of second birth had recently been celebrated in his mother's hut, and he had been born into his clan. Shortly before, his eye-teeth had been taken out to make a gap through which gruel could be poured should evil spirits ever bind together his jaws.

Through the tall grass he could see the speckled backs of his charges, and beyond, advancing quickly towards him, one animal, red-faced, seated on top of another, tall-eared. With a moan of fright he turned and fled, scuttling like a guinea-fowl through grass and bush to his father's homestead.

Matu listened to his son's incoherent story calmly, took his old and rusty spear from the back of his hut, and went out to see what had occurred.

"There are no animals here that are likely to eat you," he reassured Karanja, "but it may be that something strange has come out of the forest."

But when he saw the animal bobbing through the grass in front he turned his head and chuckled. Karanja clutched at his father's blanket for security. He now saw that behind the animal marched a line of Kikuyu men with loads on their backs and heads.

"Do you not know what this creature is?" Matu said. "It is harmless, and certainly does not eat children. It is a European riding on a tame animal. He has put a piece of iron into its mouth to bind its anger. He says to it : clk-clk-clk-clk, like a hen, and that makes it move."

Karanja had never before seen a European, for he had been herding goats in forest glades whenever one had come to the Mau.

Before evening Matu knew that this European had come to stay, for he had brought with him many goods. He was very tall, so he was called Marafu; his hair was red. One leg was stiff; for this reason he walked with a limp and preferred to be carried by animals.

Next morning Karanja herded the goats in another direction. Not for several days could he summon courage enough to venture close to the big square house. He approached delicately, glances recoiling before strange shapes; and then, without warning, a terrible noise beat upon his ears and two wild animals of the utmost ferocity leapt out at him like maddened lions. He ran desperately for shelter and barely slacked speed until he reached the homestead.

That evening, in the thingira, his father laughed at him again.

"I have seen those animals," he said. "Europeans have them in the house to keep away thieves. Sometimes they seem to value them more than children. I have been told that Europeans believe that the spirits of their ancestors dwell in these beasts. We have no name for them but in Swahili they are called dogs. You must not run away, or they will bite; if you stand still they, too, will stand; if you touch them gently and say : 'Go in peace,' they will go, and not trouble you."

Karanja heard, but it was a long time before he dared to approach the European's house again. He was kept busy herding goats and learning how to look after cattle. His father had proved the truth of the saying 'wealth is like shade'; possessions had grown as life advanced, and now he could afford a small herd of cows. Karanja was given nothing for his herding, but he observed that his mother received coins from the Indians at Njoro when she sold her surplus maize and potatoes; so he decided to start a shamba of his own. He dug a small strip of garden behind the homestead at a time when he should have been looking after goats, and worked at this for several days. The goats, however, strayed on to a neighbour's shamba and ate some young maize, and the owner brought a case against Matu before the elders' council.

Matu was very angry, but Wanja said : "Do not rebuke him, or he will not wish to cultivate any more. He shall call his friends to help; and then he can dig in his shamba early in the morning and herd goats or calves for the rest of the day." So she bought green bananas in the market, packed them in a gourd with leaves of the tree makurue to ripen, and prepared a feast; and Karanja asked boys from all the homesteads around to cultivate his shamba. One day he walked into market behind his mother with a small sack of his own maize to sell. But when he got the money he did not know what to do with it. He was not old enough to buy ornaments; so he buried it under the floor of his mother's hut.

2

SOON after the European Marafu came he called all the men to a meeting. He was unable to speak to them, but an overseer announced :

"This European, whom you must address as bwana, has bought all this land and intends to cultivate a very big shamba. Everyone living on his land must come to work for him for one month and then rest for one month, so that in every European's year a man will work for bwana for six months and go home for six months to work for himself. And for each month that a man works for bwana, he will be paid six rupees.

"Every man may cultivate a shamba and may keep his goats and cattle on bwana's land; but henceforth he must on no account cut down or injure any trees."

A few days later an officer from the Serkali came and called each man before him in turn. Matu was asked his name and circumcision age and many other questions, and told to press his fingers on to a dark substance and then on to two pieces of paper; and he saw that his fingers left black smudges on the white. He was given one of the pieces of paper and told to keep it carefully, for it would protect him from being taken or molested by the Serkali or by other Europeans. He made a little goatskin bag and kept it on a chain around his neck, thinking that if it protected him from such things it must be a very powerful magic indeed. He heard later that its name was Kipande, and that it was given away for nothing.

Every morning Matu went to dig big stumps out of Marafu's shamba. Oxen came, very big ones, and were made to drag the stumps away; but stumps were many, and the rains were approaching, and it became apparent that the shamba would not be ready in time.

One morning Matu saw, to his great alarm, a large party of wild, foreign-looking men, their hair done in plaits and a queue like Masai, walking across the shamba at the heels of the overseer Kimani. Yet they looked too savage and unkempt for Masai, and they spoke in a strange tongue. They did not know in the least how to use any implements for digging, and they made fools of themselves trying to learn. But they knew at once how to handle oxen.

That night a meeting of married men was summoned and Matu learnt that they belonged to a tribe called Kipsigis.

"These people are very bad indeed," Kagama said. "They steal cattle continually and are enemies of the Kikuyu, and they also have many very powerful sorcerers among them. The Kikuyu cannot live at peace with these thieves. We will tell Marafu that they must go."

The message was delivered, but it received a very rude reply. Marafu said that the Kipsigis were to stay, and that if the Kikuyu objected they, and not the Kipsigis, must go. The Kikuyu said nothing, but they would not approach close to the Kipsigis, and the work of stumping went more slowly still. Marafu came and shouted at them in the manner of Europeans, like an angry child, but they paid no attention.

3

THEN, as the Kikuyu had feared, cows began to disappear. A boma belonging to Kagama's brother was broken into and two heifers stolen. The owner complained next morning and Marafu sent men to search among the Kipsigis, who lived in a group of huts by themselves. But there was no sign of the heifers; whether they had been eaten overnight and the bones buried, or whether they had been hidden in the forest, nobody knew. Marafu sent a message that the Kikuyu were to cease making false accusations against the Kipsigis. This made the Kikuyu very angry, and they began to talk of leaving Marafu and finding land elsewhere.

Worse was to follow. It became apparent that the Kipsigis were making magic against the Kikuyu. Several men awoke in the night to hear mysterious rustlings in the thatch and the sound of light missiles striking the roof on the side nearest to the Kipsigis' huts. After that things began to go wrong. Kagama's youngest wife, in her first pregnancy, bore premature twins which had to be suffocated and buried, since it was no longer safe to leave corpses in the bush for fear of Europeans. The eldest child of his brother fell into the fire and was too badly burnt to survive, and two of Matu's heifer calves sickened and died within three days. To confirm the cause of these disasters—if confirmation were needed—twigs were found on several paths arranged in such a way that sorcery could not be doubted. Practically no one went to work the next day, and when Kimani came to summon the men they refused to go. Marafu sent messages that if they did not come each one would lose a month's pay; but they still paid no attention.

Kagama took a goat to Matu and asked him to lay a retaliatory curse on the Kipsigis. Matu had first to send a colleague by train to Kiambu to fetch special medicines from plants which did not grow on the Mau. He mixed them with the blood and stomach contents of the goat, put them in the spike of a mununga tree and gave them to a young man, with instructions to take the medicine three times in a circle around the Kipsigis' encampment and then to bury it under the path that they took to work.

The medicine took effect within ten days. A Kipsigis brought an axe down on his companion's leg, fracturing the bone. The man was bound up by Marafu, put in a wagon, and taken to the train at Njoro; but he never returned.

The same night another Kikuyu boma was broken into and a heifer stolen; and after that a guard of young men was set over all the cattle bomas at sunset. The youths no longer owned spears, but they had heavy-headed clubs and digging-knives. For two nights nothing happened; but on the morning of the third day the body of a Kipsigis youth was found clubbed to death in the bush not far from Kagama's homestead.

Since he had been a thief caught in the act and therefore executed legally, and without blood-price obligations, no one expected the matter to go further. But Marafu sent a messenger to Nakuru and next day a European of the Serkali arrived with two Wakamba assistants. For several days after that all was confusion and trouble. Everyone was questioned, bullied, rudely spoken to and generally annoyed. Since European law, for some unaccountable reason, seemed to support the thief, and since Marafu was known to be on the side of the Kipsigis, everyone denied all knowledge of the execution. In the middle of the disturbance the Kipsigis ran away in the night in a body, leaving a sense of great relief behind them.

When it was certain that the Serkali's agents had gone, two young men drove a goat to Matu's to be purified and have their heads shaved and rubbed with fat. Everyone then knew whose club had protected Kikuyu property against the thieves; but Marafu apparently did not notice, or at any rate said no more. He had bought a big implement made of metal discs that turned the soil astonishingly quickly, and every day the shamba grew, although by now the rains had come and the land could not be got ready in time for the crop. But this was a small matter; there would be other seasons, and Marafu, like all

Europeans, was obviously so rich that he would not be troubled
by famine if he missed a crop.

4

KARANJA had a sister called Wamboi, three years younger than
he. She was old enough to go with Wanja to the shamba and
prod the soil with a knife, or to the forest for firewood or twine,
or to the river to carry back a small gourd of water, and she had
a little pot in which she sometimes cooked beans and maize on a
fire of her own behind Wanja's hut. One day she was taken ill
and could eat no food. She lay on the bed all day, shivering
with fever. Matu consulted the beans. They revealed that the
girl's mother had a thahu. Although its cause was obscure he
purified his wife and daughter with a goat. Unfortunately,
however, some detail went wrong. Wamboi grew no better
and Karanja fell sick, showing the same symptoms.

Matu, now seriously alarmed, decided to seek help from
Marafu, who appeared to be a mundu-mugu—he kept many
medicines in bottles in his house—and might know of a way to
reject the evil spirits on his own land.

Karanja and Wamboi were led, shivering and dragging their
feet, to Marafu's house. He came out to them holding a small
white stick with markings on it which he put into Karanja's
mouth. Matu watched with interest; this was a new kind of
magic altogether. Marafu took it out and examined it, and
then frowned.

"This child go Nakuru," he said.   He had learnt a little Swahili, but spoke it badly. "Very sick. I take inside motor-car."

Matu heard this in dismay; he could not let his children go
out of his sight to be cared for by strangers.

"It is not good for the girl to go," he ventured.

"All two go," Marafu replied firmly.

He had lately brought a motor-car to the farm. It roared
like a lion on the hills and went very swiftly, although it did not
like going out in the morning. It was bright red and had a box

behind in which people might sit. Matu watched his children clambering in with great sadness. He did not believe that they were being taken to Nakuru and he never expected to see them again.

Karanja's sickness was so heavy that even the roaring in his ears and the contortions of the boards on which he sat had no power to frighten him. He remembered little until he found himself lying on a bed. Around him, instead of the warm smoky darkness of a hut, was the glare of daylight. A blanket covered him and there were beds all around, like goats on a hill, and an unpleasant smell.

He lay there for many days, waiting for death. A man came often to thrust a white stick into his mouth, and another to give him sweet milk or medicines. Sometimes a European dressed in white approached and touched his eyes, or looked into his mouth. Gradually Karanja realised that the medicine was indeed driving out the evil spirits and not killing him, as he had supposed. The fever ebbed away and strength slowly replaced it. One day a man came to wash him all over with hot water, and he took this to mean that the purification was now complete. He was surprised, however, to find that this ceremony was repeated every day.

He was given milk and eggs to eat, and was soon allowed to walk about in the afternoon. He found that in the hospital were Kikuyu attendants who knew how to use the magic of the Europeans. They could draw the shape of words and understand the markings on the white stick and mix medicines, for which no goats' stomachs were used. They were conscious of their importance, and ordered sick people about with great authority. They wore clothes like Europeans, and Karanja knew that they must be fabulously rich. He admired them with all his spirit, and was filled with a great ambition to become like them when he was circumcised.

The hospital contained many strange things. The strangest of all was a big iron box where fire was kept and on which vast quantities of food were cooked in iron pots. When Karanja realised that food for everyone was cooked together he could not bring himself to eat, fearing poison; but hunger overcame his terror.

He was disappointed when, one day, an attendant told him that he must go. He walked home all day along a wide road. His parents greeted him with surprise and joy, for they had already mourned him as dead.

"Certainly Europeans have some good magic," Matu admitted. "Evidently their white stick can repel powerful spirits. All the same, I do not think that any cure can be certain or lasting without the sacrifice of a goat."

Karanja said nothing, but in his mind he was convinced that the Europeans knew a stronger magic than his father.

A few days later Marafu went away in his motor-car and returned with Wamboi in the back. She, too, had recovered. Now no doubt was left in Karanja's mind as to the power of the Europeans' medicines.

5

AFTER this adventure Marafu's house drew Karanja as a beehive in a hollow tree draws the bee-eater. He herded the goats so close to it that they trampled a clump of bright, sweet-smelling flowers and ate several shrubs. Karanja was chased away by a man in a long white robe, and Matu was fined three rupees. He forbade his son to go near the house again.

Karanja was too fascinated to obey. The house was like a dream; there was no telling what was going to happen next. Once, early in the morning, he saw Marafu's face entirely covered with what he took to be white chalk, and he knew that some magical ceremony was going on. In the evening he watched a huge iron pot full of water being taken in, perhaps for a sacrifice or a purification. He heard that Marafu had a kind of beer not made from sugar-cane or honey, so strong that when Marafu's servant drank no more than half a horn-full, he staggered as if he had been beaten on the head and fell down unconscious to the floor. There was a great panic, for everyone thought that he had been poisoned, and the other men who worked for Marafu ran away. Marafu found out and was very angry; and after that no one dared to touch the European's beer again.

One day Marafu went away for fifteen days and returned with a wife. Everyone who worked in the house was annoyed, for European women, as a general rule, were shrill-voiced, lazy, and bad-tempered. The ways of Europeans were always inexplicable, and most inexplicable of all was their failure to control their wives. Their women did not cook for them, left others to sweep and build the fire, never worked in the shamba; yet they did not seem to beat their wives, and they allowed them to argue and disobey. The wives, moreover, were grossly lacking in respect. They ate with their husbands, even meat; and the husbands often made open displays of physical affection, a thing no decent man would do. It could only be supposed that European women possessed some very powerful and secret magic to cause injury to any husband with whom they grew displeased. Charagu, Marafu's head servant, said that this was so. He had known of a case where a husband displeased his wife by talking too often to another woman. His wife went away and left him, and shortly afterwards the man fell sick and died.

Marafu's wife soon troubled the cook. She had the comfortable smoky kitchen, with its three hearth-stones and its ample space for all comers, pulled down and a new one built. An iron box to contain fire was installed and many unnecessary instructions issued about washing pots and driving out rats. Marafu became no better than a fool. He obeyed her orders, as if he had been a woman and she a man, and waited upon her, instead of she on him. No room was left for surmise; she had undoubtedly bewitched him. Charagu and the cook were sorry for him, but they knew that they must show as much respect to his wife as to him, or else he would become very angry.

Soon after her arrival she ordered an uncircumcised boy to

help Charagu in the house, and Karanja, who had been watching for such an opportunity, was engaged at three rupees a month.

Matu was upset about this, but he said nothing. He did not know who would herd his cattle and goats while Karanja was working for Marafu and Matu's wives were busy in the shambas. In the old days a boy would not have dared to make such a decision for himself. He was angry, too, because a European from the Serkali had ordered all married men to pay a tax of eight rupees for every hut. Matu had handed over twenty-four rupees, dug up out of the floor of his hut. He had been told that all the rupees were finished and that something called shillings were to take their place; in fact that year's circumcision-age had been named Shillingi, to mark the event. It was all very confusing; things were always changing and no one could tell what would happen next. Perhaps the old days, with all their raids and dangers, had been better after all.

6

OF the many curious things that Karanja saw in Marafu's house, the most remarkable was the way in which a spring could be summoned out of a hole in the wall, and then made to cease again. He spent many hours twisting a piece of metal to cause this miracle, until Charagu found him, and cuffed him on the head. He could not find out where the water came from. Nor could he understand what was meant when Charagu brought him some of the vessels that the Europeans used for eating and drinking, and said, "Wash these." Karanja replied:

"How can I, when they are already clean?"

Charagu showed him a little dark liquid in the bottom of two vessels, and said:

"Fool, have you no eyes? Europeans will have no dirt or stain on any vessel, just as there are no hairs on the back of a lizard."

Karanja marvelled at such an idea, for at home a calabash would go many days without washing. When he went inside the European house he saw that everything was very clean. Even the ashes of the fire were taken away every morning. There was no smell save that of plucked flowers. For the first time he realised that in his own home there was a great deal of dirt. On the other hand a hut was warm, whereas the European house was bitterly cold, and he wondered how Marafu and his wife could sleep at nights. It was fortunate that Marafu was rich enough to afford many blankets, and not afraid that leopards would jump in through the open hole in the wall.

Charagu told him that he must not enter a European house in the piece of cloth, stained with red ochre, that he wore knotted on one shoulder. He was given six shillings and told to buy a shirt from the Indian, and a pair of shorts to clothe his legs. He strutted back as proudly as a cockerel, feeling that he was now just like a European. But sometimes European clothes were an embarrassment, and when he went to the latrine he left his shorts behind in the kitchen. Charagu and the others laughed at him and he ran away and hid in mortification; but after that he learnt how to deal with shorts. Charagu also gave him a lump of fat and told him to rub it between his hands in water. Karanja identified its smell as that of Europeans. He was pleased that he was now like a European in smell as well as in looks. He began to despise young men who smeared themselves with ochre, which Charagu said was very dirty. For some time he could not, however, bring himself to eat European food, which was tasteless, unsatisfying, and frequently unclean.

He soon became fascinated by the magic which he learnt to know as writing. He would sit in a rapt silence and watch Charagu tracing signs with his stick on the white bark. Charagu often sent messages in this way to his friends in Nairobi or Kiambu, and sometimes replies would be brought back by a man sent on a horse to the station. When Karanja realised that a Kikuyu like himself could do such things he was filled with wonder, as though for the first time he had heard a bird sing; and thoughts raced through him with such speed that it seemed as if a high wind was whirling overhead.

One day Charagu saw him gazing at a piece of bark covered with designs like those on the gechande, the rattle-gourd of a singer. He laughed and asked:

"Do you wish to understand such things?"

Karanja stared at him and said: "Yes."

"Then I am willing to teach you," Charagu remarked, "in the evenings, when Marafu has eaten. But I cannot, of course, do this for nothing. You must pay me half your wages."

Karanja agreed at once. He had no use for his shillings; there was nothing that he wanted to buy. Charagu gave him a stick and a piece of bark and taught him at night, when he had nothing better to do, by the light of the kitchen lamp. Karanja discovered that words could be broken into many small pieces, like grains of maize ground between stones, and that each fragment had a different shape and could be drawn. Laboriously and wonderingly he learnt the shape of each sound, and how to mix them together to make simple words. So the miracle of transforming sounds into sights was gradually revealed to him. For a long time he could not control the pencil, nor understand how the sounds of the many symbols could be bound together into one word. But after his lesson he would walk home under a brilliant moon or a great sheet of milk-white stars, more than a little afraid of leopards in the dark bush, his head dizzy with sleep but his heart filled with the glory of his own knowledge. His mother chided him a little for being out so late, and his father ignored him. But he was indifferent to their censure; for he, a boy, already understood a great magic, of which they, his elders, were ignorant.

7

WHEN Karanja had been with Marafu for two years, his father decided to have him circumcised. The ceremony was held on the farm next to Marafu's, where Matu had found a fig-tree near the river. A skilled circumciser was sent for from Kiambu and permission obtained from Marafu to brew much honey-beer.

The candidates painted their legs and chests with lime but refused to rub themselves with ochre and fat because they said it was dirty. Kagama (who had been elected mathanjiku in charge of events) and the other elders were upset at this breach of custom, but they could not say anything. All young men now cropped their hair, like Europeans, and were even ceasing to have their ears pierced and to wear ornaments in the lobes. But in all important respects the full details of the ceremony were carried out, and Matu paid his fee to the council and was initiated into the secrets of elders of the third grade.

For fourteen days before the ceremony Karanja attended dances held every night on different farms along the Mau. The elders, combining together, bought an ox from Marafu, which the youths roasted and ate. When the day came Karanja was the best-dressed candidate of all. He had collected, at various times, much finery for the occasion, but of a different kind from that which his father had used. He wore a bright-striped European jersey, and two stiff white collars in place of Colobus skins around his wrists. His legs were swathed in rattles made of small cans filled with stones. In his ears he wore yellow cigarette tins and he carried a bright malacca cane. He had also given presents to his sister Wamboi, who was circumcised on the same day. She wore a purple veil across her body draped with strings of cowrie shells, and European women's stockings wound around her head; and she carried proudly in her hand something that no one else had got: an open umbrella. The name given to the age was Gechande, in honour of a troubadour who went up and down the Kikuyu country at this season with his rattle-gourd singing a lewd but highly entertaining song.

Karanja had grown into a tall, willowy youth with long, straight legs and a light skin that came to him with his Masai blood. His face was alert and quick to change expression, and his observant eyes missed little. He knew that his good features and his skill at the dance caused the girls to glance at him with long, soft looks and to address him in high, rippling voices. Nor was his agile mind slow to invent neatly-phrased and pointed songs with which to lead the chorus. One of the youths of his age-grade grew jealous; Karanja, he said, deceived the girls with boasting lies and was at heart a coward. Karanja knew this to be untrue. He was not afraid to eat European food, to drink their strange medicines, to use a latrine or to approach a horse, all things which his father, even now, could not have brought himself to do. He laughed at his circumcision-brother and said : "Do girls seek out a coward? If the Masai came as they used to I would slay ten warriors single-handed." He was glad, however, that there were no Masai to slay.

8

AFTER Karanja's wounds were healed his father suggested that he should work for Marafu to earn his own tax, for which he would now be liable. But Karanja refused. A restlessness was on him. His feet itched to feel the dust of unknown paths, his eyes to gaze upon new things and the faces of strange people.

"Now I have become like a python in a pool," he said to his father. "The river flows down from above, but where does it come from? And it hurries on below, yet I do not know where it is going. For a year I shall do no work, but I shall walk about the world to seek its beginning and its end and to find out about all the people who are in it."

Matu disliked this talk, but he did not protest. Instead, he gave his son powerful charms to guide his feet in safety and to avert lions and rhinos. "Go, if you must," he said, "and go in peace; and may God guide your feet back to this homestead."

Karanja took as his companion on his journey a young man of his own circumcision-age called Karioki. He was a strong, thick-featured youth, with a ready smile and an even readier temper. By nature he was obstinate, and quicker to justify a breach of manners than to show regret. He was lazy, too, and preferred to gossip and crack jokes with his fellows in the shade than to attend to his father's goats or help his mother cultivate.

Whenever his father asked a near kinsman to reprimand him he would grow sulky, and disappear for several days together. But he was liked by other boys for his lively tongue and his ability to tell a story. The girls liked him too, although not as much as he believed they did, for he was very vain of his appearance.

After his circumcision he wandered, with his friend Karanja, over many European farms, dancing and singing every night. But then his father was called to work for Marafu and asked Karioki to tend the goats. Karioki looked sullen and made no reply. The next morning he disappeared. His father was shaken with a deep anger at this undutiful behaviour.

"Tell Karioki that he is my son no longer!" he exclaimed in his rage. "Only when he brings a ram in token of repentance will I forgive him, or consider the payment of bride-price for whatever girl he desires as wife!"

The elder did not doubt that these bitter words would bring Karioki back at once; but Matu, whose thoughts were deep, shook his head.

"Life is no longer the same," he said. "In your youth and mine we could not have insulted our fathers; we feared the anger of the elders, and only our fathers could provide us with wives. But now Europeans teach their magic to children, so that uncircumcised boys are like elders, and elders like infants in arms. Your son Karioki, and my son Karanja—can they not go to work for Europeans and thus themselves find shillings to buy goats to pay for their brides?"

Matu, it proved was right: Karioki did not return to his father. Instead, he disappeared with Karanja, his friend, in search of the beginning and the end of the world. They walked away together one morning in their clean new shorts and shirts, their only luggage a light stick held as their ancestors had clasped the spear. It was a year before Matu saw his son again.

CHAPTER 11

Pig's Meat

I

KARANJA and Karioki visited many places together, receiving hospitality wherever they went from women with sons of the age-grade Gechande, young men who were as brothers to themselves.

They went first to Elburgon, a land of tall, sweet-smelling cedars and deep-grassed glades. Here they saw an engine that chattered all day and a bright whirring wheel that bit into the red cedar trunks with a high scream of anger like many swarms of bees. They watched with awe as the great trunks fell apart and were carved into sections, as a man might slice a banana with his knife. Kikuyu like themselves were tending the savage tree-eater; but the cry of the great knife was disturbing and the nights were cold and spirit-haunted. Karanja and Karioki were uneasy, and they continued along the road.

They passed over a land of wild, wind-swept pastures bounded by abrupt black walls of forest, a country of horizons curved as gently as if the earth had become the body of a sleeping girl. But the winds were cold, the air light as a petal, and they walked on until they came to a land of smooth, tumbling hills, steeped in brilliant green, that lay beyond. Here, when the sun dropped half-way down the sky, a purple storm rolled out of the west, swiftly as a flight of cranes, and flung itself against the hills. At sunset the travellers looked in vain for the friendly shape of a Kikuyu hut. Strange men with long hair dressed like Masai passed them on the road. They carried spears, and gazed before them with the proud, hostile eye of hawks. These men, they knew, were Nandi, a savage race of greater ferocity even than the Masai. They trudged on wearily under a web of stars until they reached a cluster of lights centring around a station on the railway line. Here, at last, they found men of their own race, and were given shelter and food.

That evening, in the far distance, they had glimpsed the shining waters of a great lake; another world lay below their questing feet. But the next morning they turned and retraced their path. That world was full of hostile people who would not give them food; it was best left unexplored.

2

AT Londiani, on the homeward path, they met a European who offered them work. He had three long wagons and three teams of oxen, and he wished to carry many wooden cases to a distant place called Eldoret. Karanja and Karioki told him that they were experienced in the work of driving oxen. As soon as they had started, the European, who was of a different tribe to Marafu, saw that they could not wield the heavy, long-thonged whips, and was very angry; but when he had finished shouting at them he agreed to teach them the work. They found it difficult, and repeatedly wound the thongs of the whips around themselves as if they had been insects in cocoons. Slowly they learnt to crack the whip with the noise of a snapping branch, to call each ox by name in a voice which compelled it to obey, and to know at once when an animal used cunning to keep its harness taut but to withhold its full weight.

Every morning they yoked the oxen as dawn broke and walked beside them swinging their whips until the sun was high. They rested in the afternoon, whilst the outspanned oxen munched grass amid a cloak of flies. Again through the evening they took the rutted road. White dust hung above them by day, but towards evening it turned golden in the sun and a bright halo enveloped them as they lumbered onwards to the north.

At night they chopped thorn branches to make a low boma for the oxen and cooked their evening meal under the stars. The

European shared their food, and later rolled up in his blankets beside them underneath the wagons. They themselves talked of many things, often telling stories and riddles until the night was half over. One evening Karanja told his companions this tale:

"There was once a very old man who went on a long journey. He was so old that he could not walk, so he told his four sons to carry him on their shoulders. The sons did so, but the path was rough and the old man was so jolted and bumped about that he complained loudly, groaning and crying out in a high voice: 'You are hurting me, do not go so fast.' But the sons paid no attention.

"Presently he saw that there were many brown objects moving along in front. They, too, were travelling across the plain, and they always kept the same distance away. He said to his sons: 'Why do you follow these ogres? I believe you are taking me to a place where you can kill me.' But the sons went on carrying him, and one answered: 'It is all right, they are only rocks that are rolling away.'

"Then he noticed that beyond the rocks was a black object moving in front of him across the plain. He cried out again, saying: 'Why do you follow that black object, I believe it must be the devil!' But the sons said: 'It is all right, that is only a carrion crow.'

"The old man groaned again, and then he heard a loud noise in the air repeated many times. He cried out in a high voice to his sons: 'Put me down, I am frightened, there are spirits in the air coming to kill me.' But the sons went on carrying him and said: 'It is all right, the noise is made by a blacksmith shaping a knife on his anvil.'

"That night when they stopped to rest the old man was very frightened, so in the night he called on a spirit to put a lot of big stones on the path. The next morning when they started off one of the sons fell over a stone and was killed. The others said: 'No matter, we will go on, and three of us will carry him.' But the old man was heavy, he was jolted more than ever before.

Presently another son fell over a stone and was killed also. This happened to all four sons, and when they were dead the old man lay helpless in the road.

"Then a European came along and saw him and said : 'What is this useless old man doing here? He cannot carry a load, he is no good to anyone; we will take all his skins and ornaments away.' So they left him naked, and very soon he died, for there was no one to carry him to the end of his journey. Now, what is the answer to this riddle?"

Karanja's companions laughed and one said : "I can tell you the answer. The old man is the wagon, and his sons are the wheels. The rocks are the oxen that walk ahead, the bird is the boy Karoma who leads the oxen, and the blows of the smith are the sounds of the long whips. The old man groans and squeaks a great deal, but all the same he cannot go forward without his sons, the wheels, to carry him. If they are broken he will lie helpless by the side of the road and a European will come and take away everything in the wagon."

"That is the right answer," Karanja said.

3

ELDORET lay beyond a broad plain bare of trees or rivers, and they were glad to reach their journey's end. They took their wages and refused to continue, and they found themselves alone in a strange land.

Eldoret was a disappointment. It was true that there were many Indian shops full of alluring goods, a few crowded eating-houses, and a place where for a few cents they could buy mugs of beer; but they could find no youths of their age-grade, no dances, and no girls of their own race. They met a man of their tribal group who gave them a bed in a small house of mud, but it was full of lice, and cold, for there was no fire.

After a few days Karanja said : "This is a bad place; we have to buy our own food and cook it ourselves; and what sort of a life is that? Besides, we have not yet come to the farthest point to which one can travel, where the road ends. Let us leave Eldoret, and see how far the road takes us."

Their plans were overheard, and when they were standing outside an Indian shop debating whether they could afford a smart felt hat, a man came up to them and said:

"I hear that you wish to go to the farthest point to which one can travel by road, beyond which there is nothing. It so happens that I am going to that place to-morrow in a large motorcar, and I can take you if you would like to come."

Karanja and Karioki stared at the man with suspicion. He was a Kikuyu, but they did not like his looks. He wore smart European clothes, but he was fat and he wore a fringe of hair on his upper lip. They noticed with interest that his ear-lobes had been cut and sealed up so that they contained no holes for ornaments.

A man who was examining a blanket looked up and laughed. "Do not listen to him," he remarked to Karanja. "Do you not know that beyond this country there is another one called Uganda? He is trying to cheat you, knowing that you are ignorant youths."

"Ho, so here is a schoolmaster talking," the well-dressed man exclaimed angrily. " Ask him to tell you about Uganda, and about Europe, where no doubt he has been—he, a man dressed in a blanket, who does not even wear proper clothes! As for me, I know nothing—I, Robinson, who have been six times to Uganda and am a Christian, an educated man, and have a house in Nairobi!"

Karanja was half impressed, half sceptical, and began to turn away.

"If you do not believe me, I can prove to you that I am a Christian," Robinson said. "I carry this sign that I am a follower of the European God; if an enemy comes to strike me and touches this, he will instantly fall down dead."

Robinson pulled out of his shirt a small shining charm in the form of a metal cross suspended around his neck. Karanja gazed at it with interest, and, in spite of himself, with awe. It must indeed be a powerful charm, he thought, even a smith's bangle did not kill at touch. "How much does it cost to get to this place that you speak of, to the end of the road?" Karioki asked.

Robinson waved his hand. "I am a rich man, and do not take money from those I call my friends," he said. "Since, however, it is a long way, and food is expensive there, I will make a small charge; one shilling for each man to go, and one to return."

"That is a very big charge," Karanja said. "But perhaps we will pay it, if you are quite certain that we shall return in safety."

At noon next day they kept their appointment with Robinson at the Indian shop, and started out perched on top of a load of sacks and cases. There were half a dozen others with them, but they were thick-set, thick-lipped men from Kavirondo who understood few Swahili words. A little before sunset they stopped near a big house belonging to a European. Robinson said that everyone must sleep the night there and that he would arrange it; and he asked Karanja and Karioki for their shillings. They paid up, although unwillingly. He led them up to the European's house, saying that the servants would find them beds. An overseer came out and gave Robinson eight shillings. Robinson walked away towards the lorry, and Karanja never saw him again.

When the overseer asked for their kipandis, Karanja and Karioki realised that a terrible mistake had been made. They refused to produce them and an angry dispute followed. The European was sent for, and he said that they must stay on his farm and work.

"But we do not want to work for you," Karioki said. He was shaking all over with rage.

"What sort of a fool are you?" the European shouted. Neither Karanja nor Karioki liked him; he blustered, and had the manners of a baboon. "Why, then, did you come here with Robinson, whom I sent to Eldoret to fetch men who were willing to work for me?"

"Robinson said nothing to us of work," Karioki answered.

"We paid him two shillings each to take us to Uganda. Give us our shillings back, and we will go."

"You lie, you stupid fools," the European said. "Here men are beaten when they tell lies. Give me your kipandis at once. You came here to work; enough, you shall work; and if you run away I shall have you brought back and beaten."

Karioki wanted to refuse his kipandi, but Karanja said: "It is no use, we must do as he says; we were cheated by Robinson, who has sold us to this man." He handed over his kipandi and Karioki sulkily followed suit, muttering to himself. Coming in search of dances, they had found only work.

4

THE name of the European was a Kikuyu word meaning pig's meat. He was abusive and ill-natured, and his overseer was another like him. People were afraid of his temper and of his great strength; even his wife was frightened of him, his house-servants said. Still, he paid good wages, and twice a week he shot a wild animal whose flesh the men from Kavirondo ate with great relish. But if a man's work did not satisfy the overseer he received no payment at all for that day's labour. Most of the people on the shamba were Waluo—coarse, ill-behaved meat-eaters, Karanja thought—and they were too stupid to complain. But the arrangement did not suit Karanja and Karioki, who had no wish to work at all, much less to toil in the fields all day for a European they despised. The overseer disliked and bullied them, for they were not of his race.

They had come in the season of rain, and were set to work digging large holes and then carrying small trees from beds near a river and planting them in straight lines. When it started to rain Karanja and Karioki ran for shelter and sat down in a grass-roofed shed to keep dry; but the overseer came and ordered them out with angry words. Karanja obeyed, for he was frightened of the overseer; but Karioki lost his temper and went back to the sleeping-hut. The next day Pig's Meat told him that he would lose ten days' pay. Karioki glared, but said nothing; in any case he had resolved to run away.

"I think we must go to Nairobi and become Christians," he said that evening. "Then perhaps we should know what to say to these Europeans. This Pig's Meat treats us like hyenas, and abuses us as if we were birds eating his crops. Do the fathers of Europeans teach them no manners?"

"They are not all like Pig's Meat," Karanja said. "Marafu does not abuse us often and he never makes us stay out in the rain."

"Marafu is all right," Karioki agreed, "but why should we work for him at all? Why cannot we be rich as he is, and travel everywhere in a motor-car, and hire women to do the hard work?"

"How could a black man acquire so much wealth?" Karanja said. "In any case, it is easier to become rich by making friends with the Europeans, like my uncle Muthengi, than by becoming their enemy. They are too powerful to be successfully opposed."

"I shall go to a mission to learn how to speak to them," Karioki said.

"You must wait until Pig's Meat writes on your kipandi that you are no longer his," Karanja warned, "or you will be captured by police."

5

AFTER a month Karioki heard that Pig's Meat had dismissed the man who looked after his horses. Since Karioki had once performed this work for Marafu, and since it seldom involved going out into the rain, he asked to be transferred to the stables; and this was arranged. He was given a boy to sweep out the stables, carry water and clean the harness, so that he himself did not have too much to do. He fed the two horses and gave them water and every afternoon he led out the mare, who would foal shortly, for a walk.

He was able to spend much of the day in the warmth and shelter of the kitchen gossiping with the cook, a Swahili of wide education and, moreover, a Christian with a powerful charm like Robinson's. Karioki asked many questions about Christians, but did not get very clear replies. The cook said that there was only one God who lived in the sky, and that those who refused to admit this would burn forever after death, together with all Christians of the wrong kind. He himself, he said, was a Catholic, which was the right kind; the others were called C.M.S., and were very wicked. He added that all people, rich and poor, white and black, men and women, were equally important in God's eyes; but that God actually preferred poor men to those who were rich. "Then how is it," Karioki asked, "if God likes poor men better than rich (which surely cannot be true) that the Europeans are all so rich? If they wish to please God, should they not become poor?"

The cook laughed and said : "What God believes is one thing; what the Europeans believe themselves is another. Men do not, after all, behave in the same way as gods."

"It seems to me a foolish way to behave in any case," Karanja said. "If I went to my clan's ridge, should I be treated with the same respect as a son of my uncle Muthengi? Of course I should not, for his father is rich and important and mine is moderately poor. Because God loves the Europeans he has given them much wealth; it is best to become rich as quickly as possible, therefore, and so please God."

"And also buy a bicycle," Karioki said. "I should like to have a bicycle more than anything else that I have seen."

6

THE cook's wives made excellent beer, and parties were often held at night on Pig's Meat's farm. One day the Europeans went away in their car before noon, saying that they would not return until late at night, and the cook invited Karioki to a beer-drink. The boy who assisted Karioki said that he would stay with the horses all day; so Karioki left him in charge.

All through the afternoon warm beer, made from jaggoree, was passed from hand to hand in mugs, and many excellent jokes and stories were told. Karioki found that, contrary to custom in his own country, girls and married women were allowed to join the circle. He found also a young girl dressed like a Swahili who did not appear to despise him as an uncouth rustic among smarter and more sophisticated young men. She wore a printed cotton robe and her hair was parted, combed and dressed like a youth's. The beer greased his tongue so that his boasting speech flowed as easily as water over stones; and in the evening, when no one remained sober, he found that she was willing enough to go with him into the intimate darkness of a hut. He did not return to join the drinkers, but fell into a heavy sleep on his host's European bed.

He awoke next morning feeling as though his skull had been cracked in several places and stuffed with wood shavings. Groaning heavily, he dragged himself out of the hut and walked to Pig's Meat's stables to start his day's work. He was late, for the sun was hand-high over the horizon and most of the dew was off the grass; but he hoped that the boy would have fed the horses.

When he arrived he saw at once that something was wrong. The door of the mare's stable was open and several people were standing round it. Karioki hurried up, but when he looked inside he turned to run away. Pig's Meat was standing over a dead foal that lay on the ground; and the mare was very sick.

It was too late to escape. Pig's Meat saw him, but instead of shouting he said quietly to a Jaluo who was near: "Seize that man and take him to the house." Karioki felt his arms gripped from behind and all his protests were in vain.

So, too, were his excuses, when Pig's Meat had finished attending to the mare. The European's voice was high and rattled in his ears. Karioki learnt that the boy had failed him; the mare had received no food or water after her morning meal, and in the night, with no one to attend her, she had slipped her foal. He blamed the boy, the cook, a sudden sickness; it was no good. Pig's Meat ordered him to be thrown to the ground and his legs and arms held; and then the overseer, taking a whip of hippopotamus hide, beat him until his back was bleeding and his strength exhausted by his struggles and by the pain.

When it was over he retreated to his hut and lay there, without moving, all day. Karanja returned from work in the afternoon to wash the wounds and offer Karioki food. But his friend would not eat anything, nor would he speak. He lay in silence on his bed, wrapped in hatred and resentment as a bean is encased in its pod.

Next morning he woke Karanja before dawn.

"Hurry after me," he whispered, "and take your blanket; we are leaving this place of evil at once."

Karanja sat up and rubbed his head in the darkness. "It is impossible," he whispered back. "Pig's Meat's name is written on our kipandis; we shall be sent back to him to work until the thirty days are finished."

"We will burn these kipandis, fool, and get new ones," Karioki answered. "Do you think I will work here another day? I am going to find a poisoner and pay him to destroy that hyena. I leave now—for Nairobi. Come, if you wish to. If not, I go alone."

Karanja could say no more; nor could he desert his kinsman. He slipped on his clothes and stole out of the hut with his blankets over his arm. The dawn was pale as ashes above a ridge of black hills, and the wet grass underfoot was cold as the scales of a snake. Both youths shivered when the sharp air drenched their lungs.

"Which is the road to Nairobi?" Karanja asked. His low voice hung like a hovering bird on the still windless air.

"How do I know?" Karioki answered. "But fear not, we shall find it without fail."

7

THEY travelled first on foot, then in an Indian's truck, finally by train; and at last, after many days, they reached Nairobi.

When they emerged from the vast house into which, to Karanja's great surprise, the train itself went, a long road stretched away before them covered with many people, and more motorcars than they had thought existed in the world. Before them was as strange a sight as they had ever seen : a small wagon with large wheels drawn by a man, who stood quietly like a horse between the shafts.

"See, here are men like oxen, who pull wagons !" Karanja exclaimed, staring round-eyed with amazement. He watched while a European woman climbed into the cart and two men, one pulling and one pushing from behind, ran off with the woman high above them in the air.

"Where are they taking her?" he asked, amazed. " Surely they are Wakikuyu like ourselves !"

"It is indeed remarkable," Karioki agreed. "Surely all the people and all the motor-cars in the world are in Nairobi."

Karanja had never known that so many rich people could exist. Everyone wore very expensive clothes; many even had shoes like Europeans, and white hats. He saw innumerable bicycles, and Kikuyus like himself driving cars. His spirit swelled with excitement and hope. He, too, would become rich like all these men, and drive a car. He wanted immediately a pair of trousers and a white hat.

When they had walked for some time up and down the streets of shops, where goods could be seen yet not touched and everything looked very clean, Karanja said :

"Have the people in Nairobi no stomachs, then? We have walked a long time and seen many shops, but they sell no Kikuyu food ! Truly it is a remarkable thing."

It was a long time before they could find a place to eat. They came at last to a crowded, dusty section of the town where no Indians or Europeans were to be seen. For the first time Karanja sat like a European on a wooden bench and ate rice mixed with meat and a rich gravy with his fingers, and drank tea. It was a strange experience. The owner of the eating-house told them of a place where they might go to sleep. He sent a small boy to show them the way. The house was kept, he said, by one of his sisters; it was called a hotel. Here they would be comfortable, and would pay less money than was necessary elsewhere.

"Money?" Karanja repeated, by now a little dazed. "What money is there to pay?"

The owner of the eating-house laughed. "You must indeed come from a long way off if you think that you can find a bed without payment, unless of course you go to the house of a kinsman. Have you friends here in Nairobi?"

"No," Karanja said.

"Then you must pay for your bed."

"But such a thing is unheard of!" Karanja exclaimed. "Who has ever paid anything for a night's shelter? What sort of behaviour is that? Wherever a man finds himself at night, if he travels in peace, there he is given food and shelter. Everywhere that is the custom."

"Not in Nairobi," the proprietor said.

"Tell me where I can find young men of my age-grade, the Gechande," Karanja persisted. "They cannot fail to give us hospitality."

The proprietor had grown impatient, for other customers needed attention. "Very well, go and seek them," he said; "but do not return to ask me for a bed. My sister's house is quickly filled, and there is no room for fools."

Karanja and Karioki left, offended and not a little disturbed.

"I can see that Nairobi is very different from other places," Karioki observed. "All men here are rich and know how to behave just like Europeans. And I have seen many women dressed in cotton, not in skins, with hair growing on their heads like men. I think Nairobi is a good place; I am glad I came."

Karanja, however, counted over his money, wondering what he would do when it came to an end.

8

THEY were disappointed in the house of the proprietor's sister. It was a small, square mud cabin with a beaten earth floor, roofed by flat-beaten petrol tins, and not so well-swept as an ordinary hut. Bedsteads covered with old blankets crowded the walls, and everything was dirty. The blankets were full of lice and the air was heavy with the smell of unwashed bodies and stale food. All around were other huts of the same kind, without cultivation, standing as close together as forest trees.

"And for this we must pay money," Karanja grumbled. "Where do we cook our food?"

"Do you not see the charcoal brazier on the floor?" the owner answered crossly. She was fat, and wore a printed cotton dress like a European. It was too tight for her, and her bulging breasts and body pushed their way out of several splits. When she moved she quivered all over. Although she was a Kikuyu she had grown her hair and parted it into many curly squares, like a Swahili. Karanja was shocked and ashamed to see a woman so immodestly dressed. She spoke brazenly to men and did not turn her eyes away in respect. "If you complain of this house, go elsewhere," she added rudely. "You are lucky that there is room for you. Now give me your money; it is thirty cents each."

"Thirty cents of a shilling!" Karanja exclaimed. "For a bed to sleep in for one night ! I believe that you are no better than a thief."

"And we have not yet been given that for which we pay," Karioki said. "We will pay to-morrow morning, when we have slept."

"Pay now, or go," the woman answered.

Karanja was so horrified at the woman's behaviour that he

wanted to leave at once, but Karioki, after further useless argument, produced the money, and they stayed.

For the next few days they walked about the red, shadeless roads, breathing the thick dust and seeing many peculiar things.

"The houses are built as close together as yam-vines in a shamba," Karanja remarked. "What do all these people eat, when no one has enough land to cultivate?"

"Food is brought here in trains," he was told, "and by people who carry it in to the market on their backs; and there is a house where a big herd of cattle is slaughtered every day."

"Is it not a dangerous thing for so many people to live together in one place?" Karanja persisted. "If enemies came, what is to stop them from falling upon this place and destroying everyone in it?"

"Such dangers belong to the past," he was told. "There are no enemies powerful enough to fight the Europeans."

9

ONE evening Karioki won ten shillings at a game played with hard pieces of paper on which were bright designs, in a house where many people went every night to gamble. He bought a great deal of beer and gave a party for his friends. Several women came to their hotel, and Karioki told his friend to take any one that he fancied. He himself had already purchased several different women for a night, but Karanja had been afraid. He thought that such women, who obeyed no husbands or fathers, would know much of evil magic; or they might be infected with a thahu which would fall upon him if he slept in their bed. It upset him, also, to hear that they demanded money in exchange for their favours. Among his own people, he pointed out, such a thing would have been absurd. If a girl disliked a young man she would not let him share her bed; and if she liked him, for what would she expect payment?

"Here it is different," he was told. "In your country young men have to be very careful. The girl's small apron must not be lifted, for if she conceives her lover must pay ten goats. Here the women are no longer virgins, and you may do whatever you like with them on these occasions."

Karanja thought this a remarkable arrangement, but, on reflection, one that might well have its advantages, and he put his fear of thahu out of his mind. The woman he selected made him pay a shilling, but on the whole he considered it well spent.

The next evening, however, Karioki lost all his money. Karanja had only a shilling left, and suggested that it would be best to return home.

"I have a friend who helps an Indian in his shop," Karioki said. "This Indian is looking for someone to work for him. I will do so, and then perhaps I can make enough money to buy a bicycle, which I want above everything else. Let us stay a little longer, and then we will go home."

Karanja reluctantly agreed, and asked employment from many Europeans whom he saw walking along the streets. But no one seemed ready to offer work. Then he went to Europeans' houses, and spoke to their servants. Here he was successful, but when the European woman heard that he had lost his kipandi she refused to employ him until he brought another. He did not dare to do this, so he gave up asking Europeans and took a job with an Indian, unloading heavy stones from lorries at a place where a house was being built. The wages were very small and he could only afford enough food to cook one small meal a day on the charcoal brazier in his hotel. He hoped that Karioki would soon get his bicycle, so that they could go home.

CHAPTER III

Benson Makuna

I

FOR several months Karioki and his bicycle remained as far apart as ever. Karioki's wages vanished like the dust of roads after rain. Often he had nothing left for food, and shared the meagre half-calabash of ground maize or the few bananas that Karanja had managed to buy. He would have abandoned hope of the bicycle altogether had it not been for his new friends. Many of them occupied positions of importance and seemed to be men of wealth; but Karanja observed that, although Karioki boasted of their friendship, his friends never gave him food.

One whom Karioki admired above all was called Benson Makuna. He was a Christian, an educated man who could write and speak fluent English. He did work of the highest importance for the Government, work which made him exceedingly rich. Nothing was hidden from him, even the most mysterious customs of the Europeans; he knew what was in the minds of those who governed the country. The great chief of the Serkali, in fact, often asked his advice on what to do.

But Benson Makuna was not content, as many might have been, to enjoy riches great enough to buy him all the wives, the cattle, the bicycles a man could ask for. He was a friend of a Kikuyu leader whom the Government had persecuted and banished to a distant part of the country, and now he carried on the work this leader had begun. On the day called Sunday, when all offices and shops were closed, he would summon meetings and deliver splendid orations. His audience listened entranced, silent at first, then stirred by deep emotions. For Benson spoke always of injustice, of the work and hardships which his people had to endure while Europeans sat at ease in their houses, plotting new methods of oppression.

Karanja went one day to such a meeting and heard Benson Makuna say :

"Long ago, did not our fathers fight bravely when the Masai came to steal the cattle and goats of the Kikuyu? Were they not strong warriors, guarding their land and their homes?"

A murmur passed through the listeners like a ripple of wind over tall grass.

"Why then do we allow the Europeans to steal from us what the Masai could not?" he demanded. "Have not the Europeans taken away our land, and made their own shambas on stolen property? Are not many of our people homeless, because Europeans have driven them from land rightfully belonging to their clans? And who cultivates these same shambas now? Are the Europeans able themselves to plough the land, to weed it, to reap the crops? Why then do you work from sunrise until late in the afternoon in order that Europeans may become rich on land they stole from your fathers?"

"How else can we get money?" a voice asked.

"Who takes your money when it is earned?" Benson retorted. "Does it not go to pay the Serkali's taxes? Twelve shillings every year must be paid for every wife! These shillings are taken from us, and for what purpose? Do you know what becomes of all the taxes you pay? I, Benson Makuna, am able to tell you! The shillings are given to the D.C.'s, that they may buy motor-cars and send their children to school! The Europeans pay no taxes, none at all—only we are taxed! Those who cannot pay are caught by the police and taken away in iron fetters; they are beaten and starved and made to labour all day until their backs break. Or if a man fails to carry a kipandi, as if he were a criminal, then also he is captured by the police! Friends, is this justice, according to Kikuyu law?"

A deep sound shook the throats of the assembly. "It is not just!" the people cried.

2

"Who is it that oppresses our people?" Benson continued. "Who forces you to work, and forbids you to brew beer, and betrays you when you do not pay taxes? Is it not the old men, the elders, who are friends of the Europeans? Do they not claim all the land that is left to us, so that the young men, who know far better how to grow crops, cannot obtain land? A European who owns a shamba can get a paper from the Government to say that it is his. Why cannot a Kikuyu do the same? Is it not time that we, the young men who are educated and understand how unjustly we are treated, rise against these elders who obey the Government, and drive out all the Europeans, and govern the country ourselves?"

"We will make you our chief!" a voice cried.

Benson looked pleased, but he held up his hand for silence and went on:

"There is another thing. Why do the Europeans not build schools everywhere quickly, so that our children can become educated and learn to read and write, as I can? It is because they wish to keep us in ignorance so that we shall not know how to claim our rights! To a few they give education, to deceive us, but I, being an exceptionally clever man, can see through this.

"Now they are scheming to take the rest of our land away from us. They mean to drive us into poverty and starvation, and then all the young men will be killed. They are keeping this a secret, but I, who work in a Government office, have found it out. After the rains they are sending soldiers, and all who resist will be shot. Men of the Akikuyu, shall this be allowed?"

Again there was a deep stir in the audience and a cry of "Never!" One voice shouted: "Tell us, Benson Makuna, how this can be stopped."

"I will tell you," the orator cried. "I shall stop it, because I understand European ways. But can a tree grow without seed, or a man check the advance of weeds without tools? We have formed a great Association, as Europeans do, in which all the Kikuyu must join. Only thus can we resist the treachery of the Europeans! Friends, will you join this Association to protect our land and our people?"

Everyone shouted: "We will join, we will protect our land"; but one voice asked: "Will you demand money from us, Benson, if we join?"

"How can we fight the Europeans without money?" Benson replied. "Must we not pay Indians who understand European laws? Can an Association exist without an office and without clerks? Have we not a newspaper now, to bring us the truth, instead of the lies which the European newspaper tells in order to deceive us? Men of Kikuyu, each shilling is a sword that will sever the thongs with which Europeans have bound us! The fee to join this Association is two shillings."

This statement was received in silence, and one or two standing on the edge of the group slipped unobtrusively away. But most of the audience were stirred by Benson's words to fill with cents and shillings a hat that was handed round. Benson started another speech, but the word "Police" rippled from mouth to mouth and in a few moments the group had dissolved as quickly as a flock of pigeons disturbed by the bird-scarers' shouts. Benson Makuna strolled off amid his companions, swinging his cane, his hat tilted over one eye. He was slim and spruce and wore magnificent yellow shoes. At the end of the road he got into a car with a driver and went away.

"Is he not a clever man?" Karioki said. "All the Europeans are afraid of him because he knows their secrets, but they dare not kill him. I have heard that King George, who is above all chiefs, has sent for him to offer him bribes if he will stop this Association, and offering also to give him a European woman for a wife; but he has refused."

"What is he going to do with all those shillings?" Karanja enquired. "I heard someone behind me in the crowd say that he has bought a motor-car. I do not know how that will make Europeans give back our land."

"He has a motor-car, but it was given to him by an Indian, his friend," Karioki said indignantly. "You must not listen to such wicked talk. Have you not heard the saying: slander is the bead ornament of the rich man? He is a great leader, and one day he will drive all the Europeans out."

Karanja remembered a story that his father had told him a long time ago. "I think that he must have eaten the beetle of eloquence," he said.

3

KARIOKI was dismissed from the Indian's shop soon after Karanja's work came to an end. For several days they wandered about the hot streets of Nairobi seeking work, eking out their last shilling on a few cents' worth of maize flour and a banana each day. At last Karanja could stand it no longer. The floor of the lodging-house was covered with filth and some unclean woman had given him a thahu that was making him sick. He told Karioki that he was going home.

"How will you get there?" Karioki asked. "You have no money for the train."

"I shall walk," Karanja said. "Surely on the road I shall find Kikuyu people who will give me food; it is only in Nairobi that every rice-grain has a price."

"Wait for three days," Karioki begged. "Something very great is going to happen to me. In three days I shall have a bicycle, and one for you also, and we will go home."

Karanja did not believe this; but he agreed to wait for three days more before starting for home.

On the evening of the third day Karioki did not return to eat at sunset. Very late at night Karanja heard him come in, panting quickly, and go to bed. Before dawn next morning he felt his shoulder shaken and awoke to find Karioki standing by his bed.

"Come !" Karioki whispered. "We are going home."

Karanja knew that something important had occurred. He dressed quickly and went outside. Karioki was standing still in the half-light, his hands cupped around a small cloth bag. He opened the neck and Karanja peered inside. He could see the dull gleam of coins and hear the rustle of currency notes. He gasped at the sight of so much money, and then gazed at his friend. Horror, alarm, admiration were blended in the look.

"You will be caught by the police !" he whispered.

Karioki shook his head. "The police do not know me. Only the Indian came, just as we had finished ; he did not see my face. I hid behind the door and struck his head with an iron tool. He had no time to look at me."

"You have killed him !" Karanja exclaimed in dismay. Instinctively he drew back lest he should touch the hand of one contaminated with death.

Karioki laughed, but the sound was not one of a man at ease. "You are like a child," he said, "you would be frightened of a francolin in the bush. I did not kill him ; it was only a light blow. A man of experience was with me ; he had iron tools with which to break open the safe."

"This is folly," Karanja said angrily. "Now the police will seize us and we shall never see our homes again."

"How can they find me ?" Karioki said. "It is you who are a fool. This morning I will buy two bicycles, one for each of us, and trousers and shirts, and European hats and shoes. Then we will go to Kijabe, to the mission ; I wish to become a Christian and to learn to write."

"I shall go back to Njoro," Karanja said.

4

BUT all his worries sank like pebbles into a deep pond of ecstasy when the bicycle was his. It shone and glittered in the sun like a fish, it moved lightly beneath his hand like a coy woman. It filled his soul with a pride almost too great to bear. He had never dared to hope for ownership of such a thing. Its mere possession assured him a place among the aristocracy of the rich, the sophisticated, the educated men. Only clerks, teachers and the highest-paid servants of Europeans owned bicycles. Yet by some miracle, he, Karanja, was of their company. As he pushed the graceful shining machine along the street he could hardly keep his feet from a dance, his throat from song. It had cost one hundred and eighty shillings; a sum equal to twenty goats, perhaps more; half the payment on a bride.

They had bought also light brown cotton suits, such as were worn by Christians, and hats and shoes. Karioki paid for everything; his pockets were like granaries full to the roof after harvest. They ate like chiefs their first full meal since they had come to Nairobi, a big plate of rice and meat; and then, heavy of stomach but light of heart, they set out for Kijabe. Karioki had insisted on going to the mission. Benson Makuna, he said, had promised to make him a clerk in the Association; but he must first become a Christian and learn to write.

They wheeled their bicycles carefully through the streets until the houses thinned out and shambas began. When they reached a hill Karioki announced that he was going to ride. He flung his leg over the saddle as he had seen others do, and fell in a heap on to the road. Annoyed, he tried again; this time he reached the saddle, but the bicycle bolted with him and ran into an old woman carrying a basket of fowls. The woman and the hens screeched at him together, in the same tones, and he shouted back angrily, while Karanja shook with laughter on the road.

"Perhaps there is a curse upon your bicycle," he suggested when he could speak. "It does not seem gentle in its habits."

"That fool of an old woman was in the way," Karioki said. "She has less sense than one of her hens. Bicycles cannot be cursed; besides, this is a particularly good kind, it has a charm attached to it which prevents a lion from catching anyone who rides it."

Karanja knew this, for he had seen pictures of the bicycle be-

ing chased by a lion and understood that this kind was so swift
that no lion could overtake it. Nothing had been said, however,
about its behaviour towards old women.

Karanja's bicycle behaved no better. It threw him into the
road and fell viciously on top of him.

"I do not think I shall ride mine yet," he said, rubbing his
shin. "No doubt at Kijabe there will be someone who can
teach us the secret." So they walked to Kijabe, pushing their
bicycles along the road.

Kijabe was a big place with many buildings : hospitals, dor-
mitories, schools. At first, when they said that they had come
to school, the missionary rejected them because of their age.
Karioki explained that they had come from a long way off and
brought all the money they had earned for fees because they
wanted to be Christians. Finally the missionary smiled and
said that they could stay, but that they would have to sit with
uncircumcised boys in the lowest class of the school. They
agreed, and found a place to live with the father of a man who
worked on Marafu's farm. Every day they attended school,
sitting on long benches in a big light house of grass while a
teacher wrote words on a flat black stone with a piece of white
chalk.

A small group of circumcised men attended this class, but the
great majority were boys, some of them only five or six years old.
Karanja could not help resenting the indignity of being put
amongst them. Sometimes they were taught by a female, an
elderly European woman with grey hair. "If a woman can be
a Christian," he thought, "it cannot be very difficult; no doubt
I shall soon become one too." But it was much harder than
he had hoped, and he was told that it would take at least two
years.

5

HE still wore the charms that Matu had made to protect him
from lions, rhinos and evil magic. One day, when he was

bathing in a cold river that flowed past the mission on its way from the forest to the great valley that lay below, a Kikuyu dressed in a European suit came up and saw the charms lying with his clothes on the bank.

"How can you bring such things as these to the mission?" he asked Karanja in a stern voice. "Do you not know that they are very evil and come from the devil, who is the enemy of God?"

Karanja dried his lean, shining limbs slowly in the sun, and laughed.

"They do not come from the devil," he replied. "They come from my father, who is a mundu-mugu of great fame."

"You are an ignorant man," the newcomer said. "Do you not know that a mundu-mugu is the servant of the devil himself? No doubt your father has often sacrificed goats to cure people of diseases?"

"Certainly he has," Karanja said. "He is said to have great powers, although of course I myself, being an educated man, do not believe such things."

"Yet you wear these evil charms. Do you not know that those sacrifices of your father were made to the devil and not to God?"

"That cannot be true," Karanja said, "for often the sacrifices have been accepted and the sickness dispelled."

"Those offerings are to the devil, not to God, just the same. And those charms that hang around your neck are the devil's also. If you are wise you will throw them in the water before they cause you harm."

Karanja looked idly at the charms lying on his shirt: a small goat's horn, a lion's tooth and a mununga spike full of medicine. It was true that he seldom thought of them now, but without them he would feel less safe in the precarious situations into which he was led. Then a thought struck him, and he asked:

"If it is true, as you say, that these charms are not liked by God, can they perhaps bring sickness to one who wears them?"

"Assuredly," his informant said. He spoke earnestly, and

Y

as one in authority. From a red mark sewn on to his shirt Karanja recognised him as a dresser from the hospital, and therefore one who knew all about disease. "He who worships the devil is sure to fall sick, sooner or later."

"I am sick," Karanja said, "but I thought it came from having slept with a woman in Nairobi who had a thahu. If what you say is true it might perhaps be that God is angry because of these charms."

"What sort of a sickness have you got?" the dresser asked. When Karanja told him he said : "That disease can be cast out in the hospital, because the European doctor, who is blessed by God, has a medicine which he pours into your arm through a needle of iron."

"How can I obtain this medicine?" Karanja asked.

"There is only one way. You must cast these evil charms into the water at once and never think of them again. To-night you must pray for a long time to God, asking forgiveness. Come to-morrow to the hospital; and if God has heard you, the doctor will be able to cast out your disease."

Karanja thought for a little, fingering his charms. He did not want to let them go. Still, if he was to become a Christian, clearly it had to be done; and in any case he could get more from his father later on.

He got to his feet without another word, picked up the charms and hurled them into the shallow stream. The shining waters opened a white mouth to receive them, closed up, and rippled on.

"Now I am without protection," Karanja said, "save that which the God of the Christians can give. To-morrow I will come to the hospital to see what he can do."

6

KARANJA made friends with the dresser and persuaded him to restore the shape of his ears. For some time Karanja had realised that long, hanging lobes looked ridiculous with European dress. Such ears, stretched to hold heavy iron ornaments or blocks of wood, were worn only by old men and by stupid youths from far uncivilised districts, who knew nothing of European ways and dressed uncouthly in blankets.

He paid a fee of one shilling and the dresser operated on him with a razor-blade on a table made of sticks behind a group of huts. The severed ends of the lobes were sewn together neatly, and the wounds painted with a medicine that stung. It was painful, but the result was well worth while. When the lobes had healed no one could have told that they had ever been pierced and distended, and Karanja no longer felt self-conscious about them in the presence of well-dressed men.

One day the chief missionary asked to see Karanja's kipandi. When he replied that it was lost he was told to get another from the D.C. Karioki was given the same orders. Karioki asserted that the danger of being caught by the police could no longer exist; and indeed the D.C. gave them new kipandis without objection. Again they had to make marks on paper with their fingers; and Karanja was not at ease.

"These smudges are signs by which we can be recognised, as my father can tell one goat from another by the markings on its chest," he said. "I hope that Pig's Meat is not looking for us still."

"One day I shall return to kill Pig's Meat," Karioki boasted. "But I am too busy now. There is a girl in the school here who admires me very much; I am thinking of marrying her."

Some days later Karanja was called from his class to find two policemen standing on the grass outside. He looked around quickly, but saw that it was too late to run. His arms fell limply to his side and despair filled his heart. Now he would be taken away and never see again his bicycle or his father.

One of the policeman shackled his wrists together with iron fetters and the other did the same to Karioki. They were taken by train to Nairobi and left in a big building surrounded by a high wall on the outskirts of the town. Inside were many people, and policemen armed with rifles; and there they stayed for several days. Twice a day they were given food on plates, but it was full of lumps and very badly cooked and Karanja hardly dared to touch it at all.

At last they were brought before a European in the place where cases were heard. Here they learnt that evil fortune had mastered them entirely. First they were charged with running away from Pig's Meat, which they had expected; and then with stealing money from the Indian and hitting him over the head.

Karanja glanced around him in despair when this charge was read. The eyes of the police were like stars, he thought; they saw everything, and no one knew where they were looking. The Indian himself was in court to point to Karioki as his servant; and the man who had sold them the bicycles; and many others.

The European refused to judge them then. They were returned to prison to be judged later, by another man. The European pointed to an Indian in the court and said:

"This man is your friend. You must tell him everything and he will speak for you to the big judge when your case is tried in a month's time."

The month was slow to pass. Once the Indian came, and Karanja told him the whole story; but he seemed to take little interest and did not listen carefully.

"How could the police know that I took the money?" Karioki asked. "I was not seen."

"You left the marks of your fingers on the safe, and they were the same as the marks on your kipandi," the Indian said. "It was very foolish. Next time when you steal remember to cover your hands, or to wipe everything that you touch."

Karanja fell into a mood of deep dejection and could scarcely eat. He was convinced, now, that the dresser at Kijabe had deceived him. Evil fortune had clawed him like a leopard, and all because he had thrown the protection of his father's charms into the river.

7

KARANJA did not understand the trial at all. He stood with Karioki in a wooden pen. Above them was an old man in a red woman's dress with long white hair curled like that of the Swahili prostitutes he had seen in Nairobi. The Indian lawyer also appeared to have grown curly white hair. For some reason all those concerned with the trial seemed to be wearing the dress of European women, as boys imitated girl's clothing when they were circumcised. It seemed to Karanja a most undignified thing for elders in a court of law to do.

There was a great deal of talk. The Indian told Karanja that he must explain the whole story. He tried to do so, although he was frequently interrupted by the interpreter and forbidden to say things which he had already said; and he did not know who was his accuser. Everyone seemed in a hurry, and there was only one judge. At the end of several muddled hours of talk the interpreter said that he must go to prison for six months and that Karioki must go for two years.

"That is not just," Karanja exclaimed. "I did not steal anything. I ran away from Pig's Meat, but he was a bad man who beat Karioki, and I do not want to go back."

"All this is nothing to do with the man you call Pig's Meat," the interpreter said. "It is because you did not go to the police when you heard that Karioki had stolen from the Indian. Instead you bought a bicycle with stolen money."

"Why should I have told the police?" Karanja said, much surprised. "Is not Karioki of my own age-grade?"

"That has nothing to do with it," the interpreter replied. "You should have gone to the police just the same."

Karanja was taken back to the comfortless house behind the high wall in a state of deep dejection. He felt that his life was already ended, that he would never see his father and mother again.

The prison stood on the edge of the Masai plain, shadeless

save for a few scaly gum-trees. It was a place without purpose; but at first it was not as bad as he had expected. There was plenty of food, even though it was badly cooked, and his bed and blankets were cleaner than those he had been given at the fat woman's hotel in Nairobi. And he no longer had to do the cooking in a charcoal brazier, or pay for his food. But he was very upset when his clothes were taken away and replaced by a blanket, the costume of ignorant men who only understood how to cultivate a shamba.

8

WORK in the prison was not hard. Sometimes the prisoners sat in a shed and sewed thick cloth into sacks and sometimes they dug and cultivated in a shamba. For several months they were taken out of Nairobi every day in a truck to work on mending a road. In Nairobi Karanja had become weak from lack of food and from sickness, but now he grew strong again, and a doctor pricked his arm with a needle to cure his disease.

In spite of these advantages, however, he was unhappy. At first he mourned the loss of his bicycle, and then he was haunted by a desire to see his father and his family. As time crawled on he grew restless and moody, tormented by futile desire. It seemed as if a spring welled within him which could find no outlet, or as if he had been a tree loaded with ripe fruit that stood in a desert where none ventured, so that the fruits rotted and fell uselessly to the ground. Some of his companions, driven by feelings which they did not understand, turned to each other in order to blunt the edge of desire. Karanja was revolted and deeply disturbed; he had never imagined that such unnatural behaviour could occur.

Time moved like a cloud, without form or boundary, until one morning a warder gave him back his clothes. This surprised him, for he had thought them taken away for good. Then he was taken out of the locked gate alone and told that he was free. The grass of a new season's growth was green on the plain around him, and he thought: now my mother's crops will be knee-high, and perhaps after all I shall see my father again.

"Which is the road to Njoro?" he asked.

"Njoro is a long way off," the warder said. "You will need money to get there. You had better stay in Nairobi first. Now, I have a sister who can give you shelter in her house. . . ."

"No," Karanja replied, "I am going to Njoro."

The road was long and the journey hot and tiring, but on the eighth day he climbed the hill above the broad valley and reached the long-grassed, wooded country that he knew as home. News of his arrival was shouted along the road ahead and before he reached the homestead he saw his father, bent-backed and thin-legged but laughing like a young man, hurrying through the glades with a bag of medicines over his shoulder to greet his son.

CHAPTER IV

Capitalists

I

O N his father's shamba Karanja found order and peace, and escape from the turbulence of the outer world. The freedom to come and go, to eat and sleep as he pleased was sweeter than cane juice; once again events came clothed in reason and propriety, no longer naked in their unpredictability, like sudden flames. He decided that to seek the causes that lay behind them, to search for the end of any road, were foolish pursuits. How could he discover the sources of the river of events, that lay so far away amid such brutal rocks?

Matu, to whom he spoke something of these thoughts, said:

"There is an old saying: a visitor is like a stream. At night he comes, at sunrise he departs; none knows the place of his origin or of his destination. A stream cannot rest, it hurries along; only when it spreads out into a swamp can it nourish the roots of plants with its waters. Do not, therefore, wander like a visitor, or you will become thin and without substance like a stream. It is better to remain in one place, remembering the saying: he who stays under a tree knows what ants use it. Therefore you should seek a wife, and I will pay goats to her father, and then you will be content."

"I am ready to do so," Karanja answered, "but still my thoughts trouble me and I wish that I had been to school."

"Thoughts are like fireflies," Matu said. "They shine brightly but are gone before you can catch them in your hand. Those who chase them cannot see the ground before their feet and fall into pits dug for wild beasts."

Karanja asked news of Marafu's shamba, and of all that had happened during his absence.

"Marafu is stopping us from cutting down trees for firewood," Matu replied, "and I do not consider that he pays us sufficient shillings for our work. But he is no longer quite so noisy, and his voice has become softer, more like an elder's. Strangely enough, it was the woman who taught him good behaviour. Sometimes she, too, grows angry; however, she is a woman, and most women are foolish at times. But she has many medicines to cure diseases and nowadays all the women take their sick children to her. They say that she has stronger magic than I have, but I do not think that so young a woman with only one child, and that a baby, can know much about magic or curing disease."

"Marafu has a child?" Karanja enquired.

"A son. The mother suckled it for three months only, and now she gives it milk from cows. Whoever heard of babies being given warriors' food? There is something else that has come to Marafu's: a big thing that runs swiftly across the shamba and pulls the plough. A man sits on its back and it obeys his hand. It makes a great noise, but does the work of a hundred women in a day."

Karanja immediately resolved to become the keeper of the noisy object. He could ride a bicycle, and this could not be harder to control. The man who sat on its back agreed to teach him its ways for five shillings. Later, when this man left to attend to his own shamba, Karanja asked Marafu if he could be employed to drive it and the European agreed. For a year he worked as the tractor's driver, whenever there was work to do. It shook beneath him like a warrior getting ready for battle, but once it had agreed to go it was obedient. He felt like the chief of an army, like his uncle Muthengi whom the warriors had followed into battle long ago.

2

WHEN the season of dances came Karanja exchanged his shorts for a length of white calico, put a white cock's feather in his hair, and went every night to some gathering of young men and women along the Mau. The rhythm of the dance had not been killed by the alien shoes that had encased his feet. He became famous for his prowess, and for the spicy character of his songs. People came from distant farms to hear in his verses the stirring stories of his adventures : of how he had been to Mombasa and sailed in big boats; of how the Governor had offered to buy his bicycle, which flew faster than a European car, for sixty cows; of his friend Benson Makuna who had been to England and ate food without touching it with his hands; of the large number of women who had implored him to become their lover because of a charm given to him by his friend a court interpreter in Nairobi, who owned three motor-cars.

It took a year to select a bride. He watched the girls carefully in the shambas, weeding and digging, as well as at the dance. Few resisted his entreaties when he walked back with them after a dance to the doors of their mothers' huts and told them of his desire to enter. But it was hard, after all his experience, to treat them as virgins, and the question of his marriage was settled for him when a girl conceived and named him as her lover. Her father brought a case before the council and Matu paid the ten-goat fine. She seemed a hard-working, cheerful girl, and Karanja was quite willing to make her his bride. Her name was Ngima. She had not married before because she suffered from bleeding of the nose, an affliction which, the young men said, was certain to make her barren. When Karanja proved the falsity of this assumption he laughed at them as ignorant, superstitious fools. He himself, an educated man, did not believe such old-fashioned things.

The bride-price, he found, was higher than ever before. Matu had to pay eighty goats, one cow, four fat rams, a barrel of honey and a heavy blanket worth a year's tax. He complained a great deal at the price, but Karanja knew that he could well afford it. His eldest daughter Wamboi had just been married to a Masai herdsman who worked for a European on a nearby farm. This Masai had seen her at the market and although he had never spoken to her, he had sent messages to Matu offering large payments in cows. Wamboi had at first refused, but the Masai had raised his offer to a point where Matu could no longer resist. Although Wamboi cried bitterly and protested, she had to go. After a month she returned to her mother, following the custom, and said that she was happy enough. The Masai was rich and kind and there was little cooking to do, since he lived on blood mixed with curdled milk, and meat roasted on a grid.

3

In the hot months before the rains Karanja took his new wife to the land Marafu had given to him and showed her the piece she was to cultivate. She looked at it in dismay and said:

"What madness is this? Do you think you have married that engine that you sit upon? If you had five wives they could not cultivate a piece of land that size!"

"I did not say that you were to do it alone," Karanja replied. "I intend to find other women who will help."

"Whoever heard of a woman cultivating for a man who was not her husband, or her father, or perhaps her husband's brother?" Ngima said.

"Europeans pay others to work for them," Karanja answered. "Cannot a Kikuyu do so the same?"

He called together all the fathers of unmarried girls on Marafu's land and gave them a great deal of beer. Then he laid before them his proposition: that the daughters of each homestead should work for him for five days when the time of planting came. To each father he would pay ten cents a day for the daughter's services.

At first the fathers refused, saying that their daughters had plenty of work to do at home. But after they had turned the idea over in their minds for a little nearly all of them agreed. Five days, after all, could make little difference to their own shambas; and fifty cents was not to be despised. Karanja was promised a labour force of about thirty girls as soon as the rains should break.

When low black clouds gathered in the valley he called the girls together and gave them grains of maize to plant. It was good seed that Marafu had sold him, all white; there was not a single black or purple grain. The women were amazed at this, but Karanja said: "Do you not know that white maize can be sold to the European mill for twelve shillings a bag, whereas the old-fashioned coloured maize can be sold to Indians only, and for six shillings?"

All through the season of growth Karanja paid girls to weed his shamba and people wondered what would happen to him if the harvest failed. Then he would have no money left to buy food, they supposed, and he would die of hunger. Matu also looked on the venture with misgiving, but his son boasted:

"The people here are all stupid, they know nothing of modern ways. Can they not see how Europeans grow rich? When this crop is sold I shall buy a bicycle and a clock, and everyone will say: 'Karanja is a very clever man, it is we who are fools.'"

A smile flickered behind Matu's eyes and he said: "The mouth which utters a shout of pleasure is the same as that which cries for help. Remember the saying, my son: the leather cape in which a child is carried is not sewn until the child is born."

The hot weather came, and then the harvest; and many girls were called to Karanja's to pick the cobs. They neglected their mothers' shambas, where maize was also ripe, and several refused to hand over to their fathers the money Karanja gave them, spending it instead on ornaments at the Njoro shops.

It was a good harvest. Karanja watched with satisfaction while five granaries were filled. He asked Marafu if he could use the machine that stripped grain from the cob, doing in a day what the quick hands of women would take a month to achieve. Marafu agreed and lent him the machine to shell the maize, and also a wagon to take it to the European mill. An elder who heard Marafu praise him for his industry said:

"Now the European is angry because you have grown white maize like his own, and wishes you evil; he has openly praised your crop." But Karanja laughed and said: "Do you know so little of European customs? They mean no harm when they praise openly a crop, or a cow, or a child."

The old man replied: "Whatever they mean, it will bring bad luck; for how can the spirits fail to hear, and bring evil to the crop, or the cow, or the child?"

4

A few months later Marafu called Karanja to his office and said: "Your maize was good, and this year the price is good also. You sent away twenty-seven bags and each bag sold for fourteen shillings. Here are 378 shillings, paid to you by the mill."

"Ee—u!" Karanja exclaimed; the paper money, more than he had ever seen before, filled his two hands. "Thank you, bwana; this is very good indeed."

Marafu smiled and said: "You are now a rich man. This cannot happen every year, so do not spend it all at once. Why do you not take it to the Post Office and let the clerk keep it for you? When you wish to spend it, it will be there; and thieves will be unable to take it."

But Karanja rejected the idea. The Indian might keep it for himself, he said; besides, the Post Office belonged to the Serkali, and if the Serkali knew of his riches they would certainly make him pay a larger tax. He put some of the money in a tin box and buried it under the floor of his hut. The rest he took to Nakuru; and he returned on a bicycle, laughing with pleasure like a drunken elder. It was the first bicycle to come to the farm and everyone hurried to his homestead to admire its splendour.

The word of Karanja's wealth spread abroad far and wide.

Many people came to visit him, knowing that they would find plenty of food. Every week he bought fresh beef from Njoro, and his neighbours said: "Now Karanja is so rich that he eats meat several times a month; now indeed he is behaving like a European."

Such good fortune could not last. One evening Karanja returned to find his hut in disorder and the floor dug up like a shamba before the rains. With a cry of dismay he took a log from the fire and held it over the place where his money was buried. The flame lit up an empty hole.

He ran at once to Marafu, and an enquiry was held; but no one displayed the hand of guilt. Next day a policeman came from Nakuru and asked many questions. They were without result. A meeting of the elders was held. The old men were disturbed, for theft was a serious business, but they knew of no one to accuse.

"There is nothing we can do," they decided. "If Karanja sacrifices to the spirits and obtains a good charm, he may escape another time."

Matu, alone, was not prepared to let the matter rest. A son's loss was his own, and that which had been stolen must be returned, or compensation paid. It had always been so.

"What thief is willing to return his loot?" Karanja said wearily.

"He can be made to do so," Matu answered. "Is not that the way in which the law is kept? Europeans have many policemen; these men walk about openly looking for stolen property, and if they do not find it, what can they do? Theirs is a foolish, clumsy method. Before Europeans came we had no policeman, yet only in seasons of famine were there serious thefts. And I do not remember a case where a thief was not made to return what he had taken."

"Those methods belong to the past," Karanja said.

"No," answered Matu, "the power of magic will never die. I will go to our own country and find a man who will know how to curse the thief who robbed your hut."

"That is all nonsense," Karanja said impatiently. "No person has power to do as you say. People do not believe in that any longer."

Matu took a pinch of snuff and looked calmly at his son. "Always the son knows better than his father," he remarked. "Can a man bring a thief to confession by learning how to write, or to wear shirts? I shall fetch a sorcerer, and you will see."

5

MATU brought back a shrivelled, grey-haired man with a wrinkled face like worn leather and deep-set eyes as bright as a bird's. He walked with crooked back and bent knees, and wore an old-fashioned ox-hide cloak that flapped about his calves.

"This sorcerer will find the stolen money," Matu told his son, "and soon your wealth will be restored."

"What is his fee?" Karanja asked.

"It is high," Matu admitted. "I have promised him thirty shillings; but it is worth it; you will get it back."

"I shall not pay anything," Karanja said angrily. "He is trying to cheat you."

"You are obstinate and foolish, and deserve to lose your shillings; but as you are my son I will pay him all the same."

Karanja said nothing, but he watched the sorcerer's actions with suspicion. The old man sat apart under the trees telling the beans, and observed closely all that went on about him. One day Matu said:

"Come to the big acacia above my homestead before sunrise to-morrow morning; there is something that you should see."

Karanja at first refused; but curiosity drew him to the appointed spot while the sky was pollen-yellow and the mountains black before sunrise. The sorcerer was crouching over a little fire. Smoke stood up like a white vine in the still air of dawn. They waited in silence for the sun. As it burst over Nyandarua's crest, colour sprang out of the red bark of the acacia and its foliage glowed suddenly with a vivid green. The sorcerer rose to his feet, took from his bag a hen's egg, and smashed it against a fallen branch.

"May the body of the thief be broken as the shell of this egg is broken!" he intoned. "May he be broken utterly and trodden into the ground!"

Matu handed him a calabash full of water, which he lifted towards the rising sun. He tipped it carefully over the young fire and chanted:

"May the thief die as this fire dies at my feet! May life wither in his body as the flames perish in these burning sticks!"

Finally he took the calabash itself and broke it with a stone, crying:

"May the limbs of the thief be shattered as this calabash is broken into fragments!"

After the cursing the sorcerer marked the faces of his witnesses with medicine and chalk, and said: "Within a month the thief will come to you and bring the shillings; and in another month he will be dead."

A few days later the sorcerer went, taking with him thirty shillings of Matu's money. Karanja waited for some time, and then asked his father:

"Where is this thief who is going to return my shillings as the sorcerer said? I do not see him anywhere."

"It is no matter," Matu answered. "He will come."

Several months passed, and Karanja said again: "The sorcerer took your thirty shillings by a trick. Such curses are old men's tales; I told you that your money would be wasted."

But Matu obstinately replied: "It is no matter. By now the thief has certainly died, but perhaps the money was already spent. If you had bought goats instead of shillings made of paper, you would not have lost them in this way."

6

KARANJA's young brother Kaleo, although not yet circumcised, asked many questions about schools. "Why is it that we have no school here?" he enquired. "There are boys who learn to become clerks, or carpenters, or even teachers. I do not wish to grow into an ignorant man."

Matu explained that the nearest school was too far to be reached on foot every day. His young son went on herding goats, but could not hide his disappointment.

One day Kaleo disappeared. Matu had given him money to buy a new shirt at Njoro, and some sugar for beer. When he did not return next day Wanja went to look for him at the homesteads of his friends. None had seen him, or knew where he had slept. Days passed, and still he did not reappear. It was thought that he had been kidnapped and taken to Mombasa to be sold. Matu's grave calm concealed his sorrow; he feared that he would never see his son again.

Karanja was not so sure. "Kaleo may have gone to find a school," he said. "If we do not have one here soon all the boys will run away. We must ask Marafu what he means to do."

The elders agreed to this idea, and a deputation went to ask if something could be arranged.

Marufu said: "Schools belong to the missions, and the money which pays for them to the Government. But I will do this: I will give you a place to build a school, and the timber and nails. You must erect the building yourselves, and then I will find you a teacher and give him a house and his food."

The elders agreed to this plan, and a school of cedar posts and mud was built. Marafu gave two lamps to hang in it, and a big blackboard; the fathers, it was decided, must pay a shilling for each child. When all was ready Marafu sent for a teacher, and a man named Roland arrived. He was smartly dressed and at first he did not seem at all pleased with his new house and with the school. In the evenings he taught the men who worked by day. Karanja became his most persistent pupil and learnt to talk in English fluently, and to recognise the countries of the world on a map. He plagued Roland with many questions about Christianity, and foreign races, and the ways of Europeans. Some of the things that Roland told him made him begin to doubt whether it was wise to become a Christian after all.

"Is it impossible, then," he asked, "for one who has two wives, or more, to be a Christian? Must all the elders who have married several women go to this place of fires the Christians know about, and burn?"

"No, a man with two wives can still become a Christian," Roland said, "if he promises not to increase the number afterwards. But a young man with only one wife may not marry any more."

"Then," Karanja said thoughtfully, "it would be best to wait to become a Christian until several wives have been acquired."

Roland looked shocked, and remarked:

"That, however, is not what the missionaries say."

CHAPTER V

Forbidden Dances

I

WHEN the school for young men was over in the evenings, Karanja often went to Roland's house to drink thickly sweetened tea. The teacher gave him news of much that was happening in the outside world. He learnt, for one thing, that missionaries were opposing the custom of circumcising girls. They did not mind, it seemed, about boys, but for some reason they wanted girls to be left alone.

"But girls who have not been circumcised before they become women are unclean," Karanja protested. "They know nothing of the way in which women must behave; and they would most probably be barren. They are like a person who finds his way into a homestead by crawling under the fence instead of by walking through the gateway in the proper way."

"The custom is cruel and wicked, so the missionaries say," Roland replied. "No Christian should have his daughter circumcised, or God will reject him. And, anyway, the Serkali is going to forbid the practice altogether."

When this reached the ears of the elders, indignant words were used. "What right have Europeans to forbid us to circumcise our daughters?" they demanded. It was suggested that the new law was part of a plot to destroy the Kikuyu people so that the Europeans could seize the land. "Girls who are not circumcised cannot be true Kikuyu," many people said. "All would be barren, and then our race would cease to exist."

Rumours began to reach the Mau of serious trouble in Kikuyu itself. The Serkali, it was said, was going to issue orders that no more girls were to be circumcised. The missions were expelling all married Christians who refused to take an oath that

347

their daughters should be left alone. Everywhere indignation sprang up, spontaneous in each father's heart, like blades of young grass after rain. What right had the missions or the Serkali, people angrily demanded, to dictate the upbringing of Kikuyu girls?

Soon something else occurred to confirm the belief that the behaviour of the missions was part of a plan to destroy the Kikuyu people. Three Europeans came to Tetu and moved from place to place casting spells on the people with a kind of magic. This consisted of an iron machine shaped like those used at railway stations for telling the weights of sacks; but it was not the same, for it had been charged with a magic that destroyed the fecundity of all those, men or women, who touched it. These Europeans went first to missions and made all the Christians stand upon it in turn. But the news of this magic spread quickly and all who were able to escape from the mission ran away.

For some time it was not known why the Europeans were trying to deprive the Kikuyu people of their fertility. Then Benson Makuna arrived in Tetu with the explanation, which the Europeans had tried hard to conceal.

Had not Christians been taught, he said, that the Son of God, who had been sacrificed many years ago, would one day be born again as a human baby? The Europeans, Benson continued, had learnt that the time was at last at hand; and that the new Messiah was shortly to be born of a Kikuyu mother.

This child would deliver the Kikuyu people from European oppression, and would rule over a great Kikuyu nation. One day he and his followers would govern Europe itself, entering into possession of all the Europeans' fabulous riches. So the Europeans, panic-stricken, had resolved to bring sterility on all young men and women of Kikuyu, in order that the black Messiah should not be born. For this purpose they had sent the European sorcerers with their iron machine. For this purpose, also, they were forbidding the circumcision of girls. The uncircumcised women would be unclean and their babies—if they were able to conceive—would die before weaning. Benson charged all his fellows steadfastly to oppose this plot, if necessary by force, and to insist on the circumcision of Kikuyu girls according to the customs of their fathers.

2

As the season of circumcision approached, excitement mounted. Young men moved restlessly around, like bees disturbed by something they cannot see. Wild, unsettling talk flew fitfully about the homesteads, flaring here into passionate speeches, dying there into a half-forgotten simmer.

On the Mau news came in snatches, like bursts of distant music on a gust of wind. They heard that Benson Makuna and his Association were urging all fathers of girls to refuse the missionaries' oath, but to take another, no less solemn, pledging themselves to have their daughters circumcised in the fullest and most thorough way. This oath was very sacred, and was taken secretly; the Itwika snake was somehow involved. All those whose daughters attended mission schools were taking their girls away. Young men were roaming the country in small bands learning the steps of a dance called the mambeleo, and singing the words of a new and more than usually obscene song. A big circumcision ceremony for girls was being planned and a special dance for the girl candidates, the musirigo, had been invented.

Then came news that the Serkali had forbidden both the new dances and was fining all those who were heard singing the songs. Muthengi and the other chiefs had also forbidden these dances; they were sending their njamas to stop performances. In spite of this, the words were being sung everywhere : in the shambas, and on European farms; in Nairobi beer-halls, by men walking along the roads, by groups of youths gathered in front of the Serkali's offices. The verses were full of wit, and provoked keen enjoyment and laughter.

Both the song and the dance intrigued Karanja and he re-

solved to learn them in full. He obtained leave from Marafu
and went by train to Kijabe, to the mission where he had thrown
away his charms. Here he found his friend Karioki, now released from prison. Somehow·Karioki had acquired wealth,
for he was living near the mission with a young wife. He
had been baptised as a Christian, he told Karanja, and his
name was now Jehoshophat. He was employed by Benson
Makuna, whose Association had become so powerful that it
was feared by all Europeans, by the Serkali, and even by
King George.

Jehoshophat was a very busy man. Every day he addressed
meetings and persuaded elders to take the oath to circumcise
their daughters. All the young men of the district were dancing
the mambeleo and singing the forbidden song. Many of the
boys had been taken away from the mission and classes had
dwindled to a quarter of their normal size.

Among those who had stayed, Karanja found his young
brother Kaleo. The boy had used the money given him for
clothes to travel by train to Kijabe, where he had heard there
was a school. When the European missionaries learnt that
Kaleo's brother had arrived at Kijabe, the grey-haired woman
spoke to Karanja and asked for three shillings in fees.

This woman had aroused the anger of Jehoshophat and his
colleagues, for she was in charge of the girls who lived at the
school. All those fathers who had taken the secret oath had
sent young men to fetch away their daughters; but this woman
had refused to let them go.

The fathers were so angry at this that they went before
the D.C.

"This European woman has stolen our daughters," they said.
"She is keeping them in captivity at the mission and will not
allow us, their fathers, to fetch them home. Is such blatant
theft allowed by the Serkali, under the law?"

The D.C. replied: "Certainly such a thing is not allowed.
No one may steal another's child, nor keep another person in
captivity against his will. But nor may a father force his

daughter to submit to a public ceremony of mutilation if she does not desire it. A meeting shall be held, and the daughters themselves shall decide."

The old men grew still angrier and said : "What sort of a law is this, that upholds a disobedient girl against her father, to whom she rightfully belongs?"

3

THE fathers sat in sullen silence outside the mission school and the European woman brought their daughters out to stand before them. They regretted now that they had ever sent the girls to school, even though the marriage price would be twice or three times that of an uneducated girl. They were disturbed to see that their daughters had thrown away their aprons. Each wore instead a cloth dress covering her breasts but giving, it seemed, no real protection elsewhere.

The European woman stood up, her face half hidden by a big hat and her eyes screened by glass so that no one could know what was in her mind. She was very thin and her figure was not that of a woman at all. She addressed the girls in Kikuyu, saying :

"Your fathers have come to take you away to be circumcised, and you must decide whether or no you wish to go. There are more important reasons than the pain and the injury why you should refuse to submit. I have explained to you that this custom is cruel, and therefore against the wishes of God. Moreover, our bodies were made after the image of God and it is a crime to mutilate them wilfully in a way which God did not intend. Therefore you should refuse to accompany your fathers, who are like men blind and deaf and unable to understand how evil is the thing they wish to do."

The fathers murmured angrily during this discourse, and at the end one or two lost their tempers and spoke in loud voices to the European. One even threatened her with his staff, although he was prevented by others from striking. Several men tried to speak at once and there was much confusion. "What right have you, a woman, to tell our daughters that the customs of our people are cruel and evil?" they shouted. "How can you say to elders that they are deaf and blind?"

At last one man's voice gained ascendancy over the rest, and he said to the girls:

"Do not listen to this woman; her words are part of a plot to destroy the Kikuyu people. Do you not know that the Europeans have stolen much of our land, and now they are trying to make all Kikuyu women barren so that they can seize what remains? Circumcision is a very old custom of our people; it has existed since the world began. By it your fertility will be ensured; if you forgo it you will be unable to conceive and no man will want to marry you. What right has this woman to tell you which of our ancient customs is bad? Do not be deceived; leave her and return to your fathers, where you may learn to dance the musirigo and be received properly into your own clan."

A few girls left the group and went over to their fathers, saying: "We are tired of European ways. Here we are not allowed to dance with young men, and always we sleep alone as if we were covered with sores. This was not how our mothers behaved when they were girls."

The majority, however, dared not speak to their fathers, nor look at them. They turned their heads away and wiggled their shoulders, but their feet did not move.

"Why do you not answer, you disobedient girls!" their fathers exclaimed. "Have the Europeans made you dumb?"

Still the girls made no reply, until one murmured: "We do not want to come." Others, emboldened, echoed: "We wish to stay here at the mission; we do not want to be circumcised."

At this the fathers rose angrily and left in a body, striking their staffs on the ground as they walked and muttering like a thunder-cloud gathering for the storm. This open defiance from their own daughters was more than they could stand. Several cried angrily: "The European woman has bewitched our daughters !" and others added : "Yes, and stolen them from us like thieves !"

"The Serkali will not help us," another said. "How, then, can we get back our daughters?"

No one could think of a plan, and at last an old man said : "Let us ask Jehoshophat, the friend of Benson Makuna, who understands the duplicity of Europeans; perhaps he will know."

4

THAT night a number of the fathers gathered in the hut where Jehoshophat was staying, close to the mission. Karanja was also there, and several educated men. Among them he recognised the hospital dresser who had made him throw away his charms.

These young men listened to the elders' indignation, and Jehoshophat said :

"This is indeed an outrage, one that all Kikuyu must join together to resist ! Shall this European woman be allowed to break our ancient customs like a calabash broken with a stone? Are we women, always to do what others tell us? I have a plan which will teach the Europeans not to interfere. Are you ready to join in this, and to do what I say?"

The young men shouted agreement; but the hospital dresser said :

"What sort of words are these from you, Jehoshophat? Have you not been baptised as a Christian?"

"Certainly I am a Christian," Jehoshophat affirmed.

"Then why do you talk of the old customs as if you were an elder?" the dresser asked. "These elders here are not Christians; they know only the old customs, which they want to keep. But you follow the new customs taught by Europeans. Is it an old custom to wear trousers, and shoes, and hats? Is it an old custom to read books, or to eat chickens, or to smoke cigarettes? Yet all these things you do. And which of the customs do you keep? Are your ear-lobes long and full of ornaments? Is your body covered with ochre and fat? When you are ill do you go to a mundu-mugu for purification, or do you come to the hospital to be cured?"

Several men laughed at this a little uneasily and Jehoshophat tried to interrupt; but the dresser went on:

"You know that you have accepted European customs and abandoned the old ones of the Kikuyu. And indeed I know that many European customs are better, for I have seen how pain and diseases can be cured by medicines in hospital and I know that they cannot be cured by the sacrifice of a goat. Now we can see that the circumcision of girls is a bad custom; other people do not have it, and God turns his back on such things. Some customs are good, and we should keep them; but the bad ones must go. When you say you are in favour of it I think you tell lies."

Jehoshophat grew very angry at this. He seized a stick from the fire and would have brought it down on the dresser's head if someone had not held his arm.

"You are a fool. Europeans have paid you to take their part!" he shouted. "Go away from this meeting, go back to your masters and tell them that we, the true Kikuyu, are not cowards like you. Do we try to make Europeans behave as we do? Why then should Europeans try to make us behave as they do? We are not to be treated like cattle, driven wherever the Europeans wish us to go! Tell the European woman that she shall follow our custom, since she has tried to make our daughters follow hers!"

The hospital dresser went out, taking with him one or two others who shared his opinions. Karanja was one of those who left. He did not agree with the dresser, but on the other hand Jehoshophat had a way of getting into trouble, and Karanja did not want to follow him to prison again. He could see, too, that there was a certain amount of truth in what the dresser had said. He knew himself that many of the old customs, such as greasing the body with ochre and laying curses on thieves, were stupid and dirty, and no longer practised by young men. It might perhaps be that the circumcision of girls was a custom of the same kind. But even so, he concluded, the Europeans had no right to interfere. Girls were the property of their fathers; who were the Europeans to say how they were to be brought up?

5

HE awoke late next morning, and while he was eating breakfast in the sunshine outside the hut he saw a party of policemen hurry by. After he had washed in the river he strolled up to the mission, chewing a stick of cane, to see if there was any news.

The place was in extreme confusion. European officers were there, and many people were standing about watching a house which was guarded by policemen with rifles. He was horrified to hear what had occurred. The European woman with grey hair had been murdered in the night. Several people had broken into her house and found her in bed. She had been crudely circumcised in the Kikuyu fashion where she lay, and later in the night she had died from the wounds. The culprits had not yet been caught.

Karanja turned away immediately and fled from the mission. He had no wish to be seen and questioned by the police. He got into the first train he could see, and by nightfall he was back in his own homestead. He said nothing to anyone of the woman's death.

The police did not follow, and within a few days he had recovered his composure sufficiently to teach young men the steps of the mambeleo, and girls the musirigo. The elders met in council and decided to hold a circumcision ceremony for boys and girls alike on the farm.

One evening, when Karanja returned late to his homestead, he saw an unfamiliar green bicycle outside his hut; and in the thingira he found Jehoshophat drinking tea by the fire. The young man's clothes were crumpled and dirty and he himself had lost his self-confident look. He shook hands warmly with Karanja and said:

"I have come to the homestead of my circumcision-brother to rest, for I am weary after much work for the Association. Also, Benson Makuna wishes me to help the Kikuyu who live on European farms to resist any attempt to prevent them from circumcising their daughters. The Serkali is very frightened. Kikuyu circumcision ceremonies are being held everywhere, and the Serkali has not dared to stop them."

Karanja spoke little while they ate the hot food that Ngima brought them in calabashes. He was afraid of Jehoshophat, and wished his friend had not come. This man travelled everywhere with trouble for his shadow.

"Have the police caught the men who killed the European woman?" he asked.

Jehoshophat looked at him in silence for several moments, and Karanja read fear in his face.

"No," he said at last. "The police are fools; they will never catch anyone. Besides, those who circumcised her were the executors of justice, that is all. If Europeans force us to observe their customs, why should we not show them ours?"

"Is it our custom to kill women?" Karanja replied. "My father, who knows all the old customs, has never told me of that. When he was a young man he killed Masai warriors in battle; I do not think that he killed women in bed."

"There was no need for her to die. Those who circumcised her did not intend to kill."

"Perhaps the European judge will believe that," Karanja said.

6

JEHOSHOPHAT rode around Marafu's farm on his bicycle urging all the elders to take the oath to have their daughters circumcised. Most of them did so, but Matu refused. He agreed with the principle of the oath, but he did not want to find himself evicted from his shamba, and his caution was stronger than his indignation. Another supervisor for the ceremony was elected, and a date fixed. Women began to prepare for brewing and the chorus of the mambeleo was heard every evening until late into the night.

Then Jehoshophat started to tell the young men, at first in whispered confidences revealed to small groups, of a new and secret plan. The time had come, he said, for the Kikuyu to cease their abject obedience to the foreign oppressors. Were they not like oxen, yoked together by force and made to drag the heavy burden of taxes while Europeans walked beside them shouting orders and beating them with whips? Were they to continue in this servile way for ever? Were there not plenty of educated young men among the Kikuyu perfectly capable of taking over the government of the country from the Europeans, who had come here only in order to squeeze riches from the labour of the people as juice was wrung from cane?

These young men, Jehoshophat said, were alert and ready to seize their opportunity, as in the old days Kikuyu warriors had been ready to charge into battle at the sound of the war-horn. That opportunity was to be created by the fathers who would hold circumcision ceremonies everywhere for their daughters. The Europeans would send police to stop the dances; the offices of the Serkali would be left unguarded; the young men would capture them and seize the boxes where the tax money was kept. All the clerks, interpreters and telegraphists were in sympathy; it was they, and not the Europeans, who did the work. A powerful magic had been obtained to make all the European officers of the Serkali lose the power of their limbs, so that they would be unable to resist. Then the Kikuyu would rule the country and Benson Makuna would be in the Governor's house. Then heavy taxes would cease; the Kikuyu would seize the Europeans' land, their cattle, and their motor-cars.

"And you," Jehoshophat concluded, "you must lock this European Marafu into the store and seize all his cattle, and his house, and his motor-car, and then these shambas you are cultivating will become your own."

When Matu heard this talk he decided that Jehoshophat must be sent away. He could tell from the young man's manner that he was telling lies. Only harm could come of the presence on the farm of such an empty-headed fool.

"Truly the saying that the mouth can sell the head is a wise one," he observed. "This man talks like a hen; his words are all noise and no sense."

He went to Marafu's house and told him what Jehoshophat had said. "Everything will be all right here if he is sent away," he added, "but his words trouble the young men. Just as your dogs howl from restlessness when the moon is full, so his words bring disquiet into people's minds."

"These young men have not enough work to do, that is the trouble," said Marafu. "They are lazy, worthless fools. Tell this Jehoshophat that he is to come to see me at once, or I will send for the police."

Marafu was not in a good temper that morning. The cook had burnt the coffee, the rains were late, the planting delayed, and his youngest child was ill and had cried all night. When Jehoshophat arrived he was told abruptly to produce a kipandi; but he replied:

"I do not carry one. Kipandis are for men who work on shambas, but I am an educated clerk and I do not need to carry one about."

"Kipandis are for everyone," Marafu replied, angrily. "If you cannot show me yours I shall send for the police."

Jehoshophat felt confident that the European would not dare to make good his threats. He raised his voice, and answered:

"Those are not good words to use to me. You cannot refuse to let me visit my friend Karanja because you claim this land. You Europeans have stolen land from my people; you have no right to say where a Kikuyu may walk and visit."

"Leave my farm at once, you impudent hyena!" Marafu exclaimed angrily. "Do not ever set foot on my land again!"

"Do not call me a hyena!" Jehoshophat retorted. "You cannot order me about like this! I, who am a Government clerk, tell you . . ."

He could not finish the sentence, for Marafu hit him brutally in the face, and retreated into the house before he could recover. "So this is your friend!" the European exclaimed to Karanja. "You will go too, if he ever comes to my farm again."

7

JEHOSHOPHAT walked away rubbing his nose, his spirit burning with rage. Very well, he thought, this arrogant pig of a European has settled his own fate; he shall not be spared. He shall learn that the old days are over, that Europeans cannot treat an educated clerk as if he were a louse to be crushed between thumb and finger.

That afternoon, when work was over, he called a meeting of all the young men under a big tree outside Karanja's homestead, and said: "I have spoken to Marafu and I have found out that for a long time he has been deceiving you. He is a very bad man indeed, and he is making plans to seize all your crops and all your cattle for himself. You have seen that he is having a deep pit dug near the river. What has he told you this is for?"

"He says it is for cattle," one man answered. "Cattle are to jump into it and be washed with a poison which kills ticks."

"And did he tell you that your cattle as well as his would have to jump into this pit?" Jehoshophat continued.

"Yes, that is what he said," his audience agreed.

"Then you are a lot of ignorant fools to believe him!" Jehoshophat cried. "Your cattle will jump in, certainly, but do you think that they will emerge alive? Do you believe that the poison is only for ticks? Its purpose is to kill cattle! Marafu will drive your cows into the pit, and there they will perish like ants crushed underfoot."

"But why does Marafu wish to do this?" a puzzled listener asked.

"I see that you are more foolish even than I thought," Jehoshophat exclaimed. "Do you not understand that this is part of the great plot to destroy our people? The Europeans are stopping the circumcision of our girls so that they will become barren; and they are going to poison all our cattle so that we shall become poor and helpless against their strength !"

There was an outburst of discussion at this, for while some believed him, others said loudly that he was making up the whole story, and that they had often seen cattle going through a dip.

"If this is true, Jehoshophat," one man asked, "how are we to stop him?"

"On the day when you circumcise your daughters," Jehoshophat advised, "you must lock him and his wife into the store and set fire to it, so that they will be burnt. No one will know what has happened. The police will think that the fire came by accident, perhaps from a cigarette."

Karanja, who was listening carefully, said : "If you do this, Jehoshophat, will you stay here with us and yourself set alight to the store with a match?"

"I should like to do so," Jehoshophat answered, "but I cannot, for my work here is finished. To-day I received a letter from Benson Makuna telling me to go to Nairobi on very important business. If you do what I have said I will tell Benson that everyone here is supporting him, and should receive a reward."

"Nowadays it appears that the warriors fight on one ridge and their leader on another, a long way behind," Matu observed drily. "That was not so when I was a youth." Several young men laughed at this remark.

Jehoshophat raised his arm angrily above his head. "You are a lot of ignorant fools," he exclaimed. "Can one fight with pen and paper in the same way as with spear and shield? But if you cannot protect yourselves from the Europeans without me to lead you, very well. I will do so. You must follow me and carry out my orders."

The green bicycle was leaning against a tree. Jehoshophat

leapt on to it and pedalled off along a path that wound down a slope between scattered acacia and olive trees towards Marafu's house. His audience, surprised at this sudden turn of events, discussed the matter uncertainly, and a few set out on foot after their leader.

"Ee—i !" Matu exclaimed, "this is indeed a strange army, led into battle by a hen that goes : clk-clk-clk-clk-clu-i-ik-clk !"

Everyone laughed, and at that moment Jehoshophat turned his head to see if the young men were following. The bicycle swayed, wobbled, and bounded over a twist of the path like a doubling hare. Before its rider could regain control its front wheel crashed into a tree. Jehoshophat pitched forward against the trunk, fell in a heap and lay still, the buckled bicycle by his side.

The crowd ran down the slope towards him, but when they reached his crumpled body they stood around in a frightened group, afraid to touch the motionless object at their feet. Karanja stepped forward and turned the body over. The head sagged limply on the shoulders; he could see that his circumcision-brother was dead. He dropped the body quickly. In the deep silence that fell the foot-rests of the bicycle whirred, slowed down, and gently ceased their revolutions.

At last Matu broke the silence. "It is an act of God," he said.

The others, awestruck, backed away, exclaiming : "It is true, this cannot be due to anything but the intervention of God."

That night, after Jehoshophat's burial, there was silence over Marafu's farm. God had spoken, and no one dared to offer him defiance. No doubt it was the Christian God who had slain Jehoshophat, himself a Christian; it was perfectly clear that this God was on the side of the Europeans and against the circumcision of Kikuyu girls. It was clear also that he would strike down with death all those who opposed his wishes. The mambeleo was not danced again.

CHAPTER VI

The Goats Go

I

AFTER the circumcision trouble it became clear that evil spirits were gaining ascendancy in the land. One disaster followed another like vultures dropping out of the sky when an animal falls dead on the plain.

First there were two long years of drought, and then the locusts came. Cloud after cloud swept out of the sky and fell on the maize, leaving it a plundered forest of tattered stalks. Marafu lost the whole of the crop from his big shamba. His cattle were turned in to browse among the broken plants that remained. Karanja, who had employed fifty women and children to sow his land, saw his crop devoured before his eyes in two days. The locusts coincided with the third year of drought, and in Kikuyu a famine followed on the two disasters. The Serkali sent train-loads of grain from Mombasa to Tetu and Maranga to give to the people, and because of this no one died; but food was short and many hopes of wealth were shattered.

The next season was little better, for the drought broke and the crops were drowned in rain. Much of it barely ripened; and when the time came to sell, the Indians would not offer more than half what they had paid the previous year.

The following season was even worse. Locusts arrived in even hungrier hordes, and although there was a shortage of maize, the price everywhere dropped lower still. Karanja was very angry; he was convinced that the Indians had joined together in a plot to defraud the Kikuyu. He decided that he must be given higher wages by Marafu to make up for the lower prices he was forced to accept from the Indians for his maize and potatoes. But when he explained this to his employer, Marafu said:

"Karanja, I can see that you are a fool. How much do I pay you every month?"

"Thirty shillings, bwana," Karanja answered.

"And three years ago, what was it then?"

"Twenty shillings."

"Now think about my maize. Three years ago, what was the price?"

"I was paid fourteen shillings for each bag of my crop."

"I also received that. And to-day?"

"I do not know what you got, but I only received five shillings a bag. This is not a fair price at all. Why should the Indians pay one price one year, and another the next?"

"I do not like it any better than you," Marafu said. "And I do not think I understand it any better either. But the prices of all crops are very bad. How can I pay you higher wages when I myself receive so much less for my crops? In fact, if this goes on much longer, I shall not be able to pay you at all."

Karanja smiled at this, and said: "All Europeans have so much wealth that it is not possible for them to become poor."

"It is very possible indeed," Marafu replied.

Things became worse instead of better. The locusts returned, filling the air with their wings. Maize perished, and grass as well; cattle grew thin and even the goats, browsing on locust-denuded pastures, lost their fat. Food for men as well as for beasts fell short and the heads of families were forced to draw on their buried hoards of cash to buy grain from Indians. Yet, in spite of the shortage of food, the price fell even lower than before, until Indians would only offer three shillings for a full bag of maize.

At the end of the season Marafu sent for Karanja and said: "Things have become so bad that I cannot cultivate this shamba any more. Each bag of maize that goes to the station costs more to grow than I receive for it in shillings. I have insufficient money to pay the men, and some will have to go. And if I can-

not sell next year's crop for a better price I shall have to go myself. I cannot pay you thirty shillings a month any longer. I
will pay you twenty, but if you like you may seek work elsewhere."

Karanja thought for a little and then said : "No, I will stay,
as I do not want to leave my shamba, and no doubt you will give
me more money when you are able. But I do not understand
why, if you have not got enough shillings, you cannot get more
from the bank."

"Because the bank has not got any more to give me," Marafu
replied. "The shillings are finished."

2

FOR the next year things were not at all to Karanja's liking.
Marafu grew irritable and the work was hard, for the cook
and Karanja's assistant were dismissed. The motor-car stood
unused in its shed and people were obliged to walk to the
station when they had shopping to do. Even the two horses
disappeared. Marafu's wife kept everything locked up and the
houseboys were forced to buy all their own sugar and tea. The
engine that made light for the house was Karanja's special care,
and he understood its insides as well as any European; but now
Marafu himself replenished it with oil, and kept the tin locked in
the store. So Karanja's lamps went short, and the card games
that were played every night in the houseboys' quarters behind
the kitchen had to be curtailed. Although the hut-tax remained
the same it seemed to everyone as though the sum had been
trebled, so much harder was it to pay. The only way to find the
money was to work for Europeans, and for those who had shambas
on European farms two full months' wages must be set aside for
the tax on a single wife.

"Why does the Serkali not reduce our tax, since the Indians
are paying so little for our maize?" Matu complained.

"Do not ask me about the Serkali," Marafu said. "It is not
my affair. You are lucky that the tax remains the same. Mine

are to be increased, and I have nothing at all to pay them with."

"Europeans do not have taxes," Matu told him. "It is only we who pay."

"Europeans have very big taxes indeed," replied Marafu angrily. "You have no idea how big; and all are food for the Serkali's stomach."

"Everything goes to the D.C.'s," Matu agreed.

Marafu laughed. "And what do they do with so much money?" he asked.

"They spend it on educating their children. We, who are poor, cannot pay to have them taught as European children are taught in schools."

"Well, what of it?" Marafu asked, "Although European children attend schools, very few of them learn wisdom."

3

SOON afterwards Marafu called all the men on his land to a meeting in front of his house, and made an announcement.

"The time has come," he said, "when all the cattle grazing on this land must go. There is no longer room for your cattle and mine to share the same pasture. Your cows have been giving bad diseases to mine, who are English, and die very easily. And because I receive so little money for my crops, I must increase the number of my cows. Within three months you must send away your cattle, or you must sell them. Do you understand?"

There was a long silence, and everyone stared at the ground. Faces were expressionless, but innumerable thoughts darted about inside each head like bats disturbed in a cave. It was bad news, although not unexpected. The pastures were overcrowded and had been brown and almost worthless since the locusts came. But it was an abrupt reminder that the land on which they lived was not their own.

"We understand," they said at last.

"There is another thing," Marafu continued, "concerning goats. There are too many goats on this land. Can you not see that the grass is brown and short, and that on some hill-sides there is no grass at all, but only earth? This is because of goats. They are making my land worthless, and in future their numbers must be reduced. In three months' time I shall make a count. For each married woman I shall allow ten goats to be kept, no more."

There was a murmur of dismay. No one had expected such a disastrous announcement as this. Life without goats, for the elders, would be unthinkable; and ten goats to each wife was an absurd restriction. Matu, who had just taken delivery of a hundred and sixteen for the bride-price paid for a daughter, exclaimed :

"Bwana, we cannot possibly agree to that ! Where would our goats go? On the farms in that direction, and that, and that,"—he waved his arm—"there is no room for more; the pastures are full."

"Many people keep their goats with brothers or relatives in Kikuyu," Marafu suggested. "I will give you a pass to take them there."

"My brother would not keep mine," Matu said. "He is a chief, so rich that he does not know the number of his own."

"Then you must sell them," Marafu said. "For all your cattle and goats you would get perhaps a thousand, two thous-and shillings, and you would become a very rich man."

"But if I kept those shillings in my hut they would be stolen," Matu objected, "and if I took them to the Post Office, how would I know what would become of them?"

"Everyone knows now that they are safe. Karanja will tell you, he keeps his money there."

"But what is the good of wealth that you cannot see?" Matu persisted. "My eyes can feed upon my own goats; and at night I hear them breathing in the hut. The females give birth before me and I can see my wealth increase and spread as a small pool of water spreads out in the rains. Can one do this with shillings? And do shillings have increase?"

"Shillings have increase," Marafu said. "For every hundred

that you leave in the Post Office for a year, you will receive three from the Serkali for nothing."

"Then I say that shillings are like barren females," Matu retorted. "What sort of goats would they be, if out of every hundred, only three young were born in two seasons?"

"I cannot help it," Marafu said. "Goats must eat, and if the grass is insufficient some of the goats must go. I will allow you to keep ten for each wife, so that if anyone falls ill you will be able to make a sacrifice. But as the strongest tree must die and a new one take its place, so must old customs be replaced by others. Nowadays the young men no longer use goats for sacrifice or purification, and sooner or later shillings must take their place as wealth."

The old men complained bitterly, but in the end most of them had to agree. They did not want to leave their shambas. A few were able to go back to the holdings of their own clans, taking their goats with them, and lay claim to the land that their mothers had cultivated. The majority shrugged their shoulders and said: "There is no firewood now at Kijabe or Kiambu; every bundle must be bought and paid for. There is not enough grazing there, either, for goats. Here we can at least get money for taxes by working for Marafu, who, while he is often tiresome, protects us from other Europeans and does not mind our brewing beer. If we went back we should have to spend a lot of money laying claim to our land, and very likely we should fail in the end. So we will stay with Marafu, and send away our goats."

That season Kaleo came home from school to be circumcised. The name of the circumcision-age was Kenyabus, after the big buses that came to Nairobi that year. Kaleo was very clever and had reached the highest standard of the Kijabe school; his teachers said that he could now go to the Alliance High School at Kabete, if his father would pay the fees. When Matu heard how much they were he was dismayed, and protested it was quite impossible to pay so much. But Karanja said:

"If you pay this, after four years Kaleo will become a teacher or a clerk, and then he will earn as much in one month as you must pay to the school in a year. He will live in a stone house like a European, and eat meat every day. When you are too old to work he will be able to give you money for your hut-tax, and to buy beer."

"But I have not got as many shillings as that," Matu said.

"In the first year you could sell one cow," Karanja suggested, "and that would be enough for the fees. Another year you could sell fifteen goats."

"Ee-i, fifteen goats," Matu exclaimed. "And nothing in return? That is too much altogether !"

Kaleo was very upset when he heard this, and would not eat. After the circumcision he spent much of his time with Roland the teacher. He refused to attend the youths' dances, saying that they were wicked, and that no Christian was allowed to go. Besides, he said, it was indecent to wear only a length of calico, and no shorts. Every night he spoke to the Christian God with his face covered under his hands, and he complained of the smoke and the smell in his father's thingira. "At school we sleep in a big house with open doors," he said. "It is cold, but now I find this hut is too hot, and it is also dirty." So he went to sleep in Roland's house, which had doors and windows like a European's.

"He does not like the food that I give him any more," Wanja said sadly. She was growing old and wrinkled and her limbs were stiff. Although Matu had sacrificed many goats, she did not get any better. "It would be best if you sold a cow and let him go back to this school. His heart is there; it is no longer with his father and mother. My son is like a European, and I do not know how to speak to him."

Matu took a pinch of snuff and watched his wife stirring the pot. "It is true," he said. "Youths who have been educated walk by one path, and we who are old by another, and the paths do not meet. Nowadays young men can grow richer than elders, yet they are not content. They no longer put on fine ornaments and dance all night as we did. Nor are they called upon to fight. All is ease for the young men to-day, yet when have you seen Kaleo laugh and sing as I used to when I was a youth? But it is the path he has chosen, and he must find out where it leads. I will sell a cow, and he shall return to school and learn how to become a teacher or a clerk."

Kaleo was delighted when he heard this. But he did not sing or dance, and he avoided the company of many youths of his age because they were uneducated, sinful and dirty. As soon as his wounds were healed he returned to Kijabe, taking the money in a bag, and Matu never saw him again.

4

THE drought continued long into the season when rain should have fallen, and day succeeded hot, sun-flooded day like ripe fruit falling at unhurried intervals from the tree of time. The eye of heaven, unlidded by softening clouds, glared with a fierce persistency over the red earth. The lake in the valley shrank into itself, leaving a broad white ring of soda around its edges; no one could remember when it had been so low. The locust-eaten pastures peeled like dead bark to disclose grey powdered earth, and dust-devils whirled across the valley like dancers run wild. The flesh of cattle fell away from their bones, and the milk of cows ran dry. At night the stars swam so close to the earth that it seemed as if a man could shake the darkness with an outstretched hand and bring them tumbling from the branches of the night. Matu, looking upwards, said : "Now it seems that the skies are like the breast of a very old woman, shrivelled and dry. Why does God not fill them with milk to nourish the earth?"

Karanja could see that Marafu was growing very sad. His new cows, for all their strength and size, gave little milk because of the dry pastures, but all the time they had to be fed with green crops grown by the river bank. Marafu watched their fat dwindle with a morose eye. He had a fine big bull, exceedingly strong and savage, but although it was kept in a house especially built for it, where no ticks could penetrate, one day it fell ill and died.

Marafu went to Nairobi several times, but no longer to attend European beer-parties and dances as he had done in the days before the locusts came. He left his wife behind and took Karanja, who spent many hours sitting in the car outside the bank and other offices. Nairobi had swollen like a tick on the neck of a cow and the houses had grown upwards as quickly as eucalyptus trees. Everyone now was well-dressed, and many people went about in buses. A great hall, like a European club, had been built near the house where Karanja had lived, and in it dances were sometimes held at night. These were not in the least like the old-fashioned dances, however, which Christians said were wicked; they were exactly like the dances held by the Europeans in their big hotels a mile away. Karanja attended such a dance one evening and found that all the girls dressed like European women, with shiny stockings on their legs. Karanja learnt that he could hire a black evening suit such as Marafu wore on special occasions for two shillings. Everyone danced in couples, the men holding the women in the indecently intimate way of Europeans, and ate European food.

After they had returned home Marafu sent for Karanja and said : "All my shillings are finished. I have no more money to pay the men. I cannot stay here any longer, since I do not receive as much for my maize and milk as I have to pay out in wages and food, and this shamba no longer belongs to me, but to the bank. Therefore in one month's time I and my wife and children must leave Njoro altogether. I am going to a place called Kakamega, to dig something out of the ground."

"But what will become of us?" asked Karanja in alarm.

"Another European will look after this shamba. My cows I shall sell. One day, if I can find wealth in the ground, perhaps I shall be able to return. I do not know; it is the affair of God. Any of you who wish may return to Kikuyu, but if you stay perhaps this new European will give you work."

"Bwana," Karanja said, after a pause, "I do not wish to work for another European. It is now eight years that I have been with you, and I know your customs, and everything that you demand. How do I know that a new European would treat me well? I should like to go with you, and continue to be your servant."

"Thank you, Karanja," Marafu said. "But what would you do with your wife? No one is allowed to cultivate a shamba on this land unless he works on the farm; that is the Serkali's law."

"I do not want to leave here," Karanja said. "The land is fat, and my wife has a good shamba. Besides, where would she go?"

"Then you will have to stay," Marafu said, "and work for the new European."

5

KARANJA was deeply perturbed at the upheaval, as indeed were all those who lived on Marafu's farm. It had never occurred to them that their European could go. They had complained often of his behaviour—and especially of his unaccountable refusal to let them cut down trees—but now that he was going they were afraid. A way of life had been built and now it was to be broken, like a hut in which someone had died.

Gradually the shamba withered before their eyes like a plucked flower. The big cows went away to be sold. The tractor, also, was driven off and did not return. Weeds sprang up in the shamba and were not removed. The furniture of the house was packed up and taken on wagons to the station.

A morning came when Karanja helped Marafu to pile boxes containing many of his possessions into his car, ready for a long journey. Everyone had come to see him leave and to receive farewell presents of blankets and coats.

Matu had decided to give Marafu a present, and had given much thought to its selection. A fat ram, he knew, would not be appreciated by a European. At last he remembered that

Marafu had once admired the three-legged stool that hung from a chain around his neck. Matu had brought this with him from his clan's ridge many years before. Its surface was worn as smooth as a grinding-stone and blackened with the smoke of many fires. He did not want to part with it, for it had been with him since he was a young man; but he could not let Marafu go without any present at all.

"Marafu has been a good European," he said. "He has stood between me and the Serkali, and has given grazing to my goats. Let him take the stool, for I shall not need it much longer."

When Marafu saw it he shook Matu's hand and said : "I shall not forget you. One day when everything has become better, as it may, I shall return. Do not get drunk too often, and be careful that the European on the next farm does not find the goats that I told you to sell, but that you have hidden there."

Karanja saw that Marafu's wife was crying, so he said : "We will look after the farm when you have gone. As soon as you have obtained more shillings you must come back, and you will find things as you left them here."

With that Marafu waved and many people pushed the car from behind, for it was too old to start on its own. There was a loud shout of farewell, and the elders cried after him : "Go in peace." Marafu waved his hand; and, amid a great noise from the car, he drove away.

6

His departure brought evil fortune to the shamba. Soon afterwards disasters fell like hailstones on to Matu's head. He had arranged for those of his goats which had been dismissed to be grazed on the farm adjoining, where several friends lived. He heard one day that they had been discovered by the European, who had ordered them off the farm immediately and said that a fine of ten shillings must be paid. Then the new European arrived with an officer of the Serkali. He announced at a public meeting that work could not be found for everyone, and that many of the people living on the shamba would have to go.

The European then delivered the worst blow of all: he proclaimed the expulsion of all goats on the farm.

At first no one could believe such words. "Ten goats for each wife," they said, "these, surely, may be kept."

"No," the European answered. "All goats, all, must go."

"Five goats, then," the elders pleaded. "Five for each wife; surely this must be allowed."

"No," the European repeated. "Can you not see that your goats are eating everything on the shamba, that they are spoiling the land? If you will not agree, you may go back to Kikuyu, and take your goats too."

The elders stared at the ground in a hopeless silence. They were too old to go. They did not know where they would send their wealth. The younger men, however, said nothing, because they did not so greatly care. It was possible, now, to buy brides for cash. No educated man believed any longer in sacrifices and few would agree to be purified of a thahu, or even after a death. Life without goats, therefore, was becoming feasible; it was better to spend money on bicycles, clothes, and meat or tea.

Matu returned despondently to his homestead. He did not know where to send his goats.

"The time has come," Karanja said to him that night, "to return to the land of our own clan. Perhaps your uncle Ngarariga, or your brother Muthengi, will look after the goats."

"I have told you often that Muthengi will poison me if I return," Matu said.

"You have told it to me often, but it is no longer true," Karanja replied. "Muthengi would not dare to poison you now that he is an important chief. Have you thought what is to become of Kaleo when he marries? He cannot get land here. He must be given the land that belongs to you, the shamba that you inherited from your father, or he will have nowhere to cultivate when he buys a wife."

7

MATU'S legs, bent since childhood, had grown stiff, and often caused him pain. He walked with a staff's aid, and now his face was lean and lined. In spite of his stiffness he still travelled long distances with his bag of medicines to purify elders who contracted a thahu or fell sick. But few of the young men would agree to vomit out evil any more. They said that the taste revolted them, and went instead to the hospital in Nakuru if they were ill. Sometimes they were cured, and sometimes not; Matu could not see that European magic was any more infallible than his own.

Wanja, too, looked old and worn. Her ear-lobes dangled loosely above her bony shoulders and her breasts were withered and dry. Most of her teeth had fallen out, and when she laughed her face dissolved into an immense number of lines and crevices, crinkled as an elephant's foot.

At the time of Matu's worries she fell sick. Six goats were sacrificed, one by one, until Matu remarked in jest that the question of where to send his goats was being answered by God. Wanja lay quietly on her bed in the dark hut, suffering pain in silence as she had done many times before. Karanja wished to take her to the hospital, but she refused. He went into Nakuru himself to fetch some European medicine, but it did her no more good than his father's remedies. Her strength left her gradually as a pond empties slowly before the sun; and early one morning, at sunrise, she died. Karanja and Matu dug a shallow grave and buried her without ceremony, her ornaments by her side. Afterwards Matu visited a mundu-mugu to be purified. Karanja said nothing, but refused to go.

When life left Wanja's body something in Matu seemed to die too. He did not speak, but grief shook him as an old tree is shaken by a gale. He sat all day in the shade of the acacia that spread its green hands over the homestead. His two remaining wives offered him tempting hot meals, even bought millet at the market to make him gruel; but he would eat no more than the portion fit for a sparrow.

At last, when the maize crop was harvested, he sent for Karanja and said :

"Now I am old and have stiff legs, and one who cooked my food since I was a young man can no longer stir the pot. My goats also are to be taken away; I am like the rock left on the hillside after the gravel has been washed down. I do not wish to live any longer; and in three months I shall die."

"No man can decide when to die," Karanja said. "It is the affair of God."

"I have decided, all the same. I have considered your words, that I should visit the country of my clan to claim my inheritance for my son Kaleo. Those words have wisdom; and I would like to see my brother before I die. Therefore we will go, as you have suggested; I shall be ready to start in eight days."

"That is good," Karanja replied.

CHAPTER VII

Return to Tetu

I

MATU and Karanja slept one night in Nairobi on the way. Karanja laughed at his father's astonished comments and tried to take him in a big bus; but Matu refused.

"Only people with trousers are allowed," he said. "I have no trousers, so I cannot go." Karanja reassured him, but still he refused. He did not like to feel his shoulders and legs pressing against those of strangers: men of other races, of age-grades junior to his own, perhaps unclean persons, or even sorcerers.

When they were safely seated in the train that went to Nyeri, the name by which Tetu was now known, Karanja asked his father if he had liked Nairobi. Matu shook his head emphatically and said:

"No, it is a bad place."

"Why?" Karanja enquired.

"Because the roads go in straight lines in both directions, and there are no corners. That is very bad indeed."

They travelled all the morning through the red-soiled ridges of Kikuyu. Out of the window Matu, enthralled, saw women cultivating in the chequered shambas, carrying heavy bunches of bananas to market, shelling maize cobs outside their huts. Some straightened their backs and waved at the train, laughing and calling out remarks as it chugged slowly up the long hills and around steep curves into the valleys, and young men in the wagons waved back. At every station crowds of people greeted the train. Women, shouting continually in high voices, offered roast bananas, cooked yams and sugar-cane for sale. Men in European clothes swarmed over the platform, meeting friends or picking up scraps of news. Sometimes Matu saw an elder in a blanket and ear ornaments and called out a greeting, pleased to see another of his age-grade, and one clad as he was, amid so many well-dressed youths.

They arrived at Karatina in the heat of the afternoon. It was market day. People were gathered under the giant fig-tree where the market had always been held, but now many more were present; a brown sparkling wave of people was spread far and wide over the grass where often in olden times warriors had gathered for the ceremony that preceded a raid. The women seemed to throng the ground as thickly as a mass of ants swarming over a scrap of food. From the crowd arose a noise like the persistent chattering of flamingoes by a lake.

Matu stood still and watched, amazed. He did not know how so many women could exist at one time. The market was breaking up and they were dispersing in brown streams towards the hills. On their backs were loads of firewood, bananas, grain, and new-burnt pots : the same loads that his mother had carried a generation ago. But others had bottles of milk or melted fat in their hands. The men walked empty-handed (for none carried a spear) or else holding banana leaves pinned together with a wooden skewer, full of juicy meat. Elders returned with twists of snuff done up in dried banana leaf, but young men with packets of tea or cigarettes. Matu could see no lumps of iron, nor any sign of knives or ornaments offered by the smiths. He knew, indeed, that the fires of the smiths were cold, since there was no need of weapons, and smarter ornaments could be bought at Indian shops.

Far above the market, calm and light, the peak of Kerin-yagga stood out of the sky, its long shoulders cool and shrouded in a shell-white cloud. Matu looked up at it in thankfulness, for nothing about it had changed. Nor could he doubt, despite what Christians might say, that God still lived in the place of whiteness, far beyond reach of the market's chatter or of the flight of the strongest bird.

B B

2

KARANJA took his father to a small, tin-roofed house where they sat at a table and were given mugs of sweet tea. At the next table were two men in uniform, but not policemen; and Matu asked who they might be.

"They are two of the men who keep order in the market," he was told. "They see that the maize is dry and that only white grains are offered for sale. If the blue grains are mixed, as in the old days, they do not allow the women to sell their maize."

"But it is not only white grains that are good to eat," Matu exclaimed.

"Only white grains can be sold in the market, nevertheless. Women, also, must sort their beans into different kinds, according to size and colour."

"I have never heard such a thing before," Matu said, "but who can understand the Serkali's ways?"

They asked where Muthengi lived, and were directed to his homestead. "There is a wide road all the way," they were told, "which Muthengi built when he bought a motor-car."

"Muthengi has a motor-car!" Matu exclaimed, unable to believe the man's words.

"Certainly he has a motor-car; he comes in it to Karatina nearly every day to hear cases, for he is the senior elder of the council of law. His son Razimu drives him everywhere; did I not tell you that Muthengi is very rich?"

Matu was too overwhelmed to reply. He knew that no one would believe him if he proclaimed himself to be Muthengi's brother. Even Karanja was a little awed at the affluence and importance of his uncle and the attainments of the cousins he had never met.

Everything that Matu saw by the roadside was familiar, and yet it was strange. The shapes of the hills, the curves of the sun-bright rivers, had not changed. Wydah-birds still agitated the reeds and women dug for arum roots in moist swampy earth. Higher up on the hillsides clusters of round huts were built in the same way among banana plantations and on the edges of open green flats where cattle grazed. Goat-bells still tinkled across rich valleys, and the warm herby scent of bush mingled with the smell of sunbaked earth as of old. All was familiar; yet differences sprang out on him at once. The shambas crowded thicker together than ever before and were full of beans, tall ripening maize and sweet potatoes; but nowhere was there any millet to be seen.

A man of Matu's generation, returning home with a parcel of meat, was walking with them, and Matu asked:

"Do people here no longer drink gruel, then, since the women plant no millet?"

"People drink gruel," their companion replied. "There is no homestead without its grinding stones. It is brought from Ndia; two days ago my wife returned with a load."

"But why do people not sow millet themselves?"

"Are women to plant crops for the benefit of birds? Who would keep away the greedy pigeons and the grey nyagathanga, the red-beaked murugu, and other devourers of crops?"

"Is not that the children's task? When I was a boy I would stand all day in the shamba, hurling stones from a sling."

The man turned his head to look curiously at Matu. "I also," he said. "But where are you living, that you are so ignorant of modern ways? Do not the children spend all day at school, and how then can they scare birds?"

"Who, then, herds goats in the bush?"

"It is difficult," Matu's informant admitted. "I myself have two sons at school. One goes early and returns at noon to herding; the other stays with the goats in the morning and goes to school at noon."

3

On the way they came to a pasture where cattle were grazing, and Matu stopped with an exclamation of surprise. "Have

women, then, become cattle-herds?" he asked. "Surely that is
the work of young men?"

"Those are Muthengi's cattle," he was told. "Muthengi
has wives to the number of twenty-two living and seven dead.
He sends his wives to look after his cattle, which are so numerous
that they can scarcely be counted in a day."

"Has he, then, no sons?"

"He has many, but they do not herd cattle; all of them have
been to school. Some are clerks, and others teachers; one is
a policeman at Nyeri; others are married and cultivate land.
Whenever beer is brewed in this district, one gourd must be
taken to Muthengi's homestead. Muthengi is very important
and a friend of the Serkali, but his father Waseru was only a
poor man, and as a boy he used to carry pots to Ndia for his
mother, like a girl."

"Things have changed a great deal," Matu remarked.

"That is true," his companion agreed. "Now cattle are
tended by women and girls go to draw water from the river
without fear. There are no hyenas here any more, for all
corpses must be buried, so there is nothing for them to live on.
The Serkali eats taxes like a hungry lion, and the hut-tax is
indeed a great burden; but people forget what it was like to flee
from the Masai into the forest and to hear hyenas feeding close
at night in famine times. For myself I think that perhaps
these days are better, even though Muthengi orders us about a
great deal too much. But the young men do not agree."

Matu observed that the ridges were more wooded than he
remembered them to have been when he left. They were
planted with new trees that had never existed in Kikuyu before.
He had seen them at Njoro, where they had been brought by
Europeans. They were dark of leaf and graceful, like maidenhair ferns; but under their foliage the ground was brown and
bare. They had been planted in straight lines, and their bark
was red. Matu passed several women felling them with an
axe and others stripping the bark with a knife and tying it into
bundles.

"The bark, perhaps, is used for a new kind of twine?" Matu asked.

"No, it has nothing to do with twine. It is sold at Karatina and goes away by train, I do not know where to. Many people now plant wattle, as this tree is called, for the branches provide firewood and the roots are medicine for the soil."

"That is good," Matu said with conviction, looking about him. The hillside across the valley was clothed with wattle, its outline soft and feathery against a blue cloud-strewn sky. Three shades of green blended together on the wide slope. At the bottom, by the river, was the bright vivid green of the canes; above them the full deep green of banana leaves; and on the crest the dark restful green of wattle. "Now the country looks as it did before there were Europeans, when the forest still gave us shelter from our foes," he remarked.

The shadows were far extended when Matu and Karanja came to the foot of a ridge on which a great homestead stood. Bananas and wattles screened it from the road, but through the trees above they could see the gleam of thatch.

"Look!" Karanja said. "There stands the homestead of my uncle Muthengi."

Matu rearranged his blanket on his shoulder and took a pinch of snuff, trying to appear unconcerned.

"Muthengi has many wives," he said in solemn tones. "I do not know if he will recognise me as his brother."

They walked together slowly up the hill.

4

OUTSIDE the compound two big square houses stood. One was for the car and the other for the numerous njamas who ate and slept there when they were employed on Muthengi's business.

Matu and his son walked through the entrance and stood in the largest compound they had ever seen. The ground was clear of weeds or grass. In a circle were ranged twenty-two huts, and before each stood a large granary. Behind the twenty-two were many other huts, used by some of Muthengi's married sons. To the right a thingira stood by itself, but it was not an ordinary hut; it was rectangular, and had a tin roof.

It was the hour of the goats' return. A jostling stream poured in through the entrance, guided by shouts and whistles from women and boys. The whole compound became a swaying field of goats—black and brindled, white, speckled and striped. The air was full of bleating and bells. Gradually, as the sun fell behind a wood of wattles on the hill, the goats sorted themselves out into smaller flocks and each flock found its way to the hut where it was to spend the night. A red-gold cloud of dust, stirred by the trampling of many hoofs, floated over the thatched huts.

Then the compound became full of people. Women hurried to and fro, taking brands to start a fire from their neighbours, setting pots on hearthstones outside their huts. Smoke columns began to follow the dust into the sky. The drawers of water returned, big gourds silent on their backs. Others came with firewood, and uncircumcised boys bore long gourds of milk to the huts of their mothers and to the njama's house.

The two visitors stood in silence by the fence and watched with marvelling eyes. It hardly seemed possible that so many wives could belong to one man. Matu noticed that most of them wore as many twists of copper wire as a Masai, and long dangling ear ornaments, and ropes of coloured beads. The dress of every one proclaimed her to be the wife of a man of wealth.

"How many goatskins must be needed every year to make dresses for so many women !" Matu exclaimed. "How many must be slaughtered for sacrifice, and slain for capes to carry new-born infants !"

"Truly the Serkali is a good master," Karanja agreed.

A little after sunset the engine of a motor-car was heard and Muthengi returned from inspecting those of his cattle that were herded by the salt-licks at Iruri. He was tall and heavy, and walked at a deliberate, dignified pace. His expression was stern and his face bore no traces of laughter. A badge of office, a shining lion, decorated his big felt hat, and a thick great-coat protected him from cold. On his feet was a pair of shoes without laces and in his hand a polished muramati's staff. He walked slowly over to a chair standing against the wall of his thingira and sat down, ready to receive the reports of his njamas and his wives.

His son Razimu, a tall thin youth in a light brown suit with spectacles over his eyes, followed him in. Seeing two strangers in the compound he walked up to Matu and asked, after the customary greetings:

"What is your business here?"

"I have come to see Muthengi," Matu replied. "I have travelled a long way—from Njoro, beyond the mountain Nyandarua and Nakuru lake."

"I will tell him," Razimu said.

When Matu was summoned before his brother they looked at each other for a long while, speaking no word. Through their minds the past was rushing like a torrent, each drop a scene from childhood, and emotions clouded their visions like a spray. Their thoughts were formless, and too big for words.

"It is many seasons since you were here," Muthengi said at last.

"Yes," Matu answered. "It is a long time."

"You have wives?" Muthengi asked, "and sons?"

Matu pointed with his chin towards Karanja, who stood by his side.

"This son is Karanja, the eldest. I have another at school at Kabete, and others at Njoro, at school and herding goats."

"It is well," Muthengi answered. "I, too, have sons, and all of them have been to school. Here there is peace, and the crops are in the ground. My wives are fertile, and I have not yet come to the age of impotence."

"It is well," Matu said.

"My njamas will show you a bed," Muthengi continued. "There is a place for visitors, and in your honour I shall kill a sheep."

He called for one of his njamas, who came running, and instructed him to kill a fat ram immediately, that the meat might be roasted and eaten that night.

"My wives will bring you gruel and milk, and porridge of beans and maize, and sweet potatoes," he continued. "Now I am tired, and must rest; I cannot eat meat, for my stomach is bad. To-morrow, when I have returned from a meeting of the council of law, we will talk together, for there are many things that must be said. Go in peace."

"Peace be with you, brother," Matu said.

"You see, he does not intend to poison you," Karanja remarked when they had reached the njama's house.

Matu made no reply, but that evening he could not resist the roast flesh of a fattened ram. Afterwards he smiled at his son, and said: "No doubt you are right; what need has the elephant to trample the butterfly underfoot?"

5

MATU could scarcely recognise his father's land. He remembered it as a clearing on the edge of a forest glade. Now this glade was a pasture, the shamba a shadeless field of ripening maize. Near the site where Waseru's homestead had stood was a square stone house, solidly built, with windows, a veranda and a shining iron roof. In front was a small garden bright with flowers, and a bougainvillea glowed like a fire of purple above the door. Below the garden was a fenced-in pasture and at the bottom the Ragati rippled between grassy banks where maidenhair fern would grow no longer, lacking shade.

"This is the place," he said at last. "This is where my father cleared the forest. Now the land has been taken by another. Ee-i! You see, my son, that we have travelled here in vain."

"I am not satisfied," Karanja said, staring hard at the house. "This land belongs by law to you, and after you to me and Kaleo; and by law we can claim it for our own use."

"If the law says one thing and Muthengi says another, which will be upheld?" Matu queried. "The log which is burnt to ashes cannot become timber again, nor can water spilt on the ground be returned to the gourd." In spite of his son's protests he turned back, leaning much on his staff for support. Karanja crossed the Ragati by a bridge and approached the house alone. For a moment he wondered if a European could live there, but then he saw that the house was without a chimney, and too small.

As he stood by the veranda gazing at two fruit trees planted on either side of the door, a young woman in a brown dress with a handkerchief tied around her head came from the back and greeted him. They shook hands, and Karanja asked her to whom the house belonged.

"To Crispin, the son of Muthengi," she answered. "He heard that you had come—are you not his cousin, the son of Matu?—and was expecting to see you. He is away now teaching at the school, but he will be back at four o'clock."

Karanja decided to wait, and Crispin's wife showed him the shamba and the house. She had been educated at Tumu-Tumu, he learnt, and was of course a Christian; and she had worked for Europeans, caring for a small child. Now she had three children of her own; the smallest one was fed on cow's milk, and was very fat.

Crispin had a big field of wheat, thick and even, beginning to fill the ear. In less than a month, she said, it would be ready to cut. Then she would thresh it with sticks and winnow it by tossing the grain on baskets in a wind, just as millet had been winnowed long ago. A wagon would be hired to take it to Karatina, and then it would go to Nairobi to be sold. Another field, fenced like the wheat, was given over to potatoes and maize. Crispin's wife, Rebecca, dug up a few to show him; they were the largest potatoes he had ever seen. The maize field, planted in rows, was mulched with banana leaves to keep the moisture in the soil. No shamba grew the same crops two years running, she added; that was a very bad thing to do.

"Who helps you to cultivate?" Karanja asked. "Surely you cannot dig up so large a shamba alone."

Rebecca took him to a shed and showed him a small plough, and the two oxen that pulled it grazing in a field. With them were three cows. They were large, and without humps; they were not Kikuyu cattle at all.

"Crispin bought them from a European," Rebecca explained. "He has an uncle, Ngarariga's son, who works for a European at Nanyuki looking after cows."

"But you cannot drink so much milk," Karanja observed.

"I take it to the market in bottles," Rebecca said, "and for each bottle I receive ten cents."

6

KARANJA was watching her milk the cows with both hands when Crispin appeared on a bicycle, back from school. He was a tall young man with long legs and broad shoulders and a stiff, serious expression. He greeted his cousin politely, but without much warmth; it was clear that he suspected the reason for the visit. He showed Karanja round his shamba, and said:

"This land was given to me by my father, the muramati of our clan, when I returned from the Alliance High School and bought a wife. At first when I started to do the things that I had been taught at school, everyone said: 'This man is a fool, he does everything in the wrong way, and his crops will surely fail.' But when people saw that my crops were better than any others, they began to see that it was they who had been foolish, and they copied my methods. Then I bought two European heifers for four hundred shillings, and everyone said: 'Crispin is a madman, the cows will die and his father will be ruined paying for them'; but the cows have not died, and now that people see my milk they are jealous, and wish to have cows like mine. But they do not understand how much work is needed to keep cows and grow crops in the ways taught by Agricultural Officers."

"If you went to the Alliance High School," Karanja said, much impressed, "you must know everything, including English; why do you not become a Government clerk?"

"I already have a brother who is a very important clerk in Nyeri," Crispin replied, "and another who is clerk to the council of law in Karatina, and one in Nairobi working for the Indian who buys my potatoes and eggs, and also the strawberries which I grew last year in a swamp drained by the Government. But I myself cultivate the land, because I prefer that work to any other."

Karanja stayed to the evening meal in Crispin's house. They sat at a table and ate a stew of meat and potatoes, using spoons and plates like Europeans. A vase of marigolds stood beside the lamp on the table. A picture of the Alliance High School football team, of which Crispin had been a member, hung on the wall, next to a picture of a European woman with a great deal of hair, torn from a book. The children, who sat at table with them, were fat and noisy, and wore clean dresses instead of skins. When Karanja asked their names, Crispin said:

"The eldest is called Muthengi after my father, and the next is Irumu after my mother's father. I myself have a European name, and so have all my brothers: there is Robert, and Douglas, and Harold, and Solomon. But I do not think it is right to abandon Kikuyu names. Some European customs are good and others are bad, and we should take only the good ones, and keep those of our own which do not offend God. I think we should keep to our own Kikuyu names."

Karanja did not agree with this, although he did not say so. He intended to get baptised, as soon as he had bought a third wife, under the name of Harrison, a better one than his own.

7

It was some time before Karanja could speak what was in his mind, but at last he began :

"Crispin, why have you put fences around your land? Soon it will grow tired and you will have to move on. And how is it that you fence the pasture, for has not pasture always been common to all members of our clan?"

"You do not understand modern ways," Crispin replied. He spoke with heat, as though Karanja had insulted him. "There is no need for my land to grow weary, for I treat it in the European way. And as for the pasture, I say that it is mine to deal with as I choose! Only by fencing it can I make it better, as I know how to do. This land will be mine always, and no one shall take it away."

"All the same," Karanja said, "by law the land is not yours at all. You did not inherit from your father, and you have no right to keep pasture to yourself as if it were maize. Did you plant the grass, as women plant crops? And do you not know that this land rightfully belongs to the heirs of the man who first cut down the forest for cultivation?"

"It was given to me by my father, who is a chief, and also the muramati of our clan," Crispin retorted. "Have I not made the soil fatter than ever before? The land is mine because of the work and the money that I have put into the soil, and no one shall steal it from me!"

"That is for the council of law to say," Karanja replied.

"The council is made up of old men who do not understand modern customs!" Crispin exclaimed. "Can one European start to cultivate the pasture of another? Such a thing is against the law! Why should their law say one thing and ours another? Why do they teach us these methods if they let the elders take away the land we have improved? A law must be made to prevent this, and to give us a paper saying that the land we cultivate in the European way will always be ours."

Karanja did not know how to answer this outburst. He believed that by law the land belonged to him, yet he could see that the stone house, the fruit trees and other things belonged to Crispin and could not be moved. So he said nothing more, and got up to go.

"Where do you keep your goats," he asked as he said goodbye, "since you have a house into which they may not enter?"

"I have no goats," Crispin said. "Do you not know that they are very bad for the land? I hate them, and will not allow them here."

In spite of his respect for Crispin's education, Karanja was startled and even shocked. He knew that Europeans disliked goats and that Christians paid bride-price in shillings; but he could hardly imagine a Kikuyu thinking of goats with a black heart.

8

MATU did not want to bring a case against Crispin for the land. "What is the use?" he asked. "Muthengi is too powerful; no one would dare to give a verdict against his son. I am old and have decided to die, since what is the use of living without cattle or goats? You will return to Marafu's shamba, where you have land; and as for Kaleo, he has disappeared, and who knows what will become of him? Very likely he will go to Europe, or to Nairobi. You will only waste the court fees."

But Karanja replied: "This land is yours, since your father Waseru gave it to you on his death-bed. Muthengi had no right to take it for his son. It will grow excellent crops now that the Agricultural Officer will give me or Kaleo improved seed; and a plough can be bought for fifty shillings. But first we must find witnesses who will support your claim."

A visit was made to Ngarariga, now an old man, who had been present when his half-brother Waseru died. He had five wives, and a little shop which sold cloth and paraffin, tea, sugar and salt, and also cigarettes and beads. It was kept by two of his sons, and brought in a good profit.

"I would not advise you to bring a case," he said. "Muthengi would be angry, for he gave that land to his son."

"Who rules this country, then—Muthengi, or the Serkali?" Karanja asked angrily.

"Such cases do not go before the Serkali any longer," Ngarariga explained. "They go before the council of law. Muthengi is the president of this council, and I do not think you would win."

"All the same, by law the land belongs to my father," Karanja obstinately replied. "I shall bring the case."

The council met under a tree at Karatina. The elders sat together on chairs, Muthengi, massive and heavy-jowled, in the middle. Around him were other chiefs and elders, some too young to claim a rightful place on any properly constituted council of law. One, a Christian, wore a suit and a white sun helmet; another, a follower of old customs, a head-dress and cape of black ostrich feathers, a cloak of leopard skin and dangling Colobus monkey tails.

Holding a fistful of short sticks to mark his points, Matu squatted on the ground before the elders and told his story : of the land which Waseru's wife Wanjeri, his own mother, had cultivated; of his emigration to Njoro; of his son's wish to return; of his right by inheritance to claim part of the land. Karanja, who followed, told the story at greater length and with deeper feeling. No man, he said, could take another's land without payment, and Matu had received none; nor was the fencing of pasture a legitimate right.

Crispin gave evidence standing erect before his father : he spoke with passion in his tones. How could anyone talk of seizing his land, he demanded, after all that he had done to make it fertile and rich? How could the fruit-trees he had planted, the stone house, the tanks to hold water, the manure still in the land, belong to another man?

In the afternoon the council adjourned to the court-house, a big wooden building with an office and a clerk, to consider their judgments on the cases they had heard in the morning. Several elders came up to Matu to express sympathy for his cause.

"Many young men who have been to school are fencing land," they said. "What right have they to claim common pasture as their own? Has it not always been the property of the clan? What will become of our children, if all the land is enclosed and the muramati has nothing to distribute to newly married men? And where will our goats find grazing if all the fallow is fenced?"

But the young men said: "Crispin is right: we must have our own land, just as Europeans do. How can we feed it with manure and plant fruit trees, as we are told to do, if we can be driven out at any time?"

At last the council members filed out of the house on to the grass under the tree. The clerk read the verdicts slowly out of a book. To one, an award of fifty shillings; to another, a fine of ten goats. When he came to Karanja's case he said:

"Matu cannot have the land; he has waited too long to bring the case. Crispin has built a house and planted trees; Matu cannot pay him for this. The verdict is for Crispin; Matu must pay two shillings costs."

Karanja walked back with his father complaining bitterly that justice was corrupt. "Everyone is afraid of Muthengi," he said. "How can there be justice when he is the president of the council of law?"

"It is unjust," Matu agreed, "but it cannot be helped. I am too old to be deeply disturbed any more."

CHAPTER VIII

Christians

I

KARANJA decided to seek advice from Kabero, Irumu's son, an elder with a reputation for wisdom and common sense. Although Kabero carried the mungirima staff of the senior elders he did not belong to the council of law that met at Karatina. The members of this body were chosen by the Serkali not for their seniority, but for reasons of its own. Nevertheless Kabero was a highly respected elder, and one of his sons was a young man of great importance : an Agricultural Inspector, with a uniform and a bicycle, in charge of a big shamba belonging to the Serkali, and able to tell everyone what the Serkali wanted them to do as regards their land and their crops.

When Kabero had heard Karanja's story he said : "Why do you accept the judgment of the council that sits at Karatina? Why do you not take your case before the big council at Nyeri, where Muthengi is like one bean among many in the mundumugu's gourd?"

"How can this be done?" Karanja asked.

Kabero explained, and Karanja appealed against the decision of the lower court. He was told to wait a month, when he would be called to Nyeri to present his case.

But Matu refused to listen when Karanja told him that the land might yet be gained. He shook his grey head vigorously and said :

"I will not go to Tetu to appeal before this court. What is the use? Can I fight Muthengi? Is the lion worsted by the impala calf? Let the matter rest, my son; no good can come of these disputings."

"Nevertheless I shall go before the big court," Karanja persisted.

Matu had moved to Ngarariga's homestead, where he felt more at home. At Muthengi's he could not tell who had cooked his food, so many women were there; he did not know what might have been put into it. But at Ngarariga's there was peace, and Matu was able to sit all day in the shady compound gossiping to others of his generation who came to visit him. Often beer-drinks were held among members of his clan. But his bent legs grew stiffer, his chest felt dry and sore. Ngarariga gave him a goat, and a mundu-mugu was called to make a sacrifice; but the spirits who were troubling him could not be driven away. As the days passed he grew weaker, until a morning came when he could not leave the hut without support. The mundu-mugu came to make another sacrifice, but he said:

"Let the goat live; I have something that cannot be cast out." Karanja remembered that just three months had passed since Matu had said that he must die.

2

THE old man sat in the shade all through the long hot day, listening to the goat-bells and the songs of women, the voices of pigeons and the persistent fluting of a gai-ky-ngu. The season of muthakwa blossom had come again; its scent was blown up the valleys on a light breeze, and bees were busy among the purple blooms. Sometimes he muttered to himself, and once Karanja heard him speak to Wanja, his first wife, who was dead.

At nightfall he was carried into the thingira and made comfortable on a bed. After the meal was over he roused himself from his coma and called in a low voice to Ngarariga and to Karanja, his son.

"When the sun rises I shall be blind," he said, "and when the goats go out to pasture I shall be deaf to the bells. Listen to my last wishes, and remember that if you fail to keep them a curse no mundu-mugu can remove will fall upon you."

In a thin low voice Matu delivered his will.

"The land where my wives cultivate is not mine," he said, "but so long as Marafu allows them they must continue to cultivate there. They are to belong to Karanja, who must see that they will always have land. My goats and my cows will also belong to Karanja, who must buy a wife for Kaleo, and later for my other sons. But the cow Tumbo and the female goats Umu, Nyange and Njiru must never be sold, nor may their progeny be sold either. If this, my dying wish, is disobeyed, my spirit will trouble Karanja all his life."

For some time he lay silent; and then he continued : "Karanja, do not sell my goats, nor kill them. I do not know where you will take them, but they must not die, nor be sold. For if a spark should fall among paper shillings, they would be gone in smoke and no one could call them back. But goats continue; though each one will die, the flock will remain; therefore an owner of goats cannot become a pauper."

"I will do as you say," Karanja promised.

After another pause Matu continued :

"When Irumu the mundu-mugu died I heard him speak. He said : 'When women walk all day to seek firewood, and when the cultivation lies naked under the sun, then shall evil come.' But he said also : 'On the day when trees again darken the ridges and bring shelter to the weary, then shall good fortune return.' I have seen that on the land belonging to my clan trees clothe the ridges once again and the paths wind about crookedly as they used to do; so perhaps good fortune will return to the land."

There was silence for a while, and Matu's harsh, uneven breathing could be heard in the hut.

"Irumu spoke also of paths on which our feet were set," Matu whispered at last. "He said that we moved towards unknown things, away from all with which we were familiar. His words were true. The world to which the path is leading is one which we cannot understand; it was created by a strange God and it is ruled by distant people; and the young men have learnt new magic that has taken away their laughter. It is time that I reached the end of the path, for I do not know where it is going."

A little later he raised his weakening voice for the last time in a dry whisper. "Let my charms be buried in my grave, and my medicines thrown away into the bush," he said. "Their secrets, that were Irumu's, will die with me; nowadays another magic is sought by the young men."

For a long time Matu lay motionless with closed eyes. When it became apparent that he would revive no more, Karanja placed a calabash of water by his side, covered him with a blanket, and surrendered his own place by the bedside to the shades of death.

The next morning the wasted, bony body lay stiff and cold beside the still-smouldering fire. Ngarariga, Karanja and two of Ngarariga's sons wrapped it in an ox-hide and buried it quickly in the bush. Afterwards Ngarariga burnt down the infected hut and visited a mundu-mugu to be purified. His two sons laughed at their father for his old-fashioned ideas and Karanja said that he, too, did not believe in such foolish things. This was true, but nevertheless he could not be quite sure. For some time he did nothing, but one day he borrowed a goat from his uncle and visited the mundu-mugu, without telling anyone, to vomit out the thahu. It was better, he thought, to be on the safe side.

3

KARANJA, as his father's heir, decided to carry the case to the Nyeri council of law. A written summons to attend came to him to Karatina through the post, and on the appointed day he found his way to the hall of the L.N.C.,* an imposing thatched

* Local Native Council.

house shaped like an arena, around whose pit the elders sat on a high-backed wooden bench. Tiers of seats where anyone might come to listen surrounded the central place, and to one side was a platform on which the clerk who recorded all that was said sat at his desk. Muthengi sat on this council, but Karanja knew no one else by sight. Members came from every part of the country between Nyeri and Fort Hall.

When Karanja's turn came he was nervous, for many eyes were upon him, and he could not tell where the sympathies of his hearers lay. But he stood before them and let everything that came into his mind pass through his lips. He knew that he spoke better than Matu, whose mind had been confused. When one of the councillors asked him his reasons for claiming the land he told them that he wanted it for Kaleo, who was at the Alliance High School, and he could see that this made a good impression.

The court was cleared in the afternoon and the councillors debated their decisions in private. When all was ready the parties to each case were called, and the clerk read out the verdict and collected the fines. Tribal policemen stood by to keep order should a dispute arise, and to take away anyone sentenced to a term in jail.

The council had decided, the clerk said, that Karanja could not have Crispin's land; compensation for all Crispin's improvements would need to be too heavy. But the evidence showed that Matu and his heirs had a clear right to a section of land from the clan's holding. As Karanja could not be awarded the particular piece that he claimed, Muthengi must give him another piece, of equal size and excellence, elsewhere.

Karanja paid the court fee of six shillings gladly, and the clerk gave him back fifty cents to buy food. The day had been successful beyond his hopes. Next morning he returned with Ngarariga to the homestead and a fat ram was slain for a feast of celebration. After a long delay Muthengi sent for him and showed him a piece of land. It was not as big as he considered just, and it had not lain fallow for very long, but it would do; and Karanja accepted it as the final settlement of the dispute.

He had planned ahead what he would do. He had enough money in the Post Office, and goats at Njoro, to buy a new wife. He would negotiate for one, and leave her to cultivate the land he had won from Muthengi; he himself would return to Njoro. He had thought much about the matter, and decided that he liked Njoro best. He preferred to deal with Marafu, or some other European who could be easily managed, than with Muthengi and his njamas, with their constant rules, prohibitions and general interference. At Njoro there was more land, and now that a school had been established his children could be properly taught. He himself liked working inside a European's house and being taken sometimes to Nairobi in a car.

4

AT first Karanja thought that he would like to marry a Christian girl, one who could bargain astutely for him when he was away, and keep accounts. But fathers with Christian daughters were demanding prices that no one but a teacher or a clerk, or a very rich elder, could pay. He went again to dances, where he could see the girls and attract their attention by his skill and good looks. At night he danced the mugoyo around a fire, dressed in a length of calico with a white feather in his hair. His teeth were stained purple with indelible pencil and his cheeks glowed with a floral pattern of spots of lime. Christian boys and girls watched from a distance, staring a little dejectedly at the leaping figures of sisters and cousins content to forgo the prestige of Christianity for the sinful pleasures of the dance. Bright moonlight called everyone out into the warm night, but Christians could only walk together up and down the paths, disturbed by the rhythm that pulsed up the valleys until it seemed as if the whole night was beating like a full heart, and the leaves of all the trees were dancing on their own. Blood was too hot

for sleep, with the ears full of song; and as night slowly re-
volved the prowling groups of Christian boys and girls split
into pairs and drifted silently into the blackness of the wattle
groves, two by two.

After a month of dancing he decided on his bride. She was
a daughter of Kabero, small and lively, with many suitors; but
although she flirted with all, she had accepted none. Her name
was Wanjiri, and she had been to school. She showed plainly
that Karanja pleased her, for he was—as he well knew—among
the most handsome of the men. He kept his lack of schooling
secret, and impressed her with his knowledge of English and
with his experience of the world. Kabero's daughter, attracted
by his fluency, his looks, and his smart European clothes, showed
him favours above all her other friends.

But although she laughed with him, and let him take her home
after dancing, she would not listen to his talk of marriage, and
for a reason which filled Karanja's heart with despair. He was
not a Christian; and she had made up her mind to accept none
but a Christian for her husband.

Karanja knew already that to become a Christian took several
years. Even had it been possible to attend a mission for the
period required, the central difficulty remained: if he became a
Christian he would not be able to marry a second wife. That
must be done before baptism, or not at all.

5

During his stay in Kikuyu he had learnt that many people
were dissatisfied with the missionaries, believing them to be in
league with the Serkali, which was still trying to break the
strength of the Kikuyu people by destroying their old customs.
Why else, people asked, should the missions insist that Christians
must give up all the traditions of their fathers; the circumcision
of girls, beer-drinks, dances, purification from thahu, sacrifices
to God? Even the members of the L.N.C., some of whom

were Christians, shared this feeling. They spent much of the money raised by means of a tax on a big school at Nyeri and gave money to poor parents to pay the fees, so that boys could be educated without going to a mission at all.

In particular, many people rejected the missions' teaching that no Christian might marry a second wife. If the Christian God were indeed the only one in existence, they asked, how could a man be stopped from worshipping because he had two wives? And what God who loved his people could be so unreasonable as to dislike such a natural and, indeed, desirable state of affairs, one approved by men and women alike?

Christians who could read the Bible said emphatically that they could find no instructions in the matter there. A belief began to spread that the missionaries had invented the whole story as part of a subtle European plot against the Kikuyu people. Many of the young men went about saying: "Ever since the beginning of the world, we Kikuyu have married more than one wife, those of us who could afford to. It is our custom, just as it is the custom of Europeans to have only one. That custom may suit them, but it does not please us at all. This is a matter we shall decide for ourselves! Let us, therefore, take two wives, or more if we are able; and if the missionaries refuse to call us Christians then let us start our own Church, with our own services to God, and with schools of our own."

And so the Independent Orthodox Church was founded. It had an office in Nairobi, and Karanja heard that his friend Benson Makuna was one of those on the committee who was helping to spread the movement far and wide. Benson had many powerful friends in Europe who wrote to him, and now they helped the movement with money and advice. Committees were elected in each district of the Kikuyu country and clerks and preachers were engaged. The Independents, as the followers of the movement became known, collected money from all over the country. Schools were built in several districts, and teachers were sent from headquarters. Independents could have as many wives as they were able, they could attend beer-drinks freely, and they could circumcise their daughters.

One of Karanja's cousins, who was clerk to the council of law at Karatina, explained all this to him, and gave him a book written by Benson Makuna to read. It seemed to Karanja that at last his problem was solved. He would become an Independent, then Kabero's daughter Wanjiri would no longer refuse him and he could be married in the Christian way. He went to a ceremony of this kind to see what it was like. The bride covered her head with a white cloth and carried a sunshade and a bunch of flowers; she was attended by two girls dressed in the same way, and the bridegroom wore extremely smart clothes. Afterwards everyone went to a house to eat rice-cakes and tea. But it was not as easy to become an Independent as he had hoped. Although there were many teachers in the Church—young men, for the most part, who had quarrelled with the missions—no ordained preacher qualified to baptise others had yet joined.

6

JUST as Karanja was beginning to wonder whether he had better look for a different bride, he heard of a way out of his trouble. The Independents, he learnt, had become part of a big and powerful Church in South Africa, a distant land which he had heard of as the home of Dutchmen, and as a place where black men were cruelly oppressed by white. There had been an interchange of letters, and now the leader of this South African Church himself was on the way to confer with the Kikuyu leaders.

This man was an Archbishop, a dignitary second to no one in importance, unless it might be King George. A number of preachers were preparing for ordination at the Archbishop's hands. These ordained preachers would then be able to baptise as Christians the followers of the Independents, so that soon the missions, with their foolish desire to introduce European customs and their narrow-minded views on wives, could be altogether ignored. A true Kikuyu Church, unpolluted by European prejudices, would spread throughout the land until it gained control of all the schools belonging to the missions, and then European dictatorship would be at at an end.

The visit of the Archbishop was awaited eagerly throughout the country. Everyone talked of the event. The leaders of the Independents were jubilant; even the glamour surrounding distinguished people like Benson Makuna paled beside the flame of an Archbishop's prestige. But those who taught at the Tumu-Tumu schools, such as Crispin, opposed the Independents and looked on the visit with mistrust. It was the Devil, they said, not God, whom the Independents worshipped. Muthengi and some of the elders, also, were against them, both because they feared the Serkali's anger and because they considered that the Church was in the hands of conceited and foolish young men whose own advancement was their chief concern.

The Archbishop came from Nairobi in a car. He held several services in the district, attended by great crowds. Karanja went to see him, and was much impressed. His car was new and shining. He wore a black coat and trousers and a stiff black hat, and had a big beard. He preached in English, so Karanja could not understand much of what he said. But his voice was mighty, and he appeared to be a very holy man.

Before he left it was announced that a great baptism ceremony would be held early in the morning in the Chania river and that all who wished to become Christians might attend. The possession of a number of wives, the Archbishop announced, would be no hindrance.

On the appointed day a great crowd assembled by the river a little after dawn. Both men and women came, all young people, and while they waited in the cold beside a ford they sang Christian hymns. The elders shook their heads over the whole affair. They were afraid that the Serkali would come to arrest the Archbishop and his followers, and they were also disturbed when they heard where the baptism was to be. It was not far from the place where the serpent Ndamathia rose from the river's depth to display itself to chosen elders on the last night of the Itwika ceremony ; and the time for the generation Mwangi to pass on the secret to the generation Muirungu was drawing near. The elders feared that the snake would be angry at this sacrilege and send plague or famine to decimate the land. But the young men laughed, and ridiculed the elders for inventing such a foolish story; and one of the old men said : "Ndamathia will never show himself again. The secrets that we guard will die with our generation, for they concern things that the young men no longer wish to understand."

A little after sunrise the Archbishop arrived, clad for the ceremony in a long white robe. Amid shouts of greeting he waded into the cold waters where they rippled over a causeway of stones. The candidates were led out to him one by one. Two of his attendants seized each person and ducked him in the river, and the Archbishop marked the forehead of each with a cross of chalk and called on God in a loud voice to send down blessings from Heaven. Then he pronounced the new name that each candidate had selected, and the baptism was complete.

Karanja chose the name Harrison. Becoming a Christian was not nearly so hard as he had supposed. He felt elated to think that he had at last achieved it, but a little cheated that the ceremony had been so slight and swift. Perhaps it was not yet over, he thought. This, he found, was indeed the case. As he emerged from the waters, his shirt clinging coldly to his flesh, one of the Archbishop's attendants demanded ten shillings as the fee, and refused to return his trousers until he had paid.

7

Now that Karanja was a Christian, Kabero's daughter could no longer refuse to marry him. In any case he had made her pregnant, and her father had accepted the fine as a first instalment of the bride-price. Kabero agreed to take cash instead of beer. A long discussion took place to settle the value of the brews, which was finally agreed on as two good blankets, a barrel of honey and eighty-six shillings. Karanja drew the money from the Post Office, Ngarariga advanced him the thirty goats, and after a great feast held at Kabero's homestead he took his bride to a hut, of the old-fashioned kind, that he and his kinsmen had built on his new piece of land.

Karanja stayed with Wanjiri a month to break the shamba and see that all was satisfactory, and then the time came when he could delay his return no longer. He took the train from Karatina, seen off by many friends. He was reluctant to leave his new bride, who was very pleasing, and cooked well; but he had many plans for the future. His crop would be ready, now, to sell; with part of the money he would buy a small plough. Next year, perhaps, he would get a wagon as well. Crispin had given him a little seed of his best maize and of the new beans that were being grown in Kikuyu, together with the address of his brother in Nairobi who would buy vegetables, fruit and eggs.

He could see that in future, with shambas in two places, he would make more money than ever before. But now he would have to pay the tax on his father's two wives, as well as on two of his own. The thought disturbed his pleasure, as a stick dragged across the bottom of a pool will stir up mud to cloud the sparkling water. Such a thing, he reflected, was exceedingly unjust. But when a well-dressed young man on the next seat, who proved to be a clerk on the way back to Nairobi, spoke to him in English, he forgot his troubles in his delight at being able to talk on equal terms with a fellow Christian and an educated man.

8

AT Njoro the drought had broken and the new rains had been good; everything was drenched in a deep, shining green. The goats looked fat and healthy; acacias were sprinkled with pale yellow flowers, and in the shambas women had begun their patient battle with the never-dying weeds.

His way to Marafu's farm lay past the club where Europeans gathered to play games with different sizes of rubber balls, and to drink their own kind of beer. To his surprise he saw a big concourse of motor-cars gathered there, and, more remarkable, many aeroplanes, some of them very big and others small enough to be children of the larger ones.

He broke his journey to investigate, and found the largest crowd that he had ever seen at the club. People were allowed to approach close to the aeroplanes, and as he had never looked at one on the ground, he went up to a small one, painted red, belonging to a European whom he knew. He was amazed to see how small it was, and that its wings did not move like a bird's. One day, he thought, when he was rich, he would fly to England in such a machine.

Near the aeroplanes a man was selling tickets for fifty cents each. He shouted in a loud voice that out of every twenty tickets, one would enable the man who bought it to go up inside the aeroplane for a journey in the sky. Several young men, laughing and joking with each other, bought tickets; and Karanja, on a sudden impulse, did so too. He did not expect anything to come of it, but nevertheless he waited near the seller until all the tickets were gone. Then a European came with a piece of paper and the seller called out several numbers through a horn. Karanja looked at the number on his ticket and a moment later, to his great amazement, he heard it called out loudly by the seller.

"Ee-i !" he exclaimed, "that is my number. Am I, then, to go in the aeroplane?"

The European beckoned to him and he went forward slowly, not at all sure what sort of trouble he had plunged into. He had often wondered what flying was like, but now he was too frightened to want to go. But he still did not think it was possible for a Kikuyu to go in an aeroplane, so he asked : "What is going to happen, bwana?"

"You are going into the sky," the European, the owner of the aeroplane, replied. He gave Karanja a leather hat and showed him how to climb inside the body of the machine. Karanja hesitated, but the European laughed and said : "Why are you afraid? It is not going to kill you." So Karanja got in and the European tied him to the seat with a strap.

9

THE engine started with a roar greater than that of a motor-car stuck in the mud. Karanja felt the plane quivering beneath him as if it had been alive. In a panic he tried to climb out, but it was impossible, and no one heard his shouts. Then he felt the machine moving, and it was too late.

At first it was just like being in a motor-car; but then, when he looked down, he saw to his dismay that the earth had left them, and was getting farther away. He could see the tops of the roofs, and people had suddenly become round and black like ticks, and far away. He shut his eyes and tried to believe that he would return alive to earth. Another panic seized him : suppose the European should decide to fly on to England? He looked over the side to reassure himself, and felt very sick. The aeroplane was going to turn over; it was tilting at a most unsafe angle. The tops of the huts were like clusters of ant-heaps; one of the homesteads must be his own. There were objects running about excitedly beneath. They looked like small black insects, but he supposed that they were women; one might even be his own wife.

When they began to drop, his stomach went round and round and he felt even more sick. He dared not look over, for he had caught a glimpse of the earth rushing towards him and he covered his face with his hands. Then he felt the machine bumping against the earth, and presently it stopped. He jumped out, still feeling giddy, but immensely relieved to be safe. He could hardly believe that a journey in the sky could be so quickly and easily made. Driving an aeroplane could not be more difficult than driving a motor-car.

He thanked the European, and was quickly surrounded by a crowd of people enquiring what it was like, all full of respect for his courage. As he related the story, his own admiration for his bravery grew. It had indeed been courageous to entrust himself to the European, to disappear so completely into the sky. Very few people, he felt convinced, would have done it; even the smartest clerks in Nairobi did not know what an aeroplane was like. One day, he decided, he would learn to conduct aeroplanes himself, and become driver to a European.

He reached his homestead late that night. Everything was as he had left it, except that goats had died and others had been born, shambas had been dug and new seed planted. The logs of juniper smouldering on the fire of the thingira smelt sweet; they gave out the familiar smell of home.

Into his wife's hut, however, he could not enter. He had left her pregnant, and now her time had nearly come. Midwives had already entered and closed up the door. All that night no news came from it, and he began to grow anxious. Early in the morning an old mundu-mugu arrived with his bag of magic gourds over his shoulder. Karanja was angry and told him to take his devil's medicines away; but one of the midwives darted out of the hut like an infuriated hen and drove Karanja from his own homestead. One of his goats was sacrificed, and blood sprinkled around the walls. A little later he heard four bird-like trills quavering in the bright morning sunlight above the voices of the birds. He knew that a daughter had been born.

He was glad that God had decided to bless his wives with fertility, now that he had been baptised a Christian. The name of the child, he decided, should be Aeroplane. His wife, he thought, would never be able to pronounce such a difficult word; but educated people would know, and understand.

THE END

READ MORE IN PENGUIN

In every corner of the world, on every subject under the sun, Penguin represents quality and variety – the very best in publishing today.

For complete information about books available from Penguin – including Puffins, Penguin Classics and Arkana – and how to order them, write to us at the appropriate address below. Please note that for copyright reasons the selection of books varies from country to country.

In the United Kingdom: Please write to *Dept. EP, Penguin Books Ltd, Bath Road, Harmondsworth, West Drayton, Middlesex UB7 ODA*

In the United States: Please write to *Consumer Sales, Penguin Putnam Inc., P.O. Box 12289 Dept. B, Newark, New Jersey 07101-5289*. VISA and MasterCard holders call 1-800-788-6262 to order Penguin titles

In Canada: Please write to *Penguin Books Canada Ltd, 10 Alcorn Avenue, Suite 300, Toronto, Ontario M4V 3B2*

In Australia: Please write to *Penguin Books Australia Ltd, P.O. Box 257, Ringwood, Victoria 3134*

In New Zealand: Please write to *Penguin Books (NZ) Ltd, Private Bag 102902, North Shore Mail Centre, Auckland 10*

In India: Please write to *Penguin Books India Pvt Ltd, 11 Community Centre, Panchsheel Park, New Delhi 110017*

In the Netherlands: Please write to *Penguin Books Netherlands bv, Postbus 3507, NL-1001 AH Amsterdam*

In Germany: Please write to *Penguin Books Deutschland GmbH, Metzlerstrasse 26, 60594 Frankfurt am Main*

In Spain: Please write to *Penguin Books S. A., Bravo Murillo 19, 1° B, 28015 Madrid*

In Italy: Please write to *Penguin Italia s.r.l., Via Benedetto Croce 2, 20094 Corsico, Milano*

In France: Please write to *Penguin France, Le Carré Wilson, 62 rue Benjamin Baillaud, 31500 Toulouse*

In Japan: Please write to *Penguin Books Japan Ltd, Kaneko Building, 2-3-25 Koraku, Bunkyo-Ku, Tokyo 112*

In South Africa: Please write to *Penguin Books South Africa (Pty) Ltd, Private Bag X14, Parkview, 2122 Johannesburg*

PENGUIN AUDIOBOOKS

A Quality of Writing That Speaks for Itself

Penguin Books has always led the field in quality publishing. Now you can listen at leisure to your favourite books, read to you by familiar voices from radio, stage and screen. Penguin Audiobooks are produced to an excellent standard, and abridgements are always faithful to the original texts. From thrillers to classic literature, biography to humour, with a wealth of titles in between, Penguin Audiobooks offer you quality, entertainment and the chance to rediscover the pleasure of listening.

You can order Penguin Audiobooks through Penguin Direct by telephoning (0181) 899 4036. The lines are open 24 hours every day. Ask for Penguin Direct, quoting your credit card details.

A selection of Penguin Audiobooks, published or forthcoming:

Emma by Jane Austen, read by Fiona Shaw

Pride and Prejudice by Jane Austen, read by Joanna David

Beowulf translated by Michael Alexander, read by David Rintoul

Agnes Grey by Anne Brontë, read by Juliet Stevenson

Jane Eyre by Charlotte Brontë, read by Juliet Stevenson

Wuthering Heights by Emily Brontë, read by Juliet Stevenson

The Pilgrim's Progress by John Bunyan, read by David Suchet

The Moonstone by Wilkie Collins, read by Michael Pennington, Terrence Hardiman and Carole Boyd

Nostromo by Joseph Conrad, read by Michael Pennington

Tales from the Thousand and One Nights, read by Souad Faress and Raad Rawi

Robinson Crusoe by Daniel Defoe, read by Tom Baker

David Copperfield by Charles Dickens, read by Nathaniel Parker

Little Dorrit by Charles Dickens, read by Anton Lesser

Barnaby Rudge by Charles Dickens, read by Richard Pasco

The Adventures of Sherlock Holmes volumes 1–3 by Sir Arthur Conan Doyle, read by Douglas Wilmer

PENGUIN AUDIOBOOKS

The Man in the Iron Mask by Alexandre Dumas, read by Simon Ward

Adam Bede by George Eliot, read by Paul Copley

Joseph Andrews by Henry Fielding, read by Sean Barrett

The Great Gatsby by F. Scott Fitzgerald, read by Marcus D'Amico

North and South by Elizabeth Gaskell, read by Diana Quick

The Diary of a Nobody by George Grossmith, read by Terrence Hardiman

Jude the Obscure by Thomas Hardy, read by Samuel West

The Go-Between by L. P. Hartley, read by Tony Britton

Les Misérables by Victor Hugo, read by Nigel Anthony

A Passage to India by E. M. Forster, read by Tim Pigott-Smith

The Odyssey by Homer, read by Alex Jennings

The Portrait of a Lady by Henry James, read by Claire Bloom

On the Road by Jack Kerouac, read by David Carradine

Women in Love by D. H. Lawrence, read by Michael Maloney

Nineteen Eighty-Four by George Orwell, read by Timothy West

Ivanhoe by Sir Walter Scott, read by Ciaran Hinds

Frankenstein by Mary Shelley, read by Richard Pasco

Of Mice and Men by John Steinbeck, read by Gary Sinise

Dracula by Bram Stoker, read by Richard E. Grant

Gulliver's Travels by Jonathan Swift, read by Hugh Laurie

Vanity Fair by William Makepeace Thackeray, read by Robert Hardy

War and Peace by Leo Tolstoy, read by Bill Nighy

Barchester Towers by Anthony Trollope, read by David Timson

Tao Te Ching by Lao Tzu, read by Carole Boyd and John Rowe

Ethan Frome by Edith Wharton, read by Nathan Osgood

The Picture of Dorian Gray by Oscar Wilde, read by John Moffatt

Orlando by Virginia Woolf, read by Tilda Swinton

READ MORE IN PENGUIN

Penguin Twentieth-Century Classics offer a selection of the finest works of literature published this century. Spanning the globe from Argentina to America, from France to India, the masters of prose and poetry are represented by Penguin.

If you would like a catalogue of the Twentieth-Century Classics library, please write to:

Penguin Press Marketing, 27 Wrights Lane, London W8 5TZ

(Available while stocks last)

READ MORE IN PENGUIN

A CHOICE OF TWENTIETH-CENTURY CLASSICS

Ulysses James Joyce

Ulysses is unquestionably one of the supreme masterpieces, in any artistic form, of the twentieth century. 'It is the book to which we are all indebted and from which none of us can escape' T. S. Eliot

The First Man Albert Camus

'It is the most brilliant semi-autobiographical account of an Algerian childhood amongst the grinding poverty and stoicism of poor French-Algerian colonials' J. G. Ballard. 'A kind of magical Rosetta stone to his entire career, illuminating both his life and his work with stunning candour and passion' *The New York Times*

Flying Home Ralph Ellison

Drawing on his early experience – his father's death when he was three, hoboeing his way on a freight train to follow his dream of becoming a musician – Ellison creates stories which, according to the *Washington Post*, 'approach the simple elegance of Chekhov.' 'A shining instalment' *The New York Times Book Review*

Çider with Rosie Laurie Lee

'Laurie Lee's account of childhood and youth in the Cotswolds remains as fresh and full of joy and gratitude for youth and its sensations as when it first appeared. It sings in the memory' *Sunday Times*. 'A work of art' Harold Nicolson

Kangaroo D. H. Lawrence

Escaping from the decay and torment of post-war Europe, Richard and Harriett Somers arrive in Australia to a new and freer life. Somers, a disillusioned writer, becomes involved with an extreme political group. At its head is the enigmatic Kangaroo.

READ MORE IN PENGUIN

A CHOICE OF TWENTIETH-CENTURY CLASSICS

Belle du Seigneur Albert Cohen

Belle du Seigneur is one of the greatest love stories in modern literature. It is also a hilarious mock-epic concerning the mental world of the cuckold. 'A *tour de force*, a comic masterpiece weighted with an understanding of human frailty ... It is, quite simply, a book that must be read' *Observer*

The Diary of a Young Girl Anne Frank

'Fifty years have passed since Anne Frank's diary was first published. Her story came to symbolize not only the travails of the Holocaust, but the struggle of the human spirit ... This edition is a worthy memorial' *The Times*. 'A witty, funny and tragic book ... stands on its own even without its context of horror' *Sunday Times*

Herzog Saul Bellow

'A feast of language, situations, characters, ironies, and a controlled moral intelligence ... Bellow's rapport with his central character seems to me novel writing in the grand style of a Tolstoy – subjective, complete, heroic' *Chicago Tribune*

The Go-Between L. P. Hartley

Discovering an old diary, Leo, now in his sixties, is drawn back to the hot summer of 1900 and his visit to Brandham Hall ... 'An intelligent, complex and beautifully-felt evocation of nascent boyhood sexuality that is also a searching exploration of the nature of memory and myth' Douglas Brooks-Davies

Orlando Virginia Woolf

Sliding in and out of three centuries, and slipping between genders, Orlando is the sparkling incarnation of the personality of Vita Sackville-West as Virginia Woolf saw it.

READ MORE IN PENGUIN

A CHOICE OF TWENTIETH-CENTURY CLASSICS

Collected Stories Vladimir Nabokov

Here, for the first time in paperback, the stories of one of the twentieth century's greatest prose stylists are collected in a single volume. 'To read him in full flight is to experience stimulation that is at once intellectual, imaginative and aesthetic, the nearest thing to pure sensual pleasure that prose can offer' Martin Amis

Cancer Ward Aleksandr Solzhenitsyn

Like his hero Oleg Kostoglotov, Aleksandr Solzhenitsyn spent many years in labour camps for mocking Stalin and was eventually transferred to a cancer ward. 'What he has done above all things is record the truth in such a manner as to render it indestructible, stamping it into the Western consciousness' *Observer*

Nineteen Eighty-Four George Orwell

'A volley against the authoritarian in every personality, a polemic against every orthodoxy, an anarchistic blast against every un-questioning conformist ... *Nineteen Eighty-Four* is a great novel, and it will endure because its message is a permanent one' Ben Pimlott

The Complete Saki Saki

Macabre, acid and very funny, Saki's work drives a knife into the upper crust of English Edwardian life. Here are the effete and dashing heroes, Reginald, Clovis and Comus Bassington, tea on the lawn, the smell of gunshot and the tinkle of the caviar fork, and here is the half-seen, half-felt menace of disturbing undercurrents ...

The Castle Franz Kafka

'In *The Castle* we encounter a proliferation of obstacles, endless conversations, perpetual possibilities which hook on to each other as if intent to go on until the end of time' Idris Parry. 'Kafka may be the most important writer of the twentieth century' J. G. Ballard

READ MORE IN PENGUIN

A CHOICE OF TWENTIETH-CENTURY CLASSICS

The Garden Party and Other Stories Katherine Mansfield

This collection reveals Mansfield's supreme talent as an innovator who freed the short story from its conventions and gave it a new strength and prestige. 'One of the great modernist writers of displacement, restlessness, mobility, impermanence' Lorna Sage

The Little Prince Antoine de Saint-Exupéry

Moral fable and spiritual autobiography, this is the story of a little boy who lives alone on a planet not much bigger than himself. One day he leaves behind the safety of his childlike world to travel around the universe where he is introduced to the vagaries of adult behaviour through a series of extraordinary encounters.

Selected Poems Edward Arlington Robinson

Robinson's finely crafted rhythms mirror the tension the poet saw between life's immutable circumstances and humanity's often tragic attempts to exert control. At once dramatic and witty these poems lay bare the tyranny of love and unspoken, unnoticed suffering.

Talkative Man R. K. Narayan

Bizarre happenings at Malgudi are heralded by the arrival of a stranger on the Delhi train who takes up residence in the station waiting-room and, to the dismay of the station master, will not leave. 'His lean, matter-of-fact prose has lost none of its chuckling sparkle mixed with melancholy' *Spectator*

The Immoralist André Gide

'To know how to free oneself is nothing; the arduous thing is to know what to do with one's freedom' André Gide. Gide's novel examines the inevitable conflicts that arise when a pleasure-seeker challenges conventional society, and raises complex issues of personal responsibility.